"I don'[...]ela," he said
in as st[...]ut even if I
had, I'm your father, Rachel. I don't have to report to
you."

"Obviously not," she said, "given the number of times
I've heard from you since summer."

He stared. "Is *that* what's really bothering you? Rach,
I thought you were just as busy as I've been. I didn't
think you'd miss hearing from me. I'm sorry. Really, I
am."

"Oh, for heaven's sake!" Rachel said. "It's not about the
e-mail, Dad. It's about all those years when you didn't
have time for me because you were so busy fawning
over Angela. You think that didn't hurt? You think kids
don't see those things, no matter how young they are?"

"Rachel, that was years ago. Why are you bringing it up
now? I thought—God, all that time working with
Victoria, and you're *still* hurting about those things?
What does it take for you to get over it?"

"Maybe not having it start all over again," she snapped.
"Maybe getting her out of our lives once and for all!"

**"If you like Mary Higgins Clark, you'll love
Meg O'Brien!"**

—Armchair Detective

MEG O'BRIEN

CRIMSON RAIN

MIRA®

ISBN 1-55166-932-3

CRIMSON RAIN

Copyright © 2002 by Meg O'Brien.

Visit us at www.mirabooks.com

Printed in U.S.A.

ACKNOWLEDGMENTS

Many thanks to...

Cathy Landrum, for her valuable research, and to Al Wilding, retired Seattle police officer, for checking my police scenes for accuracy.

Immeasurable thanks and love to my family, who generously helped me to finish this book during a period of immobility by shopping for me, cleaning for me, running to the post office, keeping my computer going and even seeing to it that my birds in the garden got fed. Bless you all...Kevin, Robin, Kaiti, Greg, Darrell, Tiffany and Scott. Thanks also to Peggy, who makes me proud, and to her mom, Amy, who recently put herself through college and deserves huge huzzahs! Finally, a very special hug and kiss to Courtney and Jonathan, whose visits add light to our lives, and to Emily, the "Little One," who helps by just being here and keeping me laughing!

It seems I thank my MIRA editors in every book, but that's only because I love every one I've ever worked with. Many thanks to Dianne Moggy and Amy Moore-Benson, and this year in particular to Miranda Stecyk, my editor through the *Crimson Rain* revisions. Her insight, hard work and enthusiastic support for this book made the job of revising seem easy, at a time when I wondered if I'd ever be able to finish.

Finally, I extend my utmost gratitude to my many wonderful readers who have written such beautiful letters about my books, and whose support for my writing keeps me going. Please stay in touch. I value each letter and e-mail, and even if my writing schedule keeps me from answering each one, I will always treasure your kind words. You can reach me now in two ways: by e-mail (megobrien@earthlink.net) or through my Web site (www.megobrien.com).

Prologue

Life, some say, is only an illusion—an illusion we create ourselves, in our own minds, then project onto the screen of our days. Paul Bradley would wonder, later, if he had indeed, by some strange quirk of mind, created the hellish thing that happened to his family that long-ago Christmas Eve. Until then, he and Gina had seemed to have so much going for them. How, in one devastating moment, could it all have fallen apart?

A miracle might have saved them. Miracles, some say, are another thing we create ourselves. By choice, they say, we abide in either heaven or hell.

Paul might have made different choices in the years to follow. Gina might have, too. Neither of them could possibly know, however, the evil that lay in wait for them. Nor did they know that by the simple matter of making different choices, they might have been spared.

The vicious act that brought everything to a head—though no one could say it was the "true beginning''—took place sixteen years ago on a night that was supposed to be holy, but into which crept the very soul of sin. Paul Bradley stood that night with Gina, his wife of six years, in the kitchen of their historic home on Queen Anne Hill. Larger and with more property than most on the hill, it had the kind of architectural appointments the Bradleys loved. Finding it on Queen Anne Hill, one of the oldest and most desirable areas in Seattle, had been a bonus. Though some referred to the hill these days as a queen in a faded petticoat, there was talk of future gentrification on Lower Queen Anne. New and luxurious homes, apartments and businesses were going up every day.

The Bradleys had chosen this particular house because it stood in a quiet area above the fray and had a fabulous view. On good days they could see the Sound and most of West Seattle. On foggy days, the top of the Space Needle seemed to float on the clouds, like a hovering spacecraft or a ship at sea.

Never had Paul felt so content with the way his life had turned out. He had his own business, selling antiques to millionaire software executives, and Gina was on her way to becoming a successful interior designer. The Life Plan they had put down on paper before they married was working out—albeit with a few glitches here and there.

One of those glitches was that Gina hadn't been able to have children, something they had discovered shortly after they married. Since they both wanted a family, and the sooner the better, they saw no reason to wait before adopting. Rachel and Angela, fraternal twins, had come into their lives one warm August day when they were a year old, about the same time as Paul and Gina's first wedding anniversary. It seemed the Bradley family was now complete.

To be honest, there had been a few rough moments in the past year with Angela, who had shown signs of anger and hostility that seemed unusual for a four-year-old. Paul and Gina had been warned by the psychiatrist at Saint Sympatica's orphanage that the girls might have problems due to a lack of sufficient maternal bonding in their first months. They had been left on the steps of the orphanage nine months before the adoption, with nothing but a note saying that they were three months old and their names were Rachel and Angela. Nothing was known about their mother, the psychiatrist had told them.

Though the twins were not identical, they both had brown hair and clear hazel eyes that seemed to connect with Gina and Paul from the first time they held them. The Bradleys had fallen in love with them on sight, and readily agreed to provide them with all the professional care they might need.

Everything had seemed fine until, at the age of four, Angela had begun to exhibit symptoms of what Victoria Lessing—the Seattle psychiatrist they had taken her to—tentatively labeled as RAD: Reactive Attachment Disorder. Angela seemed to have no real feelings for people, and no remorse when she hurt someone, as children often did while playing. Victoria had continued to work with Angela, often including Paul, Gina and Rachel in the sessions. The therapy had seemed to be helping, and in recent months they had actually begun to relax with their child.

As for Rachel, they thanked God that she had always been quiet and shy, showing no signs of RAD.

"You might want to keep an eye on Rachel," Victoria had cautioned. "This kind of thing can suddenly appear in the teens, and even later."

So far, so good, Paul thought that Christmas. Angela seemed to be getting better, while Rachel still showed no signs of the kind of syndrome Angela suffered from. Gratefully he took Gina into his arms, and together they listened to the sounds of carols on the stereo in the living room, the twins making small noises as they played around the Christmas tree.

"How did we get so lucky?" Paul murmured against his wife's hair. She smelled of apples and cinnamon, and he loved her more than life itself. He wanted to take her to bed right then and there, and thought: *If we could just get the girls in bed early...*

That probably wouldn't happen, of course. They were too excited about Santa coming. Paul was looking forward to it, too. The twins were at an age where they understood the Santa Claus story, and he and Gina looked forward to getting up in the morning and seeing their delight over the toys Santa had brought them.

Paul smiled and slid his lips down to Gina's, pulling her against him and rocking slightly back and forth.

Excitement began to build in him, and he could feel her shudder and melt, her arms tightening around his neck as their lips moved. He took her tongue inside his mouth and began the gentle searching that he knew would send her over the top. Gina's arms tightened and she pressed herself so close there was little room left to breathe.

She did that, Paul knew, when she began to feel weak with arousal, hanging on to him as if to an anchor. He loved that feeling, the one of being needed, and his own arousal became a growing force, taking him over. Neither of them heard as the noises from the twins in the living room became louder and more intense.

The crash brought them back. That, and Rachel's earsplitting scream.

"Good God, what did they do now?" Gina half laughed as she pulled away from Paul's arms and ran for the kitchen door. Paul was close behind her, but was caught up short as Gina stopped in her tracks, her hands going to her mouth, eyes wide.

"No!" she screamed, running toward the twins.

Paul couldn't say, later, if he'd fully understood what was going on. The tableau that met his eyes was too shocking, too unbelievable.

The eight-foot Christmas tree had been knocked over and lay on its side, surrounded by puddles of water. Ornaments had fallen off and broken; fragile shards were scattered everywhere. Foil icicles glittered on the carpet, and the toy train beneath the tree had jumped its tracks.

Angela, in her white Christmas dress with its bright red sash, stood over her sister, a sharp kitchen knife in her hand. Rachel lay on her back on the floor, her arms up in a feeble attempt to fend her sister off. Her screams cut into Paul, sending pain straight through him.

Angela never looked up, nor showed any sign at all that she'd heard when Gina yelled out, running toward her. Paul ran, too, but felt as if he were moving in slow motion. His legs were like lead, and his mind could barely take in what he was seeing.

Before they could reach her, Angela thrust the knife down. Paul somehow miraculously moved ahead of Gina and barreled into Angela, pushing her to the ground and wresting the knife from her hand. She fought him with the ferocity of an animal, her teeth biting into his arm, feet kicking at his groin.

Paul closed his mind to the red-hot pain and held his ground. Looking back quickly, he saw that Gina knelt beside Rachel and was holding the child in her arms. Blood seeped through Rachel's pink Christmas dress and onto Gina's blouse.

In the background, carols continued to play. "Joy to the world, the Lord is come..."

Paul looked down into Angela's five-year-old hazel eyes and saw nothing but evil there. No fear, no re-morse. Their color now seemed darker than her hair—

huge, black orbs filled with hatred. She opened her mouth and spit into his face.

Paul's heart plummeted to his feet. To him, it seemed as if Satan, not the Lord, had arrived that night.

1

She walked into the bedroom dressed in a gold satin gown so tight Paul could see every sinewy muscle as she moved toward him. Her hips swayed, and she touched the tip of a finger to her mouth, wetting it, then pushing it farther in, sucking on it as her eyes met his in a familiar promise. The fabric of the dress was so thin, so tight, it was little more than gold sweat outlining her breasts and the deep V between her thighs.

God, she looked good. How many hours a day did it take to stay in such great shape?

Momentarily he thought of Gina, his wife, and felt a pang of remorse. He remembered the way they had been together the first year of their marriage.

But that was more than twenty years ago, and no matter how hard they had tried to hold things together, no matter how they had honestly wanted it, nothing had been the same since that terrible Christmas when Angela…

As fast as the thought came, Paul turned it off. He had learned to do that—to compartmentalize and not dwell on the bad times. Instead he turned his attention to his groin, and the fact that he was growing hard. It was almost painful, the excitement his mistress, Lacey, could invoke in him by the merest look. It was a good pain, though, telling him he was still alive. Rational thought flew out the window as she reached the side of the bed and raised one long, slender leg, straddling him. Leaning down, she swept his cheeks with her waist-length blond hair, teasing and laughing softly as her full breasts nearly fell out of their satin shield.

Paul reached up and yanked the low-cut neckline apart, his arousal intensifying as he heard the buttons pop, the thin fabric rip. Lacey gave a soft laugh. He had bought her the gown so that he could do this, playing out a fantasy that Lacey enjoyed. He could never bring himself to actually hurt her, nor did she ask for that. This pretense at roughness had become part of their foreplay, one his mistress had suggested, and the lingerie was a one-time purchase he could well afford. She threw back her head, shaking her hair in buttery waves as her body began to move over his. Reaching for him with one hand, she slid him inside her while remaining upright and giving him access to her breasts. Rocking back and forth, she moaned.

The tightness in Paul's throat grew as he grabbed her breasts firmly, the way she liked it. Squeezing her nipples until they were stiff, hard nubs he could fix his mouth around, he stroked the soft fullness of them, letting the feel of her overtake him until all coherent thought left his mind. Only a blank slate was left. A blank slate with nothing written on it—no unhappy past, no painful present, no pallid future.

When it was over, it was as if a job had been done, a commitment met, if only to himself. He had managed to hold the memories at bay.

Spent, Paul stared at the ceiling. For three months, holding the bad memories at bay had been Lacey Allison's only job. He had rescued her from a string of temporary positions as an assistant to various Seattle CEOs and had put her up in this luxury apartment. For the past three months she had waited for him every evening, whether he was able to come here or not. Even during the day, when she went out to shop, she would take a cell phone with her so that he could reach her at any time. This, too, was her suggestion. She wanted to be with him every possible moment.

As for Paul, from the day he'd made the decision to be with her—unthinkable up until then—he couldn't get enough of her. He wanted to drink her down, make her a part of him that would never leave, never go.

He reached for her, and this time an aeon passed that he wouldn't remember later. He had gone into another world, a world where nothing mattered, not even the sex. Lacey did that for him. She took him to that blank slate where, for a few moments, at least, nothing existed—not even Lacey herself.

* * *

Gina Bradley opened her front door and stood for a moment, listening for signs of movement. Shifting the bags of groceries in her arms, she shook her head and sighed. For heaven's sake, who did she listen for?

Certainly not Paul. It was only five, and he had been coming home later and later these past few months. In the beginning, she would hold dinner for him, warming it in the oven at seven, eight, nine. In recent weeks she hadn't bothered, taking a sandwich for herself up to their room and watching television or reading until he came home. Often it was after midnight when she would hear his car pull into the driveway. The Infiniti's headlights would sweep the room quickly, leaving as faint an impression as Paul's presence when at last he would tiptoe quietly into the bedroom with a mumbled apology.

His excuse, always, was that he'd been working late, and Gina had no reason not to believe it. Paul became moody and withdrawn every year before the Christmas holiday. Losing little Angela sixteen years ago had changed her husband in ways even she couldn't comprehend.

Not that she herself didn't still miss the child. But it was a long time ago, and Gina had tried to move on, to build a career she could exist inside, like a hermit crab. If her work as an interior designer didn't always satisfy, she accepted that as natural, given the circumstances. Losing a child—even a child one had adopted and lived with for only four years—had left a hole in her heart. Not just a break, the kind country-western songs were written about, but an actual hole as seen in medical journals, the kind that led to death, or at the very least, drastic surgery.

For a while, Gina and Paul thought that, because of their grief, they might actually die. However, they had somehow pulled themselves together and had been saved—if *saved* was the right word—by the surgical removal of memories. Clean, antiseptic cuts were called for, as in the giving away of clothes and toys, the burning of photographs, the removal of everything that might remind them of Angela.

Everything, that is, but Rachel, her twin.

They had wished for identical twins at first, little girls they could dress in the same outfits, a cutesy look that would have people stopping in the street to coo over two-seater strollers and rhapsodize, "Oh, how precious." They came to be grateful, however, that Rachel and Angela had been fraternal twins instead. The fact that they didn't look alike helped after Angela was gone. And as Rachel grew, she took on more of Gina's and Paul's traits, so that eventually the reminders of Angela were diluted in that way, as well.

Except at Christmastime. If they lived to be a thousand, they would never be able to wipe away the memory of Angela in her new white dress with the wide scarlet sash, the knife in her hand as she stood over Rachel, a look of pure evil on her face. Then, as Paul and Gina had screamed in unison, there was that awful, unbelievable moment as Angela had thrust the knife down, slicing at Rachel's tiny five-year-old chest, while tree lights twinkled and carols played.

As Paul had said later, it was as if the devil himself, not the Lord, had arrived that night. The devil in the form of a five-year-old girl, a girl they had raised in almost exactly the same way as her twin, whom they had adopted, too, thinking that keeping the girls together would be a blessing for all concerned.

That one of those girls would turn out to be a killer, they could not have foreseen. A "bad seed," to coin a term. But one didn't coin terms when one loved a child. One simply stood by in horror and disbelief as signs of evil began to show themselves, growing in intensity until that evil reached a crescendo on a holiday night that was supposed to be a warm, loving, family occasion.

It was all Gina and Paul could do to survive the shock—and then to remove all traces of Angela from their home.

Unpacking groceries, Gina wiped away tears. Often, when she allowed herself to remember Angela, tears sprang to her eyes and her collarbones ached from the emptiness in her heart. The last sight of that child as they turned her back over to the people at the orphanage was frozen in memory for all time.

That was the hell of it. Angela could be so sweet, so affectionate, convincing everyone who knew her that it wasn't possible she could have done something so terrible. Then there would be an incident, like Rachel falling down the stairs, or rat poison from the garden shed ending up mysteriously in Rachel's milk.

More than once, they'd had a scare like that with Rachel. And more than once, Angela had been nearby. They'd had no proof that she'd caused these "accidents" in any way, and Rachel herself said she had tripped over stuffed animals on the stairs. But the question remained, who had put those stuffed animals there, in a corner of the stairs that was so dark they were unlikely to be seen? And though it was hard to believe a five-year-old would think to take rat poison from a high shelf in a garden shed and put it in her sister's milk, who had placed the step stool by that shelf and forgotten to put it back? Who, but someone short enough to need it?

On the other hand, to suspect Angela of such monstrous deeds was, at first, unthinkable.

It wasn't until that terrible Christmas Eve that Gina and Paul were forced to admit they had a killer on their hands. That Rachel hadn't died that night was a miracle. Paul had gotten to her in time, saving her from more than a shallow wound. It was enough, though, to convince them that Angela could never be trusted alone with her sister again.

They'd had to make a decision, and it was the most difficult one they'd ever faced. On the advice of Victoria Lessing, the psychiatrist they'd been consulting for months, they took Angela back to the orphanage.

Though on the surface it seemed cold to do that, Saint Sympatica's was known for its private funding by wealthy patrons, and for having psychiatric care for its children. It was because of the high quality of care that it had been recommended to Gina and Paul when they first announced to friends their intention to adopt a child. The long flight to Minnesota to apply, then the following investigation and paperwork, were well worth it when they finally got to hold the twins in their arms.

Gina could remember the first time she realized that Angela was Paul's favorite. They both did their best not to choose favorites, but there was some link, some bond between Paul and Angela that drew them together. Angela was outgoing and could make Paul laugh with her antics, while Rachel was timid and reserved, standing back and watching while her sister danced like a windup bear and made funny faces that stole the show.

This, of course, had the effect of making Gina show more attention to Rachel so that she wouldn't feel left out. When Angela was old enough to notice this, she became angry over Gina's preference for her twin, as she perceived it. At first she threw tantrums, stamping her feet or kicking things. Around the age of four, however, she began to hit Rachel. When she blackened one of her sister's eyes, Gina and Paul began consulting Victoria Lessing. Victoria at first told them that, though a black eye seemed a bit extreme, fighting amongst siblings was normal. Perhaps Angela hadn't realized what the consequences of her actions would be? Now that she did, her love for her sister might temper her actions in the future.

The problem, as Gina saw it, was that Angela did not seem to have the usual twin's love for her sister. There were times, in fact, when Gina was sure that Angela hated Rachel.

She tried to talk to Paul about this but, blinded by love, he couldn't see it. Angela was too good at hiding her darker side when he was around, and consequently he would defend her hotly, arguing that she simply had a stronger, more assertive personality than Rachel. Paul felt this would serve her well in the future.

In all fairness, not even Gina could have foreseen the kind of terror that future would bring.

The phone rang, and Gina came back to the present with a start. Rolling her eyes, she sighed, sensing who was on the other end of that ring.

"Hi, Mom," she said, picking up the kitchen phone.

"How'd you know it was me?" Roberta Evans asked. "Oh, you've got that caller ID now, right?"

"Right, Mom," Gina lied. It was easier than explaining that she'd developed a sixth sense for trouble. "What's up?"

"Rachel's coming home tomorrow, isn't she? I forgot when her plane comes in."

"Five-oh-five in the afternoon, Mom. You want to come with us?"

"Sea-Tac at that hour, the week before Christmas?" Her mother's tone was one of exaggerated horror. "I'd rather wrestle a polar bear! How come you didn't make it at a better time?''

Gina could hear the puff-puff of her mother's cigarette, and saw in her mind the dyed red hair, the dark-lined lips. She loved her mother like crazy, even with all her eccentricities. Truth be told, she loved the eccentricities too—even more than she let on.

"That was the only flight we could get her on, Mom. She's having tests at school today."

"Well, that's the most ridiculous thing I ever heard of! Tests, with Christmas only five days away? What are they trying to do to young people these days?"

"It's something special, Mom. The term ended officially on the fourteenth, but she had to take some test for a special class."

Gina sighed and changed the subject, taking a box of cereal from a bag and putting it in the cupboard. "We're taking her to dinner on the way home," she said. "We probably won't get back here till late."

"You keep saying 'we,'" her mother commented blandly. "Does this mean Paul will be with you?"

"Of course. We always pick Rachel up together, you know that."

"On the contrary, I don't know a thing about Paul these days. Seems to me he's never home when I call you at night."

"Well, maybe you don't call on the right nights," Gina said, defending her husband out of habit.

"He's not there now, I'll bet."

"No, but—"

"And he wasn't home last night when I called, either."

Gina took down a heavy cut-crystal tumbler and pulled a spicy Chardonnay from the fridge, pouring it to the tumbler's halfway mark, then shrugging and filling it clear to the rim. *What the hell.*

"Mother," she said patiently, taking a sip, "you know Paul always works late during the holidays. It's his way of coping."

"Well, it may be none of my business, but if you ask me, it's not his only way of coping."

Gina frowned. "You're right, *Mother*. It's none of your business."

"Don't *Mother* me, Gina Evans Bradley. He wouldn't be the first man to stray."

"No, but as I've told you before, Paul isn't the type."

"Ha! All men are the type."

This was not a discussion Gina wanted to have. But to simply let it go would only add more fuel to her mother's fire.

"Paul is too tired these days," she said quietly, "to have an affair. He's worn-out, Mom. I'm worried about him."

"Are you saying he's worn-out when he's with you? You don't have sex anymore?"

Setting the tumbler of wine on the counter with a thud, Gina snapped, "Mom, that's enough! I don't want to talk about this anymore."

"Because if he is, that might very well prove my point, you know."

Gina clicked the flash button on the phone. "Mom, there's another call coming in. It could be Rachel. I'll talk to you in the morning, okay?"

"Oh, for heaven's sake! You can just stop clicking that thing. I know there's not a call coming in."

"Bye, Mom." Gina smiled as she hung up the phone. Her mother was still sharp at sixty, and at times almost psychic.

About Paul, however, she was completely off base. Paul would never have an affair. Gina knew him too well, and the one thing she knew for certain was that he simply wasn't the type.

Paul watched Lacey as he dressed, who lay on the bed and followed his every move, a mock lewd grin turning up the corners of her mouth. Her lips were swollen now from lovemaking, and with her bright red lipstick rubbed off, she looked like a little girl—an innocent child, though he knew she was neither a child nor innocent, but a woman who knew things that other women never even thought about.

Pulling his pants on, he shoved in the tail of the white dress shirt he'd worn to Soleil Antiques that day. His hands fumbled. He was depleted from their love-making, and she was beginning to get to him again. Lacey played with a nipple, her eyes smoldering. Incredibly, she was ready for more.

Paul was tempted, but he had to get home. Gina

could never know what he was doing; it would hurt her to the core, and he didn't want that. Keeping a mistress was something entirely apart from his marriage to Gina. It was like—well, like living two different lives, each of them necessary and valid but for entirely different reasons.

Lacey sat up and reached for him. He dodged her, laughing.

"Enough! What are you trying to do, put me in cardiac arrest?"

She slid from under the satin sheets and pulled bikini briefs over legs so long, they seemed two-thirds of her height. Bending over, she let her full breasts hang as she placed them in a more comfortable position inside her bra. Paul's mouth went dry.

"Cardiac arrest?" Lacey chuckled, straightening. "Not you! You're a bear. A big, strong bear." Then, squinting, she studied him through the most beautiful green eyes he had ever seen. "No…you're too tall and thin to be a bear. More like a handsome black panther. An aging panther, of course, with that gray hair popping out along your temples—"

He couldn't help himself. Reaching over, he slid a hand inside the bra and cupped one of her breasts. Stepping closer, he pulled her to him, closing his eyes and resting his chin on her head. "Oh, God, you feel so good."

Despite himself, he began to grow hard again. He glanced at the little clock decorated with hand-painted cherubs on the night table, one of the few things Lacey had brought with her from her own apartment. She hadn't owned much, having just moved to Seattle in the summer. When he'd offered to help her pack to come here, she had said, "I don't have enough to bother with. I think I'll just put most of it in storage." It had made him feel good to be able to give her a better life than she'd had in Atlanta, growing up in a home where her hardworking parents could never quite make ends meet.

It was ten forty-five, according to the clock. He calculated quickly. It would take him twenty minutes at the most to drive home, and if he left here by eleven-thirty he could be there before midnight. That gave him another forty-five minutes.

He pulled Lacey down on the bed, his tongue seeking hers, his body working quickly against her, the bra and bikini panties slipping off easily as he molded himself to her skin.

When the phone rang again, Gina thought it was Paul. Gina muted the sound of the television and picked up the cordless phone by the bed.

"Hi, Mom." Rachel's high, young voice came over the wires.

"Honey?" Gina sat straighter as alarm bells went off. "Why are you calling so late? Is something wrong?"

"No...just nervous, I guess. Flying, you know."

Gina went into automatic mother mode. "Well, but

think how many times you've done it, and you've always arrived safe and sound! I'm sure you'll be fine.''

She couldn't let Rachel know how anxious she herself always felt when her daughter was in the air.

''I made reservations for dinner at the Space Needle,'' she said. ''You can look forward to that, at least.''

Rachel's smile seemed to carry through the phone. ''Great! I'll get my first solid meal in days and a view of Seattle, too. Is, uh—is Dad coming?''

''Of course he is. He wouldn't miss picking you up with me. He never has, has he?''

''No. I just thought…he's pretty busy lately, isn't he? I haven't had many e-mails from him in the past few weeks.''

''Well, you know how busy your father always is at this time of year.''

''Sure, I guess that's it. Hey, Mom? I really need to shop for some clothes. Do you mind?''

''Of course not. We'll go on Saturday.''

''There'll be Christmas crowds, though.''

''I'll fend them off the same way I did last year,'' Gina said, smiling. ''They won't stand a chance.''

She had expected Rachel to laugh, but all she said was, ''Mom, *really*,'' in a tone that sounded like disgust.

Last year, while cleaning off the front steps, Gina had slipped on a patch of ice, spraining her ankle. When she and Rachel had gone shopping, she was recovering but still used a cane. Much to her delight, she discovered that the crowds in the stores had parted for her as if she were Moses parting the Red Sea. She had thought Rachel had enjoyed that, too, but now she wondered if her daughter had been embarrassed by her.

"I, uh…I could wrap an Ace bandage around my ankle, if that would make you feel better," she tried with a hint of humor. "No one would ever guess there was nothing wrong with me."

Rachel's voice took on an edge. "For heaven's sake, who are you, my mom's evil twin? Watch out, or we might have to cart you away—"

She bit the words off, as if suddenly realizing what she'd said. Not before her remark had shocked Gina, however. Rachel was always so careful not to talk about her twin, or say anything that might even remind Gina of her.

"Sorry, Mom," Rachel said softly.

"Oh, honey, it's all right. I know you didn't mean anything by it."

But was that true? she wondered. They had never really known how much Rachel had suffered over the loss of her sister. She was too silent, keeping too much inside. Not even Victoria had been able to bring much out. The best Gina and Paul could do was provide Rachel with all the love they had to give. And, of course, reassure her that what had happened to Angela would never happen to her.

Gina talked with her daughter a few minutes more, and then said goodbye. As she turned off her reading

light, she pulled the down comforter up over her
shoulders, feeling a chill. It was bad enough that Paul
withdrew every year at this time. What if Rachel began to do that, too?

As Paul drove home, he automatically began the
mental transition from Lacey's chrome-and-glass
apartment to the elegant house on Queen Anne Hill.
Often he would relax by listening to classical music
on a CD, but tonight, as he drove past homes decorated to the hilt with Christmas lights, the usual holiday depression set in. He couldn't keep himself from
wondering how things had turned out this way, after
such great hopes for the future. Hadn't he started out
life with all the usual excitement of a college graduate
with an MBA? And hadn't he thought, like most, that
he had the world by the tail?

Even meeting Gina had required little effort. They'd
run into each other in a campus café during their last
year at the University of Washington, begun dating
and were married shortly after graduation. They wrote
down their goals for themselves and their marriage on
crisp white paper, and mapped out their lives in the
way of young couples in the eighties: Gina would
work for a while until Paul became established and
they had a nice nest egg. Then she would quit to stay
home and raise children. They would have two children—a good number in an age where having too
many was frowned upon as not being politic, in a

world where populations had exploded and having big families was an environmental no-no.

They wouldn't get bogged down in work for work's sake, they agreed, the way their parents had. Having been born in the sixties, they remembered fathers who wore business suits and ties, fathers with gray faces who trudged back and forth to the office every day and kept their noses to the grindstone to buy a house with a mortgage that wouldn't be paid off until long after they were dead. They remembered mothers who from the age of eighteen had stayed home and been housewives, who had so many children to raise they'd become more and more worn-out as the years went by, their dreams turned to so much dust.

Paul and Gina swore they would never end up like that. Life in the eighties was going to be different. These were the Reagan years, the years of renewal, a good economy, the years when he who had the most toys won. Paul and Gina would have well-paid jobs that would give them time off to travel through Europe, take vacations, go skiing at Aspen. When Gina finally did leave her job, it would be only after they had a solid nest egg. And she wouldn't take off forever, the way her mother had. She'd get the children to a certain age and then reenter the work force while she was still employable and could command an excellent salary.

As the first months of their marriage passed, however, Paul and Gina's Life Plan had taken sharp, unexpected turns. Gina learned she was infertile—a congenital defect, the doctors said. As for Paul, though his antique business brought in the kind of money they'd dreamed about—enough, along with Gina's work as an interior designer, to enable them to buy the house on Queen Anne Hill—their work took up so much time that he and his wife barely knew each other six months after the honeymoon. They had the house of their dreams but rarely lived in it, except to sleep after the long commute home each night. They had the prerequisite two cars, but traveled in them only to work and back on bogged-down freeways.

After eight months of this, Gina began to have an itch. She wanted a baby. She didn't want to wait. They had enough money to take care of a child, and she needed more in her life than just work.

So they adopted the girls, a move that was supposed to change their lives. And it did. The hell of it was, it had changed a dream into a deadly nightmare—one from which, Paul knew, he would never awaken, as long as he lived. Was it any wonder he couldn't fully live in that world—couldn't participate in a place of so many dark memories, without some kind of light shining through?

Every day he thanked God for Lacey, who had brought him light, as well as laughter. Without her, he would never have survived. In fact, there were moments when he felt she was all that kept him alive.

2

Gina buttered a piece of toast, put it on a plate and slid it across the black granite breakfast bar to Rachel, who gobbled it down as if she hadn't had a decent meal in weeks.

Which she apparently hadn't, except for last night at the Space Needle. Gina studied her with a worried frown. Rachel had clearly lost several pounds since summer vacation. She had never been overweight, but was blessed with a trim, athletic figure that was largely from all her years of rowing. Rachel had been a rowing fanatic, latching onto the sport in her first year of high school. Gina and Paul had thought she would go to the University of Washington on a scholarship, but Rachel had surprised them in her senior year by stating that she was no longer interested in rowing, and wanted to go to college in a warmer climate. She had chosen Berkeley, in Northern California. Gina had thought at the time that her daughter simply wanted to spread her wings, put some distance between herself and home. And she had to admit, the change would probably do Rachel good.

Now, however, Gina wasn't so sure. Sitting there on the stool, with her long brown hair pulled back in a ponytail and no makeup on, Rachel looked much as she had in grade school. Gina remembered how they would sit this way in the mornings, the two of them chatting companionably till Rachel's ride arrived. Her eyes would light up at the idea of going to a movie on the weekend, or planting spring bulbs with her mother, the two of them digging in the moist earth side by side, no words needed between them.

Where had that easy companionship gone? Rachel had come home this time seeming sullen. Detached. Gina felt the loss like a shaft through her heart.

"Rachel, what's wrong?" she said now. "You've changed somehow since summer."

"And?"

"And I'm not sure I like all of it. Last night, at the airport, for instance—"

"Oh, for heaven's sake, I was just tired. I didn't mean to snap. And why didn't Dad come? You said he was going to."

"I thought he was. But I told you, honey, something came up." Gina ran her fingers through her short-cropped brown hair, inadvertently messing up the style she'd worked at so carefully this morning.

"Came up? At Soleil?" Rachel rolled her eyes.

"Yes, at Soleil," Gina said, annoyed. "Where else?"

Rachel shrugged and studied her toast, picking off tiny pieces and putting them in her mouth one at a time, chewing slowly. "Nowhere, I guess."

Gina sighed. So far, this visit was not going at all

well. "Rachel, if you've got something to say, please just say it."

Her daughter slid off the stool and took her plate and coffee cup to the sink, grinding the rest of her toast in the disposal. With her back to Gina she said, "I just think there's something wrong."

"Like what?"

"I don't know...like maybe Dad is sick, or something."

"Is that what you think? That he's sick?"

Rachel came back and slid onto the stool. Her eyes held a glint of anger. "Well, he's not acting at all like himself. Haven't you even noticed?"

"No, I haven't." Gina's brow furrowed. "What would make you say that?"

Rachel shrugged again. "For one thing, he hasn't been e-mailing me hardly at all this semester. One of my friends at school found out her father had cancer, and the only way she knew was that he stopped talking to her on the phone. He was too sick to call the way he always did."

"Well, sweetheart, I can assure you that your father does not have cancer. He's perfectly well, and when he gets down here you can ask him for yourself."

"That's another thing. Why is he sleeping so late?"

Gina gritted her teeth. This was worse than when her daughter was seven and asked so many questions that it drove her crazy, especially in the morning before she'd fully woken up.

"It's only ten o'clock," she said briskly, looking at

her watch. "And speaking of time, we should be leaving soon if we want to beat at least some of the crowds." She piled her coffee cup and silverware on top of her toast plate.

"Mom, you aren't—"

"No, I'm not taking the blasted cane!" Gina took her dishes to the sink. "Now stop annoying me, Rachel, and go get dressed. Maybe you'll meet your father on the stairs, and you can pester him for a while."

She tempered her words with a smile and crossed over to her daughter, kissing her lightly on the cheek. Rachel gave her a half smile and slipped away, her ponytail bobbing behind her as she went through the door. A scene from childhood, Gina thought. Yet it's not. It's all wrong today.

Rinsing the dishes and putting them in the dishwasher, Gina gazed out on the back lawn. The skies over Seattle could be gray in winter, but the rain at least kept the grass and the cedar trees green. Unfortunately, the flower beds were all dead, except for a chrysanthemum here and there. Gina yearned for spring, like a sailor at sea too long yearns for land.

They were lucky, though, to have this beautiful home, and to have bought it before prices went sky-high. From the front, one could see the Space Needle, and the view of the Sound was exquisite. Even with the problems they'd had with Angela, she and Paul enjoyed a life that most would give their right arms for.

As for the problems, they were over now. In the

past. They had finally reached that place they had talked about and looked forward to when they were younger—an early retirement, possibly travel, and an easing of the pressures of life.

Gina felt a wave of depression sweep over her, a feeling of being dead inside. Quickly she shook it off and went to get ready to leave. She and Rachel would stop at a drive-through espresso stand along the way to the stores. Another jolt of caffeine, that's all she needed. She and millions of other Washingtonians— victims of the barometer, and addicts all.

Paul stood at his bathroom mirror, taking in the lines of strain that had appeared around his eyes since Rachel had come home. He had seen her only briefly, arriving home himself at ten—early, for a change— just as Gina and Rachel had pulled into the driveway themselves. That had meant leaving Lacey's apartment early, and now he felt bad that he'd gone there at all, instead of helping Gina pick up Rachel. He had told himself he would stay only an hour or so, and that Gina would be fine going to the airport alone. He would meet them at the restaurant.

But that had all flown out the window once he was with Lacey. The lines of strain deepened. He felt torn between his daughter and his mistress, and weak because he hadn't chosen well.

What he didn't understand was why Rachel was so different this time. During her visits home in her freshman year, she had been the young woman he'd always known. Now she looked at him with eyes that seemed to cut right through him. It was as if she had the ability to reach inside his soul and pull all his secrets out.

Though he felt ashamed to even think this way, it almost made him not want to be around her.

Bracing himself to walk into the kitchen, Paul planted a smile on his face. Rachel was there, talking on the phone, and he crossed over to her, kissing her on the cheek.

"It's great to have you home," he said when she hung up. He hugged her.

"Is it?" She pulled back and looked up at him, her eyes narrowing. "You know, Dad, I saw a show on TV at school, called 'The Human Face.' John Cleese—you know, that guy who used to be on Monty Python?—he showed how when the muscles around the mouth don't go up and the ones around the eyes don't widen, a smile is a fake."

He stared at her, nonplussed. "What are you saying?"

"That I don't know whether to believe you when you say you're glad to have me home."

"Of course I am, honey!" he insisted. "You know that!"

"Then why didn't you come to the restaurant last night?"

He flinched at her cold tone. "I'm sorry, Rach. I meant to, but things came up."

She turned and busied herself at the fridge, taking out a bottle of water.

"What things came *up,* Daddy?" she asked, twisting the cap off the bottle with a loud snap.

It was almost as if she were making a double entendre of a sexual nature, Paul thought with a start. *What things came "up?"* But he couldn't believe Rachel capable of that. Even if she knew anything about his being with Lacey last night—which was impossible—she would never say something like that.

There was something about Rachel this time, though, that made him feel uncomfortable, off balance.

He poured himself a full cup of steaming coffee and changed the subject. "How was school this semester?"

"You want to see my report card?" she answered.

"Well, of course I'm always interested in that, but I didn't mean—"

"Because my grades are okay," she interrupted, "if that's what you're worried about."

"Rachel…" He sighed as she leaned against the refrigerator and glared at him. "What is it? What's wrong?"

"Why don't you tell me?" she said.

"What do you mean?"

"I mean I don't hear from you anymore. We used to write back and forth all the time—" Rachel's voice broke slightly. "We used to write about things that were funny, and I got so I looked forward to it." Turn-

ing her back to him, she added, ''I guess that was my
mistake.''

He set down his coffee cup and reached for her. His
hands light on her shoulders, he turned her around so
that she met his eyes. There were tears in hers, and he
couldn't stand it. ''Rachel…oh, honey, it wasn't a
mistake. I don't know why I haven't been writing as
much, except that I've been so busy the past few
months.''

''I thought you were going to slow down now,
spend more time with Mom. That's what you said
when I was home last summer.''

The tears brimming in her eyes ran down onto her
cheeks. Paul wiped them away with his thumb, just as
he had when she was a child. ''Honey, your mom's
been busy, too. We did talk about retiring, but it seems
that she's been getting more work than ever. She
hasn't been home much.''

He didn't mean that to sound like a criticism, or to
put the blame on Gina for his own frequent absences,
but Rachel took it that way.

''According to her, you're the one who's been too
busy to retire,'' she said testily.

Paul sighed. ''Things are never one-sided, Rach. It
takes a lot of work to make everything come together
in a home.''

''Yeah? Well, it looks to me like both of you would
rather work on other people's homes.''

''Rach,'' Paul said softly, determined that this not
evolve into an argument, ''I don't understand what's

gotten into you. You're entirely different from the girl you were last summer. And I'm sorry, but it's hard to believe that you're this angry just because I haven't been e-mailing as much.''

''Well, in the first place,'' Rachel said, mimicking his composure, ''I'm not a *girl,* Daddy. I'm twenty-one, and I've been away from home almost two years now. I think I've reached a point where I can make my own mind up about some things.''

''Of course you have,'' he agreed. ''Just…honey, tell me what you want me to do. How can I make things better for you?''

He recalled having asked that same question far too many times over the years, always with the nagging feeling that he was becoming the kind of parent who didn't know or care about his child's feelings. Yet he did care. He apparently just wasn't at all good at showing it.

If that was the truth, however, it was also true that Rachel had never seemed able to tell him, clearly, what she needed from him. Like a runner who sees the finish line ahead, he had always fallen just short of it—and the race, after so many years, had left him feeling winded. Inept.

Rachel had turned her back on him again, and Paul looked at her, so fragile-seeming, so young. His heart did a flip-flop. He loved her so much. Why had they never been able to reach each other?

And what might he be able to do about that now?

''Your mom wants us all to pick out the tree tomorrow," he said. "Would you like to go to lunch, first? Just you and me? We could catch up on all the things you've been doing since summer."

She didn't answer immediately. But he saw her shoulders ease from their stiff, almost military posture, and when she turned back to him she put her arms around his neck and hugged him. "Sure, Daddy," she said, her words muffled against his shoulder. "Let's do lunch."

The next day, Paul left Soleil Antiques early, determined to reach the Four Seasons before Rachel. They had planned to meet in the lobby, and he was afraid she would read too much into it if he were late. When he arrived right on the dot of noon, however, Rachel was already there, and she had other plans.

"I can't stand this place anymore," she said nervously, with a sharp look that scanned the lobby. "Let's get out of here."

Giving him no time to ask questions, she turned quickly and headed for the front doors. Out on the sidewalk, Paul said curiously, "The Georgian Room used to be a favorite of yours when you were little. What happened?"

"It's just too...much," she said. "All those chandeliers and things, I mean, after living on cheese puffs and burgers at school. Besides, I don't think the Georgian Room is open for lunch."

"You're probably right," Paul agreed. "It's been a

while since I've been there. Well, we could go to any number of restaurants. I'm not in a hurry, are you?''

For a moment, Rachel didn't answer. Finally, she shoved her hands into her pockets and said, ''I'd just as soon get this over with.''

The chill in her tone was almost as bad as the way she turned on her heel and left him to follow her down the street. Paul had to hustle to keep up with her pace, and the ring of her boots as they tap-tapped ahead of him on the sidewalk seemed to sound an alarm. He noted how thin her shoulders looked in the old camel's hair coat that she'd refused to part with for years. It got shabbier and shabbier, and the more it did, the more she seemed to like it.

She looks so thin, he thought. When did she lose so much weight?

And then, *Dear God, don't let her be anorexic.*

His fears on that score, at least, were laid to rest when Rachel stopped in front of a hole-in-the-wall greasy spoon and said, ''This'll do.''

The narrow little place had a green see-through shade on the front window, with aging black booths running along one wall and a bar along the other. The five men and one woman sitting at the bar looked as if they'd come in years ago and just never left. They eyed Rachel and Paul suspiciously, and Paul wondered if he and Rachel looked like cops. Inwardly he smiled. If I had a badge, I'd pull it out and flash it, he thought, just to clear the room. God knows, at least three of America's Most Wanted could be sitting right here in downtown Seattle, drinking away the days till they were found.

Rachel took a seat in one of the booths. Paul hesitated, looking at the cracked vinyl seat. Carefully he dusted crumbs from it with a paper napkin. Looking at Rachel, he noted the slightly mocking grin.

He gave her a rueful smile. "And to think I wore my best suit to have lunch with you."

She made no comment.

The bartender dried his hands on a stained towel he'd tucked into his waist and called out, "What can I get you?"

Rachel ordered a Pepsi and a chili dog with all the trimmings. Paul ordered a beer and a bag of chips.

"Aren't you eating?" Rachel asked.

"Not anything that human hands have touched," Paul said, smiling.

There were pool tables in the back, and the clicking of balls hitting each other resounded down the long, narrow room. Paul couldn't resist saying, "You come here often?"

Rachel shrugged. "There are all kinds of dives like this in Berkeley. Students learn to seek them out. They're cheap."

"Rach, you know you don't have to do that. We send you enough money to eat well. What are you spending it on?"

"What makes you think I'm spending it? Maybe I'm saving it for a rainy day."

"Are you predicting rain?" he asked, attempting a smile again.

"You never know," Rachel said with a tone of finality.

Paul wanted to follow up on that, but decided to change the subject instead.

"Come to think of it, I remember eating burgers and pizza when I was in school. I didn't have much money, and—"

"You've told me all about that before, Dad," Rachel interrupted. "Must we go through it again?"

Paul felt hurt at her flippant tone, but answered, "I was only going to say that I thought you'd want something a bit…oh, fancier, when you came home."

"The setting doesn't matter, Dad. Not for what we have to talk about."

Paul turned his attention to the napkin that was still in his hand. If he could remember how to do it just right, he might be able to make the figure of a bird out of it, the way he had when Rachel was a child. Maybe that would somehow help to make this day right.

The napkin, however, was too flimsy, falling apart in his hands. It seemed a metaphor for this place, this day, and the way his relationship with Rachel was going.

The bartender brought their food and Rachel devoured her chili dog in record time, washing it down with the Pepsi. Paul toyed with his chips, but drank the full mug of beer, wishing he'd ordered whiskey or almost anything that would kick in fast. The beer didn't at all help the nervousness that was growing as he waited for Rachel to speak her peace.

It finally came.

"So, Dad…what's on your mind these days? Or should I say who?"

Paul thought he had braced himself for whatever was coming, but even so, he was shocked by the frontal attack. He set down the empty mug and tried to keep his expression bland. "What are you talking about?"

"Oh, please. Mom may be too busy to see it, but when you've been away, like I have, it's plain as the nose on your face. You haven't been spending all those hours at night at Soleil, have you? You've been…shall we say, with someone else?"

His mouth was suddenly so dry he could barely speak. Taking a sip of water, he managed, "I don't know what you mean."

Her voice became icy. "You must think I'm really dumb. Mom, too."

"Rachel, I have no idea—"

"Oh, come off it, Dad. You've been paying good money to send me to college. Give me some credit for not being stupid."

"I have never once thought of you as stupid, Rachel."

"Then why don't you just tell me how long this has been going on?"

He couldn't answer. That Rachel knew about Lacey

was bad enough. That she expected him to talk about it was worse. Casting that much light on his affair—his betrayal of Gina, and yes, Rachel, too—made it impossible for him to think of it as anything but sordid.

Rachel gave a snort that broke the silence. "I know she was always your favorite, but I never thought you'd let her back into your life. Or ours."

"Favorite—?" Paul began, confused. Then it dawned on him, and he felt as if his entire body, having prepared for a long-term, drawn-out war, had suddenly ceased fire.

"You're talking about *Angela?*" he said, relaxing back against the booth. "Rachel, what on earth ever gave you an idea like that? I haven't seen Angela since she was six years old!" Paul half laughed, the idea was so preposterous.

"You lie pretty good now, too," Rachel said with a strange smile that gave him chills. "Nice going, Dad. I'm almost proud of the way you've grown."

Paul shook his head, so bewildered he couldn't speak. What had become of his daughter? Why was she saying these things?

"I don't know why you would think I've seen Angela," he said in as steady a tone as he could manage, "but even if I had, I'm your father, Rachel. I don't have to report to you."

"Obviously not," she said, "given the number of times I've heard from you since summer."

He stared. "Is *that* what's really bothering you?

Rach, I thought you were just as busy as I've been. I didn't think you'd miss hearing from me. I'm sorry. Really, I am.''

"Oh, for heaven's sake!" Rachel said. "It's not about the e-mail, Dad. It's about all those years when you didn't have time for me because you were so busy missing Angela. You think that didn't hurt? You think kids don't see those things, no matter how young they are?''

Paul, who at first was too thrown to stand up for himself, began to get angry. "Rachel, that was years ago. Why are you bringing it up now? I thought— God, all that time working with Victoria, and you're *still* hurting about those things? What does it take for you to get over it?''

"Maybe not having it start up all over again," she snapped. "Maybe getting her out of our lives once and for all!''

"But she isn't in our lives," he argued. "I'm telling you, I have not seen Angela since she was six years old.''

Rachel studied him. "You really haven't?''

"No. I swear to you. I have not seen or heard from Angela since the last time your mother and I went to Minnesota to see her. That was fifteen years ago.''

"So you haven't had a phone call from her, or a letter, or anything?''

"No, Rachel. Not a thing. If I had, I wouldn't have kept it from you.''

"Ha," she said scornfully.

"And what does that mean?"

"It means you never wanted me to know anything. You took her away and you never even let me go visit her."

Paul sighed. "We thought that was best. We've always just tried to do the best for you, Rachel. Your mother and I love you. We really do. I wish you could believe that."

Rachel fell silent. He thought she was going to argue the point, but she shrugged back into her coat and said, "Let's blow this place. Mom'll be waiting to get a tree."

Paul didn't know whether to be disappointed or relieved. He half wanted to continue the conversation, while the other half didn't want to go near it.

He put enough money on the table to cover the food and a tip. Again he found himself following his daughter as she breezed out the door. The door came swinging back and almost struck him in the face.

It was as if she were deliberately erecting a wall between them. *I can't let that wall get too high,* he thought miserably as they walked back to the Four Seasons, where they had both parked. *If she makes it any higher, I might never be able to breach it.*

At home, Gina was already cleaning out the trunk of the Crown Vic, which was big enough to put a tree in with a bungee cord holding the lid down.

"Let me help you with that," Paul said, taking a heavy flat of bottled water from her.

She threw him a grateful look and pulled her red scarf closer around her throat. She looks like she did in college, Paul thought. The cold, misty air had softened the few lines around her eyes, which were bright with anticipation. *She's like a kid about Christmas. How could I have forgotten that?*

They began the rounds of the tree farms in Snohomish, where the traffic was thinner and they could enjoy the drive. Since it was two days before Christmas, a lot of the better trees had been taken long ago. Gina insisted they make the tree shopping spree as much fun as possible, singing songs in the car as they always had, to pass the time. She seemed not to notice that Paul and Rachel were more quiet than usual. Their search spread farther and farther away from the city, until, finally, they came across a farm that hadn't been too stripped. It was their fourth try, and Gina and Rachel stood together in the mud amongst rows of Douglas firs, shivering.

"What do you think of this one?" Gina asked.

"Too skinny," Rachel complained. "I like this one better." She stood holding a branch of a wide nine-footer.

"That won't even fit through the door!" Gina said, smiling.

Paul was three rows over when he called out, "Hey, look at this!" They trudged valiantly over the rutted ground, expecting to reject this one as they had the past five.

"I love it!" Rachel said when she saw the tall, perfectly shaped fir. She cocked her head to the side and smiled. "No holes, no broken limbs. You always were the best at picking them out, Dad."

"Oh, I don't know. It's only taken me—" Paul pushed back his jacket sleeve and looked at his watch "—two hours and four tree lots this time." But he smiled, grateful that she seemed to be getting into the spirit of things. Maybe this day would turn out all right after all.

Finding the "perfect" Christmas tree had been a tradition ever since he could remember. There had been times over the years when he'd thought about leaving Gina, when it had seemed as if there was so little left of their relationship it hardly made sense to go on. Even the bad Christmas Eve memories, however, couldn't spoil the fact that there was something solid and safe about doing things like this together, and knowing they would be doing them year after year.

When it came right down to it, there hadn't been any good reason to break up his marriage. Gina might have distanced herself from him, but she still maintained a surface relationship, keeping up the house, being there for Rachel. He'd never even thought of straying...not until Lacey came into his life, offering boundless energy when he was weary, and light at a time when his very existence seemed to grow darker every year.

"Earth to Dad!" Rachel was saying. "Hello?"

Paul came back to the matter at hand. "So you really like this one? Should I start cutting?"

"Absolutely," Rachel said. "Okay with you, Mom?"

"Cut away," Gina replied, blowing into her hands for warmth. "And fast. Let's get the heck out of here!"

"Darn it," Rachel said, "I told you to wear gloves. But not to worry." She put an arm around her mom as Paul began to saw through the trunk of the fir. "We'll be at the tearoom soon. You can warm up there."

The tree fell, and Rachel cried, "Attaboy, Dad! You'd put Paul Bunyan to shame!"

Paul grunted. Looking at Gina and his daughter, at the smiles on their faces and the way they both rose to the occasion when good spirits were called for, he could only think: I wish I *were* a Paul Bunyan, a giant possessed of superhuman powers. Maybe then I could figure out a way to fix this moment in time forever.

After dragging the tree into the house and changing clothes, they drove down the hill to the tearoom. In an old Victorian house with several differently decorated rooms, it was warm and toasty from a huge fireplace in the large front room. Taped chamber music was soft and soothing, and the scents of cinnamon, apples and other holiday treats stimulated the appetite and brought back memories of traditional Christmases Paul had enjoyed as a child.

This, too, was a tradition that Paul, Gina and Rachel had followed. First the cutting of the tree—from a lot where trees were specifically grown for Christmas, to ease Rachel's concern over the destruction of the forests—and then tea, to warm themselves up.

Over the subdued murmur of voices and the gentle clinking of bone china cups against saucers, Paul looked at his wife and daughter. Rachel's cheeks were still pink from the cold, and the bright pink scarf she wore mirrored them. Her eyes shone in the candlelight. Without warning, a memory rushed in: Angela, and the way her eyes had been so like Rachel's in color, that clear, lovely hazel, yet always with a flicker of mischief in them.

Rachel was wrong in thinking he'd had some sort of contact with Angela. Yet her instincts were right. Everything about this season combined to form a gunnysack of immense proportions that he seemed destined, always, to carry on his back. He knew that if he opened that sack, more bad memories than he'd ever be able to live with would spill out.

It was one of the reasons, he admitted to himself, that he'd become involved with Lacey. In September, the stores had already been bringing out the Christmas toys and decorations. They were everywhere, and Paul had begun to dread the coming holiday even more than usual this year. There were times when he felt certain his life was over, and other times when he wished it were.

This past summer, he and Gina had barely seen each

other for weeks on end. She was working on a house up on Camano Island, more than an hour away, and she often came home late. Finally he had stopped going home after work, and had begun to have dinner in the city. His favorite place was the Gordon Biersch Brewery Restaurant, because there were always plenty of people there—young people, active and happy, or at least seemingly happy as they laughed and drank together after their day's work. Sitting in a bar drinking wasn't Paul's idea of a rousing good time, but having dinner at the bar and watching everyone around him enjoy themselves made him feel less lonely.

He hadn't started out with the thought that he might meet someone. At least, not consciously. He told himself he was merely passing the time. Then one night, a young blond woman at the other end of the bar began to make eye contact with him. At first, he was embarrassed. He hadn't been with anyone but Gina since they'd met in college. On this particular night, however, Paul found himself wanting someone to talk to. That was all, he swore to himself—just talk.

So when the woman smiled at him the third or fourth time their eyes met, instead of looking quickly away as she'd done at first, Paul took that as an invitation to move to the stool beside her and join her for a drink.

It had been awkward at first. Paul found himself at a loss for words. Funny, he thought. All this time I've been wanting someone to talk to, and now I don't know what to say.

But the woman made it easy for him.

"Hi, I'm Lacey," she said softly, holding out a hand. "May I buy you a drink?"

Paul smiled and shook her hand. "I thought the man was supposed to buy the woman a drink."

Lacey laughed and tossed her head, shaking back the lush blond hair that fell over her face on one side. Her eyes were a deep, deep green, so deep that when Paul looked into them he felt like a teenager striving for just the right poetic phrase. What he came up with was clichéd, he knew, but he honestly did feel as if he were falling into the depths of some long-forgotten, ancient sea. As for her complexion, it was creamy and flawless, except for a small half-moon scar at the corner of her right eye. She had covered it with makeup, making it less noticeable, but when she turned into the light from behind the bar, it stood out in sharp relief.

Paul was glad she had a flaw. Without it, he might have been intimidated by her beauty.

"What old-fashioned world did you come from," Lacey teased, "thinking the man has to buy the drink?" Nodding to the bartender, she pointed a finger at his nearly empty drink glass. "Don't tell me. You're married, and you haven't dated in years. And you don't want to get involved. Well, that's perfect, because I don't want to, either."

The bartender set the drink before him, and Paul relaxed. They began to talk. At ten o'clock they were still talking, and Paul, shocked at the time, said that he had to go.

"Maybe I'll see you here again," he said tentatively, unwilling to commit to an actual meeting, but hoping she would be here, nonetheless.

"Maybe," she said. "I stop by after work now and then." She touched him on the cheek with a fingernail that was bright red, like her lips. "We'll see."

That had been in August. Four short months ago, but he felt, now, as if he'd known her forever.

Their first conversation had carefully skirted personal information. Instead, they had talked about Microsoft, the Huskies, the Mariners, Boeing, the traffic...endless minutiae. In succeeding talks he told her about Gina and Rachel. She told him she had moved to Seattle in June and was working temp jobs. It had been difficult at first, but now she was established with one particular temp company, and in demand as an assistant to local CEOs. She living frugally, but was doing all right.

She seemed to want nothing from him but companionship, and that eased Paul's mind about what he was doing. By the time a month had passed, however, Paul couldn't tear himself away from the three- or four-times-a-week meetings at Gordon Biersch's. He began to tell Gina he was working late, and she had accepted that.

But then, why wouldn't she? he thought now as he looked across the table at his wife. He had never before given her any reason to doubt him.

And here she was, holding the family together as usual over the holiday—keeping the traditions and maintaining a brave facade for Rachel, even though she must know, as he did, that their marriage was falling apart.

Or *was* it a facade? Had Gina actually convinced herself there was nothing wrong? Was it possible she couldn't see how much their relationship had deteriorated?

There were times when Paul hated himself for the betrayal of his wife, and he prayed for the strength to end it.

"Can we decorate the tree tonight?" Rachel asked from the back seat as Paul swung the Infiniti into the driveway. "That tea really hyped me up."

Gina restrained a yawn. "Oh, I don't know..."

"C'mon, Mom. Talk her into it, Dad."

They had left the tree standing in a bucket of water in the front bay window of the house, facing the Sound and the city. When it was decorated and lit, it looked "awesome," as Rachel said every year, when they drove up the hill.

"We've still got two more days till Christmas," Paul said, wanting only to go to bed. "Can't it wait?"

"Boy, you two are party poopers this year." Rachel pouted. She slid from the car and ran up the front steps. "Last one in has to untangle the lights!"

She slid her key into the lock and disappeared through the doorway. Lights appeared in the hallway and living room. Gina looked at Paul and shrugged. "What do you think?"

He sighed. "At least she's smiling now. I was beginning to think—"

"I know what you mean," Gina said. "She's been a bear this trip."

"Maybe we can convince her just to put on the lights tonight. You think she'd be okay with that?"

"We can give it a try," Gina said.

Rachel's cry from inside hit them as they came up the walk. "Mom! Dad!"

Gina and Paul ran the rest of the way, following Rachel's voice into the living room. There they found the Christmas tree lying on its side, a pool of water surrounding it. The bucket lay empty on the hardwood floor.

Gina rushed forward, whipping off her woolen scarf and kneeling, trying to mop up the water before it did any more damage to the wood. "For God's sake, Paul, I told you to make sure the tree was secure enough so it couldn't fall!"

"I did," he said, bristling at the criticism. "I'll go get some towels."

"Never mind. Rachel, get me that throw cover over there."

Gina motioned to a heavy throw lying over a chair, but Rachel didn't move. Her face was pale as she stared at the tree, her eyes dark and frightened.

"Rachel?" Gina's tone was one of concern more than irritation, but Rachel's head snapped up and she took a step backward.

"Don't touch me! Get back!" Her hands rose as if to protect herself.

Gina started, and Paul stopped in his tracks to stare at his daughter.

"Rachel?" he said softly. "Rach, it's okay."

Gina rose slowly and moved carefully toward her daughter. "Shh. Shh, honey, it's all right."

Rachel's gaze rose from the fallen tree to her mother. For a moment she barely moved. Then her face crumpled and tears filled her eyes. "It's not all right!" she cried. "Nothing is ever going to be all right again!"

3

The next day, Rachel sat across from the psychiatrist who had treated her from the ages of six to sixteen. Victoria Lessing was older, of course, her hair graying now, but only a bit at the temples. Otherwise it was the same pale blond, pulled back into a twist. She still had that look in her violet eyes, too—the one that said, *I know your every thought. You can't hide a thing from me.*

"It's been a while, Rachel."

Rachel sighed. "You said it. I thought we were through with all this."

"Well, your parents are worried."

Rachel gave a shrug.

"You don't think they should be?"

"No. I just had some bad memories last night. After all, today is Christmas Eve. I think that's pretty normal."

"Normal being a relative term," the psychiatrist said, smiling.

"I suppose." Rachel fell silent.

"Have you been thinking more about your sister lately?"

"I don't know," Rachel said. "Maybe."

"Do you know why?"

"No."

"I think you do," Victoria said softly.

Rachel shrugged again. "I just thought I saw her, once. At Berkeley."

Victoria leaned forward, resting her arms on her desk. "Really?"

"Well, I was walking around on the campus, and there was this woman. She had dark hair like Angela's and mine, and…oh, I don't know. There was just something about the way she looked at me."

"Did you think she was following you?"

Rachel narrowed her eyes. "You mean, am I getting paranoid again?"

"No. I didn't mean that at all."

"But you were thinking it. *Rachel's imagining things again.*"

"No, I was not," Victoria said firmly. "You were a lot younger when you had nightmares that Angela would come back. Now that you're older, I'm sure you know the difference between being paranoid and feeling something real."

"Well, I didn't think this woman was following me, anyway. I just thought it was odd, the way she looked at me. I thought maybe Angela—" Rachel stopped talking and studied her hands.

"You thought that because she was your twin, she might have ended up at the same college as you," Victoria guessed. "The way identical twins who are separated seem to do similar things in life?"

"I...yes. I guess the thought crossed my mind."

"Of course you and Angela aren't identical."

"No. But does that matter?"

"I'm not sure. You don't have the same DNA, of course. As for other possibilities...did you try to find out if she was a student at Berkeley? Through the registrar's office, for instance?"

"No," Rachel said abruptly.

"You didn't really want to know," Victoria guessed again. "Because if it was Angela, you'd have had to do something about it. You'd have had to look her up and talk to her."

Rachel frowned. "I wish you wouldn't read my mind that way."

"That bothers you?"

"Of course it does! You've always done that, and it drives me nuts." Rachel paused, then laughed. "I guess that's not the sort of thing to say to a psychiatrist."

Victoria smiled. "We've known each other a long time, Rachel. You should know by now, you can say anything to me."

Rachel hugged herself with her arms, feeling cold even though the room was warm. "I just think it's silly, Vicky, my parents getting all worried like this. I warped back into the past for a few minutes when I saw that tree on the floor. Doesn't everybody do that sometimes?"

"Your mother said you were up pacing all night, and you didn't eat any breakfast this morning."

"Well, duh! I was upset, for heaven's sake. I'm over it now."

"Are you?"

"Yes, dammit!" Rachel gave the therapist a mutinous glare.

Victoria laughed. "I haven't seen that look since you were…oh, seven or eight."

The glare faded into a grin.

Victoria reached behind her chair and took a plate from a low mahogany filing cabinet. "Cookie?"

"Geez. I can't believe you're still plying patients with chocolate-chip cookies."

Victoria smiled. "It seems to work."

Rachel took a cookie. "This is supposed to make me more willing to open up, right?"

"Right."

She rolled her eyes. "Does psychiatry still work, even when the patient is smart enough to figure out all the moves?"

"Only when the cookies are merely a distraction, to keep the patient from figuring out the *real* moves."

"Is that what you've been doing to me all these years?" Rachel asked. "Playing mind games?"

"Why would you see it as mind games?" Victoria asked. "Why not simply as a way to help you? A way to get to the truth?"

Rachel snorted. "That assumes there's any such thing as truth."

"Are you saying there isn't?"

Carefully Rachel set the cookie back on the plate.

"Let's approach this from another direction. Do you think you've helped me over all these years?"

Victoria hesitated. "I…well, you've been going to college, preparing for the future. I certainly think you're better now than you were when you were sixteen, for instance. Or right after Angela left."

Rachel's mood changed in an instant. Jumping to her feet, she clenched her fists at her sides. "Angela *left?* For God's sake, Vicky, my sister did not *leave!* She was sent away—returned to the store, like a defective toaster oven. Why does everyone say she *left?* Does it make it easier somehow to sweep the truth under the rug?"

"So we're back to truth," Victoria said calmly, leaning back in her chair and folding her arms. "What is *your* truth, Rachel?"

Rachel threw up her hands. "How the hell do I know?"

"Do you want to know?"

"I…of course I do!" But she had paused before answering, and Victoria picked up on it quickly.

"What are you afraid of?" she asked.

Rachel sat again, rubbing her face and taking a deep breath. "I don't know. I think…I think I'm afraid of Angela. Of what I might find out if I saw her again."

"Have you been wanting to see her again?"

"I haven't even really thought much about her since I've been away at school. Then all of a sudden, I thought for sure she was there, and it all started up again."

"What started up?"

Rachel gave Victoria a shaky smile. "The fear. It was like déjà vu. It just washed right over me, like some awful wave. I started to shake, and I actually thought—"

"What? What did you think?"

"It's...it's silly."

"Nothing about fear is silly. Remember when I taught you to turn around and face the monster in your nightmares? What happened?"

"It went away," Rachel admitted. "The nightmares stopped."

"So you know you can trust me, right?"

"I guess."

"Then tell me, Rachel. What did you think when you saw—or thought you saw—Angela?"

"I guess I thought, what if she came here to kill me?" Rachel said, looking down at her hands again. They were shaking.

Victoria rested her chin on tented fingers. "And how does it feel now that you're home? Safer?"

"God, no! It feels worse. Vicky, I keep thinking something awful is about to happen. And my parents—" She paused.

"What about your parents?" Victoria pressed.

"Oh, hell, they aren't even here anymore. They're both doing their own thing, and they hardly talk to each other."

"I see. When did you first feel this about them?" Victoria asked.

"Last summer, I guess. It was so weird, I couldn't wait to get back to school."

"So let's think about this. Do you feel your parents are no longer around to protect you?"

"I don't know. Maybe."

Victoria was silent. Finally, she said, "Rachel, let me pose a theory. You're feeling vulnerable, unprotected, exposed. That could bring up old memories of the night when Angela—"

"Don't say it," Rachel interrupted. "I don't even want to think of it."

"—when Angela tried to kill you," Victoria finished, ignoring her. "Look at it, Rachel. See it. *Remember* it. Then you can let it go."

Rachel flushed. "You think I haven't been remembering it all these years? For God's sake, Vicki!"

"No, what I think is that, as you've gotten older, you haven't been remembering it the right way. We need to work on that."

"So what you're saying is that I imagined I saw Angela, because I'm feeling afraid again? My fear conjured her up?"

"Not *her,* Rachel. A woman who looked like her—" Victoria broke off. "Not even like her, for that matter, since you don't know what Angela looks like now. Perhaps just some of the same qualities you remember from childhood. Rachel, what does that sound like to you?"

Rachel closed her eyes. "Like I imagined the whole

thing. It wasn't Angela, and she hasn't come back to try to kill me again. There. Is that better?"

"You tell me."

"I don't know!" Rachel's eyes flashed, and the mutinous glare came back. "Why do I have to do all the work? You're the one getting paid for this!"

Victoria shook her head and smiled. "You may be a beautiful, grown-up twenty-one-year-old, Rachel. You may be smart, intelligent, all those good things. But I'm still seeing shades of that little girl in front of me. The one who stuck her chin out and told me to go to hell when she was ten."

Rachel hesitated, then laughed. "I did do that, didn't I? God, I must have been a handful."

"Still are, apparently," Victoria said with a smile. She picked up her appointment book and a pen. "Okay, now. Do you want us to work together while you're home on vacation, or not? Shall I put you down for the day after tomorrow?"

"Mom likes to hit the stores the day after Christmas," Rachel said. "How about the day after that?"

"Right." Victoria wrote it in.

"Uh…can I have that cookie back?"

Victoria had picked up the plate and was putting it on the file cabinet. She swung back and laughed. "Sure. Maybe it'll sweeten your mood."

Rachel stood and gathered up her coat, slipping it on with the cookie between her teeth. Then, taking it in her hand, she said, "Vicky…I know we're making light of this right now. And to tell the truth, I'm kind of relieved that we are. But I still feel, down deep, that something bad is going to happen.''

Victoria got up and came around the desk, wrapping an arm around Rachel's shoulders and walking her to the door. "You could be right, of course. But let's not jump the gun. Let's look at all sides of it first. Okay?''

Rachel nodded, drawing her pink scarf tighter as Victoria opened the door into the hallway. "God, it's raining again,'' she said, looking back toward the office window. "Now that I'm living in California most of the time, I get so depressed up here when it rains.''

"Espresso,'' Victoria said, patting her shoulder. "Get yourself some espresso. Better yet, a mocha. The chocolate will do you good.''

"I don't know,'' Rachel said. "Maybe I need some Prozac or something.''

Victoria studied her, meeting her eyes. "Maybe you do. But let's start slowly. We can talk about that later, after we meet some more.''

Rachel sighed. "Okay. See you in a few days, then.''

"Right.'' Victoria touched her cheek lightly with a pale, slender hand. "Rachel...try to have a happy Christmas.''

"You, too,'' Rachel said, stepping away.

Going down the long, carpeted hallway to the elevator, she felt awkward, as if she were stumbling. As if the hallway had shrunk, and there wasn't room now to put her feet anywhere. Or the way it felt during the occasional California earthquakes, even when they were only small tremors. It seemed for days afterward that the ground kept moving—but only slightly, so that it was hard to know whether what she felt was real or not.

She hadn't told Vicky about these "spells," which had come and gone several times over the past few weeks. She didn't want anyone to know. It was probably irrational, but the old fear was back: *If I tell them too much, they might send me away, too.*

4

Sacred Heart, the Queen Anne Hill church that Paul and Gina had been married in, was wall-to-wall with parishioners. Seats were always in demand for Midnight Mass on Christmas Eve, and ten minutes after they'd arrived it was standing room only. Gina had insisted on arriving early to assure their getting a seat, hurrying everyone along. They had made it with half an hour to spare before Mass began, and had landed a pew two rows from the front.

It was hot in the crowded church, and Gina fanned her face with the printed pamphlet containing words to the carols they would sing throughout the service. The beads of perspiration on her forehead reminded her of her wedding day and the heat wave that had come tearing through Seattle that July. She had been sure her gown would melt before the long ceremony was over. As it was, the white satin stuck to her skin when she tried to peel it off that night.

The heat hadn't dimmed her passion or Paul's, however. Gina almost blushed now, just thinking of how wanton they were on that honeymoon night.

She sighed. Where had it all gone, that passion? Had it simply dissipated with so many years of familiarity? Was that the natural order of things? Perhaps. Paul's mother and father didn't seem all that passionate about each other any longer, yet after some rocky years when Paul was a child, they seemed contented enough. Right now they were on a cruise through the Caribbean, and after that they were flying to Paris, then Rome—an anniversary gift from her and Paul.

As for Roberta, her own mother, who knew? At times, Gina thought Roberta might still be dating. Certainly that wouldn't be unusual at her age. She was only sixty, and there had been mysterious evenings lately when Roberta wasn't at home and wouldn't tell anyone the next day where she'd been. Why she'd be shy about telling anyone she was dating, Gina didn't know.

For that matter, as she looked around, Gina didn't see her mother in any of the front pews. Roberta had never, so far as she knew, missed Midnight Mass. Of course, she might have arrived late and had to settle for sitting somewhere in the back. That wasn't like her, but sometimes the traffic coming over from Gig Harbor was unusually heavy.

Roberta and Gina's father, Tony, had grown up in this Seattle parish. They had lived their lives in the old-world Catholic way, following the exhortations of the priests in those days to sacrifice and suffer. There would be stars in their crowns in heaven, they were told. Tony had suffered, all right, living for several months through a siege of cancer when he was fifty.

Gina wondered if he were somewhere "up there," and if the stars in his crown were worth it.

She knew that what had happened with the twins had taken its toll on Paul's parents as well as her own. She was glad all three remaining parents were thinking of themselves now, rather than focusing on that time when nothing made much sense and everything around them seemed to be falling apart.

When Gina met Paul, who was raised Baptist but no longer attended church, he had agreed to marry her in the Catholic church. They were both very young then, in their early twenties. Following a particular faith didn't seem to matter as much as the fact that they believed in each other. It mattered to Gina's parents, however, who insisted that being married outside the church was no marriage at all. Paul, to keep the peace, had gone along with their request.

Even so, Gina's mother had spoken of misgivings. "A man who will leave his faith behind will one day leave his wife," she had warned Gina. But that was Roberta Evans; she saw the darker side of things, always. If something could go wrong, it would—at least in Roberta's mind.

Unfortunately, in the case of the twins, she had turned out to be right. Roberta had warned Gina that adopting a child without knowing its background, both medical and familial, could be trouble. Angela and Rachel had been placed at Saint Sympatica's shortly after birth, and little was known about the woman who had given birth to them. The note she left with them in the cardboard box, on the steps of the orphanage, had said nothing that would give anyone a clue as to her whereabouts. She never went back to Saint Sympatica's to reclaim them, and the twins ended up being there several months before Paul and Gina adopted them.

"Why weren't they adopted right away?" Roberta had wanted to know. "Babies have always been in demand."

Gina had asked this question of Anita and Rodney Ewing, the couple who owned and directed the orphanage. Mrs. Ewing had seemed uneasy at the question, but had given them a perfectly good explanation. "We wanted to keep them together, and not everyone wants the responsibility of twins. Also, we've been very particular. Because the girls have been without a mother or father so long, they may need special care."

That special care was a watchful eye as the girls grew older, to ensure that they hadn't suffered from being abandoned by their mother at such a young age. For that matter, they might have been abused or neglected while in the care of their mother. If they had indeed suffered damage, they would need the best possible psychiatric treatment. This could end up costing quite a bit over the years, Paul and Gina were told, and they had assured Mrs. Ewing that they were able and willing to provide the twins with that.

Finally, they themselves went through several interviews with the Ewings and Saint Sympatica's child psychiatrist, interviews that had included psychological tests to assess their level of maturity and ability to carry through with raising the girls. They were young to be adopting, and had been married less than a year.

"Who will take care of the girls if you both work?" Mrs. Ewing had asked.

"I will," Gina had replied. "I plan to work from our house, and only part-time until they're both in school. After that, I may work longer hours, but I'll still be at home most of the time. I'll be working for myself, and I'll be able to plan my schedule to accommodate the girls."

The day they brought the twins home had been the happiest one of their lives. They did everything possible to give the girls tons of love and make them feel secure in their new home. Paul and Gina both thought they had been extremely lucky—at least for the first four years. The girls played like other children, and they seemed loving, both to each other and to their friends. It appeared that, miraculously, they had gotten through their first year of life without emotional damage. Paul and Gina attributed that to the excellent psychiatric care the orphanage afforded to the children in its care.

Then all hell had broken loose.

Gina sighed. Her thoughts had a way of drifting in church, when she should be praying. Sometimes, when making the sign of the cross she would say to herself "one, two, three, four," instead of "in the name of the Father, the Son, and the Holy Ghost." It was odd how her spirit seemed to have become a matter of rote over the years. Odd how her marriage had become that, too.

Here in this church that was so familiar to her, however, Gina sat between Paul and Rachel and felt protected with them on either side. The church was warm, and the familiar statues, poinsettias and votive candles lent a cozy air. In the crowded pew they were squeezed together, and with Paul's and Rachel's bodies touching hers, it felt as if they were truly bonded together, and that nothing bad could ever happen again.

It was therefore all the more strange when thoughts of something threatening them crossed her mind. It was a thought that had been nagging at her, actually, the past few days—ever since Rachel had come home.

Gina mentally shook herself and turned her attention to the swelling sounds of the pipe organ. Everyone rose as the altar boys came down the aisle, the lead one carrying a cross. The priest came behind them, and the choir began to sing "O Come, All Ye Faithful," their voices swelling to a crescendo at the end.

The Mass began, and Gina whispered to Paul, "Do you see Mom anywhere?"

He turned and scanned the crowds. "Can't tell. It's hard to see, it's so packed—"

He broke off and his face paled as he saw the blond woman in an aisle seat, five rows behind and across from theirs. *Lacey? My God, what is she doing here?*

His eyes met hers, and he thought he saw the beginnings of a mischievous grin. Confusion and a feeling of disaster flooded him. He couldn't let Gina and Lacey meet. Gina would know right away the place that Lacey held in his life.

Would his mistress force a meeting? Did she just want to see his wife and daughter, find out what they looked like?

As if hearing the question, Lacey gave a shrug and looked away. The procession in the middle aisle came between them as it neared the altar. Paul turned back to Gina as she tugged at his arm. "Do you see her?"

"No," Paul said, his mouth dry. "I don't see her."

From that point on he barely noticed the Mass going on in front of him. Instead, he worried about what Lacey would do.

During Communion, as parishioners filled the aisles and walked to the altar railing, Paul risked a look back again. If she met his eyes, he would try to indicate to her in some way that she shouldn't speak to him after the Mass. Perhaps just a small shake of the head would do it. Surely she'd understand.

But Lacey was gone, her seat taken by an elderly man.

Paul felt his entire body sag with relief. Then, quickly, his eyes scanned the pews in case she had simply moved to another seat. He didn't see her anywhere. *Thank God.*

But why would she leave in the middle of Mass?

To avoid having to see him with his family any longer?

That could be it.

It was several minutes before he was able to breathe normally again. He would have to talk to Lacey, though. In the three months that she had been his mistress, they had never discussed what they would do if they were seen together by Gina or anyone else who knew him. Now he would have to make sure that Lacey knew what to say if such an occasion arose: that they knew each other through Soleil. She was a client; nothing more.

Paul turned his attention back to the Mass. The priest was saying the *Agnus Dei*. "Lamb of God, who taketh away the sins of the world, have mercy on us."

Paul had little faith that anyone, God or priest, could take away his sins. He thought that he would probably go to hell by the time all this was over. He did pray for mercy, however—understanding, if not forgiveness. "Have mercy on us," he whispered, along with the congregation. "Have mercy on us."

They were on the way home when it happened. A car behind them followed too closely, blinding Paul with its headlights.

"Damn tailgaters," he muttered.

"Golly, Dad, must you swear right after Mass?" Rachel complained from the back seat.

He was too tense to answer. Between seeing Lacey

in the church, and now this, the holiday was turning out to be even worse than he'd anticipated.

Paul stepped on the brake and tapped it lightly, slowing down gradually. Maybe the car behind would take the hint and pass. The street was dark here, but there was plenty of room on either side, whereas farther up the hill, it narrowed dangerously.

But the driver behind him stayed on his tail. Dammit, why didn't it pass? Was it someone unfamiliar with the streets on Queen Anne Hill?

Paul sped up, and the other car did, too. He couldn't shake it, and now he was beginning to worry. What if this was some nut, hoping to cut them off at some point and carjack them? Or what if he was following them home to grab them in the driveway?

Even as he thought it, the car pulled out into the middle of the road and came closer, its front end nudging the left rear bumper of the Infiniti. Paul felt the bump and then heard a loud, metallic screech. The steering wheel began to slip from his grasp, and he clenched his fingers around it. "Hang on!" he yelled as the Infiniti swerved from side to side.

"Oh, my God!" he heard Gina cry.

"Daddy, what's he doing?" Rachel yelled.

Ahead was a large old cedar tree that stuck a couple of yards into the road, its trunk easily three feet in diameter. Paul saw it looming ahead of him and jammed his foot on the brake. The street was slick from the rain, however, and he could do nothing to stop the Infiniti from skidding and barreling straight into the tree.

Metal careened against wood. Glass crashed. The front air bags deployed, and Paul felt as if he'd hit a wall as the bag on his side slammed against his chest and face. Gina screamed, and Rachel flew forward. Paul felt her impact on the back of his seat.

It was over within seconds that seemed like hours. Paul sat shaken, nauseated, and as the air was automatically sucked out of the bags he looked over at Gina, who sat upright with a dazed expression on her face.

"Are you all right?" he managed.

Gina nodded. "Rachel?" she said, her voice shaking.

Rachel was crying, and though Paul was still in shock and felt weak, he managed to unbuckle his seat belt and get out, opening the back door. Rachel sat crumpled over, her face in her hands.

"Honey, are you okay?" he asked, his voice not much more than a harsh whisper. His legs shook, and he could barely hold himself upright. He grabbed hold of the door to keep himself from falling.

"Mommy," Rachel said in a strange, hollow voice. "Is Mommy okay?"

She sounded like a little girl, and tears came to Paul's eyes. He looked at Gina, who was feebly trying to reach back to Rachel.

"Yes. I think she's fine," he said, though he wasn't sure at all.

Gina began to unbuckle her seat belt and slide out. Moving slowly around the car and holding on to it for support, she reached Paul. He took her arm to steady her. Gina leaned into the car. "I'm fine, honey," she said. "Just shaky. What about you?"

"I think I'm okay," Rachel answered, unbuckling her lap belt. "My head hurts. It hurts real bad. So does my tummy."

Gina touched her gently, feeling her forehead and scalp. "I don't see any cuts. You do have a pretty good lump starting on your forehead."

"She didn't have her shoulder harness on," Paul said. "She slammed into the back of my seat. I felt it."

"Rachel, for God's sake, how many times have we told you—!" Gina broke off. "Honey, it's okay. You're safe, that's all that matters. We should get you to the hospital, though. You need to be checked out."

"No, I'm okay," Rachel said, though she clearly was not.

"We just have to be sure," Gina insisted, starting to cry.

"Your mother's right," Paul said briskly. Looking at the front of the car, he saw for the first time the full extent of the damage. The hood was crunched like an accordion, and glass from the driver and passenger side windows was all over the place.

It was a miracle, he thought, that he and Gina hadn't been badly hurt, if not killed. The windshield, made of safety glass, had held in one piece. It looked like a thousand spider webs against the beam from the headlights, which oddly enough still worked, outlining the tree.

With a shaky hand Paul took his cell phone out of his pocket, and punched the speed dial for 911. After asking if everyone was all right, the dispatcher told him it might be ten or more minutes. "We're short-staffed because of Christmas Eve, but there's a car and paramedics on the way."

Paul slumped to the ground, his back to the rear tire. Gina sat on the edge of the back seat with the door open, holding Rachel's hand and making mothering noises.

"Whoever that was," Rachel said in a tight voice, "they did that on purpose, didn't they, Dad?"

Paul hesitated. "I...we can't know that for certain. It's dark, it might have been someone who didn't know the road."

When the police and paramedics arrived, the medics checked Gina and Rachel for injuries as a young officer talked to Paul.

"This isn't the first time somebody ran into this tree," the officer said. "You see how the street starts to narrow, down there a block? People aren't prepared for it, and they think they can make it around you. You get over to the right to let them pass, but then that tree looms up and there's not enough room for both of you."

"I drive this street every day," Paul said impatiently. He wanted this to be over, and he wanted Gina and Rachel safe at home. He still felt shaky himself, and he needed a drink, a bed, some sleep. "I know precisely where this tree is," he said, "and I also know that we've asked for years to have it taken out."

"I agree with you, it's a hazard," the young cop said. "Especially at night. Seems to me I heard the city's trying to do something about it."

The uproar over this tree had been in the Seattle papers for months. The owners of the property wanted to preserve the ancient tree, and were being supported by a local preservation society.

"You know," the cop said, "maybe the person behind you was new around here. Maybe he or she didn't know the street all that well."

Paul's voice hardened. "They didn't stop to see if we needed help."

"Right. Well, I'm writing it up as a hit-and-run. You remember what the car looked like? Did you get a glimpse of the driver?"

"No. It all happened too fast, and like I said, I knew the tree was there. I was trying to keep from hitting it."

"Yeah. It's a hazard, all right."

Paul nodded. Something in his gut, however, told him that what had happened here tonight was no accident. Someone had deliberately tried to run them off the road.

At the hospital, Rachel was given a near-clean bill of health. "She may have headaches for a couple of days,'' the weary E.R. doctor said to Paul. ''Also, since she wasn't wearing a shoulder harness, the lap belt caused some bruising in the abdominal area.'' He shook his head. ''Lucky for her, you must have been able to slow the car before impact. Lucky for all of you, for that matter. If you'd hit that tree at any real speed, you might not be standing here talking to me now.''

Gina shuddered. She didn't want to think of what might have been. All she wanted to do was get home and go to bed.

I am so tired of Christmas Eve, she thought. Would they ever have a happy one again? One not fraught with some terrible event, or the kind of gloom that event left them with, like a perverse gift of some evil Magi?

Oh, stop complaining. Like the doctor said, one or all of us could be dead now.

As it was, her neck hurt, and there was a vague pain in the area of her collarbone. ''Whiplash,'' the doctor said. ''Also, probably the force of the seat belt holding you back. There's a bruise on your collarbone. It should go away in a few days.''

He had wanted to take X rays of her neck, and Paul had wanted that, too. But the X-ray department was backed up with holiday revelers who had fallen down stairs, slipped on a dance floor, rear-ended another car. It would take hours of sitting here, waiting.

''If I don't feel better, I'll come back the day after tomorrow,'' Gina promised.

Paul shrugged off his back pain as something he experienced now and then, and begged off from the X rays as well. "I really just need to get home and sleep," he said. Foremost in his mind, however, was that there wasn't any Scotch in the hospital, and he needed a drink—bad.

The Infiniti had been towed to a shop to be repaired, if possible, after being checked out at the site of the accident by the police. They had taken samples of paint that didn't match the Infiniti, and anything else the forensics lab could use.

After picking up muscle relaxants and painkillers at the hospital pharmacy, Paul, Gina and Rachel rode home silently in a cab, each deep in his and her own private thoughts.

The next morning they all slept in. When they got up sleepily around eleven and poked without appetite at eggs that Gina managed to scramble, they barely remembered it was Christmas Day. In the afternoon they watched movies on tape. Around five o'clock, when the sun had gone down, they lit the Christmas tree and made an attempt at celebration by opening each other's presents.

"Thank you, Mom, I love it," Rachel said, opening a glittery gold box and holding up a pink cashmere sweater. She didn't try it on as she normally would, but put it back in the box, on the floor.

Gina knew how she felt, and simply accepted the

thank-you, telling Rachel the same when she opened her own gift of perfume.

Paul did his best to raise their spirits by putting on his new dark green fleece jacket and modeling it, as if on a runway. He looked handsome—like a movie star, Rachel said, smiling—and Gina smiled, too, and agreed. Soon, however, they fell back into sitting silently, watching rain beat against the windows that looked out on the city of Seattle.

It's the muscle relaxants, Paul thought. They've turned us into zombies. Or maybe it's post-traumatic stress.

But he knew that wasn't the reason for his mood, and maybe not for Gina and Rachel's, either. He'd bet that they, too, were thinking: *Who would want to hurt us so much, they could do a thing like that?*

5

It was the day after Christmas, and Lacey was stretched out on the sofa when Paul let himself into the apartment. She was dressed in jeans and a T-shirt, and had kicked her shoes off. One leg was slung over the back of the sofa. In her white crew socks, she looked like a child. She was even watching the cartoon channel, like a kid on a Saturday morning.

She picked up the remote and flicked the TV off as Paul entered and hung his jacket over the back of a chair. He noted that an open bag of potato chips lay on the coffee table, and a can of Pepsi had left wet rings on the glass top.

That was one of the things he liked about being here, the fact that he could mess things up a bit. Lacey was easygoing that way, while Gina, probably because of her work as an interior designer, liked rooms neat and tidy. Even the magazines on the coffee table in their living room were chosen to look good, rather than for their reading content.

In the beginning, Paul had appreciated that Gina kept such a nice house. In time he began to weary, however, of always having to pick things up, especially when his mind was on other matters.

Before coming here, Paul had been prepared to tell Lacey they should cool things off, not see each other as much anymore. Her presence at Midnight Mass had been a bit too close for comfort. Paul honestly did not want to hurt Gina or Rachel. For that reason, he had never taken Lacey to Soleil, unwilling to risk having any of the employees gossip about them—gossip that might get back to Gina.

But now, seeing her like this, his heart melted. He had missed her spontaneity the past few days, the quick flashes of humor, her slight Southern accent from growing up in Atlanta. As much as she had tried to do away with it, Lacey had told him, she never was able to. "Guess it's inbred," she had said, laughing. "Take it or leave it." Paul had taken it. And loved it.

"That was close the other night," he said, sitting on the edge of the sofa beside her. In spite of himself, he couldn't resist stroking her breast through the tight T-shirt and feeling excited as her nipples became hard in response to his touch.

"You're sure in a hurry to get started today," she teased, pulling a pillow off the back of the sofa and smacking him with it.

He drew back, laughing, and took the pillow, putting it behind her head. Gently pushing a strand of her hair behind an ear, he said, "Actually, I didn't have that in mind for tonight."

"Oh?"

His finger paused at her ear, then traced her cheekbone. Finally he took her hand and sighed. "Lacey, sweetheart, I think we should talk."

She sat up, pulling her hand out of his. Taking another sofa pillow, she held it tight against her. "I'm not sure I like the sound of that."

Paul tugged at his tie, loosening it. Suddenly he was having trouble breathing. He felt as if he were on a precipice, about to do something that would change his life in ways he might be sorry for later.

"I, uh…I just think we should take this a bit slower. I mean, you know, spend less time together…"

His voice shook when she didn't respond. "The thing is, Rachel's home, and since the accident the other night, I think I should spend more time with her."

He had told Lacey about the accident this morning, on the phone, when he called to say he'd be coming by. She hadn't expected him on Christmas Day, of course, but it had been agreed upon that he would come here the day after, while Gina and Rachel were hitting the stores for sales. He would bring his present—a gold necklace—to her then, and spend the afternoon with her.

"Of course you need to stay home and take care of Rachel," Lacey said now. "I understand completely."

Her eyes, however, filled with tears. "That's not what this is about, though," she said in a low, husky voice. "You want to break up with me. You're saying goodbye."

"No! No, not at all," Paul said, though he wondered if that were true. His motivations weren't completely clear, even to him.

He ran a hand through his hair, which left the cowlick he tried so hard to gel down every morning standing upright. He knew this, and it irritated him. He wanted to feel in charge here today, not like a barefoot boy.

"Lacey," he said, sounding more accusative than he'd meant to, "what was all that on Christmas Eve? At the church? Why were you there?"

She dried her tears with the back of her hand, then gave him an amazed look. Laughing shortly, she said, "Why was *I* there? Paul, Sacred Heart is my parish church! I might as well ask you why you and your wife and daughter were there. The truth is, I couldn't have been more shocked. And you may remember that I left the moment I saw you."

He had to agree that was true, but added, "I guess I never knew you were Catholic."

She bristled. "Well, all you had to do was ask."

He took in her large green eyes, brimming with tears, and heard the wounded tone in her voice. She's right, he thought. We've never talked about our lives outside this apartment. That was a rule they had made. Correction—*he* had made, as if the less he knew about her, the less she infringed upon his life with Gina and Rachel.

The truth was, he had been a thoughtless, selfish bastard, thinking only of himself.

"I'm sorry," he said. "I guess my nerves have been on edge."

Standing, he walked to the window that looked out on the street, three stories down. From here, he could almost see his home near the top of Queen Anne Hill. Gina and Rachel were still out shopping, but he could picture them there later, waiting for him to come home and do all the things Rachel wanted to squeeze in before going back to school. He felt pulled in so many directions it was physically painful.

Turning back, he said, "I really am sorry, Lacey. I haven't been very thoughtful of you." He made an attempt. "You go to Midnight Mass every Christmas, then?"

"Just about. It's the only time I do go to church. No, that's not quite true. I go on Easter, sometimes. It doesn't have to be a Catholic church, though. As long as they have palms and lilies and a choir, I'm fine." She smiled.

Paul returned her smile and felt the tensions leave him. "It was just such a shock, seeing you there. It threw me off balance."

"I'll bet. You were afraid I'd come up to you afterward and tell your wife who I was," she guessed.

"No, of course not." But he flushed, and he knew that she knew.

Lacey reached for the potato chips and popped one into her mouth, chewing it with her usual gusto for food. Washing it down with a gulp of Pepsi, she said,

"And what were *you* doing there, Mr. Bradley? Churchgoing doesn't seem like your usual M.O."

"I…uh, well, Gina and I…" He flushed.

"Oh. Never mind, I get it. You were married there, huh?"

He didn't answer, and she said, "Now that I think of it, it figures, with her growing up in that neighborhood. So Midnight Mass at Sacred Heart is a family tradition?"

"Yes."

"And there I was, all of a sudden," Lacey continued with a grin. "Your worst nightmare."

"Yes…well, no, I wouldn't put it that way."

Standing, she walked over to him and pushed him lightly on both shoulders. "Well, *I* would. Look, Paul, we've talked about this before. You know you don't have to worry about me. You have to spend holidays with your family, and I understand that. Sure, sometimes it hurts. And I'll admit that at Midnight Mass I couldn't stay any longer, once I saw you there with them. I can't tell you how jealous I felt. But, hey, look at us now. You're here with *me,* for heaven's sake—not them."

Looking into those beautiful green eyes, the tremulous red lips, he hadn't the heart to tell her he couldn't stay. He thought about the fact that he had told Gina and Rachel he was going to the office, and that something urgent had come up.

How many lies had he told since meeting Lacey? How many were still to come before his wife began to sense they were lies and his entire world collapsed around him?

His guilt was nearly overwhelming. But when Lacey put her arms around him, stroking his temple with her fingertips and the hollow at his throat with her tongue, everything else flew out the window. All he could think of then was the way it was going to feel to hold her, to have her warm and naked against him.

There was no way he could ever explain this to anyone, this need for Lacey even as he loved his wife and daughter more than anything else on earth. It was if he were two men, one for Lacey and one for them. He knew that whatever this thing was that had him in its grip, it had to be a sickness. He just didn't know how to cure it—nor, at this moment, did he honestly want to. He simply wanted it to go on and on, and for nothing bad to ever happen in his life again.

Three days after Christmas, Gina sat with Rachel at the kitchen breakfast bar. They had barely touched their coffee, even though it was a new blend they'd picked up at a café down the street and had looked forward to trying out.

"I'm just saying you're living in a dream world," Rachel argued. "You don't see things the way they really are."

Gina felt attacked, and responded in kind. "Well, my dear, everyone's reality is different. That's something you'll learn, perhaps, as you grow older—and, hopefully, wiser."

"Mom, don't give me that 'different reality' thing. I know we all see things from our own perspective. I just think yours is really skewed."

Gina sighed. "And just what brought all this up?"

Rachel shook her head and didn't answer.

Gina picked up her coffee cup and took it to the sink, rinsing it out. "If you're not going to answer me, we can hardly have an intelligent discussion, Rachel."

And why the hell couldn't this visit of her daughter's just have been fun? Why was she trying to stir things up this time?

It reminded her of a period when Rachel was sixteen, and seemed intent on ruining the good spirits of everyone around her. The Spoiler, they had called her then, though not in a mean way, and not to her face. Paul and Gina would lie in bed at night and try to figure out what was bothering their daughter, and why she had to cast a negative light on everything.

Gina frowned. Her daughter was no longer a teenager. It was time to grow up.

"I'm going upstairs to collect the laundry," she said, drying her hands.

"The laundry can wait," Rachel snapped. "Mom, I'm talking about Dad."

Carefully Gina hung the dish towel on the decorative cherry-wood rod affixed to the upper cabinet, next to the sink. She had put it there the day they moved in, rather than have towels all over the counters, gathering bacteria and looking messy.

Sometimes she thought that she liked a neat house

because it was the only control she still had over her life.

"Your father?" she said, keeping her back to Rachel. "I thought we already went through all that."

"Not quite," Rachel said. She rubbed her face the same way she'd seen her father do for years when irritated, as if the source of the irritation could be rubbed away. "Mom, what if he's seeing somebody?"

"Seeing—" Gina's expression went from an incredulous smile to a glare in a matter of seconds. "If you mean another woman, Rachel, that's ridiculous. Your father is much too busy to have time for that, in the first place. And in the second place, he just isn't the type."

She was hearing her mother's words, however—*All men are the type*—and that took some of the force from her tone.

Rachel just looked at her, and after a moment, Gina said, "I'm going upstairs to get the laundry now."

Rachel stared into her coffee cup, making swirls in the cool, creamy liquid with a finger. *Round and round, round and round, down and down...like life,* she thought. *Round and round...then, at the last dizzying moment, down and down.*

Rachel dumped her jacket and purse onto the chair in Victoria Lessing's office, then asked to use her bathroom. Victoria was on the phone but waved to her, whispering, "Sure. I'll be off in a minute."

The psychiatrist's bathroom was as elegant as her

office, both of which had recently been redecorated. There were gold fixtures and an ornate mirror, trimmed in gold.

Looks like an expensive antique, Rachel thought. I wonder if she got it from Dad. Towels were in a soft lilac, the only color in the room except for a five-foot-high plant in the palm family. *Now, that—that's more like Mom's style.*

Standing before the mirror, Rachel thought she looked older than her twenty-one years. Fine lines were already beginning at the corners of her eyes, and there were dark circles that no amount of concealer had been able to cover.

Well, the past few weeks hadn't been easy. Add to that the accident the other night and the egg-sized lump on her noggin, it was a wonder she hadn't turned gray.

She washed her hands for a full twenty seconds, hoping to ward off the many germs and new viruses that were all about these days. It seemed she was forever trying to wash them away, and God only knew what she might have picked up in the coffee shop that she and Gina had stopped at on the way here.

Vicki must be worried about germs, too, she thought, because there were plastic disposable gloves in her wastebasket. Rachel smiled. Vicky had beautiful hands that didn't show her age. She probably wore gloves to bed, too, the way hand models did.

When Rachel walked back into the office, Vicky was still on the phone. "All right, all right," she was saying. "I'll let you know as soon as I know anything. Listen, I have to go."

Victoria hung up the phone and smoothed her blond hair, which hung straight to her shoulders today. Golly, Rachel thought, she looks almost sexy. Idly she wondered who the boyfriend was. There must be one. When she sat at her antique desk like that, she looked so…pure, was the only word that came to Rachel. Like someone in a painting.

Victoria's personal life, however, had always been a mystery. On one slender finger glittered a diamond and sapphire ring that she had worn ever since Rachel could remember. It wasn't on her engagement finger, though, and so far as Rachel knew, she had never married.

Rachel took a seat and settled her jacket over her shoulders to ward off the nervous chill she was feeling. Opening up to Victoria wasn't as bad as trying to communicate with her parents, but even so, it wasn't something she looked forward to.

She waited as Victoria took a stack of papers from her desk and slipped them into a drawer. Her attention was caught by something new on Victoria's desk—a bronze statue of a frog with a golden coin on its tongue. The tongue, too, was made of gold.

"Did you get that for Christmas?" Rachel asked.

Victoria's face turned pink. "Yes. From a friend. It's for good luck—especially with money."

"Do you need good luck with money?" Rachel wondered. "Sorry. That wasn't very polite, was it?"

"I don't mind," Victoria said. "And no, I guess I don't really need good luck with that. I just like frogs." She smiled. "This one may be a bit of an overkill, but I must say I love him."

They went through the preliminaries, the "how are you?" and "how was your Christmas?" exchanges. As Victoria poured tea, she said, "You mentioned that you and your parents were in an accident on Christmas Eve. How are they now? And how are you?"

"My mom still hurts, but Dad's okay. I look worse than I feel."

She stared out the window. The rain was coming down in sheets now, blotting out the view. The entire world seemed gray. Flat, with no meaning. Even the EMP—the Experience Music Project building, so oddly futuristic and blazing with color—had lost its glow.

When Victoria took a seat behind her desk again, Rachel said, frowning, "I wish I had a golden tongue."

"And why would that be?" Victoria asked.

"I still can't seem to get through to my parents. I think they're both in denial."

"Can you be more specific?"

"Well, you know what I mean. There's something wrong, and they just won't talk about it. They won't talk about Angela, either, and what happened back then. It's like that was another whole life, and somebody else lived it. If it wasn't for my grandmother..."

"What about your grandmother?" Victoria asked.

"Well, she's at least willing to tell me stuff."

"What kind of stuff?"

"You know. Like the way Daddy always liked Angela best."

"Roberta told you that?" Victoria's blue eyes widened slightly.

"Well, no, I mean I'm the one who actually brought it up. Gamma just talked with me about it. Which is more than my mother and father ever would."

"What did Roberta say about your father always liking Angela best?" Victoria asked.

Rachel shrugged. "She said parents and children are like anyone else. Like friends, you know, and sometimes you just click with one person more than another. She said my dad always loved me, though."

Rachel paused, her gaze drifting away from Victoria's. "Do you think that's true?"

"Are you saying you don't believe it?" Victoria countered.

"I don't know. I guess I've always wondered."

"Have you ever talked to your father about this?"

"I tried talking to him, but he denies it. I remember once, after Angela was gone, I got mad and said he'd never loved me as much as her."

"And how did he respond to that?"

"He didn't. Didn't say anything, I mean. He—he just started to cry."

Tears sprang to Rachel's eyes. Victoria gave her a moment, and said, "What did you do then, Rachel?"

Rachel made an effort to collect herself, wiping the

tears away with a tissue she took from a box on Victoria's desk, and squaring her shoulders. "There wasn't much I could do," she said. "He walked out of the room."

Her eyes flashed with a trace of anger. "He still does that. Walks out of the room when I try to talk to him about Angela."

There was a brief silence before Victoria said, "You seem to be asking a lot of questions about your sister these days. Is that only because of the time you thought you saw her at school? Or is there something else?"

Rachel shrugged. "I guess maybe I'm thinking about her more because I thought I saw her. At first I was shocked, and then for a minute I wanted to run up and hug her. But she disappeared, and I realized it couldn't have been her. Like, I just made it all up in my mind because I'd been wanting to see her, or something." She met Victoria's eyes. "You were probably right about that."

"So you *were* wanting to see her?"

Rachel hesitated. "I'm not sure. I keep asking myself, 'What would she be like, now? Did she get adopted again? Did she get over the problem she had? Was there even any cure for it back then? Is there now?' Nobody ever told me any of that." The note of anger in her voice returned.

"Well, you were only five when Angela left," Victoria said. "We all thought it would be best to keep it simple for you."

"Simple!" Rachel's voice rose. "So you told me my sister was sick and had to go away for a while? Didn't any of you realize that I thought she was coming back?"

"Rachel, we went through all of this as you grew older," Victoria said calmly. "We sat here in this very room when you were ten, twelve, fourteen, and we talked about it. *Many* times."

"Well, maybe I didn't understand what you said back then. Anyway, I don't remember what you told me about it."

"I told you we were all just doing our best to protect you," Victoria said. "And that we tried to do what was best for Angela, as well."

She sat forward and folded her hands on her desk. "Rachel, it was a very difficult time. I had worked with Angela an entire year before that night, and even I didn't suspect she would ever attack you that way. I honestly thought she was getting better."

Rachel nodded. "I remember. You said that kids like her can be charming, and that they can fool everyone into thinking they like them, when they don't really have any normal feelings at all."

"Because they never had a chance to bond with anyone, like a mother," Victoria confirmed.

"But Angela and I were taken care of pretty well at Saint Sympatica's, weren't we? I mean, it wasn't like some of those Romanian orphanages you hear about, where the babies were neglected from the time they were born."

"From everything I know, it's true you were taken care of," Victoria said. "Saint Sympatica's had an excellent reputation for that. There aren't many orphanages that have a resident child psychiatrist, for instance."

She refilled Rachel's cup with tea, using a napkin to keep the spout from dripping the rich amber brew onto her desk. "Rachel, your parents chose to adopt you and Angela specifically from Saint Sympatica's because of their quality of care. They hoped you would not have suffered too much from anything bad that might have happened to you in your first months of life."

"Then why did Angela get RAD? And why didn't it happen to me?"

Victoria sighed. "I don't know if I can answer that. For that matter, Angela was never definitely diagnosed as having Reactive Attachment Disorder. The psychiatrist at Saint Sympatica's and I felt that her symptoms fit that diagnosis, but there was always a tiny element of doubt. Fetal alcohol syndrome, for instance can result in similar kinds of behavior. And today RAD is still a matter for controversy. Some think it doesn't even exist, and that there are other reasons for a child to turn out to have little or no feelings for others that one would consider 'normal.'"

"What kind of reasons?"

"Well, something genetic, or some dysfunction in the brain."

"You mean a bad seed? Like that old movie where

the adopted kid turns out to be a killer because she inherited it from her biological mom, or something? I thought that was just fiction.''

''Rachel, if you're looking for an absolute answer, I'm sorry, but there are no absolutes here. All I can tell you is that Angela received the best treatment possible at Saint Sympatica's when your parents took her back there.''

Rachel's eyes narrowed. ''You know that for sure? How could you?''

''I know,'' Victoria said patiently, ''because at your parents' request I talked several times during the first year with Dr. Chase, Angela's psychiatrist. He assured me that she was progressing. Slow baby steps, but progressing, nonetheless.''

Rachel jumped on her words. ''That's all you did? You talked to him on the phone? And just the first year? What about after that?''

''After that, your parents felt they had to let go. Angela began to regress, I'm afraid, and Dr. Chase didn't feel it was safe for her to be returned to your family. Or any other, for that matter.''

''So she just grew up there, all alone?'' Again Rachel's eyes began to tear. ''Didn't anybody care that she might be missing us? That she might feel lonely and miss the only family she ever had?''

Victoria bristled. ''Rachel, your sister tried to *kill* you! Not only that, but she staged so-called accidents for an entire year before that night. It seems you've forgotten that.''

"No." Rachel returned her cup to its saucer with a clatter. "I haven't forgotten. I mean, I don't really remember that night, but I know it happened because you and Mom and Dad told me about it. I just wish…" She hugged herself, feeling cold. "Oh, God, I wish things had been different."

Victoria said softly, "Your parents wished that, too, Rachel. They had to learn to live with the fact that things were *not* different. They had to adjust to accepting things the way they were."

"My parents! Sometimes I wish…"

There was an uneasy silence as Rachel's face twisted in an expression of anger, then misery.

"What?" Victoria asked softly.

"Nothing." Rachel shook her head and looked at her watch. "Never mind. My hour's up, right? I have to get going."

Pulling on her camel's hair coat, she shoved her hands into the pockets, looking for her car keys. As she pulled them out, a slip of paper dropped to the floor. Rachel bent down and picked it up. Staring, she began to read. Then, taking a deep breath that came out in shudders, she paled. "Oh, my God."

"What is it?" Victoria asked, her tone a mixture of curiosity and alarm.

"It's…it's a note." Rachel met her eyes. "God, Vicky. It's a note from Angela!"

"Are you sure?"

"Of course I'm sure! It has to be her."

"May I see it? What does it say?"

Victoria took the note and read aloud as Rachel slid heavily into her chair.

"It says, 'So you made it through another Christmas Eve. Be careful your luck doesn't run out.'"

Victoria looked at Rachel. "It's in block print. And it isn't signed."

"No, but it's her! I know it's her!"

Victoria said calmly, "Well, I do see why you'd think it was from Angela, with that reference to Christmas Eve. But when could she have put a note like this into your pocket? Where have you been that she could have done that?"

Rachel bent forward, resting her elbows on her knees. Burying her face in her hands, she began to cry. "I don't know. Vicky, where is she? What does she mean, my luck could run out?"

Victoria shook her head. "I don't know, Rachel. What did the police think about your being run off the road the other night?"

Rachel sat straight, her teeth chattering and her voice low. "They said…they said it was a bad spot for accidents. That tree has been hit before, and they've talked for years about taking it down. The Historical Society, or somebody like that, is against it, though—"

She took a deep breath to steady herself. "Do you think Angela was driving that other car? That she drove us into that tree on purpose?"

Victoria set the note down on her desk. "I don't know, Rachel. What do you think?"

Rachel jumped to her feet. "For God's sake, will you stop being a psychiatrist for a minute and stop asking me questions? What the hell am I *supposed* to think? Is she trying to kill me, Vicky? Again?"

Rachel's face turned an alabaster-white. "Or is it worse now? Is she trying to kill Mom and Dad, too?"

Later that afternoon, Paul, Gina and Rachel sat before Detective Al Duarte in the Seattle police headquarters at Third and James. He had taken the note by a corner and laid it on the desk without touching it further. Looking around, Paul could see other officers sitting at their desks, some of them at computers, some talking amongst themselves. Phones rang incessantly, and people who looked like they'd been pulled in for one reason or another sat beside some of the desks. One played with his long, stringy blond hair, another picked at his nose, then wiped his finger on his dirty khaki pants. A young girl who couldn't be out of her teens crossed her legs and smoothed the tight red skirt she wore, then tugged at the neckline of her black sequined blouse, as if to make her breasts stand out more for the cop who was typing up a report. Her makeup was thick and dark, and her matted hair looked as if it hadn't been washed in weeks.

Paul felt his stomach turn and wished he were at home in bed.

"How many people have handled this note?" Detective Duarte asked, looking up.

"My wife and I, and of course, Rachel," Paul said.

"Vicky, too," Rachel added.

"Vicky?" the detective asked.

"My shrink," Rachel answered. "Victoria Lessing. I found it when I was in her office, and I showed it to her."

Duarte studied Rachel, but said only, "We can dust it, but I don't know about finding anything."

Looking back at the note again, he said to Rachel, "So you think your twin sister might have written this? And you say you might have seen her at Berkeley a couple of weeks ago?"

Rachel flicked a look at her mother and father, then wiggled uncomfortably in her seat. "I, uh, I'm not sure. I just thought somebody looked like her. Or maybe how she might look now."

The detective looked at Paul.

"My wife and I haven't seen Angela since she was six years old," Paul said. "That was fifteen years ago, in Minnesota. And Rachel hasn't seen her since she was five. At least, she hadn't until...well, we just learned that Rachel thought she saw her on campus. There's no way to know if it really was Angela, of course."

"Mind telling me why you didn't have any contact with this girl all these years?" the detective asked.

Gina began to speak, but Paul cut in. "It's like we said earlier, Angela wasn't well. We weren't able to take care of her."

"So you sent her back to this orphanage, this Saint

Sympatica's you mentioned? You left her there?'' Detective Duarte looked unconvinced. ''Just like that?''

''No, not *just like that!*'' Gina said angrily. ''It was an extremely difficult decision.''

The detective leaned back in his chair, lacing his fingers over his ample belly. A coffee stain spoiled the otherwise crisp green shirt he wore, and the shoulder holster made Paul nervous. He had always been uneasy around guns, and had never kept one in the house. Every now and then he wondered what he would do if he ever had to defend himself or his family. The baseball bat he kept in a corner of the bedroom would probably not stop the average burglar.

Even more nerve-racking were the questions they were having to answer now. They had avoided bringing in the police sixteen years ago by telling the doctor in the emergency room that it had been an accident, that Rachel had fallen on the knife while playing. If Angela's attack on Rachel came out here, the fact that they hadn't reported it could be difficult to explain. Paul thought that there must be a law against that, and wondered what the statute was on it.

The detective went on, ''So now you think this twin of your daughter's has come back all these years later, and wants to harm you? What would be her motive? To get even for you taking her back to that orphanage?'' His tone was doubtful. ''That was a heck of a long time ago.''

''We were run off the road on Christmas Eve,'' Paul

said tightly. "An officer took the report. Haven't you read it?"

"Got it right here." Duarte tapped a small file on his desk. "I gotta tell you, though, a hit-and-run seems more likely to me. Some drunk, maybe, it being Christmas Eve. Funny how that holiday brings 'em out."

Paul thought quickly. If they let it go at that—a drunk driver who just didn't stop to help them—this whole thing would be so much easier. He, Gina and Rachel could go home and return to their lives again. It would be as if the accident, the note and their coming here, had never happened.

After all, the detective could be right. It could have been a simple hit-and-run. Gina had insisted on contacting the police once she heard about the note, but now it felt as if they might have jumped the gun. Why stir things up anymore?

Gina broke the small silence by saying, "Maybe you're right about that accident, Detective Duarte. But what about this note? Clearly, somebody wants us to at least *think* they ran us off the road."

The detective looked at her. "Problem is, the note doesn't give us much to go on. Look, we can dust for some fingerprints that don't match yours, your husband's, your daughter's, or the shrink's. If we find any, we can run them through the computer banks. But if nothing comes up, and since you don't have this Angela's prints..." He shrugged.

"You're right, it hardly seems worth the effort,"

Paul said. "Look," he turned to Gina and Rachel. "I think we should go home and forget this."

"No, I want the fingerprints done," Gina argued, shaking her head. "I want to know who sent my daughter that note. If there's any chance at all of finding out, we should take it."

Rachel was silent. When the detective looked at her, she mimicked his shrug. "I guess I want to know, too."

"Okay." He sighed and picked up the receiver of the black phone on his desk. "Give me a number for that shrink. I'll send somebody over there, and while we're waiting, we'll get the three of you printed."

The Bradleys' prints had been taken and they were back at Duarte's desk, waiting for Victoria Lessing's prints to arrive and the computer search to be completed. Duarte, standing behind his desk, reminded them, "Like I said, you don't have to stick around. I could call you."

"I'd like to wait," Gina said. "Paul, you can take Rachel home—"

"No way," Rachel interrupted. "I'm staying right here."

Duarte sighed and everyone fell silent as the detective sank heavily into his chair, leaning back in his hands-laced-over-the-belly position, staring at the ceiling. Into the silence burst a loud gastric growl. He rubbed his stomach and met Rachel's grin. It was the first she had smiled since arriving at the police station, over two hours ago.

"You hungry?" Duarte asked.

"Starved," she admitted. "I missed lunch."

Duarte looked at his watch. "Dinner, too."

He called over to a cop across the aisle. "Hey, Joey. Got a minute? Get these folks some doughnuts or something, will you? Maybe some coffee?"

"Sure, Al," the cop answered. "I came in today just to wait on you."

"Aw, c'mon. I'm busy with these people."

"It's about time you were busy with something," the other cop said. But he got up and left, saying with a sigh and a smile, "I thought the days of slavery were over."

"Not for you, newbie," the detective called after him. "I already paid my dues, totin' that barge and liftin' that bale for the boys upstairs."

After a few minutes, the young officer came back with a tray. There were four cups of coffee on it, and a paper plate piled high with oatmeal cookies. He set the tray on Duarte's desk.

"Rosie made them," he said, nodding toward a female cop across the room. "She was up all night. Worried about her kid, you know."

The cop shook his head and smiled sympathetically. "She calls these 'aggression cookies.' Says you have to use your hands to mix 'em, and you get all kinds of tensions out."

"Yeah," Duarte said. "I wonder how much sleep

is lost every night by parents up worrying about their kids.''

"Well,'' the young cop said, "along with waiting hand and foot on you, I guess I've still got that to look forward to.'' He smiled. "Get you anything else?''

"Nah, this'll do it,'' Duarte said. "Okay, kid, dig in.'' He pushed the plate toward Rachel.

She picked up a cookie and wolfed it down.

"Help yourselves,'' Duarte said to Paul and Gina.

They both shook their heads. "Thank you, no,'' Gina said, sipping her coffee.

"You, uh, you must have other things you need to do?'' Paul said to Duarte, putting it in the form of a question.

Duarte shrugged. "I was about to take a break, anyway. I don't mind.'' Cookie crumbs fell on his shirt, and he brushed them off.

"You like these cookies, kid?'' he asked Rachel.

"They're okay,'' she answered. "When you're away at school you start to like anything that's food.''

"Yeah, I guess. These that Rosie made are pretty good, though. Maybe not quite as good as the sugar cookies my wife used to make.'' He sighed. "I sure do miss that woman.''

"Is she, uh—'' Rachel let the question dangle.

"Dead? Nah. Just gone. It's not a good life, bein' married to a cop. Shoulda known that before I married her, but you know, when you're young, you tell yourself it'll all work out.''

He looked at Paul. "So you're an antiques dealer?''

Paul nodded. "Soleil Antiques."

"Oh, yeah, I drive by it all the time. It's a good business, then? You do pretty good financially? If you don't mind me asking."

"I've done well off and on over the years," Paul said. "I started out right after college, furnishing the homes and offices of CEOs. Then the dot.commers came along, and the ones who got rich wanted the best of everything. That was before the market tanked a while back, of course."

"Pretty lucky timing," Duarte commented. "You must've inherited some money? To get a business like that started, I mean."

Paul wondered what all the questions were about. In fact, he wondered why the good detective didn't have more to do than sit here and wait with them. "Well, my wife," he nodded toward Gina, "is an interior decorator. We've worked together for years. She furnishes houses with many of the antiques I stock. We started slowly, but it's worked out well."

The detective looked at Gina. "My wife used to say she wished she could get a decorator for our house. But then she'd say it'd be a waste of money because I'd be messing it up all the time, leaving my shoes around, eatin' in front of the TV…"

"Well, I think that even when a house is professionally decorated, it should be comfortable for whoever lives in it," Gina said.

"I guess. Trouble is, what's comfortable for one isn't always what's comfortable for the other."

"How true," Paul said. Gina gave him a swift look, and Paul said uneasily, "I mean, people do have different ideas about how they like to live. Some people feel too stiff if they can't toss things around. Others get crazy if a house isn't neat all the time."

"I like a smooth, neat look," Gina replied in a tone that sounded half apologetic, half defensive. "It calms me if everything looks orderly."

"Like a showroom," Paul agreed.

"Was that a criticism?" Gina said sharply.

"Hell, no," Paul said tiredly, rubbing a hand over his eyes. "Why on earth would I ever criticize you, dear?"

It was a moment before either of them noticed that Duarte and Rachel were staring.

"Sorry," Paul said, getting to his feet and beginning to pace. "I guess I'm more tired than I realized. How much longer do you think this will take?" He looked at his watch.

"I told them to hurry it," Duarte said, "but you know, it's not like this is a life or death situation." He paused. "At least so far as we know."

"Maybe I overreacted," Rachel said. "Maybe the note was from some nut, somebody who heard about the accident somehow, and decided to play games. Like, maybe when we stopped at Starbuck's this morning. Mom, you remember that guy who kept staring at us? Maybe when we were standing in line he slipped the note into my pocket."

"Oh, for heaven's sake, Rachel!" Gina's brow furrowed. "Why would you think such a thing? It's preposterous!"

"Then why was he staring?" Rachel pressed.

"I really don't think he was. He was sitting at a table drinking his coffee, and he just didn't have anything else to look at."

"Your mother's right," Paul said. "People do that in restaurants—"

"Wait a minute," Duarte cut in. "This is the first I've heard about this."

"It was *nothing*," Gina insisted, flushing. "Just a man having coffee."

"Come to think of it, he was looking more at Mom than me," Rachel said.

"Oh, for heaven's sake, Rachel! He was staring off into space."

"Even so…what'd this guy look like?" Duarte asked.

Gina shrugged. "I hardly noticed."

"Oh, Mom. Now that I think of it, you actually blushed the first time you saw him looking at you." Rachel turned to Duarte. "He was nice-looking, about forty maybe, blond hair with a little bit of gray, wore jeans and a red sweatshirt over a white tee. Not scruffy, though, more of a nice, laid-back look—"

"What did you do, take notes?" Gina interrupted testily. She gave an embarrassed look to Paul, then Duarte, whose expression was bland.

"It happens sometimes," she said finally. "Men seem to look at me in restaurants, coffee shops, that sort of thing. I don't take it seriously. It happens to every woman.''

''Especially if they look like you,'' Rachel teased.

''Rachel, please,'' Gina said irritably. She folded her arms and looked away.

''But it's true. You're very attractive, Mom.''

There was a small silence in which Paul shifted uncomfortably in his seat. His eyes went to Gina, his expression one of a man who hasn't actually seen his wife in years. ''You, uh, I guess you have to be careful these days,'' he said. ''Right, Detective?''

''Well, it never hurts to be careful,'' Duarte said. ''Any of these guys ever come up and talk to you? Want to sit with you?''

Gina jumped to her feet. ''This is ridiculous!''

''Methinks the lady doth protest too much,'' Rachel said, in a half serious, half teasing tone. ''Mom, just how many of these admirers *have* you had coffee with?''

Gina turned her back on them and stood before a lighted, glass-paned bookcase. Her spine was rigid, unyielding.

''Hey, lighten up, Mom,'' Rachel said softly into the silence that suddenly filled the room. ''I didn't mean anything by it.''

''Your mother's just tired,'' Paul said quickly. ''Like the rest of us.''

''I can speak for myself,'' Gina said, facing them with a scowl.

"Then do so, for God's sake!" Paul said, throwing up his hands. He stood and began to pace.

"All right, I will!" Gina replied, raising her voice. "I damn well will! For instance, if it hadn't been for you—" She broke off and fell silent.

"If it hadn't been for me, what?" Paul demanded, his face only paces from hers.

"We might have brought her home," Gina said in a low voice. "We might have taken a chance."

"A chance on Angela, you mean? Is that what you wanted? To put Rachel in danger—" He broke off when Duarte leaned forward slightly, giving them his full attention.

"Mom's right," Rachel said, her own voice rising. "You could have brought her back after she had treatment. You could have given her another chance. Even Gamma says so."

Gina gave her a horrified look. "Your grandmother? She told you that?"

"At least she misses her!" Rachel cried, jumping to her feet. "You two act like she died!"

For an interminable ten minutes, none of the Bradleys had spoken. The tension in the room was so thick you could almost see it walking around, Duarte thought. He doodled on a yellow pad, then ran the eraser of his pencil across the scars on his thirty-year-old wooden desk, giving nothing away. Privately, however, he was thinking that it wouldn't take much more to send this family over the edge. He had known that from the first, or more correctly intuited it. That's why he'd decided to sit with them and wait for the prints. People in a police station were often under so much stress they said and did things they wouldn't otherwise.

Was somebody trying to send them over the edge? he wondered. Were the Bradleys right about that note? And what the hell else was going on here?

Certainly the husband and wife didn't seem all that close. The wife may or may not have been playing with fire, flirting with other guys—or at least thinking about it. The husband? He didn't even act as if he cared if she was. And then there was the kid. She was deliberately trying to stir something up. Duarte wasn't sure what, yet, but something.

Look at the three of them. They're sitting too far apart. Not even making eye contact. They look like three different people who came in here to report similar, but not quite identical, crimes. The father would have his take on it, the wife another and the daughter yet another.

Well, it wasn't his business. There was a time when he would have involved himself with this family, gone beyond the call of duty to help them out. Duarte was tired, though. Burned-out. He'd been at this job thirty-four years, since he was twenty-three, and he'd seen too much. People in families did strange things, and when he was younger, his curiosity, if nothing else, would have been piqued. He'd have gone off in search of clues like a Dalmatian at a five-alarm fire.

Nowadays, he still worked hard. He just didn't have the old passion for the job.

His thoughts were interrupted by the ringing of his phone. He picked up the receiver and talked, then tapped on the desk with his pencil point, making even more indentations in the wood. Hanging up finally, he said, "They found prints on the note from all three of you and the shrink. There's also one unknown. They ran it through the computer. Nothing came up."

No one spoke immediately. Then Paul asked, "So, what do we do now?"

"Well, if you could get me a sample of the twin's prints…"

Gina and Paul looked at each other. "I doubt they'd have fingerprinted her at Saint Sympatica's," Paul said.

"But you could call there and find out," Duarte said. "Right?"

"Yes, I suppose I could."

"Do that, then," Duarte said. "If you find out they've got the prints, let me know and I'll call them myself, get them to fax them here."

Paul looked uncertain.

"Is there a problem?" Duarte asked.

"No. No, of course not."

Paul and Gina stood. Rachel gathered up her coat and pink scarf, putting them on. She looked down at her hands thoughtfully, while sliding on her gloves.

"You know, I've been thinking," she said. "Maybe

we don't really need to go that far. Getting Angela's fingerprints, I mean.''

Her mother eyed her curiously. "Rachel?"

"Well, I'm pretty sure I overreacted," Rachel said, not meeting her eyes. "Nothing really happened to us, after all. And it was Christmas Eve, like the detective said. Drunks on the road." She gave a shrug. "I don't know, maybe we should just accept that and not, you know, go looking for trouble."

"Looking for trouble?" her mother said.

"Well, yeah. If Angela hears somehow that we're asking about her, she could turn up here..." Rachel's voice dwindled off. "I mean, if she really isn't here already, she might think we want to see her."

"And you don't want that now?" Paul asked.

"Well, do *you*?" Rachel glared at him.

Paul fell silent. Detective Duarte cleared his throat and said bluntly, "You know, folks, the fact is, it's not really up to you anymore."

All three turned to him.

"Look at it this way," he said. "We've already got a hit-and-run investigation underway from the other night. Add to that this note and what you've told me about this twin, she's got to be part of the investigation now. We can't just dismiss her."

He watched as the Bradleys' faces fell, and could almost hear them wishing they'd never come here today.

"Thing is," he added, "you've caught my interest. I'd like to help you folks out, so I'm giving you an option. Call that orphanage and see what you can find out—or I will."

He stood and took one last bite out of his cookie, then said, "Look, it's been a long day, and I'm anxious to get home and feed my cat. So if I have to stay here and work any longer, I'm not gonna be in a good mood. Which is it gonna be?"

"I'll call," Paul said tiredly. He looked at his watch again. "I have some business to take care of, though. Is it okay if I let you know how it goes in the morning?"

"Sure," Duarte said. "What is it, after six? You might not be able to reach anyone in the office there, anyway, what with the time difference."

"Right," Paul said. "Tomorrow, then."

Duarte watched the Bradleys leave, their faces pale and strained. Whether this sister—this evil twin or whatever you wanted to call her—was after them or not, they were in trouble. He wasn't really sure he wanted to be around when it all came down. Things were tough enough these days.

The next morning, Paul sat at the desk in his home office, staring out at the leaden morning sky. Thick gray fog hovered over Seattle like a harbinger of trouble. *Nothing can go well on a day like this*, it seemed to say. The only color to be seen was the top of the Space Needle, with its flashing red light. It sat above the fog like a flying saucer, resting on clouds. Closer in, his backyard called to him. Weeds he hadn't pulled in the fall were now lifeless and brown. They would come back, though, and if he didn't get them out before spring, they'd choke out the azaleas and rhodies.

Back in late August he had told Gina not to hire anyone to do the gardening; he'd looked forward to getting outside and working out. Then, in September, he'd met Lacey, and there hadn't been time to do all the things he'd planned to do before the rains set in.

Paul sighed. Nothing these days was turning out the way he'd planned. He had managed a quick call to Lacey the night before, coming into his office and closing the door behind him. He'd told her what was going on; about the note in Rachel's pocket, how they had reported it and had been tied up at the police station for hours.

Lacey's response had been soothing, "I'm sure it'll be all right, Paul. Get some rest. Things will look better in the morning."

Soothing but not realistic, he thought. Things did not look better now. He still had to call Saint Sympatica's, and he was dreading it. He had thought they'd closed that Pandora's box years ago. Opening it now was the last thing he wanted to do.

What if they *did* have Angela's fingerprints? And what if they matched those on the note? The police would look for her, and if they found her, he, Rachel, and Gina would eventually have to come face-to-face with her.

He didn't think he could take that.

What would she be like now? His last memory of

Angela was from fifteen years ago: a six-year-old girl with dark brown hair in two ponytails, her hazel eyes brimming with huge tears as he and Gina said goodbye for the final time.

No one had told the child that this was the last time she would ever see them, but Angela seemed to know. She had clung to them as if they were the only thing between her and some awful terror they would never understand. Paul had finally been forced to pry her loose from Gina's arms. It nearly killed him to hear her cries as Dr. Chase led her away.

They had turned to go back to their car, and looked behind them only once, in time for Paul to see a fleeting expression of anger as Angela's mouth tightened into a thin line. She was standing on the steps of the orphanage, her hand in Dr. Chase's. They watched her yank away from him and stomp up the steps to the heavy front doors, slamming them behind her as if they weighed no more than feathers.

Her physical strength was mind-boggling, and just as frightening as it had been the night she had tried to kill Rachel.

Paul had to keep reminding himself of that on the drive home that day. *She tried to kill Rachel.* It was the only way he had managed to keep his foot on the gas and not go back there, sweep her up into his arms and carry her home.

He pulled himself together and looked at his watch. Nearly ten in the morning. With the two-hour time difference, if he didn't call Saint Sympatica's now, they would probably be at lunch. Besides, he needed to get to Soleil. There were orders to fill, people to consult with.

Sighing again, he pulled out his address book, picked up the phone and punched in the Minnesota numbers he had thought he would never need again. As the phone rang on the other end, it seemed every muscle and nerve in his body went taut. He felt he must be on the alert for bad news, though he wasn't sure why.

A receptionist answered and put him through to Anita Ewing, who surprised him by remembering immediately who he was.

"I wasn't sure you would still be there," Paul said.

"Well, it's true I have thought several times of retiring," Mrs. Ewing answered, "but it seems there's always a new child here who needs our help. It would be difficult, you know, to just turn our work over to someone else."

"Your husband is still there, too?" Paul asked, wondering if the other owner and director of Saint Sympatica's had passed on, yet not wanting to be so blunt as to put the question into words.

"Oh my, yes, Rodney just never gives up. We had a bit of a scare a year ago when he had to have a pacemaker put in, but he's fine now." She paused. "What can I do for you, Mr. Bradley? Is everything all right with...let's see, Rachel, isn't it?"

"Yes, everything's fine. At least we think it is. Mrs. Ewing, we're wondering if you know where Angela is now? Also—and I know this sounds like an unusual question—but did you ever take her fingerprints?''

There was a small silence at the other end. ''What has Angela done?'' Mrs. Ewing said finally, in a low, worried tone.

''We don't really think she's done anything,'' Paul answered quickly. ''We're just trying to rule out the possibility that she was involved in a…well, in an accident here.''

''An accident.'' Mrs. Ewing's tone was flat.

''It's really nothing,'' Paul said, wondering why he felt a need to protect Angela, even now. ''An automobile accident. We think it was probably just a drunk driver, but the police want all bases covered.''

Another silence. Finally Anita Ewing said, ''Mr. Bradley, I don't know that I can help you. You and Mrs. Bradley gave up your rights as adoptive parents years ago, and in accordance with our policy, Angela's whereabouts are confidential now. As for fingerprints, no, we never did that here.''

''No, I suppose not,'' Paul said, not knowing whether to be disappointed or relieved.

''Do you mind if I ask why you would need fingerprints?'' Mrs. Ewing said. ''If it was only an accident…''

Paul decided suddenly to level with her. If she were to be any help at all, she needed to know. ''There was a note,'' he said.

''A note?''

"With…well, with a fingerprint on it that didn't belong to any of us."

"What kind of note?" Anita Ewing asked sharply.

"It, uh, seemed to indicate that our car was run off the road on purpose."

"Oh, my God," the director said softly.

Trying to quell her alarm, he added, "It could have just been a prank, of course. In fact, I'm sure that's what it was. But you might be hearing from the Seattle police. They might want to know where Angela is now. Would you be able to give them that information?"

"It depends," the director said after a moment. "I'll have to talk with our lawyers. And frankly, I'm not sure we even know where Angela is."

"I understand. Would you…would you please do that as soon as possible?"

"Certainly." A small pause. "Mr. Bradley, how is your wife doing?"

"Well, after all these years I guess you learn to focus on other things. Even so, I don't think you can raise a child for five years and come to love her, then just forget she ever existed."

"Still, with the passing of time…" Mrs. Ewing suggested.

"It gets easier, yes. It just doesn't disappear."

A sound of papers being ruffled came through from the other end. "Well," Anita Ewing said in the brisk, efficient tone Paul remembered, "we'll see what happens, won't we?"

"Yes. Yes, I guess we will," Paul said.

A feeling of doom swept over him as he hung up the phone. The brooding Seattle skyline now seemed light compared to his mood. He placed a call to Duarte's office. When the detective's voice came on with a grouchy "Duarte!", Paul debated about just hanging up. Why not forget the whole thing, pretend nothing had happened? Maybe it would all go away.

Instead, he told the detective simply, "The orphanage never took prints. The director said she couldn't tell me where Angela is. She has to talk to her lawyers, and then maybe she'll talk to you."

"Damn." Paul could hear the pencil tapping. "Well, I'll let you know when I hear from her."

"Okay," Paul said. He was starting to hang up when Duarte spoke again.

"What about those newborn footprints they take in the hospital? Do they have those?"

"I didn't ask, but the babies were three months old when the birth mother left them at the orphanage. Saint Sympatica's never mentioned her leaving any newborn prints there—" Paul broke off. "Why, what good would they do?"

The pencil-tapping stopped. "Well, if she, uh... ended up in the morgue."

Paul sat hunched over, his eyes covered by one hand, Duarte's words ringing in his ears. Angela, in the morgue? She was only twenty-one. God, no. *Please!*

They left it that Duarte would talk to the orphanage and take it from there.

After hanging up, Paul's depression deepened. Again he was jolted back to that last day with Angela. He could still see himself and Gina sitting with her on the broad expanse of lawn in front of Saint Sympatica's. In so many ways it had seemed a normal spring day, with robins hopping along the grass amidst a carpet of yellow dandelions. Baby birds chirped in the trees, and a fountain with angels in the middle of a circular driveway tinkled in the background.

"Why can't I go home with you?" Angela had pleaded for the hundredth time. "There isn't anything wrong with me, honest!" Her large hazel eyes brimmed with tears.

Paul had held one of her hands, Gina the other. "The doctor thinks you need to stay," Paul had said, at a loss for words that would make any sense to a six-year-old. Angela had been here a year, and for a year he and Gina had been coming every month to visit. How could he possibly tell her this would be the last time?

"But when can I go home?" Angela had pressed, one huge tear slipping down her cheek. Her lower lip shook and Paul noted that her complexion had grown pale; the rosy glow of babyhood was gone.

Of course, the winters were harsh in Minnesota. There wasn't much sunlight for months on end. That, and being separated from her family, probably accounted for the change in their daughter—the haunted look when they'd first seen her this time, and the new physical fragility. She had lost weight, and no longer seemed like the little girl they had raised till the age of five. There was a sharpness in her eyes, and an angular, hungry look to her face.

"It's part of her illness," Dr. Chase, the staff psychiatrist, had said, pushing back a thatch of brown hair. He was young, with a bland face and not a lot of personality, Paul had thought. In bearing he seemed tall when sitting, but lost inches when he stood. "She would be this way," he added, "even if you had kept her at home. In fact, she might well have become worse."

Gina had answered Angela's question, biting her lower lip. There were tears in her eyes, too, Paul remembered now. "We don't know when you can come home, sweetheart," she had said.

"You're coming back, though?" Angela had asked, the sadness in her tone almost more than Paul could bear.

"I...we don't know," he had said, avoiding an outright lie.

Sadness turned to anger as Angela yanked away from their hands, her eyes flashing. "You mean you're *never* coming back!"

"Daddy didn't say that, Angela," Gina said soothingly. "We just don't know how things are going to go."

But that was a lie, and Angela was too bright not to know it. Standing before them, she clenched her fists and cried out angrily, "Why isn't Rachel here? She should be here!"

"Honey—"

She stomped her foot. "I want to go home! I hate it here! Why can't I go home?"

Neither Paul nor Gina knew what to say. They had been through this on every visit, and always before they had left with hope in their hearts. Each time they had been able to tell their daughter that next month things could be different. Dr. Chase might give her a clean bill of health, and they might finally be able to take her back to Seattle with them.

This time, that hope had been crushed.

"She simply hasn't continued to improve," the psychiatrist had told them. "I strongly recommend that you not remove her from our care."

It was final, then. Angela might never be able to live in a "normal" home. She still had no conscience to speak of, Dr. Chase had said. No remorse, none of the feelings people normally have. She could be a danger to anyone, at any time.

Paul sat at his desk, his heart aching just as it had that day. The ache was one of emptiness, a hollow feeling where love used to be. He had thought, back then, that this was what one felt when one's heart "broke," and over the years he had stuffed back that ache, telling himself it was gone, it was healed, he would never feel it again…if only he could manage not to think of it.

Still, it never went away entirely. It popped up at

odd times, like when he saw another little child who resembled Angela with her dark hair in ponytails, walking along the street with a man who might be her father. Or when he and Gina went to school plays that Rachel was in. It had seemed so strange—almost un-natural—not to see Angela beside her sister.

Not to see Angela at all.

"Paul, you all right?" Gina tapped on his office door. They'd had an agreement for years that she would always knock before walking in, in case he was working. And Paul did the same for her. Without that, neither of them would ever have gotten anything done at home.

"I'm fine," he answered, surprised that his voice even worked. It felt as if his throat muscles were con-stricted, that there might not be enough room for air to pass through. "Be out in a minute," he added, his voice cracking.

Burying his face in his hands, he wept.

Paul sat in Victoria Lessing's office, clenching and unclenching his hands. For some reason, he couldn't keep them from shaking. He had just asked Victoria for more water, but when she poured it he'd had to put the glass down to keep it from spilling.

"I thought I had put all that behind me," he said. "I thought I was all right, that I'd never feel this way again."

"An odd expression," Victoria observed, "'putting it all behind you'. Do you know I've actually had patients who developed lower back problems from thinking they'd put their troubles behind them, when in fact they were still carrying them around?''

"You're kidding. Back problems?'' Paul's right hand went automatically to his lower back, which had been hurting lately when he stood too long.

"Well, troubles are a terrible weight,'' Victoria said. "There are books about it. Throat problems, for instance. They can come from being afraid to speak up, from swallowing anger. Leg troubles? Being afraid to move forward. Even medical doctors have begun to look at the connection between the emotions and illness, Paul. But to get back to you...''

He managed a small smile. "I thought for a minute we *were* talking about me.''

Victoria smiled. "So now we have to get to what you're carrying around. The true essence of it, that is, not just the veneer. The human mind, you know, is much like this antique furniture you work with. If a piece has been painted over, it doesn't tell you much about what's beneath. You have to remove that coat of paint to get to the rich old wood, the pine, maple, mahogany—all of which may tell you a story about the provenance of that piece, its history.''

She paused and looked at him earnestly. "You need to uncover that history in yourself, Paul. Then you have to find a way to let it go.''

"Easier said than done,'' he observed.

"True. There's that trick of putting one's troubles in a brown grocery bag by the bed every night, rather than lying awake thinking about them. Unfortunately, human curiosity is something to behold. People will inevitably take their troubles out again in the morning and go over and over them, like snapshots in a photo album of people they're afraid they'll forget.''

She studied him, her blue eyes narrowing. ''Paul, what is it that worries you most?''

''I'm not sure. I guess I'm afraid that Angela really has returned and is trying to harm us in some way. If that's true, I'll have to deal with it. It isn't something I can simply brush off.''

''Not brush off,'' Victoria said. ''There's a difference between that and letting go. You do what you can—in this case, turning the matter over to the police—and then you go on with your life as calmly as possible.''

She held up a restraining hand. ''Never mind, I know that can't be easy. What does Gina say about all this?''

He shrugged. ''I imagine she feels the same. We haven't talked about it.''

Victoria's brows went up. ''Really? Why not?''

''Well, it's hard,'' Paul said, taking a sip of water and setting the glass down carefully. ''She still blames me for making the decision to take Angela back. She thinks we could have done more for her.''

''And you? What do you think?''

''I don't know,'' Paul said softly. ''Sometimes I agree with Gina, I guess. Other times, just thinking about what might have happened if we'd kept Angela another single day…you know, Vicky, it chills me to the bone.''

Victoria nodded. ''Why are you here?''

He met her eyes. ''Because you're the only one who agreed with me. It was you, in fact, who told us she had to go back. Do you still feel we made the right decision?''

''Oh, Paul, who can say? We have to live with what we did and go on from there. Looking back and casting blame is a thankless task.''

''I wish you could convince my wife of that,'' he said.

''She's not the one sitting in that chair. You're all I have to work with at the moment.''

''I tried to get her to come with me. But since last night at the police station, it seems that she doesn't want to think about it anymore. Neither does Rachel.''

''Well, see if you can get her to come in,'' Victoria said. ''I'll do my best. With both of them. But, Paul—'' She hesitated.

''Yes?''

''Sixteen years is a long time to grieve for a child. I'm not saying it ever goes away completely—but you might want to ask yourself what's really going on.''

''What do you mean?'' he asked.

''This distance between you and Gina. Are you sure you haven't both been using Angela's loss to cover up a more basic problem in your marriage?''

Paul's first instinct was to be angry. ''I didn't come here to have my feelings invalidated,'' he said curtly.

"And I don't mean at all to invalidate them," Victoria said reasonably. "Paul, I know your grief was genuine. And certainly it's understandable that you'd think of Angela during the holidays. But think about this, too. What if you and Gina are both using Angela's loss as a handy excuse for not looking at what's really wrong?"

Paul frowned. "What are you saying?"

"Not very much," Victoria admitted. "I'm not a mind reader, Paul. It's just a suggestion. But I would like you to think about that before you come in again."

Paul nodded and stood. "I'd better get back to Soleil."

When he reached the door he turned and said, "Vicky? At the risk of using the 'A' word again, what do you really think? Not as a doctor, but as a friend. Is she back? And if she is, will she try to hurt us?"

"As a friend?" Victoria sighed. "I'm not sure, Paul. I would urge you to watch your back. Do you know what she looks like now?"

He shook his head. "I asked if Saint Sympatica's had any photos of her. Mrs. Ewing said there was a group photo they took on the twentieth anniversary of the orphanage. Angela was in it, but she was in a back row, Mrs. Ewing said, since she was one of the tallest. She said it's not very clear."

"How long ago was the photo taken?"

"About five years ago. When Angela was sixteen."

"Is she sending you a copy of it?"

Paul shook his head. "The police had to ask for it, so she's sending it to the police here. I'll go down to the precinct and try to get a look at it."

"Well, see if you can make anything of it. Watch for anyone who could be her. And keep in mind, she may try to change her appearance."

"You really think she'd go to that extent?"

"Paul, if the grown-up Angela is anything like the Angela I knew as a child, I think she would be capable of anything. Anything at all."

6

That same morning, Roberta Evans lay on the massage table at the Rose Arbor Spa, trying to relax. If she didn't relax, the massage would be wasted, and she couldn't afford that. She had a tough job ahead. Things were going crazy, and she felt as if her neck were being pulled halfway around the globe by a rubber band.

"How was your Christmas?" Andie asked. Her competent hands ran over the muscles in Roberta's back, feeling for knots and other signs of tension.

"Better than most," Roberta answered.

"Did you have it with your family?"

"No. That's why it was better than most."

Andie laughed. "Troubles, hmm?"

"No more than usual at this time of year. Ouch!"

"Take a deep breath," Andie suggested, pressing hard with her thumb on a point in Roberta's upper back. "Breath in from the diaphragm, and hold it till I tell you to breathe out."

"Oh, for God's sake, I know how to breathe, Andie!" Roberta said irritably. "We've been doing this for years!"

"I know you know," the massage therapist said patiently. "You just don't always focus." She chuckled. "Pretend you're having a baby."

"Humph." Babies were the last thing Roberta needed to think about.

When Paul and Gina had taken Angela back to the orphanage all those years ago, neither of them had seemed to consider how losing the child had affected her grandmother. Roberta had come to love both girls more than life itself, and over the first two years they were in the family, her worries about their having been adopted had subsided, washed away by the overpowering love she had for them.

It was Angela, though, who became her precious "grandbaby" from the time Gina and Paul had brought the twins home. It was Angela who reminded her of herself as a child—breaking the rules, testing her parents' limits, but always with a huge, saucy grin on her face. Rachel was quiet and demanded less attention, while Angela would always tug at her knee, asking her "Gamma" to read a story, play a game, or sometimes simply hold her.

As Angela began to show signs of temper and even violence, however, Roberta was the first to point out to Gina that this might be cause for worry. Gina didn't want to hear it, and Paul was even less willing, to the point of putting a distance between himself and Roberta rather than listen to her worries. Finally Roberta was able to talk Gina into taking the girls to a psychiatrist. She knew of Victoria Lessing through a friend, and assured Gina that she came highly recommended.

"Just let her see Angela and talk to her," Roberta had urged. "What harm can it do?"

Victoria was the first to put a tentative label on Angela's illness—Reactive Attachment Disorder, or RAD. It was most likely the result, she said, of her not having had a mother or anyone loving to bond with the first months of her life. Though the Ewings were nice people and meant well, Victoria said, it was possible—even likely—they had been overwhelmed by the sheer amount of work it took to run an orphanage that was full to bursting with more children than they could handle but hadn't had the heart to turn away. Unfortunately, they had only private funding, and during the year Angela and Rachel had been left there, they had been going through a budget crunch. There wasn't enough in the coffers to hire additional staff to help with the children.

At first they had all—Victoria, Roberta, Paul and Gina—pulled together to help Angela, thinking this problem might be something they could get past. But then there was that horrible incident on Christmas Eve. As soon as they could make arrangements, Paul and Gina took Angela back to the orphanage in Minnesota. Roberta hadn't seen her since.

Just thinking about it brought tears to her eyes, even now. That was the thing about being a grandmother. Children often didn't consider what it did to grandparents when they were wrenched apart from a beloved grandchild. Even those first months when Paul and Gina went back to Minnesota to see Angela and talk to her psychiatrist, Roberta wasn't allowed to go along. "Dr. Chase doesn't think it would be a good idea," they had said.

Good for whom, dammit? Roberta had wondered then. *Certainly not for me.* She still longed to put her arms around the child and love her, despite what she had done. And Angela, regardless of her illness, must surely be missing her grandmother.

"We grandparents have become second-class citizens, Andie," she said with a bitter sigh. "Our children say they want us to be close to their babies, but when it comes to having any say about what happens to them, like where they live or any other important life decisions, we aren't consulted."

"You can say that again," Andie confirmed with a sigh. "Mine just moved to Boston. Three thousand miles away, they took that child! I'll be lucky if I get to see her once a year."

"It's as if they think we can turn love off and on at will," Roberta concurred. "If they move away, we're not supposed to hurt. If they're *sent* away, as Angela was, we're supposed to forget them overnight."

Andie chuckled. "But then, if we ever do manage to put them out of our minds, they say we're hard-hearted."

Roberta grunted her affirmation as Andie pushed

with her thumbs on another pressure point. Taking a deep breath, Roberta let it out slowly.

Well, she had done her best to get over the loss of Angela, throwing herself into activities just as Gina and Paul had. It was Rachel who made it difficult, though, Rachel who asked the hard questions about what had happened to her sister. She asked them of her grandmother because Gina and Paul would tell her not to think about what happened, to just forget it.

Well, maybe *they* could. But Rachel had relived that last moment with Angela for years, in her nightmares. There were times when she needed someone close to talk to, to tell her the truth about things.

Not that seeing Victoria all that time hadn't helped, but Victoria was a psychiatrist, not a member of the family. She couldn't know everything that went on inside the home.

Nor had Victoria ever had a child. It was easier for her to tell Rachel that her parents were right, that she did need to forget.

Well, Roberta hadn't forgotten. A grandmother never does. And now...now, thank God, she was being given a second chance.

7

Gina was deep in thought when Rachel entered the living room. It suddenly dawned on her that her daughter was simply standing inside the doorway, watching her.

"Rachel! How long have you been there?"

"Not long." Rachel crossed over to her and rested a hand on her shoulder. "Mom, you don't mind, do you, if I spend the night at Ellen's?"

Gina set aside the invoices she was going over at the Louis XV desk. The sun, for once, had made an appearance, filtering through the Christmas tree in the bay window to bounce off the reading glasses she wore. Gina removed them, smiling at her daughter, who was dressed in jeans and the pink cashmere sweater Gina and Paul had given her for Christmas. Pink was Rachel's favorite color, and she wore something in that shade every day. Her dark hair was pulled back into a ponytail, and that, with the sweater, made her look like the Rachel she remembered from years ago, before the world and its influences had carried her away.

"No, of course I don't mind," Gina said, though truthfully she would have preferred that Rachel stay home and spend the morning with her. Christmas break went by all too fast, and it seemed as if they'd had far too little time together since Rachel came home.

"I mean, you're going up to Camano Island today, aren't you?" Rachel asked. "To work on that house for a client?"

"Yes, but not till later. Actually, I had hoped..." She stopped, not saying that she had hoped Rachel would spend the morning with her.

"And Dad will probably be working late," Rachel said reasonably. "This seems like a good time. I haven't seen Ellen since summer."

Gina smiled and put her arm around Rachel's waist, pulling her close. "It's a perfect time," she said, trying to keep the wistful tone out of her voice. "You *should* see your old friends when you're home."

Rachel gave her a kiss on the cheek. "I'll just be overnight. And it's not as if she doesn't live right across town."

"I know. Do you want me to drive you over there?"

"No," Rachel said. "I'll take my old Mustang. In fact, I can't wait to drive it again."

"Then *go*," Gina said, pushing her away with a playful shove. "I'm up to my ears in work, anyway."

"What time do you think you'll be home from Camano?" Rachel asked.

"Oh, probably not much later than seven. Depends on the traffic. I could call you." Gina knew that Rachel always liked to know where her parents were, even when she herself wasn't going to be around.

"No, don't call," Rachel said quickly, then bit her lower lip. Laughing, she said, "I mean, don't be silly, it would only embarrass me. After all, I'm a big girl now. I don't need Mommy checking up on me. Besides, we'll probably be out at a movie."

"Okay." Gina smiled. "Well, have a good time, then." She went back to her pile of invoices as Rachel headed for the door.

It wasn't until after Rachel had gone that Gina raised her head and stared out the window at the last traces of fog breaking up under the insistent morning sun.

What was that about? she wondered. Why doesn't she want me to call her at Ellen's?

But then she shrugged it off. It's just like she said, Gina told herself—she's a big girl now.

Gina slung her briefcase into the back seat of her comfortable eight-year-old Crown Victoria, the car she had bought for driving long distances. Camano Island was an hour and a half away, but the smooth drive and big, cushy seats made her feel as if she were in her own living room. Add to that a good CD, and the driving time seemed minimal, the traffic bearable.

Paul had urged her to use the Infiniti when they first bought it, but Gina didn't like change. She was used to the Vic, and she wasn't concerned with what her clients thought of her driving it, the way Paul felt he needed to be. Her clients might be as wealthy as Paul's, but they were usually older, many of retirement age, and more interested in comfort than appearances. By the time they came to her, they already had their success well in hand.

Take the Albrights, who had hired her to redo their thirty-year-old home on Camano. Ted and Amy Albright had bought it when they hit it big with Microsoft stock. There had been down times with the stock, of course, but Ted had been smart enough to get out of the market before the bad times hit. He'd cleverly taken all he had and put it into more stable investments, and now he was retiring. He and Amy were currently in their condo on Maui, and during their absence they wanted Gina to redesign the two-story beach house on Elger Bay for easier living, with a master bedroom and bath downstairs. The upstairs rooms would now be used only for guests.

The job had been more difficult than she'd expected, Gina thought, and she would have to finish it before the Albrights returned in March. That meant some long hours between now and then.

She pressed hard on the accelerator north of Everett, and the Vic, which she fondly called the Silver Bullet because of its color, moved up smoothly to seventy miles per hour. She set the cruise control and thought about the happenings of the past few days as the countryside sped by.

Was it possible that Angela was back? And if so, had she come here with an intent to harm them? Gina gave a shudder. Their entire lives could be changed overnight.

Unlike her sister, Rachel had never been any real trouble. There were, of course, the childhood years when she was recovering from having been separated from her twin, and then the teenage years, when she seemed sharp as a prickly pear, always on the defensive, an argument for everything.

But that was normal, and Gina had done her best to be patient. Even so, she couldn't stifle a sigh of relief when Rachel chose a college out of state. Not having the responsibilities of day-to-day parenthood would be a welcome change, she had thought, although of course she would miss her. She would just have to find a new life of her own.

Which she had done, in a way. But not with Paul. He was much too busy, and they had drifted apart, each going in separate directions.

Gina sighed. She had never wanted to hurt Paul, but she needed more than he was able to give her. She didn't even blame him; it was just the way things had turned out. They kept their marriage intact partly for Rachel, partly for the business, and partly because divorce after all these years would take more effort than simply going on.

Although, sometimes the facade was extremely difficult to keep up. She'd had an uneasy moment at the police station the other night, when Rachel was asked by Detective Duarte about the man in the coffee shop.

"Come to think of it, he was looking more at Mom than me," Rachel had said.

I covered well, though, didn't I? Gina asked herself now. Paul didn't suspect a thing.

While Gina was driving to Camano Island, Paul was making the rounds of the five huge warehouse rooms that comprised Soleil Antiques. The name, which meant "sun" in French, came from a large eighteenth-century wooden sign Gina had given him the day he opened what was then a very small shop. Composed of a large sun with rays issuing from it, the sign had originated in France. Dark spots of wear on the face made it seem as if the sun were smiling.

"It's to make *you* smile during the dark winter days," Gina had said, standing on tiptoe to kiss him. "You know, the kinds of days when you can't bear to drag yourself to work. You'll park, get out of your car, and this will be greeting you, rain or shine."

Those were the days when they still had their lives and the entire world ahead of them. Since then, the business, at least, had gone well. Paul now owned three buildings at this end of the block, each connected to the other. The main building was three stories tall, with stairs going both up and down from the first floor, where customers entered.

He had been incredibly lucky, he knew. It had been a matter of timing, and he'd done the right things at the right time by depending on a certain intuitive sense about the way things were going, both in business and with the world.

It had taken a while to acquire this amount of inventory, of course, but now he had one room dedicated to Chinese antiques: altar tables, cabinets, chests, screens and small accessories like wooden plates and food buckets. Another room held English antiques, and yet another a mixture of Early American and Colonial. These included nineteenth-century maps and engravings, lamps, quilts, pewter—a sampling of the kinds of accessories a client might want. There was a scattering of Civil War memorabilia, jewelry and vintage china, as well as some collectibles that weren't expensive, but that clients bought in order to fill their homes with a bit of the past.

A fourth room held art deco pieces, which always seemed to be popular. Paul stocked but personally didn't care for the Billy Haines revival—furniture of the forties, designed by the actor-turned-designer who'd been "found" by Joan Crawford. Its sharp angles and metal and plastics were too hard-edged for him. In decor he preferred the Hollywood "Glamour" era: the soft pastels, crystal water carafes, penguin cocktail shakers in glass and sterling silver, and soft creamy draperies. It was a style that always reminded him of the old *Thin Man* movies of the thirties, which he had loved watching on TV as a kid. When he walked into a room decorated in this fashion, it was as if the stars of yesterday were saying to him, "We know what it's like to feel nurtured, and now you do, too.''

This, then, was Paul's business, and he had been content enough with it. It was the fifth room, the closest to his office, however, that he truly loved. Called the Crystal Cave, it was an entire room dedicated to hundreds of pieces of art glass from a variety of periods. Paul and Gina had spent innumerable hours designing just the right lighting to make every piece sparkle at any time of the day. His personal favorites were the Gallè vases, and the contemporary pieces by Dale Chihuly, of which he had only a few. Still they seemed to overshadow everything else in terms of beauty, and Paul had made a special alcove for them. He had visited Chihuly on his houseboat hot-shop on Lake Union some time back, and had been held in thrall by the long hallway ceiling he had lined with a wild array of some eight hundred pieces of brightly lit glass, the most beautiful art forms Paul had ever seen. While he knew that the work behind Chihuly's art glass must be monumental, the end result seemed whimsical and light, as if it had come together out of a spirit of fun.

Paul deplored the fact that there was little whimsy left in contemporary life, and every morning when he first arrived at Soleil he would enter the Crystal Cave and stand stock-still, as if listening for some ethereal voice, or the notes of a forgotten song. This room had been inspired by memories of a book he'd read when he was small, about a cave that had gems of all sizes

and colors hanging from the ceiling. They would tin-
kle at the slightest breath of air, like fairy wind
chimes, and Paul had imagined having a room like that
one day. Lying in bed at eight, nine, ten years old,
with the sounds of his parents arguing in the next
room, he would squeeze his eyes shut tight and vow
to himself that he would one day, in some way, have
something magical in his life. A place to go where
there were no sounds, no violence.

The Crystal Cave had become that for him. On difficult days, when the bad memories settled down
around him like a dark cloud, he could always escape
into this room for a few brief moments and soak in its
beauty and peace. It had also become a favorite of his
clients, who never failed to remark upon its warmth
and radiance.

When the earthquake struck in Seattle, Paul had
panicked. He was in his office at the time, and it took
him no more than a minute to run from there to the
Crystal Cave, his heart beating wildly. Catching his
breath, he saw with relief that only a few pieces had
toppled to the floor. Since he'd purposely put in deep
grooves to hold the plates on their shelves, and thick,
lush carpeting in the event a customer should drop
anything, the few pieces that had fallen had not even
suffered a scratch.

Later Paul learned that businesses on either side of
him had been damaged, and he had thought that perhaps the gods had smiled on him that day. From that

point on he had not entered this room even once without a deep feeling of gratitude.

The house on Queen Anne Hill, however, had been furnished by Gina with older, more traditional antiques. "It cries out for the elegance of Queen Anne, Chippendale, Hepplewhite," she had argued. Gina had excellent taste, and for that reason Paul had gone along with her. But when it came time to furnish Lacey's apartment a few months ago, he had decorated it in the 1930s Hollywood style of his own taste. Lacey had loved it, and sometimes he wondered how it was possible that he and Lacey had so many more things in common than he and Gina did.

Yet, he loved Gina. They had survived so many bad times together over the years, and the one thing he knew for certain was that Gina would always be there. With Lacey, he felt as if, like a butterfly just breaking out of its cocoon, she might disappear one day—fly off to have a life of her own. That wasn't at all unlikely, and he knew that when he was with her, he had to make every moment together count.

Gina pulled into the semicircular driveway at the Albright house, which overlooked the Sound and, across the way, Whidbey Island. A few sailboats dotted the water, and sunshine skipped over the wakes they left behind. The air was unusually warm for December. When days like this appeared, people in Washington took advantage of it. There were far too many of the other kind.

She unlocked the white double doors with the key Amy Albright had left with her, and walked through the foyer into the living room. Whether the sun was shining or not, the tall wall-to-wall windows in here always set her back a moment or two. Her own house in Seattle had heavy draperies to close out the dank weather, and she always felt as if she were safe and cocooned there. Here in this harsh, bright light, she felt stripped, exposed, as if every flaw, every wrong-doing were laid bare.

Guilt rose in her throat and almost choked her, but she forced it back down. Guilt never helped anything, or so the priest at the small, out-of-the-way church Gina had sought out last year had told her. At least not without a confession of sins and a vow not to sin again. Gina hadn't been able to do that. She couldn't explain why, but she needed her sin, the way a fish needs water or a bird its tree.

Frowning, she shook off the dark thoughts and made a quick pass through the house, retaking measurements for new ideas she'd come up with. Then she shot new photographs to work from at home. Most of her work here had already been done, but she had thought of some changes she would like to suggest to the builder. He wouldn't be happy with getting her ideas this late, but she thought the Albrights would love them—especially since they would add significantly to the value of the house.

Ending up in the former den downstairs, Gina stood still and felt the change in vibrations, the *feng shui*.

The den had already been expanded and turned into a large master bedroom. It was a wonderful room now, she thought, so different from the formerly dark, paneled one. The walls were done in a wallpaper that was white with light sprigs of blue flowers, which was what Amy Albright had asked for. Though this wouldn't have been Gina's choice, she believed in pleasing her clients. She also knew precisely what accessories she would bring in to give the room the country look her clients had asked for.

Amy Albright particularly loved a Louis XV armoire that they'd had for years, and she wanted it left against a wall. Gina thought she could make it fit into the new decor, especially if she leaned toward a French country look. Large blue-and-white checks on a sofa angled in a corner would work, leaving free the broad expanse of glass that looked out onto a flagstone terrace and the Sound. Only Ted Albright's telescope would go there, and both inside and out there would be wooden containers filled with bright, vibrant flowers. An old dining room table in the garage could be cut down and refinished, then distressed, to serve as a large coffee table in front of the fireplace.

When appropriate, Gina liked using an occasional piece belonging to her clients, and didn't mind doing the work of making them look like antiques to match the rest of the room. Her clients appreciated the fact that she kept an eye on costs, and when the job was finished they never felt as if they were walking into a showroom, but rather their own, comfortable home that still had some familiarity to it. She would find paintings and other accessories with blue hydrangeas, Amy Albright's favorite flower, and in the new connecting bathroom she had already placed thick white towels with blue hydrangeas on the border.

Some designers would call this look too "cute," but again, it was what the Albrights wanted. Genuine antique tables and a bed would come from Soleil. Gina had already picked them out with Paul's help, and when they were moved up here, he would come with the delivery truck to assure that every single piece arrived unscathed. Paul had built a successful business by giving clients this kind of personal attention, and over the years that was one thing that had never changed. Gina was proud of him for that.

She had finished her work today early, and she headed into the new bathroom to look around. It was a large room, with a big, square jetted tub, and windows on three sides. The windows didn't face the Sound, but rather the street and neighbors. Amy had asked for an atrium to be built on all sides, for privacy. Gina thought she would be delighted with the plants, trees and flowers she and the landscape gardener had come up with.

At least in this small way she could please someone. The burden of guilt became a tenth of an ounce lighter.

She was tired, and her limbs ached from running around this past week with Rachel, not to mention all the work of the holiday. The new tub called out to her, and at first Gina hesitated. Then she thought wearily, why not? Amy was a great person, and they'd become friends. She wouldn't mind if her designer stole a moment or two in her bath.

But had she locked the front door? She thought so, and could almost see herself turning the dead bolt. Yes, she was pretty sure she had done that, and she was much too tired to walk all the way back through the house and check.

Gina put her cell phone on a white wicker table by the tub. Then, shrugging out of her suit jacket, she bent over and turned on the new but old-style chrome water faucet. Removing her blouse, skirt, stockings and underwear, she stood before the large new mirror. Looking at herself, she thought, not too bad for forty-one. My face looks tired, but the body has held up pretty well.

She gave credit to the exercise classes she'd been taking at the sports club, since Paul had been so busy and she'd had time to kill after work. Three days a week, regular as clockwork. She hadn't missed until this week, when Rachel had been home, and she now had well-developed muscles in her arms and legs to prove it. Not to mention great abs, she thought with satisfaction. It was her strength that pleased her most, however, not the aesthetics of having a good body— the feeling that no matter what happened, she might be able to handle it.

When the tub was nearly full, she turned on the jets and slipped into the warm, welcoming bubbles. Laying her head back on the rounded edge of the tub, Gina closed her eyes. She had just started to drift off when there was the soft sound of a click at the front door. Gina didn't hear it, or the footsteps that moved softly over the plush, padded rug in the living room. When the bathroom door opened, that too was drowned out by the noise from the tub's jets. It was only the motion of a shadow against her eyelids that warned her she wasn't alone.

Her eyes flew open and she jerked to a sitting position. "Who—!" But the word was barely out when hands from behind closed over her eyes. Gina screamed. The hands moved down to cover her mouth.

"For God's sake!" she heard. "You'll rouse all the neighbors!"

Twisting, she saw gray-blond hair, a navy blue T-shirt and jeans.

"Julian!" she cried when the hands over her mouth lifted. Her heart was thumping like a jackhammer, and she could barely hear herself. "What are you trying to do, give me a heart attack?"

"No, my love," he said against her ear, his hands slipping down to her breasts. "I am trying to *steal* your heart."

"Well, you didn't have to do it that way," she said, laughing, though her voice was still shaky. "Anyway, you've already got my heart."

He came around and stripped off his clothes. "Christening the spa today, are we?" he said. One long, muscular leg came over the tub, and Gina shifted to make room so that he could sit beside her. His arm came around her shoulders and he pulled her to him.

"Something like that," she said against his lips. Pulling back, she added, "God, Julian, you nearly scared me to death. Look at me, I'm still shaking. What are you doing here?"

"I was driving by and saw your car. I thought I'd just drop in and take a look at my sweet little things." He kissed one nipple, then the other.

"Stop," she said, barely able to think straight. This wasn't a safe place to be doing this. Better his house on the other side of the island, where they usually met.

But his hand slipped down between her thighs, and all sense left her then.

Twenty minutes later, they were still in the tub, with Julian's back against one side and hers against his chest. Julian's hands rested on her breasts, lightly caressing. This ability to linger was one of the things she liked most about him. It was so different from Paul, who, as his business grew, seemed to want to get sex over with as quickly as possible and get on with "more important" matters.

"I have to let Paul know I won't be home," Gina said, feeling guilty at the mere thought of him.

"Will he care?" Julian asked, rubbing his cheek against hers.

"Probably not. I'm sure he'll be working late. It's just...oh, you know, one of those little courtesies we try to keep."

She had told Julian about the accident on Christmas Eve, but not that she, Paul and Rachel had made a pact since then to keep in closer touch, let each other know they were all right when they weren't home. That was why it was odd when Rachel had asked her not to call Ellen's. Odd enough that it kept nagging at Gina's mind.

"Sweetheart, for the hundredth time, why don't you leave him?" Julian asked.

"And for the hundredth time, because I don't see any reason to. We have to be able to go on working together, after all. Besides, there's Rachel."

And you and I are never going to marry, she thought but didn't say aloud. It's never going to be any more than it is right now. An interlude. A way to make it through the day, knowing I'm cared about and loved.

A sin.

"Rachel is a big girl," he said, stroking her arm with his blunt nails, making her shiver. "I understand why you felt protective of her when we first met, but she was only seventeen then. Sweetheart, we waited till she went away to school. I think I proved I could be patient. But now..."

"Rachel may be *older* now," Gina pointed out mildly. "That doesn't mean she's ready for her parents and her home to break up."

"That's not really it, though," Julian said. "You're afraid you'll lose her, too, aren't you? The way you lost her twin."

She didn't like talking about that, and turned away.

Julian hadn't been in her life when it happened; he couldn't possibly understand. It was for that precise reason that she had chosen to be with him. No shared memories, no reminders.

That, and the fact that he made her feel wanted, right from the first.

They had met when she worked on his apartment in Seattle. Julian was a lecturer in geology at U-Dub—the University of Washington—and traveled around the world giving talks at various colleges and businesses. When he came home, he wanted his "nest" to be peaceful, and to look as if it had been there forever. Since his "nest," as he called it, was a modern high-in-the-sky apartment of glass and chrome overlooking the Sound, that wasn't an easy job. He had bought it fifteen years before, he said, because of its unusually large size, the view, and the fact that the price was good.

Gina had introduced him to Paul, who, together with her, had looked at the apartment. Then the two of them consulted with Julian, to learn more about what he wanted. After that, Paul had come up with the Mayan, Aztec and Chinese pieces Gina recommended, some of which he'd had to travel and search the world for.

By the time Julian's apartment was ready to be moved into, he and Gina were in love. They fought their feelings for a year, until Rachel went away to school. Then, with Paul gone so much, and Gina so lonely she couldn't stand it, Gina had called Julian. They had met in a restaurant and talked. The talk ended when they became so aroused by the simple touching of hands, they had run out into the rain together, still clinging to each other, as if one or the other of them might disappear and ruin this miracle of their finding each other again.

That night ended in a hotel, but ever since then they had been meeting at Julian's house on the other side of Camano, whenever Gina came up to work here—as well as some days when she didn't, but simply used the excuse of work to drive up here and be with him. It was Julian, in fact, who had introduced her to the Albrights—good friends of his—and recommended her for this job.

It was also Julian that Rachel had seen the other day in the coffee shop. That was an accident, however. Julian had sworn he hadn't known Gina would be there. She couldn't hide her nervousness in Duarte's office, however, when Rachel said that "the man" in the coffee shop had been looking more at her, Gina, than at her daughter.

I'll never feel entirely right about this, she thought. The betrayal of a marriage, no matter how empty it had become, could never be explained away or excused. She shivered and began to draw away from Julian.

"Hand me the phone, will you?" she asked, turning off the tub's jets.

He reached past a fern on the corner of the wide ledge, his strong, tanned fingers closing over the cell phone. Gina couldn't take her eyes off them, couldn't stop herself from wanting them on her body, doing things to her that let her know she was alive.

Doing her best to close out that thought, she took the phone. When Paul answered at his office, she sat upright in the tub. Julian's hands slipped from her breasts, and she felt ice-cold, suddenly. In this position, she couldn't see his eyes, couldn't know what he was thinking.

That she was being too much of a mother? A wife? She could seldom read Julian's thoughts, the way she could Paul's. She told herself that was just as well. It helped to make their relationship less complicated, more about the physical aspect than logic and reasoning.

"Hi," Paul said when his assistant put her through.

"Hi." Gina swallowed her compunction over the lie she was about to tell. "Rachel's staying overnight at Ellen's, and I'm still on Camano. I think I'll stay up here tonight. I'm tired, and I'd only have to drive all the way back here in the morning to finish up."

"That makes sense," Paul said. "I'll see you tomorrow night, then?"

"Yes. Will you call Rachel and let her know I won't be home till tomorrow? Do you have Ellen's number?"

"I'm sure I do, somewhere."

She could hear him turning carefully the pages of the well-worn antique leather address book she had given him for their first anniversary, twenty-one years ago. Gina had saved enough from the design projects she had that year to give Paul something that would have real meaning for him. Though the provenance had never been positively established, the plain-paged book was purported to have been owned, but never used, by Thomas Jefferson, whose brilliance with architecture and invention Paul had always admired—if not some of the aspects of his personal life.

"Here it is," Paul said. "I'll tell Rachel to call me on my cell phone if she needs anything, okay?"

"That sounds good. Thanks. I'd call myself, but you know how spotty the cell service can be out here. I wasn't sure I'd even get through to you."

"Sure, I understand."

Paul was so good about it when she had to "work late." But the memory of that address book and the moment she had given it to her husband, his thrilled response and the lovemaking afterward, made her feel even more guilty about what she was doing here today.

"Paul…"

"Yes?"

Julian began to massage her neck and shoulders with an oil Gina had bought for Amy Albright, and she could feel herself relaxing, becoming one with the light musky scent.

"Is there something else?" Paul asked. "I'm late for an appointment with a client."

His hurried tone and obvious eagerness to get on with business wiped out any remaining traces of hesitation.

"No, nothing," she said just as briskly. "See you tomorrow night."

They hung up, and Gina turned to Julian, touching his lips gently with hers. His arms tightened around her, holding her so close there was nothing left between them, no air, no water, nothing but skin. She thought she had never felt this safe and this loved—at least, not for many, many years.

Paul pressed the End button on his cell phone, then punched in Lacey's number. When she answered, he said, "Would you like company tonight?"

"Tonight? You betcha. But where's the family?"

"Rachel and Gina are busy. I'll see you—" he looked at his watch "—in half an hour, okay?"

"Even better, fifteen minutes," Lacey said, chuckling. "We'll try out that red teddy you gave me."

In his mind's eye, Paul could see her in the sheer teddy—every inch of her, and all of it waiting there, just for him.

"Make it five," he said. "I'll scare up a Batmobile."

Lacey laughed in that way he loved, the full, free laugh of a child who was ready for an adventure, any adventure. "Oh, Batman!" she said huskily. "I can't wait!"

Paul hung up, a smile on his face. Then he remembered that he had to call Rachel. Picking up the phone again, he called Ellen's number.

Gina was just stepping out of the tub when her cell phone rang a few minutes later.

"Let it ring," Julian said, putting down the sponge he'd been using to scrub her back and holding his hand out. "Come back in." His tone was teasing but thick with desire. "We were just getting warmed up."

"Can't. It might be important."

She wrapped herself in a towel and reached for the phone.

"Thank God, I got through to you," Paul said, his voice sounding strained. "I wasn't sure, and I was about to call the island sheriff's office and get them to go over to the house—"

"Sheriff's office?" Gina interrupted, her hand tightening on the cell phone. "Why? What's wrong?"

"I just called Ellen, and she hasn't seen Rachel. She didn't even know Rachel was supposed to be there today."

"What do you mean, she didn't know? Rachel told me this morning that she was going over there and she'd be staying overnight."

"Well, for whatever reason, she failed to tell Ellen that. Gina, I called home, and she's not there. She isn't answering her cell phone, and Roberta hasn't seen her, either."

"You called my mother? What did you tell her?"

"Only that I was looking for Rachel, to see if she'd be home for dinner. I didn't want to worry her. Gina, where in the name of God is she? I can't help feeling…"

He didn't finish the sentence, and a long pause filled the line. For several seconds, Gina thought the service had gone down.

"Paul, are you there?" Her voice rose. *"Paul?"* Her voice and her hands were shaking.

"Sorry. Yes, I'm still here. You know, I'm probably just overreacting. Maybe she was going over to Ellen's but then changed her mind. She could be with some other friend, or shopping."

"Shopping? All day?" Gina said doubtfully. "And if she went to someone else's house, after she told me she was going to Ellen's, I think she'd call."

"That's what I thought, too," Paul admitted. "She's always been good about letting us know where she is."

"Let's not panic," Gina said. "There has to be some reasonable explanation."

She stood for a moment and thought back. "Paul, she took her Mustang. Maybe it broke down. Maybe…" But she couldn't go on. Her throat was tight with fear.

"She would have called one of us if she'd had car trouble," Paul said.

"I know," she whispered. The words on the note left in Rachel's pocket blazed across her mind: *Be careful your luck doesn't run out.*

"When was the last time you saw her?" Paul asked.

"This morning. Ten or eleven, I think. I didn't look at the clock."

"I should call Duarte," Paul said. "We've already lost way too much time."

"Yes, you're right. Call him now. I'll get home as fast as I can."

Hanging up, she saw Julian's distressed face. He had gotten out of the tub, dried and was pulling on his clothes. "Something's happened to Rachel?" he asked. "What can I do?"

"I don't know," Gina said, tears filling her eyes. He reached out to hold her, but she slipped away. "I have to go home."

Gina all but flew along I-5, not caring if she were stopped for speeding. If it came to that, she would explain and ask for an escort.

Reaching Queen Anne Hill, she skirted the tree they had run into the other night, gripping the wheel firmly and nearly taking the last corner on two wheels. Ahead was her driveway, and her heart began to race. A silver Crown Vic was parked there, similar to hers. It was a model, she knew, that the police often used.

Racing up the front steps she threw open the front door and called out, "Rachel? Rachel, are you home?"

Paul came from the living room, his face pale and haggard. Her heart ached, seeing him like that.

"She's not here," he said. "Detective Duarte's in the living room."

Gina followed him in and saw the detective sitting

in a chair by the fireplace, the same one Rachel always chose when they had tea in here, afternoons.

Her legs went weak. "You haven't heard anything at all?"

Duarte shook his head. "I'm sorry."

She looked at Paul. "What about the hospitals?"

"They don't have anyone fitting her description," he said.

"But that can be good news," Duarte pointed out.

"Did you try her cell phone again?"

"Several times. She's not answering."

Terrible scenes flashed before her eyes. "I don't understand," she cried out, losing control. "What are you doing here? Why aren't you at the precinct, getting a search organized or something?"

"You have to understand, Mrs. Bradley. A young woman that age, we don't assume right off that she's met with foul play. She had a car, she could have taken off—"

"What the hell are you talking about?" Gina cried. "You met her, you know she wouldn't do that sort of thing. You know about the note she got. For God's sake, why aren't you *doing* something?"

Paul put a hand on her shoulder.

She shook him off. "No, don't touch me! I want to know where my daughter is, and I want someone to act as if they care!"

"Mrs. Bradley," Duarte said patiently, "if I didn't care, I wouldn't be here. Please sit down."

Gina swallowed hard. It felt as if her throat had

closed up, and she began to panic. Paul took her arm and led her to the sofa, where he sat beside her, rubbing her back.

"I was about to say that in most cases," Duarte went on, "we don't figure on foul play right away. But in your daughter's case, there was that note. We can't just dismiss it. And to be honest, your daughter seems like a real sweet kid. I wouldn't like to see anything happen to her."

"He's been asking me about her friends," Paul explained, "anyone at all who might know where she is. I've been making calls." His voice shook. "No one's seen her, Gina."

"Of course, she might have met someone new," Duarte said. "Somebody you folks don't know about yet. Has she mentioned anyone?"

Gina shook her head. "Only Angela. Angela's the only one I can think of who might..."

Her voice failed, and she stiffened her spine, willing her lips to stop trembling. "Angela's the only one who might have hurt her."

"*If* it was Angela she saw and who put that note in her pocket," Paul said quickly, taking her hand. "We can't know that for sure."

Gina let her hand rest in Paul's, and for the first time in a long time she felt they were together in something.

"I've been doing some poking around," Duarte said. "I talked to the director at Saint Sympatica's and got some information from her."

"You didn't tell me that," Paul said, looking at him quickly.

"No, I was waiting for Mrs. Bradley to get here. The thing is, this director, this Mrs. Ewing? I talked to her and she says she really doesn't know where Angela is. It seems Angela was never adopted again. She lived at Saint Sympatica's till she was sixteen."

"Sixteen?" Paul and Gina said simultaneously. "My God," Gina whispered. "All that time?"

"Then she ran off," Duarte said. "Nobody's heard from her since."

He sighed and added, "I hate to have to say this, but I think we can assume she may have been on the streets a while, got hooked up with maybe some bad people..." He spread his hands in a shrug. "A lot can happen to a kid like that."

"Oh, God," Gina said again, covering her face with her hands. "Oh, my poor, poor baby." In that moment, she wasn't sure if she was thinking about Rachel, Angela, or both.

"Do you know why she ran away?" Paul asked Duarte. "Did she leave a note? Tell a friend why she was leaving?"

"Not a word," Duarte answered. "Just disappeared one day. Personally, what I think is, you should go and talk to the people there. They might open up to you more than anybody in authority."

Paul stood and began to pace. "I don't want to leave here until we know Rachel's all right."

Duarte cleared his throat and met his eyes. "What

I'm saying is, I think you, Mr. Bradley, should go there right now. See if you can get a lead on this twin's whereabouts.''

Paul stared. ''You really think she's done something to Rachel, don't you?''

''Let's just say I have a hunch,'' Duarte said. ''And I've learned to listen to my hunches.''

''I guess I could make a quick overnight trip,'' Paul said uncertainly.

''If you're going,'' Gina said, standing, ''I'm going with you.''

''If I could make one more suggestion,'' Duarte said, coming to his feet and facing them, ''I think you should stay here, Mrs. Bradley, and wait for word.''

''You mean from Rachel?'' Gina said. ''In case she calls, or comes home?''

''From anyone,'' Duarte said.

From Angela, he means. In case she's got Rachel. The knife that went through Gina's heart felt just as real as the one Angela had thrust into Rachel sixteen years ago.

Dear God, keep her safe, she prayed. *Keep them both safe.*

That night, Paul caught a red-eye to Minnesota. Arriving too early in the morning, he had breakfast at a café until he thought the Ewings would be up and around. Then he drove along Summit Avenue in Saint Paul, one of the most exclusive areas in the city. Mansions of all sizes and styles lined the street, most of them backing up to the river and with rolling green lawns in front. Making a turn near the end of the street, he saw the large mansion ahead that housed Saint Sympatica's orphanage. It had been willed to the Ewings for this purpose over twenty years ago, by a wealthy donor who had no family and wanted to support their work with orphaned children. Set on several acres of landscaped grounds, it overshadowed most of the luxury homes on Summit Avenue. The donation had been a lucky break for the dedicated Ewings who, up until then, had been taking care of children in their own rather small home and barely making ends meet.

They had done a good job, no doubt about it. After a few years their work had been featured in the local newspapers, and other wealthy donors had appeared almost overnight. Finally a board had been appointed, and the Ewings had only to see to the children; the business end was taken care of for them.

Several minutes later Paul sat across from Anita Ewing, who alternated between twisting her hands to toying with papers in front of her. She hadn't yet met him fully in the eye.

Well, I can't blame her for feeling uneasy, he thought. He himself felt as if he were about to jump out of his skin. He wanted to get this over with and get home. He needed to be doing something more, and if he were at home, he could go out and look for Rachel himself. He would scour the entire city, if that was what it took.

"It's been a long time," he began conversationally, trying to put the director at ease.

"Yes. Fifteen years or so," Anita Ewing agreed. "Time does have a way of speeding by, however."

"It seems as if you have less staff now than when I was here last," he noted.

"Well, we've had to cut back a bit," she said, her tone defensive. "But we still give our children very good care."

"I wasn't criticizing," Paul said quickly. "Just noticing a difference."

Anita Ewing nodded and seemed to relax. "Our support has dwindled a bit in past years. Some of the donors who gave so freely when we first opened Saint Sympatica's lost money in the stock market a few years ago. Others have died." Her smile was rueful. "Young people these days don't seem to donate to as many causes as their fathers and grandfathers did. I suppose they have tight budgets, children to put through college." She sighed. "I'm very grateful for the check you've been sending us each year, Mr. Bradley. It's helped enormously."

"I'm glad to be able to do it," Paul said. "After all, you gave us a beautiful daughter in Rachel. And you cared for Angela all those years."

Mrs. Ewing picked up a cobalt-blue paperweight that she held in her palm and studied, rather than look at him, it seemed. "I'm afraid we didn't do so very well with Angela."

"But that wasn't your fault," Paul said. "I'm sure

you did everything you could.'' He sat forward. ''Mrs. Ewing, I really need to know more about Angela. It's urgent, now.''

''Urgent?'' Her gaze swung up to his.

''Yes. Rachel…'' He could barely say the words. ''Rachel has disappeared.''

She seemed to not comprehend his words. ''I don't understand. Why would you think…'' Her eyes widened. ''Disappeared? Rachel is gone? How? When?''

''She's been home in Seattle for Christmas vacation,'' Paul said, ''but we've had no word from her since she left the house yesterday morning. We think Angela might…well, that she might know where Rachel is.''

The director dropped her paperweight with a thud. ''What you really mean is that you think Angela has done something to her. Again.''

''I don't want to think that,'' Paul said quickly. ''But the thing is, Rachel believes she saw Angela on the campus at Berkeley in California, where Rachel has been going to school. We need to know if it really was Angela, or if Rachel just imagined it. Because if Angela *has* been hanging around, there's no telling what she might do.''

''Good God.'' Mrs. Ewing paled and visibly shook herself, then became businesslike suddenly. ''Tell me what I can do.''

''Well, for one thing, I'd like to talk to Dr. Chase, the psychiatrist. And I'd like to see that photograph you have of Angela when she was sixteen. I believe you told Detective Duarte from the Seattle police department that it was taken shortly before she ran away?''

"The photograph won't be a problem," Mrs. Ewing said. "I faxed a copy of it to Detective Duarte this morning, in fact. And the original is here in my files. Unfortunately, Dr. Chase is an entirely different story."

"He's no longer with you?" Paul asked, disappointed.

"Dr. Chase, I'm afraid, is no longer alive."

"He died?" Paul couldn't hide his surprise. Lewis Chase had been around his own age, a young doctor in his first years of practice when he and Gina adopted the girls from here. "He was ill?"

"Not ill," Anita Ewing said flatly. "Dr. Chase was murdered."

The director suggested they walk to a bench near the bank of the river and talk there. She wore a heavy winter coat, but Paul, more accustomed to the mild temperatures in Seattle, had to pull his short jacket tighter around himself to fend off the cold. His Reeboks crunched on snow that had fallen and then frozen in the night. Gray skies hung over the river, and he knew why he could never live in the Midwest or the East. His spirits, already flat, felt crushed by the lowering clouds.

"It's a long story," Mrs. Ewing said, casting an eagle eye toward a group of children who played in

the snow at the bottom of the hill. A young woman—
a recreation assistant, it seemed—was with them. The
children were throwing snowballs at one another, running away, laughing, then attacking again. Mrs. Ewing
smiled and turned her attention to Paul.

"I know you must be in a hurry to get home. But
I think you should hear this, and I wouldn't want to
talk about it inside where some child might overhear."

They sat, and Mrs. Ewing scraped a handful of snow
off the bench beside her. Working it into a ball, she
rolled it between her hands, over and over in a nervous
gesture. Finally she let it drop to the ground and began
to relate to Paul a story his mind could barely take in.

"The children were all at breakfast," the director
said, "when we heard one of the housekeepers scream.
I ran from the dining room and up to the second floor,
where it seemed the scream had come from. When I
got there, the housekeeper, May, was standing outside
Dr. Chase's bedroom door, her hands covering her
mouth. I ran up to her, then looked into the room as
she pointed. She was shaking all over, and I put my
arm around her. It was a horrible sight, Mr. Bradley.
Dr. Chase lay on his bed, his arms and legs outstretched. He had been tied to the bedposts with pil-
lowcases that were wrapped around his elbows and
ankles. He was naked, and there were cuts all over his
body. Cuts and stab wounds. Blood had spattered the
walls and soaked into the sheets. There was blood on
the floor, on the nightstand...everywhere. His hands

lay over his genitals—which had been severed from his body.''

Paul's stomach turned as Anita Ewing continued. ''Some of the children had followed me up there, and May and I had our hands full keeping them from seeing into the room. Rodney came running from the gardens, and it was he who called the police and waited for them there. May and I ushered the children down to the dining room again. It was then that it struck me.''

She paused and looked at Paul. ''Are you sure you want to hear this?''

His heart was pounding, but he nodded. He felt certain he already knew what she was going to say.

''Well, the children had all heard May's screams, and everyone knew something terrible had happened. The ones who hadn't followed me up the stairs were already buzzing about it, talking back and forth with each other excitedly in the dining room. Except for Angela. Angela was sitting in her chair, eating her breakfast as if nothing had happened. My first thought was, *She hasn't missed a bite. Her plate is almost clean.*''

The director folded her arms tight against her chest and shivered. ''Of course, Angela's attachment disorder, if that's what it was, kept her from having normal feelings for people. But even so, it seemed strange to me. No reaction, nothing at all. Not even when we had to tell the children that Dr. Chase was gone.

''We didn't go into detail, of course, but they knew.

Somehow, children always do. Over the next few days I watched for some sort of acting out by Angela. She had spent more time with Dr. Chase, perhaps, than most of the other children. Only she and a couple of the boys needed the kind of intensive psychiatric care he provided. I thought she might have developed an attachment to Dr. Chase, or at least a bit of a fondness for him. They used to take walks out on the grounds together, and it seemed to me that perhaps he had taken on the role of a substitute father to her. I thought that had to be a good thing—Angela developing an attachment to someone, anyone at all."

She paused, took a deep breath and went on. "There was a police investigation, of course. The older children were all questioned and cleared. You asked me earlier about fingerprints. There was so much blood, the police couldn't find any that were legible. There never was any proof that any of the children here, or for that matter, any of the adults, had murdered Dr. Chase. And there was no reason to suspect anyone. Or so we thought. But then a few weeks later, one of the older girls came to me. She said she had heard Dr. Chase and Angela arguing the day before the murder, and that Angela had screamed at him, threatening to kill him."

Paul stared off into the icy river. When he could find his voice, he said, "How old was Angela at the time?"

"She had just turned sixteen."

"My God."

Anita Ewing nodded. "I was appalled, of course, and to be honest, I didn't know whether to believe it. The girl who told me this wasn't entirely reliable. She had been in constant trouble here."

Paul thought of something. "You said a couple of the boys were under Dr. Chase's care. Were they questioned?"

"Everyone was questioned, with no exception. Both boys left here when they were eighteen. One of them, Billy, seemed a nice enough boy, always trying to please. A bit too much so, in fact. He was placed with us at the age of thirteen, when his father and mother were killed in an auto accident. According to Dr. Chase, Billy's mind wasn't a place you would want to journey in. Underneath the pleasant exterior, he apparently could be quite deceitful. At any rate, Billy swore he never went near Dr. Chase's room the night he was murdered, and there seemed no reason to disbelieve that. Billy had never been violent, and there were no witnesses who could place him at the scene of the crime."

She reached over to Paul and touched his arm. He saw that there were tears in her eyes. "Even though you had returned Angela to us because she tried to kill Rachel that night, I really thought she had been improving. She was such a delightful child, you know, so bright and funny...so easy to love. I'd come to care for her as if she were my own.

"I did tell the police," she added, "what the girl—Mary, I think her name was—said about the argument between Angela and Dr. Chase. But I also told them about Mary's penchant for causing trouble. The police questioned Angela for hours, and came to the conclusion that she knew nothing about Dr. Chase's murder. Shortly after, Angela left here. She disappeared one night, taking only a few clothes and forty-eight dollars from my petty cash box. I haven't heard from her since.''

There was a long silence while Paul sat with his hands shoved deep into his jacket pockets. He felt frozen, not from the frigid temperature, but Anita Ewing's story. Finally he said, ''May I see that photograph of her?''

''Certainly. I can allow that, since Angela was never adopted and she's come of age now. Besides, under the circumstances...''

The director stood and Paul followed her back into her office. Crossing over to a file cabinet, she motioned to him to take a seat, and pulled out a folder. ''I'm afraid it's a group photo, and not very clear. I don't know how much it will help you.''

Paul took the photograph and searched the children's faces. There were four rows, perhaps forty children in all, but no one he recognized as the Angela he remembered.

''Which one is she?'' he asked softly. All these years he'd been thinking that he'd know her on sight. It seemed incredible to him now that he didn't recognize her at all.

Mrs. Ewing pointed to a tall girl in the back row.

"This is Angela, the one with the dark hair all the way down to her waist. Bangs, too. She cut them herself, but never would let me cut the rest. In fact, she fought me all the way when I suggested it, because some of the children had lice. 'I'll pick them off and eat them if I have to!' she raged. 'You aren't cutting my hair!'"

The director shook her head. "She frightened me at times with that anger. But then she'd change in a split second and have me laughing. That girl had so much spirit. There were times when I actually admired that about her."

Looking at Paul, she said, "I've never told you about the twins' mother, and what they were up against from birth. At the time you and Gina adopted the girls, it seemed best to put the past behind them. But perhaps now it would help in some way. Would you like to hear about that?"

"Yes, I would very much like to know," Paul said.

"Please sit down, then. It isn't a pretty story, I'm afraid."

Mrs. Ewing sat at her desk, folding her hands and clearing her throat. Stark winter light from the frosted window behind her touched her silver hair, turning it white.

"As you know," she said, "the twins were left on our doorstep with little information about them, so what I'm about to tell you came from a friend, a civilian with the local police department."

She paused, as if expecting Paul to object to her not

telling him this before. When he didn't, she continued. "Rose, the twins' biological mother, was apparently 'normal' until she was a teenager. There is a kind of mental illness, I'm told, that doesn't show up until adolescence. A young girl can be a good student, a great daughter, someone everyone loves. Then one day in her teens, she—or he, it can as easily be a boy— picks up a knife and kills his or her mother, father, siblings. Or takes a gun to school and shoots everyone in sight."

"Yes, I've heard of that," Paul said.

"No one seems to fully understand," Mrs. Ewing said, "what causes a child who, up to then, has seemed like every other child, to do this sort of thing. My personal view is that it has something to do with hormones. It's the only thing that makes sense to me. If I had my say, we'd be putting all children on medication to even out their hormone fluctuations from the time puberty sets in."

She waved a hand. "Sorry. I have a tendency to get on a soapbox at times. Another theory is that there's something in the brains of these children that kicks in during the teenage years. So far as I know, there isn't a cure—in other words, nothing that can be done to prevent this before it happens.

"As for Rose, who was seventeen at the time she became pregnant, I was told that she never wanted a baby in the first place. She confessed to the police that when she learned she was carrying twins, she actually tried to kill them in the womb. She would beat on her abdomen, fall down stairs, anything she could think of to abort. Nothing worked.''

"My God. Why didn't she have a medical abortion?"

"Apparently, she didn't have the money for it. Also, her parents had raised her to believe that abortion was a sin."

"Yet she tried to kill them in the womb? That *wasn't* a sin?"

"Well, as I said, she was seventeen and apparently mentally ill. A mind in that condition doesn't work logically. In her torment, Rose might have been able to convince herself that if she 'accidentally' fell down the stairs and aborted, that would be all right."

"Even though it wasn't really an accident."

"Even though."

"That's appalling," Paul said, shaking his head. "I can't believe a mother could do something like that."

"Well, for all practical purposes, she wasn't a mother then," Mrs. Ewing pointed out. "She was a young girl with something growing inside her, something she didn't want. To be blunt, she did everything in her power to get it out."

Paul thought of Rachel, and how empty his and Gina's lives would have been if she'd never existed.

"What happened after the babies were born?" he asked, dreading the answer.

"For the most part, Rose pretended they weren't there. She...are you sure you want to hear this?"

"Yes. Go on."

"Well, she was living in an abandoned house. One night a neighbor called the police and said there had been cats crying in that house, day and night. She couldn't stand it any longer and wanted them to do something about it. The police were going to turn it over to the animal control people, but one officer who was on duty and didn't have much to do that night said he'd go check it out. He found the babies alone, in a bedroom with the door shut, whimpering like little kittens. That was what the neighbor had heard."

She sighed. "When Rose came home the house was full of police and welfare people. She told the investigating officers that she had kept the babies in cardboard boxes since they were born, and every other day or so she would go into the room and…clean up their 'mess,' as she put it. She seldom fed them or talked to them, just cleaned them up. Not nearly enough, however. When the police found them, they were filthy, lying in their urine and feces. An ambulance was called, and the babies were taken to the hospital. They were judged to be about two months old. It was hard to tell, because they weighed only four pounds each—probably not much more than the day they were born."

"Oh, my God," Paul murmured. "What happened to the babies after they were found?"

"They were in foster homes for a few weeks, and they could have been adopted. Rose gave up all parental rights, and the father, apparently, was a vagrant who'd raped her and then moved on. No one, however, after hearing the story of how the twins had been found, would take them. Not that they didn't sympathize, but the child welfare people had to tell them honestly that the girls could end up with severe emotional problems. Finally, when they were three months old, it was decided to place them here at Saint Sympatica's for long-term care."

"But then we came along a few months later and adopted them," Paul said. "And you never told us any of this. You said they had been left here on the steps."

"To be honest, I was afraid to tell you," Mrs. Ewing admitted. "You and your wife looked like just the right people to adopt the girls, and I hoped they'd have a good life with you. I did tell you, if you recall, that they might need psychological care, and that they never had a chance to bond with anyone during their first few months."

"True," Paul agreed. "You told us that, but nothing about how terrible their circumstances were."

"Mr. Bradley," Anita Ewing sighed again. "Would you and your wife have taken them, if you'd known?"

He hesitated only a moment. "Yes. At least, I think we would have."

"But you can't be sure."

"I...I suppose not. We might have been afraid they would be too much responsibility." His tone took on an edge. "On the other hand, if we'd known what we were really up against, we might have been able to protect Rachel from Angela. Now our daughter is missing, and possibly in danger. Or worse."

"You're quite right," Mrs. Ewing said, meeting his eyes. "I really am very, very sorry for the trouble you're having now. My husband and I have tried so hard to do the right things for our children. I wonder if you can understand how difficult it is at times to know what's right and what isn't. Not that I'm making excuses, but it isn't always possible to give our children the kind of attention we would like to give them. We started out with a dream, Rodney and I, and I'm afraid we weren't very practical about it. We never allowed room, for instance, for a lack of funds and not enough staff—"

She broke off. "Well, that's neither here nor there now, I'm afraid. Mr. Bradley, I hope you find Rachel soon. And I pray she's all right." She stood and held out both her hands, and Paul took them in his. "I don't know if any of this will help," she said. "But I hope you can find it in your heart to forgive me for not being more forthcoming with you when you adopted the twins."

"I'm not in any position to judge you, Mrs. Ewing. When we find Rachel, I'll have a lot of making up to do."

On the way home to Seattle in the plane, one thought kept running through his mind: *What might Angela, daughter of Rose, have done to her sister? Was life of no value to her? Had she inherited a soul bereft of any conscience at all?*

Paul was back in Seattle by ten o'clock that night. He had kept in touch with Gina by cell phone while he was gone, and he knew from his last call, made the moment he disembarked at Sea-Tac, that Rachel had still not been found. She had now been gone two days, and his steps were as heavy as his heart as he pulled into the driveway on Queen Anne Hill.

The silver Crown Vic that was almost the same as Gina's was parked on the street. Duarte was here, then. Paul had called him from the airport and asked if he was free, and whether, as a favor, he might meet with him and Gina at the house.

"I'm just now getting off a twelve-hour day," Duarte had said, "and I'm bushed, but I'll stop by for a few minutes on my way home."

Dropping his keys onto the mahogany table in the hallway, Paul found them both in the kitchen. Duarte was drinking coffee and Gina was feverishly rolling out dough for a pie, her movements rapid and jerky. There were sliced apples in a white enamel bowl, blueberries in another, and the scent of chocolate chip cookies drifting from the oven. Flour coated Gina's arms and nose and, as he walked in, she barely looked up.

He hadn't seen her this way since the week they'd taken Angela back. There had been pies, cakes, cookies all over the kitchen the morning after they'd returned from Saint Paul. "I couldn't sleep," Gina had said, exhausted and hollow looking. In the following weeks this pattern was repeated so often he finally begged her to see someone. She had begun to go for therapy with Victoria, who had put her on medication. From then on, the nightly baking raids had stopped.

That was when Gina first began to be "quiet," as he thought of it. She withdrew into herself and stopped talking to him, except for the times when they had to work together. Then she would be brief. Businesslike. Later, when Paul looked back, he thought that this was when their marriage first began to dissolve.

His heart melted, however, seeing her this way again. Despite the cheery cotton apron she wore, she looked frail and small and seemed to have lost weight in just these past twenty-four hours. There were dark circles under her eyes. Paul walked over to her, took the rolling pin from her hands and gathered her up into his arms. "It's going to be all right," he said. "I promise you, we'll find her. It's going to be all right."

Gina wiped away tears with the back of her hand, smearing flour around her eyes. Paul reached for a paper napkin on the counter and wiped it and the tears away.

"I'm so afraid," she whispered. "I don't know what to do."

"We'll figure it out," he said softly. "We'll figure it out together."

She pulled away, saying, "I have to finish up here."

"No. No, you don't. Come sit down, honey. This can keep."

At the word of endearment she looked at him briefly, blinked, then gave in. He led her over to the kitchen table and poured them each a cup of black coffee. Only then did he nod to Duarte and say, "Thanks for coming. I'm so exhausted I didn't think I could make it to the precinct."

"No problem," Duarte said. "I went home during a break and fed my cat. Funny thing about that cat. She's got food there all day, the dry stuff. Won't eat, though till I get home. You ever hear of that?"

Paul shook his head, staring down into his coffee.

"Anyway, I'd just be sitting around watching the eleven o'clock news," Duarte said conversationally. "Hell, I see the news in front of my face all day long. No point in watching it on a screen."

When neither Paul nor Gina responded, he sighed and said, "Okay, let's get down to business. What did you learn there?"

"Well, first off, I brought the original of the photograph, in case your crime lab can enlarge it and bring out some more details." He took the photograph from his briefcase and handed it to the detective.

Then he told them both about Dr. Chase—including the awful details about the way he was murdered. Gina's face paled, and he hated having to tell her all this, but she needed to know what they might be up against.

He went on to tell them the way Angela had responded, or rather not responded, to Dr. Chase's death before leaving Saint Sympatica's shortly after, in the dark of night and without a goodbye. When Gina bent over and covered her eyes, he knew she was doing her best to deal with the thought that Angela might well have murdered the doctor, and that she might now do the same to Rachel. He reached over and touched her shoulder.

"What's your take on this Dr. Chase's murder?" Duarte asked after glancing over the photograph.

"Well, I think Mrs. Ewing suspects Angela did it. But there wasn't any proof, and the investigation never went anywhere."

"And this girl who heard the argument between her and Chase?"

"I asked where I could find her, and she didn't know. She left there when she turned eighteen, and she'd be in her early twenties by now. She could be anywhere."

Duarte sipped his coffee, then sniffed the air. "I think your cookies are burning, Mrs. Bradley."

Gina nodded but didn't move.

"You want me to take them out?"

"Okay," she said dully.

Duarte heaved himself up from his chair. Going over to the stove, he picked up an oven mitt and used it to take the sugar cookies from the oven.

"They're burnt around the edges," he said, "but not too bad."

Taking a spatula, he lifted each one carefully and put them on a plate.

Paul shook his head and gave him a half smile. "Do you always do these sorts of things for people when you're investigating a crime?"

"Only when those people have a kid missing,"

Duarte said, putting the plate of cookies on the table between them and sitting down again with a heavy sigh.

"Look, folks," he said, "I think we have to agree that this isn't a typical kidnapping. Up to now there's been the possibility that anything could have happened. Your daughter could have been grabbed at an ATM, for instance, on the way to her friend's house. Or, there could have been a carjacking. But carjackings are usually witnessed by someone, and no one's reported any in the last day or two. We've checked all the hospitals, and she hasn't been seen at any of them, so we can rule out that she got sick and passed out, and that someone found her and called the paramedics. Also, we checked the streets between here and the friend's house. They're all residential, and we've gone over them twice now. She's not there in her car unconscious, or anything."

Gina began to cry, and Paul reached over automatically and took her hand, holding it tight.

"Detective, what you're saying is that you think Angela's done something to her."

"No. All I'm saying is that we have to take a serious look at that now. We've got to find this twin, see where she is and what she's doing these days. If we discover she's in the Seattle area...well, we'll rev up the investigation, smoke her out and take it from there."

He picked up a cookie, took a bite off the edge and

said, "Not bad. I think I might even like them better this way."

Then, setting it down, he added, "There's one other possibility, of course."

"Oh?" Paul said.

"Well, it could be that Rachel, for some reason, went somewhere on her own."

"She wouldn't do that," Gina said, coming to life. "Rachel would never worry us that way. She would let us know she was all right."

"That may be," Duarte said. "But I have to tell you, it's been known to happen."

The next morning, Paul knew he should call Lacey and bring her up-to-date about what was going on, but he wasn't up to it. They had just told Gina's mother about Rachel, and that hadn't gone well.

"What do you mean, she's missing?" Roberta had nearly yelled into the phone. Paul and Gina were on separate phones in the kitchen and study, so they could both talk to her.

"We haven't seen or heard from her since the day before yesterday, Mom," Gina said.

"Did you do something?" Roberta asked, lowering her voice.

"Do something?" Paul asked wearily.

"Yes, do something!" Roberta snapped. "Like maybe she got tired of the two of you barely talking to each other and decided to go back to school."

"Mom, that's ridiculous!" Gina said. "Of course

she didn't go back to school. She wouldn't do that without telling us."

"This is serious, Roberta," Paul said quietly. "The police are looking for her."

There was a small silence.

"You really think something's happened to Rachel?"

"Mom, we tried to tell you yesterday, but your machine said you were away for a few days. Where did you go? We haven't seen you since Rachel came home."

"I, uh…decided to spend Christmas with a friend," Roberta said.

"But we always spend Christmas together," Gina said.

"Well, this year we didn't!"

"I just don't…" Gina began.

"That doesn't matter now," Paul said briskly. "What does matter is Rachel. And Angela."

"Angela?" Roberta's tone changed. "What about her?"

"We think she may be back," Gina answered, her voice cracking. "We think she might have done something to Rachel."

"Oh, my God." A longer silence this time.

"Mother? Are you still there?"

"Yes. Yes, I'm here," Roberta said quickly. "Why do you think this? Have you seen Angela?"

"No, but Rachel found a note in her pocket that we think is from her. And on Christmas Eve we were run off the road. Mom, Paul went back to Minnesota and talked to Mrs. Ewing at Saint Sympatica's. Angela ran away from there when she was sixteen. No one's seen or heard from her since.''

''Well, one can hardly blame the child for running away! It's not as if she had a real home there, after all.''

The criticism was clear.

''Roberta,'' Paul said, trying to calm himself, ''she ran away shortly after the psychiatrist there, Dr. Chase, was murdered.''

Roberta made a soft sound of exclamation. ''Murdered! Are you telling me *Angela* murdered this man? No, I don't believe it! I mean, when she was five and hadn't any self-control yet...but surely she outgrew—''

''That's not what I was saying,'' Paul interjected. ''In fact, there was never any evidence that anyone at Saint Sympatica's was involved. But Mrs. Ewing had a feeling—''

''A feeling!'' Roberta exploded. ''A *feeling?* Is that supposed to be some kind of proof that poor child has done something to Rachel?''

''Mom,'' Gina said quietly, ''we all know how you felt about Angela. But please.'' She caught back a sob. ''Rachel is missing! Don't you even care?''

''Oh, God, of course I care,'' Roberta said softly. ''I love that child more than you'll ever know.'' Her voice filled with tears. ''I'm just afraid, I guess. Oh, God. What are you doing to find her?''

"As I said," Paul answered as patiently as possible, "we have a police detective looking into it. He's keeping it quiet for now because we don't really know what's happened, and if Rachel has just gone off somewhere on her own, we don't want to embarrass her. But if she doesn't turn up soon..." He left the rest unspoken.

"What can I do?" Roberta asked, clearly gathering herself together. "Tell me what I can do."

"Just let us know if you hear from Rachel," Gina said. "Or Angela, though that probably isn't likely. And if you think of anything that might give us a clue about where Rachel is, call us right away."

"I'll do better than call," Roberta said. "I'm coming over there. And don't even begin to argue with me about it."

"I'm not about to argue," Gina said tiredly. "I've been up all night baking, and I haven't the energy for it."

Roberta made it to Queen Anne Hill from Gig Harbor within the hour. While she and Gina sat at the breakfast bar and picked halfheartedly at the crusty edges of pies that would probably never be eaten, Paul took his shower. It was an oversized shower, and he recalled the way they had designed it, when they bought the house—big enough for two, so that he and Gina could use it together, and with a view of the Space Needle. They'd had many romantic nights in this shower that first year, before the twins came. After that, things changed. At first he had felt left out, almost jealous of the time Gina spent with them. But he'd come to love them so much, their roles became almost reversed. He was the one who taught them how to walk, played with them, read to them at bedtime. The romantic showers together became less and less frequent, and finally, after Angela was gone, they stopped altogether.

Did he stop spending time with Rachel then, too? He couldn't remember. It seemed as if he and Gina were both home less, desperately trying to lose themselves in their work. From the time Rachel was five until she was twelve, Gina had hired a full-time housekeeper and nanny. She was a wonderful woman, and he and Gina had relied on her for just about everything. Had they done so to the point that they'd neglected Rachel—emotionally, if not physically?

And why had she seemed so different since she'd come home this time? Could Roberta be right? Had Rachel decided to teach them a lesson, to make them sit up and take notice?

Duarte had said he'd contact Berkeley and find out if anyone had seen her down there. She would have gone back in a few days, anyway. Had she decided to go back early and not tell them? Make them worry for a while?

But if that were so, where was her car? Duarte had said there was no sign of it at the airport. But surely she wouldn't have driven all the way from Seattle to Berkeley, which was across the bay from San Francisco. That would take days, and the Mustang was not in shape for a drive like that.

He realized, suddenly, that they had been focusing on Angela too much. If Rachel had indeed decided to drive to Berkeley, the old Mustang could have broken down along the way. She could be stuck along the road in an area where her cell phone didn't work. Worse, she could have gone off the road and become trapped beneath her car. Or…someone could have stopped to "help" her.

And done something to her instead.

Paul dried himself quickly, dressed and placed a call to Duarte. He got the detective's voice mail and said, "I need to talk to you as soon as possible. I think we need to look into the possibility that Rachel tried to drive back to school and had an accident or a breakdown on the road. Could you contact the authorities between here and Berkeley? Please call me on my cell phone, or leave a message at my office or home."

Leaving all three numbers in case the detective called in for his messages and didn't have them handy, Paul set the receiver back down on its cradle. Turning in his chair, he stared out the window. Not far from the bottom of Queen Anne Hill was Lacey's apartment. He had put off calling her, feeling separated from her now by so many degrees that it hardly seemed as if she were still in his life at all.

How could things change so much in just a matter of days? He supposed he felt that Lacey couldn't possibly understand what he and Gina were going through. And aside from that, he didn't want to lay his burdens on her. Lacey was young, with her whole life ahead of her. She didn't need his problems to deal with.

All the same, Paul thought, he should talk with her. He punched in her number, which he'd never put on speed dial in case Gina were to use his phone and accidentally dial it. Lacey answered with her usual perky "Hi, it's me, whoever you are!" and he couldn't help smiling. It was the first time he'd felt a genuine lift of spirit in two days.

"How do you know there's not some pervert at the other end of the line?" he had asked her once. "Why are you so damned friendly to everyone?"

"And who says I can't be friendly to a pervert?" she had countered. "I might just say, 'Hey, how's it goin'? I've been waitin' my whole life for you!' Golly, Molly, it'd probably blow his mind and he'd hang right up!"

That was one of the things he liked most about Lacey. She always saw the funny, if odd, side of things.

"It's me," he said now. "I'd like to come over. Just to talk."

"Well, you sure know the way," she said. "You want coffee? And I've got apple pie."

"Pie is probably not a good idea this morning," he said, groaning. "But coffee sounds great. Make it strong."

Lacey had a small glass table beside the window in her living room. They sat there on the zebra-striped

1930s chairs Paul had brought over from Soleil and drank coffee, while Paul brought her up-to-date on what was going on.

"God, Paul, I can't believe it! And I can't even imagine what you're going through. You *and* Gina. To have a child missing…" She reached for his hand. "Even at Rachel's age, it has to be the worst thing in the world."

"It *has* been pretty bad," he said. "I'm glad you understand why I may not be around as much for a while."

"Well, of course not." She reached for his hand, and her long blond hair fell over one shoulder. "Paul, you'll need to put every ounce of energy into finding Rachel. I understand that perfectly. And you're not to worry about me. I'll be fine."

"Thank you," he said, deeply grateful she was taking it this way.

"And if there's anything I can do, please just let me know."

"I will."

"Geez. I just wish I'd known sooner. Not that I could probably do anything except send you good thoughts. Was it awful in Minnesota?"

"Awful to hear about Dr. Chase's murder," he said, "and to think that Angela could have done it. It makes Rachel's disappearance all the more frightening."

"Oh, Paul. She wouldn't really do something that terrible to her own twin sister, would she? I mean, you said it was years ago that she tried that, and now that's she's grown…"

Paul shook his head. "I don't know what she'd do at this point. I just don't know enough about her."

Lacey brushed back her hair and said, "Okay, look, maybe I can help you with that. All I do is sit around here most of the day, anyway. Let me try to track her down for you. You and the police need to focus on looking for Rachel, in case she did just take off on her own. I'll track down Angela. And I promise you, I'll find her."

He looked into Lacey's sea-green eyes and wondered what he was going to do about her. Every time his guilt rose up and he thought of leaving her, of just letting her go, she did something that touched his heart.

"It's wonderful of you to offer," he said with a hesitant smile, "but I don't know…"

"No buts. Just give me someplace to start. In fact, don't bother. You said the police are checking out Berkeley? Well, I'll go on the Net and see what I can find. It's pretty easy to locate people these days, you know. I might even be able to turn up an address for Angela that way. Paul, this could go more quickly than you think."

"That would be great," he said, feeling a weight lift from his heart.

"Well, I know the police will do a good job. But Paul, there are all kinds of ways of tracing people on the Net, and sometimes you can find someone on your own, in a way the police don't have time or the resources to think about."

He smiled. "I didn't realize you knew so much about computers."

She grinned. "Well, sure. What do you think I do here all day—watch tv and eat bonbons?" Making a face, she admitted, "Well, I guess I do a little bit of that. But not all day." Gesturing to the computer he had given her when she moved in, she said, "Most of the time I'm 'Surfin' USA.'"

Paul smiled again. How could he ever think of leaving this woman? And how could he ever have thought of her only as solace for his grief? The longer he knew her, the more he saw the many different sides of her, and the more he cared about her.

He sighed and braced himself to say, "I have to go now." Gina needed him, and he needed to be with her, too. Feeling more torn than ever, he gave Lacey a long hug at the door and kissed her forehead. "I don't know how to thank you for this."

"Don't thank me," Lacey said, stroking him on the cheek. "Let's just find Rachel—before it's too late."

Paul made a stop at Soleil to check his messages Gina often left them on his machine, as his cell phone didn't always work when he was in various parts of the warehouse. There was nothing from her, however. And nothing from Duarte.

The warehouse was nearly empty. It was usually slow over the noon hour, and his assistant, Janice, and two of his four clerks had gone out for lunch. His floor manager and another clerk were in different rooms, either taking inventory or arranging new pieces of furniture that had recently arrived. Except for them and Annie, his receptionist in the front lobby, Paul was alone.

Taking this opportunity, he went through the Japanese room and into the Crystal Cave. He'd had a comfortable chair brought in years ago, and on particularly bad days he would sit there in quiet meditation. In recent years it had helped to give him enough balance to keep going.

It had been a long time since he'd done that, however. Life had a way of moving in on one. Business, phone calls, other obligations...

It was impossible to clear his mind today. Fear overrode everything, with images of Rachel at the hands of a crazed Angela, or lost on a back road somewhere between here and L.A.

Alive? *Oh, God, let her be alive.*

He tried to think the way a detective would. If Rachel really had just decided to take off, where would she go, if not back to school? Paul tried to recall everything she had said since coming home. Was there a clue in her conversations with them? Anything at all?

She had seemed happy the day they cut down the Christmas tree and went to tea. But that was before the accident, and the note.

Vicky. Rachel had been seeing Vicky, and so far as

he knew, no one had informed her of Rachel's disappearance yet. Had Rachel told Victoria anything in their sessions that might help?

He pulled his cell phone from his pocket and called her office, remembering the number from so many calls over the years. Her voice mail was on, and he left a message that he'd like to see her as soon as she returned from lunch, that it was urgent—about Rachel—and could she please make time for him?

Paul sighed. It seemed impossible, the way life went on. Impossible that Rachel could be gone, either in peril or worse, while people were having lunch in the usual way. Talking with friends, drinking wine, perhaps, tasting foods that Rachel might never taste again.

He shook himself and stood. *I've got to get out of here, do something productive.*

His floor manager, Daniel Britt, tapped lightly on the cherry-wood frame of the door. Paul turned. The young man was tall but slight, with warm brown eyes and thick, wavy brown hair. Creases in his forehead seemed to indicate that life had taken a toll on Daniel, though he was only twenty-three. He had been with Paul four months, and in that time he hadn't spoken to anyone about his personal life, so far as Paul could tell.

He saw a great deal of potential in Daniel, however, who had walked in one day and asked Paul to take him on as an intern. His résumé listed excellent skills and experience in other jobs, but his love was antiques.

He would work without pay, he had said, for the opportunity to learn the antique business.

As it turned out, Daniel had learned so quickly, and had been such a hard worker, it wasn't long before Paul had taken him on as a full-time salaried employee. He even dared to dream that Daniel might turn out to be like the son he would never have, someone who might take over the business one day.

"Sorry to interrupt," Daniel said softly, "but we don't know what to do with this lap desk."

He was holding a beautiful old travel desk, or lap desk, the kind that people in the horse-drawn carriage era would take with them on trips. It looked like a simple box, but when opened its slanted top provided a writing table, and inside were drawers for paper, pens and ink.

"Where did it come from?" Paul asked. He took the travel desk from Daniel and set it on a small table next to the chair, looking it over.

"We, uh…we don't know. It was on Annie's desk when she opened this morning."

Most mornings, Annie arrived before anyone else. Though it wasn't expected of her, she made a pot of coffee for everyone and often brought in doughnuts or Danishes, as well. The other clerks teased the receptionist about "mothering" them, but no one, so far, had complained.

"I should say," Daniel went on, "she found it there when she went back out to her desk after she made the coffee. Someone apparently came in and just dropped it off.''

Paul's trained eye told him that it was a valuable piece. There were other lap desks from the 1800s era still around, but this one was especially well crafted and made of fine rosewood with an inlaid satinwood design. It had many small drawers inside, where people would hide their private letters and jewelry, in the event bandits stopped them along the way.

He opened the two largest drawers, thinking he might find the owner's name and phone number in one, but both were empty.

''No note or anything?'' he asked.

''No…'' Daniel shook his head and hesitated, but said no more.

''Well, put it on my desk for now. We'll probably hear from the owner later on.'' Soleil Antiques had been in this neighborhood for so many years, it wasn't unreasonable to think that someone in a hurry, perhaps on his way to work this morning, had trusted him to take care of the piece until he could call about it later.

Daniel nodded and took the travel desk. ''I'll try to find room in your office. Things are kind of piling up in there.'' He hesitated again. ''Uh, Paul? You haven't been around much since Christmas. Is anything wrong?''

Paul hesitated for only a moment. ''My daughter is missing,'' he said.

Daniel looked confused. ''Daughter…you mean Rachel?'' he said after a moment. ''She's missing?''

"We haven't seen or heard from her in three days."

"That's terrible," Daniel said. "I'm so sorry. I had no idea."

"The police are looking for her," Paul said. "We've been trying to keep it quiet, in case…well, you know, in case she just decided to get away for a day or two. She could turn up anytime, and we wouldn't want to embarrass her by having it all over the papers that she'd been kidnapped, or—" Paul squeezed his eyes shut, and felt Daniel's hand on his arm.

"If there's anything I can do…" Daniel said. "Anything at all."

"Thanks." Paul managed a slight smile. "Just help keep things running here for me."

"Of course. Would you like me to go through the paperwork on your desk, see how much of it I can clear up?"

"That would be great."

Daniel left quietly, shutting the door behind him. Paul shoved his hands into his pockets and looked around the Crystal Cave. Walking over to a Lalique vase, he stared into it as if it were a crystal ball. "Where is my little girl?" he whispered. "Where are both my little girls?"

The vase was not a crystal ball, and it had no answer for him. For just another moment he soaked in the quiet brilliance of this room that had always given him so much rest. When he left this time, however, he was more confused—and more afraid—than he had ever been before.

From Soleil, Paul stopped at the police station, hoping to find Duarte there. The detective was at his desk, working on a pile of papers.

"Reports I've been putting off too long," he said, looking up briefly as he wrote on one with a black pen. "Have a seat. Be with you in a minute."

Paul took a seat, and for the first time he noticed a photograph in a silver frame on the detective's desk— a young Duarte, it seemed, with a woman and a small child. When Duarte looked up, putting the papers into a box labeled Out, Paul said, "Family?" nodding in the direction of the photograph.

"Was," Duarte replied. "That's Laura, the one who left. Brad, there, he's my boy. Thirty-five, now. He went with his mom, and I'd take him to Mariner's games, Little League, that sort of thing on the weekends. I don't see him much anymore."

The detective's voice held a hint of sadness, and Paul could empathize. "It's hard to connect with grown kids these days. From what some of my friends tell me, they're all pretty busy with their careers."

"True," Duarte said. He leaned back in his chair and studied Paul. "What about you and Rachel? Have you always gotten along?"

Paul realized that, despite the detective's seemingly casual air, there was more behind the question than simple curiosity.

"Well, with all that's gone on in our family—you know, with Angela and everything—it's been difficult. Nothing's ever been exactly 'normal,' if you know what I mean."

"I know from what you've said that Rachel's been in therapy a lot," Duarte said. "Is that just because she lost her twin?"

They still hadn't told Duarte about Angela's attack on Rachel at the age of five. With Rachel missing now, however, and with Angela possibly being responsible for whatever had happened to her, Paul felt he could no longer hold back that information.

"No. There's more," he said. He told Duarte the entire story. "I'm not sure why we didn't mention this before, except that we lied about the incident when we took Rachel to the hospital. We loved Angela, despite what she'd done, and we felt it wasn't her fault that she'd grown up with that streak, as we thought of it then. And we didn't want what she did to become a matter of public record. It seemed enough to take her back to Saint Sympatica's, where she'd get good care."

Duarte surprised him by agreeing. "That makes sense, I guess, kid that age. Five, right?"

Paul nodded. "Now that Rachel's missing, of course…"

"Now that Rachel's missing," Duarte said, "it's even more important to find Angela. Especially after what you told me about that shrink at the orphanage being murdered, and Angela disappearing right after that." He took a large gulp from the coffee cup on his desk. "I've been talking to the lab guys about the photograph." He pulled it out of a file folder and handed it to Paul. "I'm afraid I may have given you false hope. They say the quality isn't good enough to do much with it. Too fuzzy, and when it's enlarged it just gets worse."

"I was hoping they could enhance it somehow," Paul said. "Bring out more features? Then age it?"

"Well, it's not as easy as it looks on TV. With a decent original, we can do all kinds of things now. Change the hair color and style, and even age her face to tell us how she might look at the age of twenty-one."

Duarte leaned over and tapped his pencil at the tall girl in the back row. "You see how her hair is half covering her face? With a decent original we could reconstruct that side of her face by computer, using the other side as a model. You say you burned Angela's photographs from when she lived with you?"

"I'm afraid so. There was nothing mean about it. We just thought it would help to forget."

Duarte nodded. "On other fronts," he said, "I got your message a while ago, and I'd already thought about the possibility Rachel might have taken off for California. I've alerted the highway patrols in Washington, Oregon and California—all up and down I-5 and 101—just in case anybody's seen her. Or does see her."

"Thanks," Paul said, relieved. "By the way, I have

a friend helping to look for Angela. She's used to going on the Net and she said she can cover a lot of bases in a short time that way.''

''A friend, huh?'' Duarte's face remained blank, but there was more than casual interest in his voice.

Paul shrugged. ''Just someone I know.''

''Uh-huh. Would you like to give me this someone's name?''

''I...not really,'' Paul said.

''Uh-huh.''

''It's just that I wouldn't want Gina to know my friend is doing this,'' Paul said awkwardly. ''I mean, I wouldn't want it on your records here somewhere.''

Duarte sighed and came forward in his chair. ''You know, Paul—may I call you Paul? I been through a lot of tough cases, and this one could be the toughest. I liked your girl, Rachel, the minute I met her. And I could see the other day that she was dealing with something she didn't want to talk about. Fine. People need their secrets, sometimes. But now she's missing, and if she'd talked to us more openly, we might have found her already. See what I'm saying?''

''You're saying that secrets can slow things down.''

''Or worse,'' Duarte said. His voice hardened. ''You want your kid coming home to you in a body bag? Dammit, man! This is no time to play games.''

''I know, I know,'' Paul said, rubbing a hand over his face. ''Look, if I could just tell you and you didn't write it down anywhere—''

''Oh, for—'' Duarte slammed his palms down on

his desk. "All right, I'll tell you what I'll do. You tell me the name of this person who's supposed to be helping out, and I'll keep it to myself. I just want to talk to the woman, see what she's doing. Frankly, I don't give a damn that you're sleeping with her."

Paul blinked. "I didn't say that."

"You didn't have to. You think I didn't know from the first time you sat in that chair that you and Mrs. Bradley don't always get along?"

Paul was silent.

Duarte shook his head and picked up the name plate on his desk. "You see this word, here? It says 'Detective.' I didn't get this made up at some school carnival, for Christ's sake."

Paul couldn't help smiling.

"What's that for?" Duarte growled.

"I was just picturing you at a school carnival," Paul said. "I bet you'd drive those guys nuts, the ones with the phony games you never can win."

"Not at my son's school," Duarte said, grinning. "They know better."

Paul shook his head. "Okay," he said, giving him Lacey's name, phone number and address.

Duarte wrote the information down. "I want to talk to this shrink of Rachel's, too," he said, scanning the yellow pad. "Victoria Lessing. Does she know Rachel's disappeared?"

"No. I'm going there when I leave here. I'll tell her what's going on."

"You know this woman well?"

"Angela was treated by her for a year, before she went back to the orphanage. Gina and I have both seen her now and then. Rachel, too."

"So you trust this woman?"

"I...yes. I've never had a reason not to trust her."

"But you hesitated," Duarte pointed out. "There must be something."

"No...no, not really. I don't know why I hesitated. Vicky has become almost like a member of the family. Not that she's ever been anything but professional, but Roberta, Gina's mother, knew her even before we did, so it's been a lot of years—"

"Gina's mother," Duarte said, interrupting. "I'll need to talk to her."

"Sure," Paul agreed. "I can arrange for her to come in. She's just as worried about finding Rachel as we are."

"You know where I can reach her now?"

"She was at my house when I left there a while ago."

Duarte pushed the phone toward him. "You mind?"

"No, of course not." Paul looked at him curiously. "You don't want to call her yourself?"

"Let's just say I'd like to keep it as informal as possible. Nobody needs to feel like they're a suspect and get all uptight about coming in."

"And the more informal it is, the more they'll open up to you, right?" Paul guessed.

Duarte shrugged. "Dial," he said.

Paul punched in the number to the house, and Gina answered. "Is Roberta still there?"

"No, she left shortly after you did."

"I thought she was going to stay and keep you company."

"I'm not very good company today, I guess."

"Do you know where she is now?"

"No. Why?"

"I'm down here at the police station. Duarte would like to talk to her."

"My mother? Why?"

Paul looked at Duarte. "Nothing special. It's just that she might remember something that could help."

"Well, you could try her at home. I didn't get the feeling she was going there, though. She said she'd be in touch in a few hours."

"Okay. Well, if she calls you, will you tell her Duarte would like to talk to her, and find out what her schedule is? Keep it casual, let it be her choice to set the time. But tell her to make it soon, okay?"

"Okay. Paul? When will you be home?"

"I'm not sure. I just remembered that Victoria doesn't know Rachel is missing. I thought I'd go over there from here and talk to her. Maybe Rachel said something to her that could give us a clue."

"Oh, God, you're right. I hadn't thought of that myself. I just haven't...oh, been tracking right, I guess. Mom put me through the wringer."

"Oh? In what way?"

"About not being accessible enough to Rachel, not

home enough, not close enough to her to know what she's been thinking about or experiencing. You know how she is."

"I'm sorry she put you through that," Paul said. "Are you all right now?"

"About as all right as I can be, I guess."

"Try to get some rest. I'll get home as soon as I can."

"Okay."

"Wait. Gina, did Roberta say anything about herself? Has she been close to Rachel recently? Enough to know what's been going on with her?"

"Well, she always talks as if she knows our daughter better than we do, but you know she's been acting like that for years."

Paul sighed. "Maybe Detective Duarte can get something out of her. More than the usual harangue, that is."

He met the detective's eyes, and Duarte nodded.

"I'll try to get home as soon as possible," Paul said. "I'll just run over to Victoria's and talk to her, then I'll come straight home."

Gina said, her voice thick with tears, "Paul, we've got to find our little girl."

"I know," he said softly. "We'll find her. Hang tight. I'll be there soon."

"Let's go," Duarte said when he'd hung up.

"*Let's* go?" Paul repeated.

"Well, look at it this way. When I asked you about this shrink and whether you trusted her, you hesitated.

That's enough for me. I say we both go and talk to this lady.''

Duarte told the officer next to him that he'd be out awhile.

"If she's not there, we wait," he told Paul. "Sometimes that's all detective work amounts to, cooling your heels while the perps keep you waiting."

"You don't really think of Victoria Lessing as a perp, do you?" Paul said, startled.

"I think of everybody as a perp until it's proved otherwise," Duarte said, ushering Paul through the door ahead of him. "Even you."

As they walked to the parking lot, Duarte couldn't help wondering what the hell he was doing. He never got this involved in cases anymore. There was just something about this one. Maybe it was the kid, Rachel. Something about her intrigued him, something secretive that her parents didn't know about. He would swear to it. Maybe he wasn't like a Dalmatian anymore, dashing after that five-alarm fire. Maybe he had become more like Lazybones, his cat. Curious, that's all. Nothing wrong with that.

Duarte frowned. *Except that curiosity was what had killed the cat.*

Victoria had received Paul's message, and had kept the hour open.

"I am so sorry to hear this," she said, after Paul

told her about Rachel. Her brow furrowed. "When was the last time you saw her?"

"Three days ago, around ten in the morning. She told Gina she was going to a friend's house, but she never showed up."

"We hoped she might have said something to you that would give us a clue to where she might have gone," Duarte said.

Victoria turned to him. "You mean you think she just left? Went away somewhere without telling anyone?"

"Unless maybe she told you," Duarte said.

Victoria shook her head. "Not a thing. In fact, it's hard to believe that's what she did."

"What about the twin? Angela? You think she could have done something to Rachel?" Duarte suggested.

Victoria's eyes widened. She looked at Paul, who nodded.

"He knows," Paul said. "You can speak freely."

"Only to a certain extent," Victoria countered a bit stiffly. "So far as I know, Rachel is still my patient. There's a matter of confidentiality."

"I understand that," Paul said. "But if you know anything that could help us find her... Vicky, she might be in danger."

She seemed to be thinking it over, and finally she said, "Well, I can tell you that Rachel has been worried since she saw Angela on her campus at Berkeley. At least, since she thought she saw her."

"How did she react to that?" Duarte asked.

"Somewhere between curious and frightened, I think," Victoria answered. "She was afraid Angela had come back and would harm her. At the same time, I think she would have liked to see Angela, which is natural enough. They are twins, after all."

"Do *you* think Angela might have done something to Rachel?" Duarte asked.

"That's hard to say. I haven't treated Angela since she was five years old."

"You were in contact with the psychiatrist at Saint Sympatica's, though, right?"

"Well, yes, but only by phone. Paul and Gina asked me to stay in touch with him and let them know how Angela was doing."

"And how was she doing?" Duarte pressed.

"Angela had a hard time adjusting to the orphanage after having lived in a real home," Victoria said. "She insisted she hadn't done anything wrong, and she didn't belong there. She missed Rachel, too. She kept asking when Rachel was coming."

"To the orphanage? To visit?"

"Yes. Apparently, every time Paul and Gina went to visit her, she expected that Rachel would be coming, too."

Duarte turned to Paul. "Did you ever take Rachel there?"

"No. We never felt it would be good for her, and Dr. Chase agreed."

"Speaking of Dr. Chase, Paul, he's the person you

really should be talking to,'' Victoria said. ''He would have more of a fix on whether Angela might still be a danger to Rachel.''

''I forgot, you don't know,'' Paul said. ''Dr. Chase is dead.''

''*Dead?* My goodness, what happened? He was young, wasn't he?''

Paul told her about the way Chase had died, and how Angela subsequently ran away from the orphanage.

''Was Angela a suspect?'' Victoria asked.

''Let's just say her actions were suspect,'' Paul said. ''They never had enough proof to make her an actual suspect.''

''But you're thinking she was the one who did it,'' Victoria guessed. ''And now you think she has Rachel. Or worse.''

Paul wet his lips, which had gone dry. ''We don't really know, Vicky. But it's possible.''

Victoria tapped at her lower lip with a bright coral thumbnail. ''The only thing I can think of,'' she said, ''is that it seemed as if Rachel really wanted to see Angela again. I know I'm not giving away anything if I say that Rachel has always had to deal with guilt over being left with you, while Angela was sent away. It's a common survivor syndrome.''

''I know. We've talked about that.''

''Well, she may have felt that she needed to see Angela to apologize in some way. I wonder if Angela did make contact with her. And if Rachel met her somewhere. You say she told Gina that she was going to meet a friend?"

"Ellen Stanaway. She and Rachel have been friends since high school."

"Have you talked with Ellen?"

"Only over the phone. Ellen said that she and Rachel didn't have plans that day. In fact, she hadn't heard from Rachel since she came home for the holidays."

"So Rachel lied about that."

"So it seems." Paul met her gaze.

"Dear God. I can see why you're worried."

Duarte spoke. "It's possible Angela contacted Rachel, and Rachel made plans to meet with her. Then..." He shrugged and a small silence filled the room. "That's what we have to find out," he said finally. "What happened then."

Paul felt cold, suddenly. Terrified. And at fault. If only he had been a better father. If only all the moments he'd spent with Lacey since Rachel came home had been spent with her instead. If only he'd taken more time to e-mail her at school.

Suddenly he knew beyond a doubt that he himself had caused all this to happen. Rachel's disappearance was some horrible kind of punishment for his sins.

"Paul?" Victoria's voice came through to him. He forced himself to focus.

"All of this is only speculation," she said. "We don't really know that Rachel went to meet Angela. It could have been anyone. A boyfriend from school..."

He shook his head. "Rachel would have told us if that were the case."

"Rachel is a grown woman now," Victoria pointed out. "She might not tell you everything that's going on in her life."

"Did she tell *you* anything about a boyfriend?" Paul asked.

"No. But that doesn't mean anything, either. Patients lie to their psychiatrists all the time. Often, they want us to think they're more well than they really are."

Duarte stood and leaned over the desk to shake Victoria's hand. "Appreciate your time," he said. He took a card out of his shirt pocket and handed it to her. "Please call me if you think of anything."

"I will," Victoria said, standing. "And Paul? Anything I can do, anything at all…"

"Thanks, Vicky. Just let us know if you hear from Rachel."

"Of course." But she avoided his eyes, leaving Paul to wonder why.

With a sinking heart, he followed Duarte to the door.

Once in Duarte's car, the detective suggested they stop somewhere for coffee and a sandwich. "I don't know about you, but I haven't eaten all day," he said. "Besides, we need to talk."

Paul called Gina on his cell phone to check in, telling her he was with Duarte and that they might have lunch, if she was okay. Gina assured him that she felt much better and asked about Victoria. "She wasn't able to be much help, I'm afraid," he said.

"Well, you had to try."

He agreed, and asked if she was certain she'd be all right while he had lunch with Duarte.

"Sure," she said. "I feel better sticking by the phone, and I have some work to do, anyway."

"The Albright house?"

"No, just some ideas I want to put on paper. It helps…well, you know. Paul? Tell Detective Duarte I really appreciate his help."

"I'll tell him," Paul said. "And Gina? Thanks."

"Sure," she said. "I'm putting a pot roast in for dinner. Comfort food, you know."

Paul smiled and hung up. He turned to the detective, who was sliding the Vic into a parking place in front of a diner. "Been eating here for twenty years," Duarte said. "Not many of these things left, you know."

They seated themselves at a booth along the window and made more small talk after the waitress took their orders. Finally Duarte said, "All right, give."

"Give?" Paul raised a brow.

"What's going on with you? You look like a man who's carrying around a heavy weight."

"You might have noticed," Paul said shortly, "my daughter is missing. She might be…" He couldn't say the words.

"Yeah, I think I noticed," Duarte said. "That's not

what I mean. You practically drifted off the screen for a few minutes back there.''

Paul shook his head and stared into his coffee cup. The waitress brought their sandwiches, and he slid the cup aside to make room for his plate. Toying with the toothpick in the club sandwich, he said, ''Are you Catholic, Detective Duarte?''

''Not so's you'd notice. But yeah, I was baptized, a thousand years or so ago. And by the way…call me Al.''

Paul nodded, but was silent.

''You need a priest?'' Duarte guessed. ''I'm used to hearing confessions.''

''Maybe that's it,'' Paul said. ''The truth is, I haven't been to confession in years.''

''Well, something like this tends to send people running for God,'' Duarte said. ''Or at the very least, absolution.''

''Absolution.'' Paul's voice was bitter. ''I just feel I brought this all on. Like, if I'd paid more attention to Rachel, she wouldn't have disappeared. Have you ever felt that way? If you just didn't take your eyes off someone, they wouldn't go away?''

''Sure,'' Duarte said. ''I feel that way every time I see my son.'' He took a bite of his grilled cheese and bacon sandwich, chewed and swallowed, then said, ''This isn't exactly about Rachel, though, is it?''

''What do you mean?'' Paul said.

''That girl. Lacey? The one you told me about?''

Paul shrugged. ''I'm beginning to realize that I've

got to break it off with her. I can't split my loyalties anymore. Shit, Al, losing Angela had such an effect on us, it's a wonder Gina and I are still together at all. We can't go through the loss of another child and survive.''

"You want it to survive?" Duarte asked. "Your marriage, I mean?"

"I don't really know how to answer that. I know we've got problems, but I don't want to lose Gina. That's the bottom line, I guess. I don't want to lose her.''

"And you think it'll all be on you, if something happens to Rachel? You'll be to blame for everything?''

"Well, like I said, I can't shake the feeling that whether she left on her own or Angela's got her, it wouldn't have happened if I'd been paying more attention.''

"Sure," Duarte said. "I know how that works. Anything at all that happens to our kids, we gotta be at fault.''

"But it's different this time," Paul said. "This time, it's true.''

"So what do you want to do about all this?" Duarte asked.

Paul looked through tears at his untouched sandwich. "I want to go home and hug my wife," he said.

8

Rachel stood at the cabin window, looking out. Snow had fallen in the night, and it lay on the cedars and the ground as far as the eye could see. There were no other cabins, no homes, no birds flying overhead.

She was completely alone.

She turned back to the potbellied stove, opened it and shoved another log on the fire. The stove warmed the entire one-room cabin, and there were cans of food in the rustic cupboards that could be heated in a pan on top of it. There was also an oil lamp, an old musty-smelling cot, a rickety little table and chair, and a small corner area with a toilet and sink. No gas or electricity, and no fridge. No milk, no fresh foods.

A spartan existence, she thought. Just enough to keep me alive.

But for what purpose? That was what frightened her the most.

She wasn't sure how many days she had been here. Two, now? Or was this the beginning of the third day? She decided to start making marks on the wall each night, to keep track. Wasn't that what prisoners did in the movies?

She couldn't remember how she had gotten here.

The last she knew she was in her car, wondering why the car ahead had stopped. Then the driver had stepped out and come to her window. Rachel had rolled it down, asking, "Is there something wrong?"

The words were barely out before the driver's hand, holding a strange-smelling rag, came down over her nose and mouth. Her head was shoved back against the seat to keep her from squirming away, and though she tried to strike out with her arms and legs, they went weak. The next thing she knew, she was here in this cabin. Alone.

She thought she knew who the driver was. She hadn't actually recognized her, but there was something about her expression, something familiar just before Rachel blacked out.

Angela. It had to be Angela.

Damn her stupidity! She should have told her parents about taking Angela's call the other day.

"I'd like to see you," Angela had said. "I've missed you, Rach. Haven't you missed me?"

Rachel could hardly believe it. She really had seen her on campus, then! It hadn't been a figment of her imagination.

She had wanted to see her sister. But she feared her, as well. There were things she couldn't quite remember about the night that Angela had tried to kill her, things that were like a nightmare she could only remember snatches of the next morning. The one thing she knew for sure was that there was more about that night to be afraid of than she remembered.

She had agreed to meet Angela at a restaurant, out in public where nothing could happen. She told her mother she was going to Ellen's house, so that she wouldn't worry. And worse—she had told her she was staying overnight. Her mother wouldn't even have been looking for her till the next day—if then.

Her plan had been to meet with Angela, and if the talk went well she would go home and tell her mom and dad about it. If it didn't, she could always drive over to Ellen's and ask to spend the night. That way, if she were upset, at least she wouldn't have to answer a lot of questions.

Stupid. Stupid, stupid, stupid! Angela had been a step ahead of her all the way. Rachel never did make it to that restaurant. Instead, she had woken up here.

For about the hundredth time she beat her fists against the one window of the cabin and was forced to admit that she was only wasting her energy. The window didn't give an inch. The glass was thick and unbreakable, and the door, made of heavy timber, was apparently locked or barred from the outside. Her hands were already swollen and bruised from trying to force either of them open. If only there had been a poker for the fire—anything she could use as a tool, or even a weapon.

But Angela had been too smart for that. Nothing worked—not the cans of food, the can opener, the few plastic forks in the kitchen drawer, the logs of wood that she had tried pounding against the window and door like a ram....

And because she had been such an idiot, her parents would never find her. Even when they realized she was missing, they wouldn't know why.

They might think to blame Angela, of course. But Angela had changed. She didn't look at all like the twin sister Rachel remembered, or even the woman she had seen on campus. She looked like someone else entirely now, and her parents would never recognize her—even if she walked up and spoke to them on the street.

It was sometime in the night that Rachel heard a noise at the door of the cabin. She had left the oil lamp on with the wick turned low. There was no telling how long the oil would have to last, and she knew she should try to preserve it. Still, her worst fear was of waking up in the night, in the dark, with Angela standing over her. There were times, in fact, when she would drift off and then wake suddenly, certain that Angela had been there.

Now, bolting upright on the cot, she stared at the door as it slowly opened. Her heart beat wildly in her throat, and she remembered how she had planned to leap up if Angela came back, grab a piece of firewood and slam her with it.

Brave plans, made in the cold clear light of day. Instead, she could barely move. Her whole body was frozen with fear.

"Hey, little sister," she heard the husky voice of

the grown-up Angela say. "I've brought you something."

She was dressed in a leopard-print jacket, jeans and
boots. The jacket was open, and around her neck was
a gold locket with the initial *A* on it. In her right hand
was a long silver knife, flashing a sickly yellow in the
dim glow of the oil lamp.

Angela came toward her, the tip of the knife pointing at Rachel. Rachel squeezed back against the log
wall as far as she could, pulling the musty blanket up
to her neck. "What do you want?" she cried. "Damn
you, Angela, what do you want with me?"

"I brought you a surprise," Angela said, reaching
into a pocket with her free hand. From the leopard
jacket she pulled a shiny red apple, holding it up.
"You always liked apples, didn't you, Rach? Remember how we used to share them? Mom would say,
'Don't cut your own apples, girls, I don't want you
playing with knives.' But we'd sneak a paring knife
out and sit in the backyard under the willow tree,
where she couldn't see us."

Angela came closer, pressing the knife against the
soft flesh beneath Rachel's chin. "Remember that?"

Rachel nodded. Her teeth were chattering, yet she
barely felt the blade on her skin, she was so numb.
Numb and distant, as if she were floating on a glacier,
but the glacier was in the sky and she was floating
farther and farther away from home.

"Oh, for heaven's sake, snap out of it!" Angela
said. She turned on her heel and strode over to the

small table by the stove, where she began to cut the apple. When it was in quarters, she counted them out in a singsong voice. "Eenie, meenie, miney, moe... catch a doctor by the toe."

She laughed. "Get that, Rach? Doctor?"

Rachel didn't answer.

"Now, don't tell me you don't remember, little sister." Angela grinned. She tossed two pieces of the apple at Rachel. "Here, eat up. You'll be needing your vitamins."

Rachel didn't touch the apple slices. The thought struck her that they might be poisoned.

"Not hungry?" Angela said in a mock-teasing voice. "Must be nice. I can't tell you how many hungry days and nights I've had since last we met. Let's see now...that would have been when we were both sixteen, right? The night you managed to sneak away from summer camp and visit me at Saint Sympatica's?"

Angela laughed, and the sound of it chilled Rachel. "What a night that was," Angela said. "Remember now, little sister? The night you killed Dr. Chase?"

Rachel's mind reeled. What was Angela talking about? And who was Dr. Chase?

"That's—that's crazy," she said. "You're crazy!"

"I could very well be," Angela agreed indifferently. "But that doesn't mean I'm not right."

"I—I didn't," Rachel stuttered. "I—I n-never did anything like that. How could I?"

"Uh-oh," Angela said, a strange, hollow smile

sweeping over her face. "Oh, dear." She toyed with the knife, tapping the point as if testing it for sharpness. "Don't tell me you've forgotten, little sis. You blocked it, right? Just the way you blocked that Christmas Eve night?"

Rachel began to cry. It felt as if all the underpinnings of her life were falling away beneath her. Everything crumbling, all at once.

"I'll never know how you got away with that night," Angela said, beginning to pace. "Except that you were the least likely suspect, of course. Little Rachel, so sweet and quiet, never causing any trouble..." She laughed. "Or so they thought. And me? They sent me away to pay the price for you. I wasn't as sickly sweet as you, I guess."

Her face twisted into a mask of anger. "Holy Father Christmas, Rach! Who would believe you tried to kill me? And all I did was defend myself."

Rachel covered her eyes and began to sob. "You're lying! I never did anything like that. I *couldn't* do anything like that!"

Angela ignored her. "You have no idea what it was like at Saint Sympatica's. I would wait in fear every day, knowing he would call me into his office and do those things to me. Or make me do things to him. One day he took me out into the woods along the river, Rach. I was maybe ten years old. He made me pose for pictures. Then he made me lie down on a blanket and open my legs so he could 'just touch me,' he said. But he did more than touch me, Rach. He pushed himself into me, and he said he was only going to do it a little, but he lied. He pushed and pushed until I screamed, it hurt so damned much. Then he put his hand over my mouth so no one could hear me scream. I can still smell that hand, Rach. It had a salty, coppery smell. I didn't know why until I saw that there was blood on his hand. My blood.''

Her voice became thick with tears, which she wiped away with the hand that still held the knife. ''Steady, Angela, steady,'' she murmured to herself. She paced in ever-decreasing circles, coming closer and closer to Rachel. ''That was the same day it rained blood,'' she said, standing directly over her sister at the edge of the cot. ''The rain came down in buckets, and it was red, a bright crimson red. When I got back to Saint Sympatica's I was covered in it. It had soaked into my blouse, my skirt, my hair, everything. I thought somebody, Mrs. Ewing maybe, would run up to me and say something like, 'Oh, my God, Angela! What happened to you?' And I would be able to tell them then, because I had proof. I would say, 'He hurt me, he hurt me real bad, and God made it rain blood to punish him.'

''But no one even noticed, Rach. They were all gathered in the recreation room watching television, and the man on TV was saying how scientists thought a meteor had passed overhead and left some sort of minerals behind that made the rain red. I tried to tell Mrs. Ewing that wasn't the reason, and that God had made it rain blood to punish Dr. Chase, but then the rain stopped and she was rushing out to hose off the porch. I tugged at her arm and said, 'Look. Look at me,' and she did, but for only a second. 'For heaven's sake, Angela!' she said, 'go up and get out of those clothes! Bring them down so I can wash them before they stain.'

"And that's when I realized that no one would believe me if I said God had turned the rain to blood. I think maybe somewhere down deep I didn't believe it anymore, either. And if God hadn't turned the rain to blood to punish Dr. Chase, there was only one thing I could do." She took a deep, ragged breath. "I would have to figure out a way to punish him myself."

There was a long silence, broken only by Rachel's sobs. "I—I'm so sorry," she said at last. "I d-didn't know."

Angela bent over her and said softly, "But you did know, little sis. You found out when you sneaked in to see me, that night when we were both sixteen. You found him doing things to me there in his room, and you killed him. Then you ran. And that's why they never could prove that anyone at Saint Sympatica's killed him, Rach. No one did. It was you, all along."

"That's crazy!" Rachel cried. "I never was at Saint Sympatica's! Never!"

But even as she tried to deny it, snatches of memory began to flit through Rachel's mind. A room in a big house. Angela pinned to a bed by a man who was shoving himself into her. Angela crying, "Please don't, oh God, please don't!'' The man smiling. ''You know what to do. Do it, Angela, do it.''

She remembered her own head filling with rage, everything going red. Then blank. Blank until this very moment.

Angela smiled. ''Aha! It's coming back, isn't it? Now you know. And now you've got to pay the price for murder, little sister. Just like I've been paying for your sin, all these years.''

9

They were in Rachel's Mustang, on a deserted mountain highway. Rachel thought she recognized the pass as one connecting western and eastern Washington, over the Cascades. From the position of the sun, which was rising, she knew they were heading east—away from home, not toward it, and the road signs told her they were possibly three hours, at least, from Seattle. The cabin had been closer to home than she'd realized.

She tried to think what she could do to escape Angela, but her hands were bound behind her back. If she tried kicking with her feet, they might go off the road and over a cliff. Her only other hope had been that they might reach a part of the highway that was blocked because of the snow, and she might get a message to someone on the road crew. That hope had been dashed when she saw the banks of snow, however, on either side of the road. The crew must have come through in the middle of the night.

If only she'd stop talking, Rachel thought desperately. With every word, she fell deeper and deeper into despair.

She stole a glance at Angela, trying to see in her the sister she had loved and remembered. Angela's hands, in leather gloves, were tight on the steering wheel, her mouth a grim line. Her waist-length hair was tucked up into a knitted cap. In the leopard coat, jeans and boots she looked so stylish—more like a movie star than a murderer. She really is beautiful, Rachel thought. How can someone so beautiful be a killer?

"I went blank myself after that Christmas Eve," Angela was saying. "At least that's what Dr. Chase said. I was like dead or something. I didn't know what had happened until a few days later at Saint Sympatica's, and then I didn't even know where I was. The only thing they told me was that Gina and Paul—the only parents I'd ever known—had brought me there, and then returned to Seattle to be with *you,* the so-called *victim.* Can you believe it? All that time they thought you were the victim." Angela's laughter was hollow.

"But if I really did do it, why didn't you just tell them at Saint Sympatica's that it was me?" Rachel asked.

"Oh, I told them all right. Over and over. Dr. Chase, anyway. He said I was sick, and not to tell anyone at all what I'd just told him. He said I was imagining things, that my mother and father saw *me* do it, not you, and if I told anyone that it wasn't me who started the argument that night, they'd say I was crazy and keep me there forever. I'd never go home, he said, and I'd never be adopted by anyone else."

"But you never did come home. Or get adopted."

"Oh, for heaven's sake, Rachel! You sure grew up stupid. No, I did not get adopted, and I never went home. The good doctor made things up so I'd look unadoptable. That way he could keep me there for himself. The Ewings were nice enough, but they were too busy to notice, or they trusted him, or something. Who knows? It's like when kids are molested by their fathers and the mother never knows. It's easy to cover something like that up. Especially when a kid starts out with people thinking there's something wrong with you in the first place."

Rachel's eyes filled with tears. She had never been so terrified in her life, yet at the same time anger began to build. If Angela was telling the truth, she would never forgive her parents for just assuming Angela had attacked her, and not the other way around. Nor would she forgive herself for not remembering and speaking up.

What would it have been like? she wondered. What if she, Rachel, had been the one to be sent thousands of miles away? To be molested and raped?

And if she had been lucid at the time, would she have confessed to starting that fight? Would she have protected Angela?

She didn't know. But Angela was her twin, and the same bond that had left her yearning for her sister all these years made Rachel want to help her now. It didn't matter what Angela had done, or if she was lying now. They were sisters, twins, and what happened to one would always impact the other.

She was starting to remember how she had ended up at Saint Sympatica's when she was sixteen. On her sixteenth birthday, in fact. She had been away at a music camp in Wisconsin, a camp she herself had purposely chosen because of its proximity to Minnesota. By that time she had too many questions that weren't being answered. Her grandmother was the only one she could talk to about Angela, but only about the time when Angela was sent away. She didn't have any up-to-date information at all. Rachel wanted to know how her sister was. She wanted to see her. Talk to her. Make sure she was all right.

She knew that Angela might not be at Saint Sympatica's any longer. But that day in August was Angela's birthday, too, and finding her was a chance Rachel had to take. If her sister had been adopted and was living somewhere else, she would try to make the people there tell her where Angela was.

She had gotten a friend to cover for her at camp that afternoon, and had thumbed a ride to Saint Paul. Her mother would have died if she'd known about it—not just that she was going to see Angela, but that she was alone at night on the road, at the mercy of strangers. Rachel herself was scared to death as it grew dark that night; she had to keep telling herself she'd be all right, that if anything bad happened, she had the steak knife from dinner the night before, right there in her backpack.

She recalled now that a truck driver, a nice woman who had taken to the road herself in her teens, dropped her off at Saint Sympatica's. How she had made her way inside without being seen, however, was still a blank. She remembered standing outside on the lawn, in the dark, waiting for the lights to go out. It had seemed peaceful there, the August air soft and warm. Lightning bugs lit up the shrubbery, and frogs somewhere nearby sent out their *ribbit* songs.

Then, suddenly, there was a boy. She remembered that now, too. But who was he? What was he doing outside while the orphanage was dark and everyone else was apparently in bed? Had he been the one to tell her where Angela's room was? Rachel couldn't remember. She did remember finding Angela in a room, with a man pinning her to the bed. Angela crying softly, begging him to leave her alone.

Oh, God. Was it true that she, Rachel, had killed that man? The one Angela called "Dr. Chase"? Vague bits of memory were coming back. She saw herself running across the room, screaming silently, deep in her heart, as she beat on the man's back with her fists. And then she remembered blood. Blood all over the place.

There was something else, though.

"Angela," she said uncertainly, "who was that boy?"

Angela gripped the wheel and looked straight ahead. "What boy?"

"There was a boy, wasn't there? That night at Saint Sympatica's?"

"No," Angela snapped. "There was no boy."

"But I think I remember seeing someone—"

"Look, you want me to leave you right here on the side of the road? For God's sake, shut up, Rach! Stop being an idiot."

It was a full half hour later when they reached the outskirts of Spokane. Angela pulled off onto a narrow side road. She stopped the car, slipped the knife she'd had the night before out of her jacket and turned to Rachel, resting it against her cheek.

"Last stop, little sis. You know, I'm kind of sorry it has to be this way."

She pushed Rachel forward and slid the tip of the knife down her back till it came to the rope that tied Rachel's hands. Cutting through it with a sawing motion, she said, "You know what you have to do. Right?"

Rachel rubbed her wrists and nodded. "Right."

10

That morning, Paul sat with Gina at the breakfast bar, waiting for the coffee to brew. Paul was across from her, on the stool usually filled by Rachel. He took both her hands and told her how sorry he was that they'd drifted apart—not only the past few months, but the past several years.

"I don't know why we've been going our separate ways instead of growing closer," he said. "I just know it isn't right. And I know it's been my fault. Gina, I want to start doing better. Whatever's happened, whether Rachel's been kidnapped or she's just gone away, I have to believe she'll be back. And when she does comes back—" his voice broke "—I want our daughter to know that her parents are together and behind her, every step of the way. I...I want you to know I'm behind you, too."

Once he'd begun speaking, Paul hadn't been able to stop the words from pouring forth. He felt drained, as if he'd run a marathon.

Gina's eyes shifted away from his.

"You, uh...you want that, too, don't you?" Paul asked uneasily.

"Well, of course I want us to be united for Rachel,"

Gina said. "I…I'm just not sure it isn't too late, Paul. For us, I mean."

The color drained from Paul's face. "Are you saying you think it's over? That we should separate?"

She bit her lower lip. "No. I mean, I just don't know. It's hard…it's hard to know what to do, with Rachel gone. It just doesn't seem like the best time to make a decision like that."

His hands tightened. "I don't want to lose you."

She looked at him, surprised. "I…I don't want to lose you, either," she said hesitantly. "It's just that…oh, Paul, I just can't think right now of anything except getting Rachel back."

"Of course," he said. "You're right, I'm rushing things. We should take it day by day."

She nodded, looking down at their intertwined hands. "Day by day." A tear fell on one of her hands, and Paul lifted it to his cheek and held it there.

The rich scent of French roast filled the room and Gina stirred. "The coffee…"

Paul squeezed her hands and put them gently back onto the breakfast bar. He went to get the pot and filled both their cups. He had barely finished pouring when the phone on the kitchen wall rang. He grabbed it, hoping it was Rachel.

"Paul, you'd better get over to Soleil," Daniel Britt said, his voice shaking. "There's been some trouble."

"What kind of trouble?"

"Just come on down. Trust me."

The tone of Daniel's voice filled him with dread.

"Is it about Rachel?"

Daniel seemed bewildered. "Rachel? No. But Paul? You need to see this."

Paul told Gina that something was wrong at Soleil, then kissed her on the cheek and said he'd let her know what had happened. She hugged him.

"Call me right away," she said. "Promise?"

"Promise."

It took him less than fifteen minutes to make it from home to Soleil. What could have happened? he asked himself over and over as he pulled into his personal parking space in the back. Did it have something to do with Rachel, after all, and Daniel just didn't want to tell him?

When he walked through the door, Annie gave him a strange look. "What's up?" he said tersely.

She seemed nervous, unable to meet his eyes. "Daniel asked that you wait for him here, Mr. Bradley." She pushed a button on the phone and, over the speaker, Paul heard Daniel answer.

"Mr. Bradley is here," Annie said.

"Tell him I'll be right out," Daniel answered.

Annie hung up and again she gave Paul a look that seemed to him almost pitying. *Oh, dear God,* he thought, *don't let it be Rachel.*

"Just tell me," he said harshly. "Whatever it is, just tell me."

She stared down at her desk, then looked up with relief as Daniel rushed in.

Seeing Paul, he slowed down and took a breath. "I am so sorry," he said. "Paul, I am truly sorry."

Paul's fear mushroomed. He followed Daniel through the large front room to the door of the Crystal Cave, his feelings fluctuating between relief and dread.

It's not Rachel. It's bad, though.

Daniel opened the door to the Crystal Cave and Paul stood on the threshold, stupefied.

Glass littered the floor. Hundreds of glittering pieces, thousands of them, shattered to bits. Not a single plate, cup, glass, or vase remained on the shelves. Instead there were mounds of shards, glistening in the light like an ugly crystal beach, stretching from wall to wall.

Without thinking, Paul took a step forward. He felt pain crease his ankle. Looking down, he noted that blood was seeping through his khaki pants. He was standing in a foot-high mound of glass, barely identifiable except that he thought he saw part of a Chihuly sea form wedged up against a Gallè vase.

As if from a distance he heard Daniel say, "Don't go in there, Paul. It's not safe." He tugged at Paul's arm to hold him back.

But Paul didn't have to go in. He knew nothing was salvageable. Like Humpty-Dumpty, there would be no putting these pieces back together again. All these beautiful, irreplaceable pieces of artwork, some of it created by masters hundreds of years ago, destroyed forever. He felt a thrust to his heart, a blow that physically pained him.

"Who did this?" he whispered. "Who would do this?"

"We, uh…we don't know," Daniel said. "It…it was like this when Annie got here this morning."

"The security alarm?"

"Disabled."

Paul turned to him. "No one knows the code except you, Annie, Janice and me." He broke off. "Where is Janice?"

"She called in sick today. She has the flu."

"Did you call the police?"

Daniel nodded. "They're sending someone."

Paul's eyes fixed on something long and dark in the rubble. "What's that?"

"It's a tire iron," Daniel said. "I walked in a little at first, but then I realized I shouldn't disturb anything until the police got here. I did get a good look at the tire iron, though, and I think that must be what they used."

Paul turned on his heel as anger set in. "I'll be in my office," he said.

Once there, he called Gina and told her what had happened. She was as horrified as he was. "I can't believe it!" she said. "Oh, Paul, I'm so sorry."

They talked a few minutes more, then he called Duarte and filled him in.

"I heard," Duarte said. "There's a car on the way. I was just getting ready to leave here."

"Al? This was done deliberately. It looks like they even left the tire iron they used to smash everything."

"Hang tight," Duarte said, and hung up.

Paul put the receiver down and rubbed his face with his hands. He kept seeing it—all that beautiful glass, like so much refuse now.

He would have to call his insurer. But it wasn't the cost of all the breakage that mattered. It was wondering who in the name of God would do such a thing.

Angela? It popped into his head without conscious volition.

A long-forgotten scene came to him, from the early years with Angela. She was sitting in his lap and he was reading to her. *"Humpty-Dumpty sat on a wall…"* When he came to the end, she had asked, "Who are all the king's men, Daddy? Why can't they put Humpty together again?" And he had answered, "I'm not sure, Angel. Maybe they didn't care enough."

"Do you care about me, Daddy?" Angela had asked in that sweet, high-pitched voice. Her eyes—so like Rachel's in their light hazel color—had darkened with tears. "If I fell down, would you care?"

He had kissed her on the forehead and said, "Of course I would, Angel. I would never let anything happen to you. I promise."

Oh, God. He had failed her. He had broken his promise, and she had suffered for it.

Daniel stood at the door. "The police are here. They want to talk to you."

"Tell them I'll be right out," Paul said. Casting an eye around his office, he wondered what he'd been thinking all these years. The hard work, the long days spent putting together the business, traveling around the world looking for antiques and pieces of art. Leaving his family, leaving Rachel…

It all felt like dust on his tongue now. Nothing had gone right. Nothing was the way it had been planned. *If there is such a thing as karma,* he thought—*what goes around comes around—this must be it.*

When Paul walked into the reception room, he was brought up short by the look one of the two uniformed cops gave him. It seemed cold and laced with suspicion. The questions were even worse, as if he might have done this thing himself to collect insurance. He answered their questions and told them as calmly as he could that he had no idea who might have done it. That was something he'd talk only to Duarte about.

Dammit, anyway! Where was he?

The cops wanted to know Janice's home address and phone number. Annie, innocently enough, had told them that Janice almost never took sick leave. Since she hadn't come to work on the one day the vandalism took place, she was suddenly under a cloud of suspicion.

Poor Janice. She was hardworking and loyal. She'd never do a thing like this. He tried to tell them that, but they said only that sometimes those are the ones you had to watch out for. The "least likely suspect."

They took information from him, Daniel, Annie and the other floor clerks as they began to arrive. They told everyone not to touch anything until the detectives arrived.

Paul was impressed by the thoroughness of the two officers, and he wondered if they were always this careful. It wasn't until Duarte and another detective came through the front door that he realized Duarte must have given them a heads-up.

Duarte spent a moment with the two cops and spoke to the other detective, leaving him to handle things. Gesturing to Paul, he said, "Let's take a look. We can talk in your office."

Paul led the way, stopping at the door to the Crystal Cave. He didn't want to look in, and in fact dreaded having to see it again.

Duarte whistled. "Holy God. Whoever did this was one angry sonuvabitch." He glanced at Paul. "Or bitch."

He didn't go in, but followed Paul down the hall to his office. "You got any coffee?" he asked. "Any that's thick and black?"

"I'll see." Paul called up to the front and asked Annie if she would bring them both coffee. "Yesterday's, if you have any left over."

"The officers won't let me leave the room," Annie said.

Duarte barked to the two cops through the speaker phone, "You think she's gonna smash the pot, for Pete's sake? Let her do it!"

He and Duarte sat in silence as a Seth Thomas clock

on a bookcase ticked the minutes away. *One, two, three...*

Paul drummed on his desk, while Duarte wiped imaginary crumbs from his tie, which hung loose around his neck. Finally Annie appeared with two cups, one fixed the way Paul liked it and one black as pitch. Duarte sipped that one and closed his eyes, saying dreamily, "Perfect. Marry me, Annie."

She blushed and left the room without turning around, just backing away like a subject before a king. Paul had never been able to break her of that habit, no matter how hard he had tried. Annie was only in her thirties, he guessed, but she read only Regency romances on her lunch break, and in her heart she was from another century. That was what made her such a trustworthy receptionist. Her instinct for antiques was so good, she was able to weed out nonvaluable pieces from valuable ones before they ever reached the back rooms.

When she was gone, Duarte took another gulp of the coffee, then set it down on a piece of scrap paper on Paul's mahogany desk. "Wouldn't want to ruin this great finish," he said. "Which reminds me. You think you could get me a new desk? A new old one, I mean? Something nice. Not so scratched up."

"I could," Paul answered with an attempt at a smile. "But if you doodle on it the way you do the one you've got, it won't be nice for long."

Duarte nodded. "Yeah, I guess you're right. Oh, well. It was just a thought."

He gave Paul a sharp look. "You think Angela did this?"

"I don't know. Maybe. What do you think?"

"Well, we've got to check out your staff. Especially the ones you say have the security code. Of course, any of your employees could have left the alarm off before they went home last night. Deliberately left it off for somebody else, that is. There could be two of them working together. You know who was the last to leave?"

"No," Paul said. "But Al, we're like a family here. I trust the people who work for me. I can't for a minute believe any of them did this."

"Maybe not," Duarte said. "But we've got to question them, anyway. Meanwhile—" he took a deep draft of coffee "—we haven't got a lead on Angela. Or Rachel. Not a clue. Plenty of false alarms, but nothing's panned out. I'm sorry."

Paul shook his head. "I don't know what to do anymore. I'm so damned worried about Rachel, and now this—" He broke off. "I didn't want to say it, but actually I'm pretty sure Angela did this."

Feeling a bit foolish, he told Duarte the Humpty-Dumpty story. "It may sound silly, but I think she was sending me a message. I'm not exactly sure what the message was, unless she just wanted to torment me with the fact that she was here and could destroy me, my business…whatever."

He couldn't bring himself to voice his worst

thought. *Rachel*. Was Angela telling him she could destroy Rachel...or that she already had?

"Maybe it's just part of the whole package," Duarte said. "See, the thing is, Rachel's been gone, what, four days now? And there hasn't been any ransom note, no contact from a kidnapper. Now, either she's gone off by herself, the way we talked about, or the evil twin—sorry—grabbed her and she isn't interested in ransom. She just wants you and your wife to suffer."

Duarte sighed. "Paul, I don't think that little girl of yours—Rachel, I mean—would have done this to you. I don't think she'd have just gone off without telling you, or at least calling. I've seen a lot of teenagers who do that sort of thing when they're pissed off at their parents. But Rachel? She's not a teenager. Besides, she didn't seem the type."

Paul tried but couldn't meet his eyes. "You think Angela's got her, don't you?"

"I know you don't want to believe that, and I can't blame you. But we gotta be realistic about this. It's time to move forward, Paul."

"Meaning?"

"I'll get an APB out on Rachel, and I'll notify the FBI we've got a probable kidnapping."

"It'll be all over the papers," Paul said. "There'll be crank calls, too, won't there? People claiming they've seen her."

"A lot of false leads," Duarte agreed. "Are you saying you're not up for it?"

"God, no," Paul said. "If only one lead proves to be true and helps us find Rachel, it'll be worth it. I'm just...I'm really worried about Gina."

"My guess is she's a gutsy lady," Duarte said. "You might be surprised to discover that about her. You might be surprised by some other things, too."

Daniel and the other employees were told they could go back to work. Paul sat in his office, thinking, while Duarte helped the other detective bag evidence in the Crystal Cave.

"I don't think we really need the crime lab here," he had said. "The chance of finding any clean prints on this stuff is practically nil. First off, there are too many pieces. Hundreds, maybe even thousands of them, if you count all the smaller shards. It'd take a year to dust them all, and we haven't got the manpower. Chances are it'd be a waste, anyway, because the perp probably didn't even touch them—just went around swinging that tire iron. We'll take the tire iron, of course, and check for prints on it. Other than that, our only hope is that we might find something else significant. Something personal the perp dropped accidentally, for instance."

Paul called to let Gina know what was going on, and that he was going to stay at Soleil until the detectives left and things settled down. There had never been so much as a theft at Soleil, and the clerks and Annie were all having a hard time concentrating. He also wanted to hang around in case Janice tried to reach him here after the police talked to her. Janice had been his assistant for years, and while it was true that she almost never took a sick day, Paul didn't believe for a moment that she was in on this vandalism. It had to be a coincidence that she had taken today off.

"We're pretty sure Angela did this," Paul told Gina. "In fact, Duarte said to tell you that he's sending an officer to the house. He'll be outside in a car."

He didn't say that if Angela had done something to Rachel, Gina could be next. His voice was calmer than he felt when he said, "Don't open the door to anyone you don't know, even the police if they don't have ID. I'd rather you didn't go out today, either, at least until I get home and we can go together."

Gina agreed, and promised she'd be careful. "I just can't believe it," she said sympathetically. "That someone would destroy something that means so much to you...? I'm so sorry, Paul. You must be heart-broken."

Getting an officer to watch the house had been Duarte's idea, and he'd had to tell his lieutenant the whole story about Angela, in order to get someone assigned to that duty. Rachel's disappearance was official now; as Al had said, there was no keeping it quiet any longer. An APB had been issued throughout Washington State, and the FBI had been called in.

Before hanging up, Paul told Gina that he loved her. The words sounded strange to his ears after such a long time.

"I love you, too," Gina said softly.

He could tell she was crying. He tried to think of other words to say, but nothing seemed right for this moment. He set the receiver down gently and rested his head on his folded arms, praying. *Help us. Somebody, please help.*

Several minutes later, Duarte entered Paul's office. "We've got something, but I'm afraid it isn't good news."

"What is it?"

"You know that tire iron? There weren't any prints on it, but it had a Ford stamp, showing it was issued from the Ford factory, probably when the car was new." He paused a moment. "Rachel was driving a Ford car. A Mustang, right?"

"What are you saying?" Paul asked. "Don't tell me you think that Rachel did this! For God's sake, Al, there must be thousands of Fords on the road, right here in Washington State."

"Yeah, but how many of them have drivers who wanted to destroy that room in there, something you held near and dear?"

Paul's nerves were on edge, but he tried to temper his anger. "Rachel would not have done this, Al. She loved that room, too."

"Well, that brings me to the alternative," Duarte said, not quite meeting his eyes.

"Which is?"

"Which is, maybe Angela's been driving Rachel's car."

Paul stared at him. Just the thought of Angela driving around in Rachel's car, and what that might mean, made him feel light-headed. Sick.

"You mean that she's gotten rid of Rachel," he said. "That's why she's got the Mustang."

"Or, she could have just holed her up somewhere," Duarte said. "Long enough to make you suffer, thinking she's dead."

Paul fell silent, and Duarte leaned forward and ran his finger over the satin inlay on the travel desk. "What's this?"

"It's called a travel desk," Paul said. "Or a lap desk. Someone left it here the other day."

"Just left it? Without saying anything?"

"Yes."

"Don't you think that's sort of odd?"

Paul sighed. "I guess I haven't had much time to think of it at all, lately. When it first came in, I figured the owner was in a hurry and would come back later. When he or she didn't, I forgot about it. I haven't been here that much. Anyway, it's not important."

"You don't think so? Aren't those cherubs, there, in the design?" Duarte said.

Paul looked—really looked—at the satinwood inlay for the first time. "Yes," he said. "Cherubs and flowers. Why?" His brow furrowed with bewilderment.

"Well, *think*, man," Duarte said, obviously trying

hard to contain his impatience. "What are cherubs? Angels, right?"

Paul's face cleared. "Right."

"Don't tell me you didn't even look inside it," Duarte said. "Didn't it occur to you that Angela might have left this? That it might be important somehow?"

"No, dammit, it didn't!" Paul said tersely. "I just told you, I forgot about it."

"Okay, okay," Duarte said. "I just wondered if you looked inside."

"No. Well, actually, I did, but I had other things on my mind, and I didn't check all the drawers. Just the two larger ones."

"You mind checking the rest of them now?" Duarte asked, drumming his fingers on the desk.

Paul gave him an irritated look but pulled the travel desk closer. He studied the outside before opening it. Approximately ten inches deep, twenty wide and eighteen long, the desk was in excellent condition. Opening the rectangular box, he set it up so that the cover slanted to make a writing surface. Then he pulled out every obvious drawer.

One still held two silver candleholders, in excellent though tarnished condition. Another held an empty crystal ink bottle with a silver cap, and a similar bottle filled with sand for drying the ink.

"These longer drawers," he said as he pulled them out, "would have held paper and envelopes. See, there are red wax drippings showing that a wax seal was used at one time."

While Duarte watched, he began to pull out the smaller drawers and feel around inside the cavities they left. "Often, these desks have secret drawers," he said. "Travelers used to hide their jewelry and other valuables in them when they were on the road. Usually there's some sort of spring mechanism." He frowned. "This lap desk seems to have been rigged differently, however."

He found the first secret drawer by pressing on the right side of a cavity until the drawer popped out. The second and third secret drawers worked the same way. They were all empty, however, and with the fifth, Paul was ready to quit. If Angela had meant to send him a message, he couldn't imagine what it was.

Carelessly he pulled the fifth drawer out for one more try, and felt a jolt like electricity run through him. A yellowed candid snapshot lay in the drawer.

He pulled it out and stared at the little girl, perhaps eight or nine, who stood alongside a stream, surrounded by the feathering leaves of trees. She had long dark hair and her features were very much like the Angela he remembered at the age of five.

"My God," Paul whispered. "Al, look." He held the photograph up for the detective to see. Duarte studied it a few moments.

"Damn," he said. "Sonuvabitch. Is that Angela?"

"She's older, and she looks different, of course, but the hair, and something about her expression...yes, I think it's her."

Under other circumstances, this could also have

been a halcyon scene: a little girl in the countryside, enjoying a warm summer day. But the girl was entirely naked. Only the dappled shade from the trees covered her, and that just slightly. Her hair was long and dark, and her expression, Paul thought, was one of part fear, part shame. She was slightly stooped, her hands together in an obvious attempt to hide her groin area. Her breasts were bare. They protruded slightly, casting a small shadow.

Paul's hands shook. *Who the hell took this?* was his first coherent thought. Then, *Why?* His mouth went dry and tears filled his eyes. Was this Angela? And if it was, who had done this to her? Who would have made her pose unwillingly for such a photograph?

And what else had that person done to her?

Paul closed his eyes, clenching his fist. The photograph twisted and crackled. *What did we do? What did we leave her to?*

And what is it she wants from us now?

"Paul?" he heard from a distance. "Paul, snap out of it."

Duarte's voice reached his ears, but he seemed unable to bring his focus back. He felt numb all over. Numb, and without any emotion whatsoever. He thought that if he did start to feel something for the little girl in this photograph, he would crack—like Humpty-Dumpty—and nothing, or no one, would ever be able put him together again.

11

As the numbness wore off, determination replaced it. If Angela was the girl in that photograph, and if she was playing some sick kind of game, it was all that much more important to focus on finding Rachel now. Angela might or might not be involved in her disappearance, but either way, Rachel had to be found. All of his efforts must go to keeping her safe.

Paul pointed the rented Pontiac, which he'd been driving since the accident, in the direction of Lacey's apartment. Taking the elevator up to the third floor, he geared himself to tell her that he had to make an attempt at saving his marriage. He wouldn't be able to see her any longer. He would keep up the apartment for her, and all her expenses, until she found a good job and could take care of herself. He wouldn't just walk off and leave her with nothing.

Paul hoped she would be all right with this. She had, after all, said from the beginning that she knew what they had couldn't last. In fact, she had told him that if he ever needed to leave her, she just wanted him to tell her so, rather than lie about it.

When she opened the door and he smelled her perfume, saw the golden halo of blond around her head, he almost lost his resolve. But he stepped inside, kissed her on the cheek and let her take his coat and gloves.

"Golly Molly, Paul, your hands are freezing, even with gloves!" she said, holding them both. "It must be below freezing out there."

"I guess," he said, realizing for the first time that he was chilled clear through.

"Let me get you some brandy."

"Coffee's okay," he said, wanting to keep his head straight for this.

"No," she insisted. "You need something to warm your blood, not your stomach."

He acquiesced and watched her pour a hefty amount of brandy into a snifter.

"Here, sit down," she said, leading him over to the sofa. "You drink this while I take your shoes off. Where in the world have you been, Paul? And why didn't you wear boots? Your feet are soaked!"

"You know I never wear boots," he said. "It doesn't usually snow here."

"Maybe not, but it sure is wet. You know, when I was a kid we had to wear boots ten months out of the year. Anybody who could afford them, that is." Momentarily her face clouded over. "Anyway, I can't get used to people out here just walking around in the rain like it didn't even exist..."

Her brow furrowed. "Paul, what's this on your pants? It looks like blood."

"It is. I cut myself on some glass."

"Oh, you poor thing! Let me make it better." She lifted his pants leg and planted a soft kiss on the cut, which had dried over. Then she reached up a hand and stroked his cheek.

Her touch was soft as a feather, calming and soothing. Between that and the brandy, Paul felt his nerves begin to relax. But as her hand slipped down to his belt, then farther down, stroking, he pulled away awkwardly.

Standing, he carried the brandy snifter to the peninsula between the living room and kitchen, setting it down.

"I just stopped by to see how your computer search was going," he said, his mouth dry and his hands shaking.

Lacey was still where he'd left her, on her knees by the sofa. She looked at him quizzically. "You aren't yourself today. What's wrong? Beside the obvious, I mean...Rachel and all that."

He told her about the vandalism at Soleil. "I can't think what else to call it," he said, "though vandalism doesn't seem to be quite strong enough."

"Oh, Paul! That beautiful room, especially the Gallè vase, the one that was so hard to find. Was that broken, too?"

"Everything," he said, sighing, but grateful that she cared. "How did you know about the Gallè?"

"You and your memory!" she said in a mildly teasing voice. "We drank to your finding it, one night at Gordon Biersch's. We had just met, and you were so excited. You said you didn't have anyone else to talk to about it. Remember? Gina wasn't home, and Rachel was away at school.... I think it was the second or third night after we met.''

He shook his head. ''My mind must be mush, after all that's happened lately.''

She threw a wet sock at him. ''Men! They never remember the important things.''

He smiled and caught the sock. ''Important?''

''You mean you don't remember what we did after we had that drink?''

He shook his head and she threw the other sock at him. ''That was our first night together, silly!''

He thought a moment. ''Oh! Well, by Jove, I believe you're right!'' Laughing, he took both socks and went after her. She climbed over the sofa and stood behind it. ''Catch me if you can!'' she cried.

''Oh, I can,'' Paul said. ''Believe me, I can.''

But when he reached her and held her, catching his breath, it was Gina's face he saw in his mind, not Lacey's. Gina, who needed him more now than ever.

He kissed Lacey on the forehead and said, ''How about that coffee now?''

They sipped the pungent Fidalgo Bay roast at Lacey's computer, with Paul sitting next to her on the zebra-striped chair. ''I was hoping you'd come by so I could tell you what I found,'' she said. ''If you hadn't, I was going to call you on your cell.''

"Sounds important," Paul said.

"Well, intriguing, anyway. I'm not sure how important it'll turn out to be."

She set her coffee down and clicked on an icon to connect to the Web. While it was loading, she said, "First of all, Angela still uses your last name, Bradley. They never changed it at the orphanage, and that made it easy for me to do a search. She also has an interest in antiques, believe it or not. Maybe as a way of still feeling close to you?"

"That's remarkable," Paul said. "How did you find all that out?"

"Simple," she said. "But also kind of weird. Angela actually has a Web site."

"A personal Web site?"

"Yes."

"And it says that she's into antiques?"

"Big time. I'll show you." She typed in the Web site address.

While they were waiting for it to load, Paul said, "But she was only five when she left. Children that young usually don't even know what their parents do."

"Well, did you ever take them to Soleil? Show them around?"

"I...yes, I suppose I must have. But that was a long, long time ago."

"Not for a kid who's trying to cling to her past," Lacey said. "Someone whose only good memories were from before the age of five? Something like that, a kid never forgets."

Paul watched the Web site load and wondered what other surprises it held. "I suppose you're right," he said.

"Trust me, I am. And Paul, like I said, it's kind of weird." Lacey handed him a printout to read. "There are pages on the Web site about antiques, and Angela's interest in them. But she's also written this bio, and it's not like anything you've told me about her."

"In what way?"

"Well, she says she was raised in a loving family and given everything a child could dream of. Right on down to singing lessons. Three years of them."

"Singing lessons?" Paul felt confused. "We gave Rachel singing lessons when she was a teenager. Rachel had a wonderful voice."

"Had?"

"Well, she almost never sings anymore. I forget when it was that she stopped." Paul thought a moment. "When she was fifteen, sixteen, maybe. But Angela almost never sang. She was tone deaf."

"Look at this," Lacey said.

He focused his attention on the screen and read down to where Lacey pointed.

I lived in a beautiful house on Queen Anne Hill in Seattle, and when I was sixteen, my parents sent me to a music camp in Wisconsin, where I could sharpen my skills. I always wanted to be a professional singer. In fact, it's the only thing I ever wanted.

"This is crazy," Paul said, feeling as if he'd just slipped into another dimension. "It sounds more like *Rachel's* life than Angela's. We sent Rachel to a music camp in Wisconsin one summer. It was her choice, the only thing in the world she wanted. I remember she was about to have her sixteenth birthday, and we wanted to celebrate it with her, but she was determined to go away." He smiled. "We tried to talk her into a camp closer to home—God knows there were plenty of them—but she pushed and pushed, and finally we gave in."

"Why do you think she did that?" Lacey asked.

"I don't know. I thought at first it was just some teenage whim. She said she had heard about it from her music teacher, and that it was one of the best. Gina and I looked into it, and Rachel was right. The camp *was* one of the best. But when she came back…"

"What?" Lacey prompted when he drifted off, thinking.

"That must be when she lost her interest in music," he said. "When she came home, she had changed completely, and she didn't seem to want to sing anymore. She stayed in her room a lot, the rest of that year. In fact, as I remember, she didn't even go out with her friends from school."

"Do you have any idea what was wrong?" Lacey asked.

"Not really. I guess I thought at the time that it was just one more teenage mood. A phase."

"Look at the rest, Paul."

He forced himself to continue reading.

It was after Wisconsin that I knew what it was all about. Music meant nothing. Life meant nothing. The only thing I wanted to do then was die.

The bio ended there. Paul, shocked, said heavily, "It sounds as if Angela is writing about Rachel. And it sounds like she knew Rachel better than I did."

He felt a hundred years old, yet as if he had never learned a thing. As if all the lessons—lessons he'd thought had brought him to a point in his adulthood where he could claim to be a man—had been a total waste.

He looked at the bio again. "Except," he said, "that Rachel *wasn't* given everything a child could dream of. She didn't have that kind of perfect family. First she lost her twin, then Gina and I...we grew apart." He opened his eyes and said, his voice full of pain, "We turned Rachel over to a nanny to raise her. It must have been so lonely for her, growing up."

Lacey held his hand, saying quietly, "So, Paul, what do you make of this?"

"I don't know. It just briefly crossed my mind that this might not be Angela's Web site at all—that it's Rachel's. And she's written about a fantasy life, a life she wished was hers. But why would she have a Web site under Angela's name?"

"I don't know, Paul. It's really strange."

"And it tells me nothing, really. Except that Rachel was horribly depressed that summer."

"Paul...why was she depressed?"

"That's the hell of it. We never knew." He stared at the computer's monitor, as if looking for a clue. "Are you saying you think she wants me to find out?"

Lacey pushed back her chair. Getting up, she went into the kitchen. "Would you like more coffee? I can make a fresh pot." Her voice was oddly muffled.

"Yes, thanks," Paul said. "Make it strong."

After a minute, he called to her. She didn't answer, and he thought she hadn't heard. He called again and rose to follow her, but she came from the kitchen, wiping tears from her eyes with a paper towel.

"What is it?" he asked.

She shook her head and didn't answer, just sat at the desk staring at the computer screen. From behind her, he put his hands on her shoulders.

"What is it?" he asked again.

"Poor little girls," she said softly. "Those poor little girls."

He was struck by the deep emotion in her voice.

"Yes," he said just as softly. "Both of them. Poor little girls."

12

The mood in the Queen Anne house was somber when Paul walked in. Gina and Roberta were sitting opposite each other in the living room, in overstuffed chairs. The fire crackled and spit. To Paul, the room seemed overly warm, and he pulled at his necktie, loosening it.

As he came closer to Gina he saw that tears had run down her cheeks and dried there. Gina never wore a lot of makeup, but the small amount she'd put on that morning—war paint, she had called it, to prepare her for anything—had darkened the tears, accentuating them.

He noted that she was still in her robe. Roberta wore an unusually somber gray suit, compared to the bright colors she ordinarily flaunted like a banner, announcing her appearance. She looked at Paul and shook her head, as if to say that she hadn't had much success at comforting her daughter. Roberta herself didn't look so good, he thought. He reminded himself that Rachel's disappearance was wearing on her, too. All too often, he left her out of the equation, simply because he didn't know her well enough—or, to be honest, hadn't taken the time to know her. Gina had always issued the invitations to holiday dinners and bought the birthday gifts. When Roberta came by on weekdays, he was usually at Soleil.

But Roberta was partly to blame for that. Her personal life was something she kept to herself. There was a mysterious air about her—as if the critical, somewhat nagging mother-in-law and mother had an entirely different side to her that existed outside of his and Gina's presence. Now that Paul came to think of it, he had no idea what she did with herself from day to day or year to year.

Paul sat on the arm of Gina's chair and stroked her hair. She began to cry, wiping at the tears and laughing softly. "Remember that old shaggy dog joke, about life being a fountain? Well, I feel like that fountain. I can't seem to stop."

"You don't have to," Paul said gently. "Let it out."

She began to cry harder. "I just don't—I don't think we're going to find her," she said between sobs. "It's—it's been too long. Maybe we should have let Detective Duarte make it official sooner. Maybe we should have told the newspapers, so people could be watching for her—"

She broke off and swallowed over and over, as if there were a lump in her throat that just wouldn't go down. "They say that if you don't find someone within the first few hours, they're probably—they're probably—"

"Never mind what 'they' say," Paul interrupted,

pulling her close. "They don't know our daughter. She's a fighter. She wouldn't let anyone harm her."

"You don't know that!" Gina cried angrily. "She could be lying in a ditch somewhere! What if she's still alive but can't move because she's been injured? She could be freezing to death out there in that rain. Or Angela—"

Paul cut her off. "Don't think that. It won't help. Look."

He drew a printout of the Web site bio from his shirt pocket and handed it to her, trying to steer her in another direction. If she could find something to put her energies into, even this questionable lead, it might help. Gina had always been strong in times of emergency. In fact, if the truth were told, she was the one who had held their family together all these years, while he just went along, following her cues.

"This bio is on a Web site under Angela's name," he told her, looking at Roberta as well.

Gina dried her eyes with the already soggy Kleenex she held in her hand. Tucking it into a pocket of her robe, she took the paper and tried to read. "My contacts are blurry," she said. "Could you read it to me?"

"Of course." Paul did so, looking up now and then at their faces for a reaction.

When he had finished, Gina seemed more mystified than worried. "How did you find this?" she wanted to know.

"One of the investigators," he said vaguely.

"Oddly enough, it wasn't difficult to find. Angela still uses the name 'Angela Bradley.'"

"Let me see." Gina rubbed her eyes and reached for the paper.

"I'd like both of you to read it," Paul said. "Tell me what you think."

Gina scanned the page. "This—this is crazy," she said. "This can't be Angela."

"Give me that," Roberta said, reaching for it and pulling her reading glasses from her purse, which was beside her on the sofa. Small noises of surprise escaped her throat as she read it to herself.

"It's beyond strange," Roberta said. "It's almost as if—" She hesitated, looking at Paul.

"What? Tell me what you think, off the top of your head."

"Well, it seems to be written by Rachel, not Angela," Roberta said. "Gina?"

"I thought the same thing," Gina said. "Paul, remember that summer when Rachel came home from camp and seemed so depressed? I thought she was just going through something temporary, that maybe she'd met a boy there and didn't know how to handle it. You know how those summer romances are. I thought if she'd met someone at camp, she might be depressed because she couldn't be with him after she came home."

"Actually," an unusually calm Roberta said, "Rachel wasn't really all that interested in boys that year. I tried to tell you—"

At Gina's expression, she broke off. "This isn't the time to get into that. Suffice it to say, Rachel had something else on her mind that summer."

She looked down at the bio again. "There are ways to find out who owns a Web site. Through the server, for instance. The police could find out."

Paul and Gina both looked at her, surprised.

"Server, Mom? Since when have you been into computers?"

"I'm into all kinds of things you don't bother to know about," Roberta snapped.

"I suppose we could check with the server," Paul said. "Or rather, get Duarte to do it. They probably wouldn't give any information to us."

"I do think Mom may be right," Gina said, "that this sounds like it was written by Rachel. I mean, how could Angela have written it? She had no way of knowing what happened to Rachel that summer. I'm wondering if Rachel wrote it, and for some reason just put it under Angela's name."

"But why would she?" Paul asked. "What would she hope to gain by doing something like this?"

"I don't know," Gina said worriedly. "I just think we have to admit that we don't know our little girl as well as we thought we did."

"Putting it mildly," Roberta said.

Changing the subject, Gina asked, "Where have you been all afternoon, Paul? I thought you were coming right home after Soleil."

"I was there most of the time," he said. "It just took longer than I thought."

Gina didn't press the matter, for which he was grateful.

13

Paul called Duarte first thing the next morning and asked if he had a few minutes. "I have something I'd like to show you that I need your help with."

"Good timing," Duarte said. "I'm taking some time off, but I've got a few things to clear up first. Come on by."

"I'll be right over," Paul said. He wondered why Al was taking a vacation at such a busy time of year. He felt disappointed, too, that the detective wouldn't be around in case he needed him. It was funny, how he'd come to depend on Al in such a short time.

At the precinct, he found the detective with his desk looking cleaner than he'd ever seen it before. There was some good-natured grousing directed his way from a couple of other cops about all the work he'd pushed onto their plates, but Al didn't seem a bit bothered by it.

"I've been holding up your end way too long," he said, catching a balled-up wad of paper that was thrown at him and tossing it back. "It's time you sniveling little kids grew up."

Paul dodged another paper projectile just in time as he sat down at Duarte's desk.

"Okay, okay, back to work," Duarte said. "If you babies didn't whine so much, you could get a hell of a lot more done."

He looked at Paul. "So, whatcha got for me?"

"Take a look at this." Paul pulled the Web site page from his coat pocket and slid it across the desk.

Duarte studied it. "I don't know a lot about computers, but Angela's name is here at the bottom, after the www. That means it's her page, right?"

"Web site, yes. Ordinarily, that would be true. But I'm not so sure about this, Al. She knows way too much about Rachel—more than Angela could ever know. Gina and I think that maybe Rachel wrote it and used Angela's name for some reason."

"Yeah? You got any idea what that reason might be?"

"None at all. We talked about it last night and couldn't reach any logical conclusion. I was hoping you might have some ideas."

Duarte sighed. "You know, Paul, there might not be anything logical about this at all. Sometimes, when you're dealing with troubled people, like this Angela person, you have to think outside the box. One thing that occurs to me is that maybe the information on this Web site isn't the important thing. Maybe it's the person who was meant to read the Web site."

"Meaning, Angela—or Rachel?"

"Neither one. Meaning you, Paul. Maybe we were intended to find this site when we started looking for Angela. Maybe it's not coincidence you found it, and maybe there's some sort of message here for you. The thing you gotta ask yourself is, who would want to send you this message? And what the hell *is* the message?"

Duarte leaned back and stared at the ceiling, a troubled look on his face. "Anyway, that's one idea. You might come up with something else. You just gotta let your mind roam, see what it comes up with."

"Well, one thing that occurred to me is that there is a contact page on the Web site. One of those things where you click on a box, or just the word 'e-mail,' and it takes you to an e-mail page. We clicked on it, and the address was just a nickname, or whatever it's called. You know, like a CB handle—Loverboy, or Redhead. This one was Twins, with four numbers after it, then the 'at' sign and the name of the server."

Al shook his head. "You've lost me there. How do you know so much about this stuff?"

"My friend, Lacey...she's a computer whiz. She's the one who found this."

"Yeah? Well, good for her. I still haven't had a talk with her, by the way. Or your mother-in-law. I figured on doing that this afternoon. Maybe I'll go over and see the girlfriend first. Have her show me the Web site while I'm there. You say there are more of these 'pages' on it? Maybe there's a clue somewhere."

"She wrote about her love of antiques on one page. Then this bio, and the e-mail page. I don't remember anything else. But then, I wasn't looking at much, after I saw the bio. My mother-in-law seems to know something about computers, and she says you can find out from the server who it is that owns the site.''

"Sure, that much I do know. I'll ask one of the guys to get it started.''

"Thanks. I'm sorry to drop this in your lap, especially since you're taking time off.''

"Hang on,'' Al said. He went to talk in an undertone to a cop two desks behind him. Then he motioned Paul over. "This is Detective Hal Barnes,'' he said. "He's gonna follow up on the Web site, find out who owns it. He'll call you when he has the information.''

"Thanks,'' Paul said, extending a hand. "I appreciate your help.''

"Al tells me it's your little girl who's missing,'' Detective Barnes said, adding, "I saw the APB. Let me know if you need anything else. I'll do whatever I can to help.''

"I guess she's not really my *little* girl,'' Paul said, feeling both sad and embarrassed. "Rachel is twenty-one. But she's missing. Her mother and I are very worried about her.''

"I've got a kid of my own,'' Detective Barnes said, nodding. "Eighteen. When they're in trouble, they're always our 'little kids' again. Funny how that works. Funny—and scary.''

Paul nodded his agreement.

"I'll bring you up to speed on the case when I get back this afternoon,'' Al said to Barnes. He motioned to Paul. "Come walk with me. We'll grab a hot dog somewhere.''

As they went down the hall together, he said, "Like Hal mentioned, if you need anything else along those lines, let him know. Meanwhile, you and I will be doing the real work."

"The real work?" Paul turned to him, bewildered.

"Yeah, well, the lieutenant's been complaining about me being out so much. He said I couldn't spend so much time on your case. The FBI's on it now, and Rachel's twenty-one, after all. Like you said yourself back there, she's not a kid. For all anybody knows, she could have taken off on her own and she's perfectly happy somewhere. Lieutenant says there are more important cases hanging fire while I'm spinning my wheels on this."

"I don't get it," Paul said. "If you can't work on the case…"

"Well, I figure what the lieutenant doesn't know won't hurt him. And if I'm on leave, he won't know what the hell I'm doing." He grinned at Paul.

"Al, you'd do that? Take a leave to help us out?"

"Why not?" Duarte said, shrugging. "God knows I've got plenty of time coming to me. I haven't taken a real vacation since L.B.J. was in the White House."

"L.B.J.?" Paul smiled.

"Well, maybe Reagan. Seems like I've never had time off. My life's been all about work. Which, in case you haven't guessed, is why my wife left me."

"You said you still see your son, though."

"Not as much as I'd like. See, back when he was born, I didn't know what I was missing. I'd come home from work and he'd be in bed, and the next morning I'd be gone before he woke up. I was either missing in action or too tired to feed or change him at night, any of that daddy stuff. I figured that was my wife's job. So it wasn't like I ever really knew him, you know?''

''Yes. I know.'' Paul thought back to all the trips he'd taken around the world when the twins were little, looking for antiques to establish his business. He did do his best to spend time with them when he was home, but Gina bore the full brunt of responsibility when he was gone. That was something he'd never questioned. Their ''jobs'' had seemed clear-cut.

And, like Al, the end result was that he didn't get very close to the girls those first couple of years. It wasn't until they turned two or three and Angela began to seek him out that he started to feel like a real father. She was always at him. ''Daddy, do this, do that.'' And she was so irrepressible, he couldn't resist.

There were times when he wondered if he would ever have become a real father to his children if it hadn't been for Angela, pushing him all the time, not letting him off the hook. Now, looking back, he realized how left out Rachel must have felt.

''Paul?''

They were at the vending truck outside, and Duarte was asking him something.

''Sorry,'' he said. ''I was drifting.''

''Well, don't drift so far you lose sight of shore,''

Al warned. But he smiled. "I wanted to know if you want everything on yours."

"On what?"

"Your *hot dog*," Al said, rolling his eyes. "Lunch. I'm paying."

"Sure, I'll take everything. In fact, I'll fix it myself, thanks," he said to the vendor. "Al, did I hear you right back there? Were you saying what I think you were saying?"

"That I plan to spend the next three weeks—or hopefully less, if things go well—finding that little gal of yours? Hell, yes. I'll be on vacation. What else will I have to do?"

Paul concentrated on taking his hot dog and piling it high with condiments. He didn't look at Al, and hoped the detective wouldn't see the grateful tears in his eyes. Damn, it was annoying how close he was to breaking down these days.

"I don't know how to thank you," he said.

"Not to worry," Al responded promptly. "I know just the thing. Buy Old Lazybones a toy. Something flashy and red."

"Let me guess," Paul said. "Old Lazybones is your cat?"

"Yeah. She punishes me something fierce when I'm gone too long."

"Really?" Paul, who was more of a dog man, said. "Cats do that?"

"Every time. Well, she learned it from my wife. And the worst of it is, I can't divorce Old Lazybones."

14

Duarte left Paul at his car in the parking lot, after they'd finished their lunch. He was already burping his up. He reached into his pocket for a Tums as he walked down the thickly carpeted hallway to Apartment 803 in one of Seattle's best high-rise condo buildings.

Pretty nice digs, he thought to himself. Wonder what makes a woman worth all this? Or was it just that Paul Bradley had so much money, he couldn't resist sharing it?

Either way, he had a feeling this little arrangement was nearing its end. Bradley was too decent a guy to keep carrying on this way, especially under the present circumstances.

He rang the bell and listened for footsteps crossing the room inside but didn't hear a thing. Good construction, he thought. Or she's not wearing shoes.

He couldn't stop thinking like that—figuring things out as he went along. Most cops he knew did the same thing. It was a trick they learned early on, so as not to be taken by surprise under any circumstances.

He knew, for instance, when she was on the other side of the door, looking through the security eye. He was careful to stand in front of it and hold his badge up where she could see it. In his experience, people got nervous if you stood off to the side, even a little, and the subsequent interview could go downhill from there, because they never quite trusted you.

The doorknob turned and the door opened wide. "Detective Duarte?" Lacey said, extending a hand. "Nice to meet you! Paul's told me a lot about you."

He shook her hand, noting how soft and white it was. "Thanks for making time to see me, Ms. Allison."

He had to look up, she was so tall. And with that outfit on—the black workout tights and bare midriff sweater—she looked as long and slender as a vanilla pod.

Yikes. He hadn't thought of a woman in terms of food in years. In his heyday, that was a sure sign his appetite was on the point of rampage.

"Oh, please, call me Lacey." She smiled. "C'mon in. You say you want to see that Web site I found?"

"Right," Al said, though seeing the Web site was only an excuse to get his foot in the door and see what Paul Bradley's squeeze was all about. "I thought there might be some clue there that's been overlooked."

She led him over to the computer desk and pulled up a black-and-white zebra-striped chair. Duarte noted how different the rest of the room was from the house Paul Bradley shared with his wife. He must have set it up this way on purpose, to strike a line of delineation.

"Have a seat, Detective," Lacey said. "After you called about coming over, I brought the site up for you."

Duarte looked askance at the furry black-and-white chair, but figured it probably wouldn't bite. He sat down facing the computer and wondered if animal prints were Paul's choice, or hers.

God knows she's young enough to be on the wild side, he thought, and then immediately reminded himself not to go down that road. Even if she weren't already taken, and even if she would entertain his interest—an unlikely scenario—this was more woman than he could ever handle.

"I showed Paul the page where she wrote about her love for antiques," Lacey said, standing behind him. "But except for the travel desk, I don't think you'll find much. It's the bio that really caught Paul's and my interest. And of course there's the e-mail page for people to contact her from the Web site. I'm sure he told you about that."

She leaned over his shoulder and moved the mouse, changing the pages so that he could see each one in turn. As Lacey had said, the travel desk that had been sent to Paul was pictured on the Antiques page, as if to say *Yes, it was me. I sent it to you.*

Angela—or Rachel—must have been pretty sure Paul would eventually see this, Duarte thought. What if Lacey hadn't come across it? Was there anyone else in Paul's family who was familiar with Web sites?

Someone who might have been expected to find it and bring it to Paul's attention?

The grandmother. Roberta Evans, the one he hadn't talked to yet. She was the one who'd told Paul that the police could get the server to turn over the name of the owner of the site.

"Did you by any chance send her an e-mail?" Duarte asked, looking at that page.

The green eyes widened. "You mean Angela? Me, send her an e-mail? Heavens, no. It's not really my place to do that. Besides, what would I say to her?"

Duarte shrugged. "Maybe, 'Your father is looking for you'?"

"Oh." She shook her hair back. "I...I guess I never even thought of doing that."

"What about Paul, when he was here and you showed him the Web site? Did he send her an e-mail?"

"Come to think of it, no. Why do you ask?"

"Well, if you or he had sent one, you might have gotten an answer from her by now. That could have been a real big help."

"You're right, of course," Lacey said, frowning. "How stupid of me to not even consider that. Do you think I should send one now?"

"If you wouldn't mind," Duarte said. "I'd do it myself, but I'm all thumbs when it comes to typing."

Lacey leaned farther over his shoulder, saying, "No problem." He watched her slender white fingers on the keys as she tapped out a message. *Dear Angela,*

Please let me know where you are. She signed it simply, *Paul.*

Pausing, she turned to Duarte. "Is that enough, do you think?"

"That should do it," he answered, trying not to react to her closeness and the fresh, clean scent of her perfume.

"By the way," he said, "did you ever meet Rachel?"

"No, I never did. From everything Paul says, though, she's a wonderful girl."

"It's a shame about this other kid, though," Duarte said. "Angela, I mean. He told you what happened to her?"

"Yes. I can't even begin to imagine the pain Paul's been in all these years. Gina, too, of course."

She clicked on the button that sent the e-mail. Despite himself, her perfume did a number on Duarte that he hadn't felt for a long time. He wondered if she noticed that he'd expanded a bit since sitting down here, but she seemed perfectly nonchalant as she told him, "There, it's done. Now all we have to do is see if she sends us an answer."

She turned to him and laid a cool hand on his forehead. "Detective, are you all right? You seem a bit flushed. Paul's always complaining that I've got it too hot in here."

I'll bet he is, Duarte thought. That doesn't have anything to do with the thermostat, though. *Down, boy. And holy crap—who knew you were even still alive?*

"I'm fine," he said aloud as she touched his cheek with the back of her hand. The hand was cool, yet he felt burnt to a crisp, as if he'd been standing in water and a bare electric wire had fallen and wrapped itself around him, frying him from head to toe.

"So," he said, clearing his throat and moving back from her hand, "this is it? There's no address for her or anything?"

"Well, no, people don't usually put their addresses on a personal Web page. The whole point, usually, is to be able to say what you want to say without anyone knowing how to reach you. There are a lot of weirdos out there, you know. Some of them might take issue with some point you're trying to make. You wouldn't want them coming to your door."

Somehow, Al found the strength to push back from the computer and get to his feet, but not without brushing up against Lacey Allison's left breast. Her sweater was made of some kind of furry stuff—cashmere, he guessed. Suddenly he was getting all weak again.

Weak in the head, he told himself firmly. *Get this over with and get the hell out.* He still had to meet with the mother-in-law, and God help him if she didn't turn out to be some frumpy old lady with no more sex appeal than a turnip.

"About that anonymity thing, though," he said, "there really isn't as much as people think. Just about any law enforcement agency is able to get the Web site owner's home address and phone number from the server."

"Really?" Lacey said, the green eyes widening again. "They can do that? Good grief! Well, I'll have to be very careful not to do anything illegal if I ever have a site of my own! Either that, or I'll need friends in high places."

She touched his arm and smiled. *Like you,* the gesture seemed to say, but only in a teasing way.

Al smiled back. The thought occurred to him that Paul's girlfriend, who knew so much about computers, might have put this Web site together herself. He'd known women who, for various twisted reasons, did things like that in the middle of an investigation. They would go to extraordinary and sometimes criminal lengths to show how much they knew and how much help they could be, in the hope that this would enhance their importance to the men in their lives. In doing so, they often set up problems, just to be able to solve them—like some super-woman detective who knew more than the police or the FBI.

Lacey, however, had revealed no tendencies in that direction. From what Paul said, she had found the site the way anyone with some computer skills might have—by searching Angela's name. And she hadn't gone any further than that. No e-mail to Angela, no suggestions for finding her...

No. Lacey Allison, in short, was beautiful, sexy and just a bit of a tease. But other than that, she seemed to have no other agenda but to be honestly helpful.

Which, for Paul Bradley's sake, Al had to be grateful.

He had other questions he had meant to ask her, but after the many changes his body had just been through, he couldn't remember them now. Luckily, he'd written them down.

He took a notepad out of his pocket while she sat at one end of her long white sofa, pushing aside a small bag from a local pet store, a potato chip bag and some magazines. Opening the notebook, he read practically verbatim the questions he'd written down, in order to get them over with as quickly as possible.

"Do you know of anyone who might have wanted to harm Rachel Bradley? Any friends of the Bradleys? Relatives? Before this, has Paul Bradley ever told you anything about Rachel that would lead you to believe she was in danger—or that she might have some reason to disappear on her own?"

To all of his questions, Lacey simply shook her head and smiled. "I wish I could have been more help," she said as she stood. Taking his arm, she led him to the door. "If there's anything else, please feel free to call or come over. Anytime."

She knows what she's done to me, he thought. And she's getting a kick out of it.

Once outside the door, he leaned against the wall to gather his composure, then let out a deep sigh of relief.

Not that Lacey Allison had really meant anything by all that laying on of hands and stuff. A lot of women were like that, he knew, especially when they were already secure in a relationship with a man. It was all just a game with them—a test, to see if they still "had it." Besides, what would somebody like her want with an over-the-hill guy like him?

Al shook his head to clear it. *Paul Bradley sure has his hands full with that one. Gina Bradley is one of the nicest women I've ever met. Talented, too. Even so, Lacey Allison's kind of body heat has to be a hard thing to give up.*

If he'd expected to be able to relax while interviewing Roberta Evans, Al soon realized he was dreaming. Roberta, Paul had told him, was sixty, which made her a few years older than him. But unlike the tired old lump he'd become, she was one hot firecracker. If she didn't have Lacey's brazenness, she made up for it with a sharp intelligence that made Duarte wonder if her daughter and Paul really knew her. Sometimes parents were put in little mental compartments labeled Good Cook, Reliable Baby-sitter, Can Be Counted On To Show Up In Times Of Trouble. Or, as Paul had said, "Can Be Counted On To Stir Up Trouble."

Roberta Evans, he thought, might be all that. But she was also something else—and he for one couldn't wait to find out just what that something else really was. The only thing he knew for sure was that she wasn't the woman she pretended to be. No woman this side of Broadway could be so incredibly odd. Could she?

Paul's mother-in-law wore a long caftan of some sort of bright reddish-purple material, with gold braid trim on the neckline and sleeves. Once she had seated him on an overstuffed orange sofa with a cup of espresso in a small gold-rimmed cup, she took up pacing from one end of the living room to another and talking nonstop. She continually raised a long, silver cigarette holder to her lips and lowered it just as quickly. There was no cigarette in it, and thus no smoke emanated from it. Her hair was dark red and full, in tight curls down to her shoulders. Her lipstick was green—although it seemed to change to purple and back to green again, right before his eyes—and her cheekbones were sharp and tinged with a blush that matched her red hair.

Al was mesmerized. He sat facing a broad window with a knockout view of Gig Harbor, but after the first second or so, he hadn't even looked at the view. The show in this room was worth more than the price of the surrounding real estate.

What the heck was this woman hiding?

Something, he was sure of that. Beneath the fascinating camouflage lay all kinds of stories she'd rather not let anyone know. Even her conversation was shrouded, revealing little of the kind of information Duarte was seeking. Within five minutes he'd heard more about the history of Gig Harbor than he'd ever known or wanted to know. He knew that she didn't think much of the Gig Harbor area law enforcement, but he wasn't certain what her complaint was. He knew that her daughter, Gina, didn't want to hear her opinion about the disappearance of her granddaughter, and that this was nothing new. Gina and Paul, it seemed, never wanted to hear her opinion about anything.

It was she, Roberta told him, who knew enough about computers to tell them to find out who owned that Web site, and she who'd had people looking for Rachel long before Paul and Gina had been willing to make her disappearance known to the public.

It was at this point that Al snapped to and stopped her.

"You told people that Rachel was gone?"

"Well, of course I did! One does not sit around and do nothing when a child is lost."

"It wasn't my impression that any of us were sitting around doing nothing," Al said with an edge.

"And how would I know that, when no one tells me anything?" Roberta argued, standing in front of him with her arms crossed.

"Who did you tell about Rachel's disappearance?" Al asked irritably. "Didn't it occur to you that telling the wrong people might harm Rachel in some way?"

Roberta's eyes flashed. "I would never do anything to harm that child."

"I'm sure you wouldn't, knowingly," Al countered. "But you just said yourself that no one tells you anything."

Within moments, her demeanor changed. "When I said no one, I meant Gina and Paul," she said quietly. "I did not mean that I don't have my own... connections."

"And by connections, you'd be talking about—?"

Al broke off midsentence as a thought struck him. "Ms. Evans, have you been in touch with Angela?"

"Now, what on earth makes you think that?" Roberta said.

"Look," Al said worriedly, "I know you had a hard time accepting it when Angela was sent back to Saint Sympatica's."

"Did Paul tell you that?" she snapped, glaring.

"No, Gina told me, the other night. We talked in her kitchen when we were waiting for Paul to return from Saint Sympatica's. She told me how close you were to Angela, and how much you disapproved of her having been sent away."

"It—it wasn't that I thought she should stay here," Roberta said. "It was the way they did it, overnight, and without ever letting me see her again."

She sat in the chair across from him, the few lines in her face deepening. "I don't expect you to understand that."

"No, I don't imagine anyone could fully understand the pain you've been in," Al said gently. "And you know, it's understandable too that if Angela has come back to Seattle, you'd want to be in touch with her. Make up for lost time, so to speak."

If he thought he could draw her out—get her to confide in him about whether she knew where Angela was, or if she'd talked to Angela about Rachel—Al had underestimated Roberta Evans.

Roberta's mouth trembled and tears filled her eyes. The proud, haughty woman who had met him at the

door less than a half hour ago seemed to crumple before him now. She covered her eyes with her hands
and shook her head back and forth. When she looked
up again, she said, "I like to think I can handle things
better than anyone else. I'm the mother, after all. I
should be able to handle things. But I can't anymore.
I don't have it in me."

The tears in her eyes spilled down her cheeks as she
pleaded with him. "Just find Rachel, Detective Duarte.
Find her and bring her home to us...before it's too
late."

Before it's too late. Her words shook him, but after
that he couldn't get anything out of her. Roberta
Evans—who, at first blush, had seemed wacky but
brave, peculiar but intelligent—had become in a few
short minutes a sad, frightened woman beyond her
prime...someone whose power to "handle things"
had been whittled down over the years, until there was
nothing left now but a shell of a woman who trembled
in fear.

God, what a gal! Duarte thought, shaking his head
as he drove back to Seattle. What an act! When this
was all over, he'd have to have a talk with Roberta
Evans. With her chameleon skills, she'd make a splen-
did undercover cop.

The only downside, however, was that she'd been
too good, even for him. He hadn't gotten anything out
of her that was useful.

Or had he? As he thought of the day's events, there
was something nagging at him, something that he'd

put away in some corner of his mind to remember later. But then he'd been distracted. And now he didn't know if he'd gotten it from Roberta—or Lacey.

The Bradleys went to bed early that night, knowing that the police and highway patrol were now looking for Rachel all over Washington. Duarte had also notified authorities in Oregon and California. Paul and Gina didn't expect to sleep, but their nerves were wearing thin, and Al had warned them that if they didn't get some rest it would be that much more difficult to handle what might come.

Paul didn't want to think about "what might come", but of course he knew what Duarte meant. Just the thought of it made him ill, filled him with dread. Still, he knew they had to be prepared. To let it blindside them would almost assuredly break the few fragile bonds that remained between himself and his wife.

He'd seen it happen over and over. A couple's child died, either from natural causes, accident or murder, and the marriage ended. As if the death of a child wasn't enough to handle, the parents had to deal with media hounds, or well-meaning people who gathered around to lend support but who couldn't keep the fear out of their eyes. *What if this happens to me,* they seemed to be thinking.

Paul knew this because, several times, he had been one of those people who stepped forward to support someone else in their grief. Annie, for instance, had lost her mother a few months ago. He remembered the flat, helpless words he had used when he hugged her and patted her back. It was the only thing he knew to do, but even as he did it he felt that it wasn't enough. The instinct was to say "this will pass," and "time heals all wounds," and all the other platitudes he'd learned over the years in similar circumstances. But people didn't want to hear that, he knew. When it came right down to it, the hug was enough, and a gentle "I'm sorry." Why had he thought, in Annie's case, that he'd had to do or say something more?

In bed that night, Gina tossed and turned, unable to sleep. Paul managed to drift off by midnight, only to have a nightmare. Rachel was there, dressed in a ghostly-white dress with a scarlet sash. She had fallen into a half-frozen lake and was trapped beneath the ice. Her hands beat against the ice as if to break it, to set herself free.

Why don't you save me? she seemed to be crying, though her lips moved silently. Paul tried to reach her, but the ice broke under his feet and the cold dark waters sucked at him, dragging him over the edge. At the last minute he managed to grab Rachel's hand, and he realized with a deep profusion of sadness that they would drown there together. He had been too late, just as he always was. Too late to keep the vows, too late to save anyone, ever.

Then, suddenly, Gina was behind him on the ice, grabbing for him, hanging on for dear life, much the same way she'd hung on to him when they first met and he would take her up into the mountains on his motorcycle.

He hadn't thought of that motorcycle in years. Or of the time the back wheel had hit a patch of oil on a narrow road, and had begun to slide out from under them. With a hill on one side and a steep cliff on the other, Gina had screamed and tightened her grasp around his waist. A close call, but it had turned out all right. Shaking, they had both dismounted. Standing side by side, they looked down the cliff to its bottom, some three hundred feet below. Though he was white and shaky at what might have been, Paul had taken Gina into his arms and promised her that from that moment on he would never let her come to harm. He would take care of her. Always.

"Always?" she had asked, trembling like a small frightened bird in his arms.

"Always," he had said. "I swear, Gina. I will never let you down."

Paul woke with that promise on his lips. He lay on his back staring at the thin, fluttery shadows of a tree on the bedroom ceiling.

How many vows had he broken? Not just the big one, but all the little ones that a marriage is based on. The ones that you promise each other in the heat of nightly passion and then forget in the long, cold reality of endless passing days.

He didn't know he had drifted off until he felt Gina shaking him, pulling at his arm. In the strange world of half sleep he was back in the nightmare—except that it wasn't a nightmare now. Gina was saving him from falling through the ice. Not only him, but Rachel, too. And as he woke fully, he knew with a cold and certain finality that Gina was the only one who *could* save him from the mess he'd made of his life.

"Someone's at the door," she was saying. She slid from the bed and pulled on her bathrobe, the faded and worn red one that she wore every day until the last moment before dressing for work.

Paul sprang from the bed, pulling on his jeans and a sweater. The doorbell continued to ring.

"Let me get it," Paul said. "It might be reporters." They had turned the answering machine on while they slept, because ever since the APB had gone out on Rachel they'd been inundated by calls from reporters. Rachel had their cell phone numbers, and even though she had never answered their attempts to call her, they had kept their phones by the bed. Al had their numbers, too, and he had promised to let them know if there was any news about Rachel.

Paul hurried downstairs, cursing himself for not having a security eye put into the front door. Releasing the dead bolt, he held the door slightly ajar without taking off the chain and asked, "Who is it?"

"Duarte," he heard. "I've got something for you."

Paul slipped the chain off and opened the door farther. "Al?" For the first time he looked at his watch. It was 3:14 a.m. "Do you know what time it is?"

The question was never answered, and Paul felt shockwaves run through him as Rachel stepped into view.

15

"Hi, Dad," Rachel said coolly. "You really didn't have to send the gendarmes after me. I'm perfectly okay."

Stunned, he reached for her, dragging her into his arms. "Rachel, thank God! We thought—we didn't know what to think. We've been so worried!"

"Gina," he called out, "it's Rachel!" He held her back a bit to look at her. "Are you all right? Where have you been?"

Gina came running down the stairs. "Oh, thank God. Thank God." She ran forward, enveloping Rachel in her arms. "Never mind all that. Just tell us you're okay." Tears flowed down her face and into Rachel's hair.

"I went to visit a friend in Spokane," Rachel said, pulling away. "Geez, you guys. I left you a note."

"You left a note?" Gina said, half laughing and half crying. She shook her head. "We never saw a note."

"Spokane?" Paul said. "Who were you visiting there? I didn't even know you had a friend in Spokane."

He looked at Duarte, as if for an answer.

"The Spokane PD found her hanging around a convenience store. They recognized her from the APB, took her in to the precinct and called. I went and got her."

"I don't understand," Paul said. "Why didn't you let us know?"

"Because I told him not to!" Rachel snapped. "You think I wanted Mommy and Daddy showing up at the police station like I was some little kid? I'm a grown woman, Dad—even if you and Mom don't want to treat me that way!"

Duarte rolled his eyes and shrugged. "I talked to her on the phone from downtown. Told her I was gonna call her folks and let them know she was all right. Well, she said she'd take off again if I did that. The officers who picked her up said she didn't have a car or any money, and I didn't want her on the street, so I agreed to go and get her."

"Some favor," Rachel complained.

"Yeah, well, I said I'd come and get her, but only if she let me bring her here."

"You didn't want to come home?" Paul asked.

Rachel didn't answer.

"Honey, I'm trying to understand. What were you doing hanging around a convenience store in Spokane?"

Rachel made an irritated noise. "You don't have to make it sound like I was trying to rob the place, for heaven's sake!" She had drawn away from Gina and planted her hands on her hips. "My car got stolen, and so did my money and my cell phone. I panhandled some quarters and tried to call you from a phone booth, but the coin slot was jammed. If the cops hadn't shown up when they did, I'd have hitched a ride home.''

"Oh, thank God you didn't have to do that!" Gina said, beginning to cry again. "We've been so worried since you disappeared." She reached out to stroke Rachel's hair, but Rachel pulled away.

"Mom, don't be so dramatic! I didn't *disappear*. I told you, I was just visiting someone. Then, when I got robbed, all I wanted to do was get home."

"Well, it's about time," Paul said tightly. Now that the rush of relief from seeing her safe and sound was over, he was angry with her for frightening her mother.

"It's all right," Gina said, hugging her. "We're just glad you're back."

"It's not all right," Paul said. "You've had us worried to death. Why didn't you let us know you were going out of town? We didn't know if..." He shook his head. "Never mind."

"Honestly, you both are being so silly." Rachel laughed, shrugged out of her jacket and slung it over her shoulder as she headed for the stairs with a jaunty swing of her hips.

"Hold it," Paul said. "Don't you dare go up those stairs. You owe us an explanation, Rachel. Your mother has been worried sick."

"And that would bother you?" she asked, turning

around. "Since when do you worry about the way Mom feels?"

He heard Gina's shocked intake of breath, and for a moment, Paul almost lost control. His gut reaction was to go after Rachel and shake her. But he had never struck her, had never even given her smacks with a wooden spoon, as was the "approved" punishment in the days when Rachel and Angela were toddlers. He believed that hitting a child only taught that child to hit.

"Rachel," he said as calmly as possible, "please do *not* go upstairs. We need to talk."

"Your father's right," Gina said. "Let's go into the living room."

Rachel cast a look at Duarte. "They can't make me do anything, right?" she said. "I'm twenty-one. I can do whatever I want. Right?"

Duarte shrugged. "Sure. Anything you want. I gotta say, though, you looked pretty cold and unhappy back there in the Spokane precinct. So maybe you don't do so well, sometimes, on your own. Hell, what's it going to hurt if you do what your parents want? You're in their house, after all."

Rachel took a few steps up the stairs, then hesitated. Finally she shrugged and came back down. Throwing them all a hostile glance, she sauntered into the living room. Duarte, Paul and Gina followed. Rachel tossed her jacket onto the floor and slumped into a chair.

"I don't see what all the fuss is about," she said.

"When I'm in California, you don't know where I am and what I'm doing all the time."

"That's different," Gina said. "When you're here, it's impossible not to worry. Rachel, we even agreed, all three of us, that we would tell each other where we were at all times."

"That was a few days ago," Rachel argued, studying the toe of her boot. "I thought I didn't have to do that anymore."

Gina looked at Paul, who was staring at Rachel as if he'd never seen her before. Meeting Gina's eyes, he shook his head slightly and addressed Duarte.

"Al, can you fill us in on any of this?"

"Only thing I know—and this is just from talking to the cops at the station there—is that the manager of the store said your daughter'd been trying to hitch a ride back to Seattle with some customers. He didn't feel comfortable with her hanging around that way, and he called 911. Like I said, the guys who answered the call recognized her from the APB. They gave her a little ride to the station and had her sit there while they called Seattle. The call came through when I was at the precinct cleaning up some things before I left on vacation, and I talked to them, and then her. You know the rest."

Paul looked at Rachel, who still did not meet his eyes. He turned back to Al. "We have a lot to thank you for," he said.

"He's right," Gina added, her eyes tearing up. "Thank you so much, Al."

Duarte looked uneasy. "Yeah, well, I told you I'd do everything I could to find her for you...." He shrugged.

Paul wondered what the detective was holding back. "Al?"

But Duarte was getting up and heading for the door. "I gotta get home," he said, yawning. "It's been a long day, and Lazybones will make me pay for it."

Paul followed him into the hallway. "You must have been up all night, to make that long drive over there and back, Al. Why would you do that?"

Duarte shrugged again. "I didn't have much else to do. Besides, you've got a good kid there."

"I know that, Al. But I'm not buying her story any more than you are. At least, I'm guessing you don't buy it. There must be more to it. What aren't you telling me? Was she with someone?"

"You mean, like Angela? I didn't see her anywhere."

"But you looked?"

"Sure, I looked. That was the first thing I thought of."

"Did you ask the guy at the convenience store? Or the cops who picked her up? If they saw anyone else, I mean."

"Hell, no," Duarte said irritably. "I didn't ask anybody that. What do you think I am, a detective or something?"

Paul had to smile.

"No one saw anybody else," Al said. "Rachel was all alone."

"What about this friend she said she was visiting?"

"Well, now, that's a funny thing. I'm not sure there was a friend. Rachel wouldn't say, and it's not like she committed a crime, so we really couldn't force her to talk."

He opened the door and stepped outside. "Look, just be glad you've got her back. Don't worry too much about what she was up to. Parents can get old real fast that way."

Paul shook his head. "I don't know. I don't think I could feel any older than I do right now."

Duarte nodded and gave him a pat on the back. "Hang in," he said. "I'm sure it'll turn out okay."

"Are you?" Paul asked. "Al, do you really feel that way?"

Al hesitated. "Let's just say it'll turn out. That's the only thing we can ever be certain of, Paul. It'll turn out. Meanwhile, we sit in the question, as the Buddhists say."

Paul nodded and murmured his thanks again.

"No problem," the detective said. "Call me, okay? We still have a lot of loose ends to tie up."

"Angela," Paul said heavily.

"Or somebody," Duarte answered, going down the walk.

Closing the door, Paul turned back to find Rachel standing right behind him.

"What about Angela?" she asked.

"Well, honey, some other things happened while you were gone. It's nothing to worry about now. Let's go back into the living room."

"I'm tired," Rachel said. She walked away and headed for the stairs again.

"We haven't finished talking," Paul said.

Rachel hesitated but didn't face him. "I'm really tired, Dad."

"I can understand that," he said. "Even so, your mother and I deserve an explanation. You can't just leave without telling us and not come home until you're found by the police. Where in the name of God have you *really* been, Rachel? Why did you leave that way?"

When she turned back to him, he saw that her eyes were filled with tears. Her face was contorted from the effort of holding them back.

"What do you care?" she said softly. "What did you ever care about me?"

16

It was nearly five in the morning, and Paul and Gina were exhausted. When they were certain that Rachel was settled in, they went back to bed. Paul held Gina close. She hadn't broken down yet, but she was shaking. "I don't even know her," she said softly. "I don't even know her." Her voice, muffled against his shoulder, was thick with tears. Her face was burning up.

"Let me get you some aspirin and a cold cloth," he said.

"No! Don't leave me. I don't want to be alone."

"I'll be only a few steps away, in the bathroom. I'll be back before you know it."

But she dug her nails into his back and held him closer. "Don't go."

"Okay," he said softly. "I'll stay right here. Try to sleep, Gina. Close your eyes."

"I can't," she said. "I see terrible pictures. First there's Angela, with a knife at Rachel's throat. Then there's *blood*." Her fists tightened. "Paul, there's blood all over the place."

"It's just the season," he said reasonably, though his voice shook. "It's natural that you'd remember what happened."

"No! It's not that Christmas. It's now. It's something that's going to happen, Paul. I've felt it since Rachel walked through the door."

"Shh. Honey, everything's all right now. Rachel's home, she's okay…we're okay."

"Are we? Are we really?" she whispered.

He kissed her forehead. "Yes," he said. "Or, if we're not, we can be. We can do something about it, if we want to."

But Gina was silent, which left him unsure. Was it that she couldn't forgive him for being AWOL from his marriage, so much of the time?

Or had she just lost any feelings for him? Had she accepted what they had—or didn't have—and no longer wanted anymore?

He drew her closer and promised himself he would make things right. With that promise, he felt as if a burden had been lifted. He felt his muscles relax and his eyelids begin to grow heavy. He heard Gina mumble something, but he couldn't make it out. "Hmm?" he said, just as an earsplitting scream came from Rachel's room. He looked at Gina. Together they jumped out of bed and ran down the hall.

"What is it?" Gina cried, certain she was going to see the same scene as the one by the Christmas tree, sixteen years ago. She knew that was crazy, but even so her mind insisted that she would find blood all over Rachel, and Angela standing there with a knife in her hand.

There was no blood, but Rachel stood in the middle of her bed, screaming. Gina followed the direction of Rachel's pointed finger. A mouse skittered across the floor and ran under a Queen Anne highboy dresser.

"Oh, my God!" Gina said, patting her chest and heaving a deep sigh of relief. "Rach, it's only—" But when the mouse stuck its head out, she screamed, too, climbing onto the bed next to Rachel and pulling her nightgown above her knees.

Paul stood watching them, a fascinated expression on his face. Finally he burst out laughing. "He's only a baby," he said. "He's harmless, the poor little thing."

Rachel and Gina both gave him scathing looks. "Oh, you think he's a harmless little thing, do you?" Gina said. "Then get him!"

"Get him?" He laughed. "How am I supposed to get him?"

"I don't know, just get him!" Gina shrieked.

"Get your baseball bat, Dad!" Rachel cried. "Hurry! I don't want him going under my bed again!"

Paul couldn't stop laughing. "You want me to whack him to death?"

"Daaad! Please!"

"Paul, she's right! Get your bat. And stop laughing. This is serious."

"Serious, huh? I don't think you'd say that if you could see the two of you standing on that bed."

But he managed to contain himself long enough to

walk down the hall to his room and come back with the bat.

"I really don't see how I can 'get' him with this, but if it makes you feel better—"

The mouse ran out and came straight for Paul. Gina and Rachel screamed, and Paul yelled, *"Aaaiiiee!"* in a poor imitation of Bruce Lee as he struck out with the bat and hopped up and down at the same time. The mouse ran past him into the hall, and Gina and Rachel looked at him, their mouths open.

"You let him go!" Rachel cried.

"And what the hell was *that?*" Gina said.

"What?" Paul said.

"Yeah, Dad. What was all that hopping about?"

"I wasn't hopping," Paul said, taking a dignified stance. "I was chasing him out, and I didn't want him running up my pants."

"Running up your pants?" Gina laughed. "Why on earth would he run up your pants?"

"Well, now, I don't know," Paul said. "Anymore than I know why he'd run up your nightgown."

"Well, they do," Gina said haughtily. "Everyone knows they do."

"Run up women's nightgowns?"

"Up any kind of skirt! Right, Rachel?" She turned to her daughter, who was laughing along with her father.

"Sure, Mom. Anything you say."

There was no sleeping after that, so all three went to the kitchen and sat at the breakfast bar, drinking coffee and eating hash browns and eggs that Gina and Rachel cooked up together, while Paul made the coffee and toast.

It was almost like old times, Gina thought, looking at the two of them. Except that there was still the specter of Angela hanging over them.

And what about Paul's and her marriage? She had heard him a while ago in bed, and had mumbled her agreement that they should try to make things better. But, wide-awake now, she wondered if it were really possible. Should she tell him about her affair with Julian? Would he ever be able to forgive her, if she did?

No. Paul would never understand. She had never had a moment's worry that he would be unfaithful. How could he possibly understand that his wife had come to a place in her life when she was so lonely she had looked elsewhere for love?

At least, that's the way it seemed to her now. Or was loneliness only a justification? In her heart, she knew she loved many things about Julian, and she knew he truly cared for her. She could never bring herself to be sorry that she'd met him.

She could, however, be sorry for her unfaithfulness. Further, she knew she could never leave her family for Julian. And since that was so, she should end it immediately. It was the only thing to do.

An hour later, Rachel stood in her shower, taking more time than usual. The night before, she had been so tired from the trip home, she'd fallen into bed without even brushing her teeth. Then there had been the mouse-capade—which had at least eased some of the tensions in the house.

It seemed as if she'd been walking a tightrope for ages. First, Angela calling, then grabbing her off the street and taking her to that miserable cabin.

She turned the cold water faucet on, hoping it would wake up her mind, help her to think straight about the thing she had to do. But aside from making her shiver and jump out of the shower, reaching blindly for a towel, it had little effect on her.

She wrapped herself in the towel and sat on the edge of the tub, replaying in her mind how quickly things had gone bad. And how much worse they were going to get.

When Angela had forced her to get out of the Mustang on the outskirts of Spokane, she had never been so afraid in her life. She had made her way to the convenience store as quickly as possible. But the phone booth had been vandalized, and the manager wouldn't let her call from the phone inside.

Damn Angela, for taking her cell phone and her tote bag with her money in it, as well as her car! She could have left her with *something*. Anything. How did she expect her to—

But Angela had wanted her to thumb a ride; her story would be more believable that way.

"Or, you could get your beloved daddy to come for you," she had said. "He'll love it, Rach. By now, he must believe that you're in a ditch somewhere, dead. He'll be thrilled to hear from you.''

Rachel could have told her that her parents were almost never home, but she didn't. And she couldn't call her grandmother. Roberta had something going on, something she didn't talk about. She had her own life. All Rachel knew was that the one person she'd always turned to was her grandmother—and for that very reason, asking her to go out at night to wire money for bus fare would be asking too much. Rachel just couldn't do it. She was a big girl, and she had gotten herself into this. She had to stand on her own two feet.

She had begun stopping people as they left the convenience store. ''Are you going to Seattle?'' she had asked, over and over, like some of the homeless kids she'd seen on the streets of Seattle. Remembering the kinds of warnings she'd grown up with, she approached only couples and women for rides. Given her luck lately, getting into a car with a strange man would probably only make things worse.

As if they could possibly get worse.

No one was headed west, however, and after she'd stood outside the convenience store for a couple of hours, shivering and squeezing up tight against the window to escape the driving rain, she was ready to give up and call her grandmother after all. The weather in Seattle had been mild the day she left to meet Angela, and she'd worn only a thin jacket with a sweater beneath. The jacket barely kept the wind out here in

Spokane, and her hope faded each time someone shook their head. "Sorry, I'm heading east."

Then, suddenly, a police car had swooped down on her. Two cops jumped out and came toward her. For an eternal minute, Rachel stood frozen in space, her hands half-raised and her blood so cold she thought there must be icicles hanging from her arms.

What could they possibly want from her? She hadn't done anything. Not yet. There was no way they could know—

But the cops had only smiled, asked for her ID, which she didn't have, and told her this was no night to be out on the streets.

Besides, they said, her mom and dad were worried about her. There was an APB out on her, in fact. That was how they'd recognized her.

A wave of relief swept over Rachel. They were here to help, not arrest her. Thank God. The cops put her in the squad car and turned the heater up high so she could get warm. One of them went into the store and got her a cup of coffee and a hot dog.

"Here, this should help," he said. He was friendly and cute, and she thought how bizarre things were now; at one time, she might have flirted a little with him. Now she just had to be careful not to let anything slip about Angela.

The cop, Officer Pete Lopez, told her that the Seattle police had put the APB out on her. Her parents were terrified that something had happened to her. They wanted her found and brought home.

His partner wasn't quite so easygoing. He kept asking her questions, and she was certain he was suspicious of her vague answers.

So she told him the story she and Angela had practiced—that she'd been visiting a friend in Spokane and was on her way home when her car, her money and her cell phone were stolen.

The "good cop," as she came to think of him, said that since she was twenty-one, of course, she'd broken no law in leaving home without word. Would she please come to the station with them, though, until her parents were notified? He'd like to make sure she stayed safe.

Rachel almost refused. Being around cops now was the last thing she needed. But she had to be realistic. This might be her only chance to get home tonight—and it had started to snow.

So she'd gone with the cops and stayed dry, at least, while they tried to reach her parents at the home number she'd given them. The answering machine, however, was the only response they got. Maybe she should have told them, "Don't expect too much. They really don't care. They just have to pretend to." But that sounded self-pitying, even to her. In the end, the police had simply called the Seattle police.

Finally, after several hours, during which they put her in a holding cell at her request, so she could lie down on a cot and rest, Al Duarte had arrived to pick her up.

At the beginning of the drive home, Al tried to tell

her that her parents were in bad shape. Sick from worry. As if he felt he needed to make excuses for them. "If you're planning on disappearing again, I want to be able to warn them," he had said. "Nobody should go through the kind of hell you've just put them through."

Rachel had stolen a sideways look. Duarte's face, in the light of the dash, seemed cold and angry. There were tight lines around his mouth and something about his eyes was all wrong. He wasn't at all like the nice, friendly cop she'd met at the precinct in Seattle.

They were barely into the long drive over the Cascades to Seattle when the snow turned to a freezing rain, making the partially cleared off highway a thin, dangerous sheet of ice. Duarte had gripped the wheel and cussed every time they began to swerve to the side of the road, but that didn't seem to slow him down. The only good thing about that hair-raising drive was that he was so focused on the road, he stopped asking questions after the first few minutes.

Sitting beside him, Rachel had experienced moments of real fear. Why had she ever agreed to let Detective Duarte take her home, anyway? After all, she didn't know much about him, just that he was a cop. And that her parents liked him.

What kind of a reference was that?

Not that Rachel herself was known for making the best decisions. She was the one who'd agreed to meet Angela without telling anyone, after all.

It occurred to her suddenly that Al Duarte might

somehow be working with Angela. Had he found her? Been taken in by her?

Angela was beautiful. And when she wasn't threatening to kill someone, she could probably turn on the charm. Wrap any man around her little finger.

Eventually Rachel had fallen asleep in the car, and the next thing she knew they were at her home. Her parents were at the door, looking as if they'd been run over by a truck.

Rachel felt sorry for the trouble she'd caused. But that didn't change anything. She'd have to keep herself on track, not let herself be overcome by emotion. Because chances were, her parents could be feeling worse before this thing was over.

A lot worse.

17

Gina sipped her morning coffee at the desk in the living room. As hard as she tried, it was impossible to keep her mind on the work before her. Rachel was upstairs taking a shower, and Paul had gone to Soleil to take care of problems that required his attention. He wanted to finish up and get home, so he could spend some time with Rachel. On the surface, things seemed to be returning to normal—whatever "normal" was. For one thing, they hadn't even talked about when Rachel would leave to return to school. It seemed as if, without discussing it, she might have decided to stay home.

Gina hoped that was the case. She would love it if Rachel stayed here and transferred to U-Dub. They could spend time together and perhaps heal some of the old wounds. The fact that Rachel had needed to leave home like that, and her anger at being brought back, told Gina that her daughter still needed help. It would be good if she continued to see Vicky and had the opportunity to work through whatever it was that troubled her.

The thing that bothered Gina, however, was why Rachel was still "acting out," as Vicky had called it when Rachel was younger. Shouldn't her pain over losing Angela have diminished by now? Enough so, at least, that she could live a more normal life?

She heard Rachel's footsteps on the stairs—taking them slowly, not running as she once might have done. As Rachel entered the living room, her energy took over, filling up the room from corner to corner. Gina sighed quietly, setting her coffee cup down and pushing her work aside. Rachel slumped into the chair next to the Christmas tree and began fingering the tinsel, all the while staring at her mother.

"What are you looking at?" Gina asked when she couldn't stand it any longer.

"Nothing. I just wondered what you were doing today."

"Well, honey, I was going to ask you what you wanted to do."

"Were you?"

"Yes. Why? Did you think I wouldn't?"

"I don't know, Mom. I don't know anything about you anymore."

Gina took a moment to calm herself before speaking back. "I guess I could say the same about you, Rachel."

"Why?"

"Well, I still don't know why you drove all the way over to Spokane, especially with the weather the way it's been."

"I told you, I went to see a friend from school."

"You mean, a friend from Berkeley?"

"Yes."

"But why didn't you tell your father or I you were going?"

"I just thought I could get back the next morning, and it wouldn't make any difference because you thought I was spending the night at Ellen's. And I was going to do that, but then I changed my mind. And when I was in Spokane it snowed and the roads were closed, then I got robbed—"

Gina was remembering an old adage about lying—that it was best to keep the explanations short. When a person explained too much, it was almost certain to be a lie.

"Rachel, why didn't you just call from your friend's house when you first got there?"

"Why, were you worried?"

"For God's sake, of course we were! Honey, I'm trying so hard to understand. Why did you do this?"

Rachel jumped to her feet, strode over to the bay window and folded her arms, looking out. "Maybe because I got sick and tired of the two of you and your games!"

"Who? What games?"

"You know what I mean!"

"Rachel, I don't! Spit it out!"

"You and Dad! I've been trying to tell you ever since I came home. Do you think I don't know what's going on?"

"Well, if you do, you're way ahead of me," Gina

said. But she was beginning to feel queasy. Had Rachel somehow found out about her affair with Julian?

"I'm talking about the way you aren't even acting like you're married anymore. And you, Mom. You haven't even been around much. You've been up in your office most of the time since I got home. Either that, or off to Camano Island."

"Rachel, honey, we went shopping together! We cut down a Christmas tree, we went out to dinner and to the tearoom. We've spent a *lot* of time together! I even asked you to go to Camano with me once."

"Why would I bother?" Rachel said. "You wouldn't really have been with me. Your mind would be somewhere else."

Gina bit her lip to keep from snapping back. She knew that what Rachel said was true this time, but it hadn't always been this way. Since she was small, however, Rachel had always been so hard to please, like a bottomless well that could never be filled. She needed reassurance all the time, and even when Gina and Paul gave it to her, she wasn't happy. She had always needed more than anyone could possibly give.

That was one of the reasons they'd let her continue on with Victoria even as she grew older. There were times when they couldn't put money into their businesses because of the cost of psychotherapy, but they paid for it gladly, even when they weren't sure she really needed it. After all, Rachel was easygoing in most ways, certainly not trouble in the way Angela had been.

But Vicky hadn't been so sure. There were times when she had wondered if the same RAD syndrome that had left Angela without a conscience, not caring for anyone, had done the same to Rachel. Perhaps, she said, it just took a while to show itself. There was a similar syndrome, for instance, that appeared only in the teenage years. Gina forgot what she had called it.

Over the years she and Paul had learned a lot about RAD, however, and one of the things that had remained uppermost in Gina's mind was that children with RAD could be either outgoing and charming, as Angela was, or quiet and shy, like Rachel. The same symptoms of nonattachment could affect either one.

She remembered now that she had wondered about this when Rachel had returned from camp that summer when she was sixteen. She had been terribly depressed and withdrawn, but Gina had explained it away as the result of a summer crush on a boy she wouldn't be seeing again. Everything seemed all right after a while, and then, by the time Rachel left for college last year, she had seemed fine.

They had Vicky to thank for that, Gina thought. Vicky seemed to have a knack for reaching Rachel, for making her believe she was liked, even loved. Rachel had formed a bond with Vicky.

In a way, Gina thought now with a pang, she and Paul had turned their daughter over to the psychiatrist, whom they'd come to think of as a family friend. Had their actions been similar to the way they'd relinquished Angela? Rejected Rachel, much the same way they'd rejected her twin?

Gina had never thought of it that way before. She had honestly felt she was doing the best thing for Rachel. Now, looking back, she simply didn't know.

Holding back tears, she said, "Rachel, I have always loved you. I'm so sorry if you didn't know that, and if I didn't show it. You were all I had, after Angela—"

"All you had!" Rachel made a scornful sound. "You didn't love me because of *me,* but as a bad substitute for Angela. Daddy, too. He always loved her best."

"No, that's not true—" Gina began, but Rachel whirled back on her, the anger on her face contorting the lovely lines.

"Of course it's true! If it wasn't, he wouldn't still get so withdrawn every year when Christmas rolls around. He'd think of us, and have a good time with us instead!"

Gina couldn't restrain herself any longer. She was beginning to feel like a punching bag. "Rachel, I cannot do this with you anymore. Dammit, it's time you grew up!"

Rachel narrowed her eyes. "Oh, don't worry, Mother. I've grown up a lot this time home. More than you'll ever know."

Rachel left, stomping up the stairs, and Gina covered her face with her hands and sat that way for a long moment. Then she looked down at her wedding ring, twisting and turning it on her finger.

This wasn't the way it was supposed to be, she thought, all those years ago when they'd laid out their Life Plan on paper. And it wasn't Rachel's fault the way things were now, though she did have to bear part of the blame for being such a spoiler. Couldn't she ever just lay down those arms and armor, and give up the fight?

What was it she was fighting for, anyway? Herself? Or some long-lost childhood dream of a perfect family, like the ones she'd seen as a child on TV? The kind that lived together, loved together, and never had a bad day in their lives?

Of course, her attitude since arriving home last night wasn't entirely unexpected. She was cold, tired, and she'd been dragged home. She never would have admitted she'd actually been saved, and by a cop. No one would be happy under those circumstances.

The incident with the mouse had, temporarily, returned some of the humor to the house. It reminded Gina of when Rachel was a preteen, times when the three of them laughed and played like that together. When and why had things changed, so that a silly scene like last night, with the mouse, was now something unusual, to be appreciated as a gift from on high? Still, it was gravy on the real gift—her daughter's safe return.

Her prayers had been answered, and Gina understood that she had been blessed. She understood, too, from her childhood years in Catholic school, that some kind of thanks was required. A simple prayer of gratitude for something as huge as Rachel's return would not suffice. It required a great deal more. A sacrifice.

She sat and thought for a long time. Then she picked up the phone and dialed Julian's number on Camano Island. *God, let him be there. And help me do the right thing.*

"Hi," he said, his voice softening when he heard hers. "What's up?"

Gina fought back the smile that automatically came to her lips every time she heard that voice. "I need to see you," she said.

"Sure. Is something wrong? Do you want me to come down there?"

"No. I'll be at the Camano house tonight, around five. Could you come over?"

"Of course I can. Gina, what's wrong?"

"I can't talk about it over the phone," she said.

"Okay." His tone turned to one of bewilderment. "I'll see you tonight, then. Around five."

Gina lay down the phone and pressed her fingers against her eyes. "God," she whispered, "I know I've asked for a lot lately, and you've answered my prayers and then some. I haven't any right to ask for more, but it's not for me—it's for them. Let me do this in a way that Paul never has to know. That's all I ask. Don't let Paul or Rachel ever find out what I've done."

18

Rachel didn't come down for lunch, and Gina had no appetite. She forced herself to eat a banana and two saltines, washing the crumbs down at the sink with the cold dregs of her morning coffee. She had a couple of hours before she'd have to leave for Camano, and she decided to spend that time catching up on work in her upstairs office.

On her way up the stairs she checked on Rachel, to see if there was any way she could possibly patch things up. She found her in her bedroom, lying on her bed and staring at the ceiling. Her eyes were red, and Gina knew she'd been crying. On a better day she might have commented on that and tried to soothe her daughter's feelings. But something in the air told her that ignorance, this time, might be called for.

"Hi," she said. "I missed you at lunch."

No answer.

"I just want you to know I have to go to Camano later on."

"Of course you do, Mom."

Gina bit back a testy retort. "I'm only going so I can finish something up, Rachel. Something really important. That way I can be home and not have any work at all to do until you go back to school. I thought you'd like that. We can spend more time together. In fact, I've been wondering if you'd like to transfer to U-Dub and not go back to California at all.''

"Whatever," Rachel replied.

Gina gritted her teeth. "Did your father call when I was in the shower before lunch?''

"No."

"I tried to reach him at Soleil, to let him know I won't be home for dinner. I thought it might be nice if he took you out.''

"Uh-huh."

"Anyway, I left a message for him to call home.''
No answer.

"Rachel...please try to meet me halfway, at least.''
Rachel turned on her side, leaving her back to her mother.

"All right, then," Gina said tiredly. "I'll be in my office working till I have to leave. If you need me, though, don't feel as if you're interrupting. Okay?''

A muffled, "Okay."

"I won't be gone long tonight. In fact, I should finish up there by six and be home by seven.''

Gina closed the door quietly and walked down the hall to her office. Never had the hallway seemed so long, or the two rooms so distant from each other.

Rachel managed to nap in shorts spurts as she waited for her mother to leave the house. Every so often she woke up feeling that knife against her throat.

Angela's eyes were always only inches from hers, and they were cold and full of hate. Now and then she would think Angela was in the room with her, only to wake to the murmur of her mother's voice on the phone in the other room. She knew from the familiar clipped cadence that Gina was on a business call.

Finally she heard her mother open her door quietly. She kept her eyes closed and didn't move, but her mother had always known when she was awake. "I'm leaving now," Gina said softly. "I have to do a few things before I go up to Camano."

When Rachel didn't answer, Gina closed the door again. Rachel listened as the sound of her footsteps faded down the stairs. She looked at the clock on her bedside table: five after three.

As soon as she heard the Crown Vic pull out of the driveway, she got up and went to the bathroom, rinsing her face with cold water. She looked at herself in the mirror. I don't seem any older, she thought. How can that be? I feel a hundred.

She went down the hall to her mother's office and looked for the address of the house on Camano. It was in Gina's black appointment book, the one she always left at home. Rachel copied it down onto a slip of paper.

Back in her room, she sat on the edge of the bed and called her father at Soleil. She was so nervous her hands shook, and her voice was husky, as if she had a cold.

"Hi, Rach. Are you okay?"

"Sure. Where have you been?" she asked. "Mom was trying to reach you."

"I just got in from a long lunch meeting with a client," he said. "I haven't had time to call her back. What's up?"

"Mom wants to know if you'll meet her tonight at that house on Camano Island she's been working on."

"She does?" He sounded surprised. "Did she say why?"

"She says her windshield wipers aren't working. It's supposed to rain tonight, and if it does, she won't be able to drive her car home."

"Oh, okay," Paul said. "Come to think of it, I need to make a trip up there, anyway, to check on measurements for a new sideboard I just found for the Albrights."

"You have the address, then?" Rachel asked.

"Yes, I've got it right here. Where is your Mom now?"

"She just left, but she said she won't be there till five, and she plans to be ready to leave around six."

"Okay. Would you like to ride along with me, Rach? You and your mom and I could stop for dinner on the way home together."

"I...I've got something I have to do, Dad. But thanks."

"Are you sure? I don't like the idea of leaving you alone, your second night back."

"No, I'm sure. I've got plenty to do," she said.

And that's no lie, she added, but only to herself.

Her stomach was so upset she thought she might throw up, and her head felt as if someone had run a meat cleaver through it.

But she'd be okay. She had to be. She would do what she had to do.

Picking up the phone again, she dialed the private cell phone number Angela had given her. "Nobody in the world has this number," Angela had said. "Do not give it out to anyone—and I mean *anyone*."

She answered on the third ring.

"Okay," Rachel said. "Here's the deal. Mom has to go up to this house on Camano Island to do some work. It's an empty house—the owners are away. I called Dad and made sure he'd be there, too. I told him between five and six. Mom says she'll be leaving there at six."

She gave Angela the address.

Angela chuckled softly. "You've done well, little sis. Keep this up and I may even forgive you for stealing my life."

"I need my car back," Rachel said. "You said you'd drop it off here."

"Well, I couldn't very well do that while Gina was home, now, could I? How would she think it got there?"

"She's not home now," Rachel said firmly. "I want my car!"

"Okay, okay. Golly Molly, Rach, relax! I have to go out anyway. I'll drop it off in a little while."

"I need it *now*, Angela. With Mom and Dad gone,

I don't have a car to use, and I told a friend I'd be at her house by five.''

"My, oh my…cold little fish, aren't we? Going off to play, while…'' Angela's voice hardened. "I'll drive by the house in twenty minutes. Look for the car at the end of the block.''

She hung up, leaving Rachel to sit with her arms around herself, trying to get warm. When that didn't work, she went downstairs and paced back and forth in the living room, watching through the front window for the Mustang to go by. She wasn't able to relax until she saw it pass the house. Running to the hall closet, she took out her black coat and a warm knitted hat and gloves. She had already changed into a black sweater and black pants, and though her hat and gloves were pink, they would have to do. The night was supposed to be bitter cold.

On a hook next to the closet was her extra set of keys, including those for the Mustang. Rachel grabbed them and took off running down the street.

19

Al Duarte entered his apartment at approximately four o'clock that same day. It was already getting dark, which depressed him. He couldn't wait for summer to come again, and the nights when it stayed light until ten-thirty, eleven. Summers were the best time of the year in the Northwest, if for no other reason than that the days were so long. He hung his winter jacket carefully on the clothes tree in the corner of the hall, where the rain would drip onto the square of tile and not hurt the carpet.

Funny, he thought, how hard old habits die. Laura had kept after him about being neat when they were married, and even now, after all these years of living alone in this drab little apartment, he was still hearing her voice in his head: *Pick it up, Al. It's no harder to do that than dropping it on the floor. Take it to the wash, Al. Don't leave it for me to do.*

Not that Laura was a nag. The truth was, he had needed some shaping up. When they first got married, he honestly thought wives were supposed to pick up after their husbands. After all, that was the way his mother had raised him.

Laura had opened his eyes about that in short order—opened them real wide. He was thankful for that, now. If he hadn't learned to take care of himself, if he'd continued to expect her to do it, he'd be knee-deep in rubble by now. Probably wouldn't even be able to find the floor.

Al chuckled. *God, I miss that woman.* They had seemed such a great match. Made in heaven, some said.

So what had gone wrong? It wasn't another woman for him, not like Paul Bradley. And he was pretty sure Laura never wanted another man. According to Laura, they had just married too young. As the years went by, they began to think less alike, see the world and their place in it in different ways. It happened to everyone who married young, Laura said. At least, everyone she knew. It was time to move on. Create new lives for themselves.

Laura had done pretty good with that, too. Last year she had married a man she met on a cruise. The guy was an accountant for a big corporation, as different as she could get from marrying a cop. Al had been suspicious of him at first. But then, he had gotten to know the guy, and he seemed like a nice enough fellow.

As for himself, Al didn't have much energy for creating a new life. His job took just about all of it. His job, and Lazybones, his cat.

He wondered why old Lazybones hadn't been at the door waiting for him. Poor thing, she really *was* getting old. There were days when she didn't even move from the couch.

With a yawn, Al made his way down the short hall into the kitchen. It was a small apartment, befitting, he thought, a man alone. Not too much upkeep, and not too much walking back and forth. That was a blessing, given that his knees were almost shot. He didn't like to let anyone in the department know about that, because they might think he was ready to be put out to pasture. In this small space, however, he admitted to himself that his days of being a cop on active duty were probably growing short.

Which might be the best for all concerned. He'd already passed the usual retirement age, and more and more he enjoyed—if that was the right word—helping people out on a personal basis. Like the Bradleys. And that poor kid, Rachel. Maybe he'd hang out a shingle and become a private investigator. And then again, maybe he wouldn't, given that part of him would just as soon sit in the sun a while. It was something to think about, though.

In the kitchen, Al made himself a cup of instant coffee, dark and hot, the way he liked it. He thought about cooking a chop or a burger, but instead he opened a bottle of whiskey and dropped a hefty amount into the coffee. Taking a sip, he felt his muscles begin to grow warm and relax. Duarte was not a heavy drinker, and it didn't take long to cross into a space where everything was grand and nothing at all mattered except a warm drink and his cat.

Speaking of which, he looked down at Lazybones's food dish, and saw that she hadn't eaten much today. He made a noise with his tongue, calling her out from the bedroom or whatever tiny space she'd been sleeping in. "Hey, Lazy! Where are you?" He whistled softly, but she didn't come.

It crossed his mind that she might be sick. Damn! One more thing to do, if he had to take old Lazy to the vet tomorrow.

Not that he really minded. She was his child, his companion, the only one he'd had for a long time now. He figured one time around the marriage block was enough; he'd had his chance and he'd blown it. Now the best he could do was try to help out people who were in some sort of crisis. He wondered if the Bradleys would get back together when all this was over.

It didn't look good. Yesterday afternoon, before he'd gotten the call from Spokane, he'd interviewed Lacey Allison, the woman Paul Bradley was seeing. She was bright, sharp, and had a good sense of humor. Duarte could understand what Paul saw in her.

Gina Bradley, on the other hand, was carrying a heavier burden than just the disappearance of her daughter—as if that weren't enough. She was involved in something secret; he would swear to it.

But did it have anything to do with Rachel? Was she in any way to blame for Rachel's disappearance?

Duarte dropped down into his old, cushy reclining chair and stared at the blank TV screen. He hadn't bought much furniture since Laura left and took most of what they had with her. There never seemed to be enough time to shop. All he really needed was this one great chair, anyway.

It would be nice, he supposed, to watch the news on CNN. But he hadn't eaten since breakfast, and this drink was really starting to floor him. It was too much of a stretch to even reach for the television's remote.

With a frown, he wondered why he still hadn't seen Lazybones. Where the hell was she? Again he whistled for her. His lap felt empty without his old friend on it. What was wrong with her, anyway?

Sighing, he set his drink down on the end table and heaved himself out of the chair. He would find her, he was pretty sure, underneath his bed. Or sleeping on his pillow. She would stretch and yawn when he woke her, and he'd feel so glad she was okay, he'd probably just fall into bed himself, rather than disturb her any more. Like the Bradleys, when they got Rachel back.

Damn, he just couldn't get them out of his mind. Did Gina Bradley even have a clue about what her husband was up to when he didn't come home till late at night? And Paul Bradley. How long did he think he could keep his affair with the Allison woman quiet, before it all came to light and the shit hit the fan?

She would be pretty hard to give up, of course. Pretty as a picture, and with a strong urge to please. The kind he himself might have gone for when he was a callow youth, just graduating from the academy. He wasn't bad looking himself, then. But thirty-odd years of police work had taken their toll. He'd seen too much, and the things he'd seen had left him with deep furrows on his brow and crow's feet like the canals on Mars around his eyes.

Entering his bedroom, he still didn't see Lazybones. There was nothing on his bed but a mound of clothes. Had he left his room like this? Damn that drink. He couldn't remember. Still, he was certain he hadn't left things in such a mess.

A cold draft of fear touched the back of his neck, making his hair rise. *Someone's been here. Someone's been in my room.*

But why would they take clothes out of the closet? Stepping closer, he saw that the sliding door was half-open. He always closed it to keep Lazybones out of there. She left behind hairs on his shoes and the open crates that held his sweaters. Also, it was hard to reach the corners to clean in there.

Duarte's instincts—to get out of the apartment and call for backup, in the event an intruder was still in the apartment—took a back seat to his curiosity.

He reached for the closet door. But before he could open it farther, the all too familiar sound of a gun with a silencer on it reached his ears—a soft *pow, pow.* Though he didn't feel anything, Al knew that he must have been hit when he spun halfway around and fell sideways over his bed. Spots of blood bloomed on the green and white comforter. For a long moment Al lay with his head on the comforter, staring at those spots. He was going down, and he knew it. But he had to at least try. Using every bit of strength he could muster,

Al pushed himself up with his hands and tried to stand, tried to see his attacker. His limbs failed him, though, and all he could do was stumble into the open closet. He tried to catch himself on the clothes. Hangers rained down around his head—hangers, shirts, pants...

As he hit the floor he felt his life oozing away, and thought, *Oh, God, not now. Not now!* He struggled to get up, but couldn't move in any direction. Even his vision was fading.

The last thing Al saw was a feather in a corner of the closet, red and bright. Flashy. It was lying on the still, white body of Lazybones, his cat.

20

Before leaving Soleil, Paul told Daniel that he was leaving early to drive up to Camano.

"Gina asked me to give her a ride home," he said, "in case it rains. Her wipers aren't working."

"You're going to the Albright house?" Daniel asked. "Tonight?"

"Yes," Paul answered. "Why? Is there a problem here?"

"No...no, I guess not," Daniel said.

"I'd like to take another look at the house anyway," Paul told him. "Gina's work is nearly finished, and I want to make sure the pieces I've picked out for the Albrights still fit."

He looked up from his desk, studying the young man's face. Daniel seemed tired and drawn.

"Is everything all right?" he asked. "You're sure you don't need me here?"

"No...no, go ahead. As soon as we get the chance, though, I really need to talk to you about some things."

An odd young man, Paul thought later as he pointed the rental car north on I-5. Quiet, almost to the point of being secretive. But nice. Dependable, too. He hoped Daniel wasn't going to tell him he was quitting.

As a classical CD started to play, he began to remember the way it used to be with Gina, the good times they'd had working together. He really wished he'd been more forceful about telling Lacey he couldn't see her anymore. Leaving it up in the air the way he had meant he would have to go back again, try to find the words all over again.

He had already hurt so many people. He didn't want to hurt Lacey, too—not when she'd been nothing but good to him. But he had to focus on Gina now. And Rachel. He would do whatever was necessary to convince Gina that they needed to go back, remember how they had begun, the hopes and dreams they'd had.

Surely they could find that again. For Rachel's sake, if no other. They hadn't had much to go on in recent years, and that was mostly his fault, he knew. The important thing was that Gina had stuck with him. That had to mean something. It had to mean she still cared.

Slowing down along the dark road, he looked for the house he remembered from his one time here before. He and Gina had come together then, consulting with each other about the kinds of antiques the Albrights would like, and what would work best with Gina's ideas for them. That had been months ago, and he expected he would find a lot of changes since then, given all the trips Gina had made up here.

The house was where he remembered, and there

were lights on. He saw Gina's Crown Vic in the driveway. He saw another car, too, but didn't think anything of it. Gina had told him she often met with other people who were working on the house up here; that was why she could never be sure what time she'd get home.

He parked his car in the driveway and went up the three flagstone steps to the front door. Finding it unlocked, he let himself in, in case Gina was in a far corner of the house and didn't hear his knock. He smiled, remembering how much she appreciated little things like that. Anything that would save her a moment, a step, an unnecessary trip when she was tired.

He couldn't be all that bad if he remembered those kinds of things about her, could he? The kinds of intimate things that only husbands and wives learned about each other, that came with years of being together and caring for each other?

Rachel shivered on the back terrace of the Camano house. She had parked the Mustang blocks away, so that no one would know she was here. Now that her plan had become a reality, however, she was beginning to think she was crazy to have tried this.

"I want to talk to them," Angela had said. "I have a lot of questions for them, and I don't want to be interrupted."

"Why don't you just come to the house?" Rachel had countered.

"No. They've got some police detective hanging

around, looking for me. Arrange a meeting someplace away from there. Work it out, Rachel!''

When Rachel had refused, Angela had threatened her, first with that knife—and then with something worse. ''You owe me, little sis. Either you do this, or I'll tell them you were the one who tried to kill me that Christmas Eve. I'll tell them about Dr. Chase, too. You think they'll want anything to do with you after that?''

Rachel wanted to argue that they *would* still want her, that Angela was wrong. Even so, she couldn't take that chance. If her parents found out the truth about her, they would have her locked up. It wouldn't matter how much they said they really loved her. They had loved Angela more from the first, and look what had happened to her.

So Rachel had agreed, thinking that somehow Angela might show her true colors in front of her parents. And as soon as they saw how mean and vengeful she was now, they wouldn't love her anymore. It was the ghost of her they'd loved all these years, anyway, not the real Angela. Angela was the one who had stayed a child forever in their minds, a child they felt they'd abandoned.

How could I ever fight that? I can't. Unless they see it for themselves, I'll always be second best.

She just hadn't expected this all to come together so fast. When her mother had decided to come up here to Camano Island tonight, it had seemed the perfect opportunity. An empty house, away from the city where telephones rang and people like Detective Duarte might drop in without any notice.

She was shaking now, though. Maybe she *should* have told Al that Angela had kidnapped her, and what she wanted her to do. There had been plenty of time during the drive home from Spokane, and she was sure he knew she wasn't telling the truth about visiting a friend there, anyway. If she had told him, he could have gone after Angela, and she could be in jail for kidnapping by now.

But he wouldn't have believed her. No one would believe her, against someone as pretty and sure of herself as Angela. She just would have said that her sister had lied, and that Rachel was a killer.

It always came back to that.

Al had given her his cell phone number on the way home from Spokane that night. "Just in case you need to reach me in a hurry sometime," he had said. She hadn't thought much about it at the time. She could still call him, though. It wasn't too late for that.

Rachel began to panic. After what Angela had done to her, she never should have believed that all her sister wanted was to talk to her parents. She was planning something bad, Rachel was sure of it.

Angela was right about me. I'm stupid. I should have taken more time to think about what I was doing. I just thought I was smart, getting this over with so I wouldn't have to bother with her ever again. That's me, all right. Stupid.

She felt dizzy, sick. Her mind wasn't working right,

and it hadn't been all day. There were times when she had wanted to tell her mother she loved her and was sorry for causing so much trouble. But there were times, too, when she felt as if she were falling, as if the sky were pressing down and might crush her. Nothing made sense when that happened. She barely even remembered who she was.

Now and then, though, her mind would clear. Like now. She knew what she had to do.

Rachel felt for her cell phone. It had been on the seat of the Mustang, and she'd stuck it into her jacket pocket earlier, out of habit. What was that number Al had given her? Something easy, like four numbers the same. Or, no—3-4-5-0. That was it. But what was the prefix?

She remembered it, she thought, but then the balloon drifted away. That was the way she remembered numbers; she put them on bright red balloons. But the Duarte balloon kept floating in front of her, then bobbing away. Each time it came close she would see one number. Then another. But where were the rest? *Where the hell were they?*

Suddenly, the string on the balloon was in her hand, and the numbers were there—all three. Rachel opened the cell phone and turned it on. No one was here yet; her mother hadn't even arrived. There was still time.

She crept across the terrace and down the five steps to the strip of grass between the house and water. If anyone came, they wouldn't hear her or know she was there.

Punching in the number, she waited as the phone rang. Her stomach clutched. *C'mon, Al! Where are you?*

Or did she have the number wrong, after all?

Just as she was about to give up, Al's answering machine clicked in. Rachel wasn't sure whether to be relieved or afraid when she heard his voice. What could he do, anyway? By the time he got her message and got up here, her mom and dad would be gone. Angela, too. And she, Rachel, would have been even more stupid for telling him anything.

But what if she kept it vague? Something she could always brush off later with some kind of explanation?

With a voice that shook, she said quickly, "Detective Duarte? It's me—Rachel. You said I could call. I...I'm on Camano Island, and my mom and dad are supposed to be here soon." She remembered to give the address, and the time of her call. "We'll only be here about an hour, and I know you might not get this message in time. I...I just think they might need some help."

Jabbing the end button, she stood there, shaking. The phone felt like a snake in her hand. Had she done the right thing? The sky came down on her again. This time she pushed it back, cussing at it silently. Dammit, leave me alone! Leave me alone!

It seemed to take all of her strength to think straight again.

A light went on in the house. Rachel watched as more lights came on from room to room. Some of it fell onto the terrace and strip of lawn, just next to where she stood. It illuminated the grass and the edge of the Sound.

She could see now that the room closest to the terrace was a living room, and she realized that the back of the house, facing the water, was really the front. Her mother had told her once that most beach houses were made this way, to take advantage of the view.

In the fringes of that beam of light, she made her way back up onto the terrace, making sure to stay in shadows. The living room seemed empty, and Rachel stood at a corner of the terrace that allowed her a view of both the living room and the driveway. On either side of her were tall evergreen trees in barrel-sized pots, which she did her best to use as cover.

Rachel jumped, startled, when her mother came into the living room. She walked straight toward the big window as if she could see Rachel. But then she stopped, looking out, and Rachel could see she was weeping. Tears rolled unchecked down her cheeks, and Rachel's hand went up as if to soothe her mother, though there was still much more than a whole plate glass window between them. What's wrong? Rachel wondered. What is it?

Moments later another car swept up the driveway, one she didn't recognize. A man got out and let himself into the house without knocking, as if he belonged there.

Had the owner come home early? Or was it one of

the carpenters or other workmen her mother consulted with?

Rachel hadn't counted on anyone else being here. *This could wreck everything.* Her stomach was in knots, and her teeth chattered so much she was afraid her mother would hear them.

She watched as the man entered the room. When he came into the light, she thought, *I know him.* But from where?

He said something she couldn't hear, and her mother turned and spoke to him. He didn't look like anyone who'd come here tonight to work. He wore jeans and an expensive-looking sweater, and had blond hair just tinged with gray.

Like the man in the coffee shop, who'd been staring at her mother before Christmas.

No, not *like* him. He *was* the man from the coffee shop.

Rachel stood, fascinated, as the man walked toward her mother and took her into his arms. He reached into his back jeans pocket for a handkerchief and wiped her tears away. Then he kissed her—long and hard. Her mother's arms wrapped around the man's neck as he pressed her close.

Rachel felt as if she were watching a movie, with no one in it that she knew.

But then her mother pulled away, shaking her head and pushing the man back. "I can't," Rachel barely heard through the roaring in her head and the lapping of water on the shore. "I can't do this anymore."

With those words she was Rachel's mother again, and questions that had been thankfully held back out of shock tumbled around in Rachel's mind like a thousand gnats.

Who is this man? Is my mother having an affair with him? Oh, God! Does my father know? Is this why Daddy's never home anymore? Because he can't stand to live with an unfaithful wife?

The man began to argue with her mother. "It'll be all right," Rachel heard him say. "We'll work it out."

"No! It will never be all right!" Gina answered. "It never has been, and it never will be."

He murmured something to her and took her into his arms again. Her mother stood motionless this time, her head against his chest. Rachel could hear her sobbing.

She didn't notice the other car that pulled into the driveway, so involved was she in the scene before her. She only saw, suddenly, the figure of her father in the doorway to the living room. He stopped in his tracks, then stumbled into the room, his face pale. He looked as if he'd been slapped.

Paul had been feeling good as he passed through the large center hall and glanced into the living room. Nothing, therefore, could have prepared him for finding his wife in the arms of another man. If he had been able to form words in his head, he might have stolen a phrase and said that his heart stood still.

It wasn't possible to formulate words, however,

with a mind and heart that had all but gone dead. He could only make a sound deep in his throat, a sound of despair mixed with absolute shock.

His wife heard him. She stepped back from the man quickly, her face paling. He could tell that she had been crying.

Was this someone she worked with, after all? Had the man merely been comforting her about something? Rachel, perhaps, and all that had been happening the past few days? That made more sense than—

"Gina," he began, gathering his wits about him. "I—"

"What are you doing here!" Gina interrupted in a tone that was part accusation, part horror. "Paul? What on earth are you doing here?"

"I...Rachel..." Paul's tone was unsure. "Rachel told me you wanted me to...to pick you up in case...I, uh...she said your wipers weren't working."

By this time, he knew from the look on the other man's face and the way he put an arm around Gina that this was no co-worker comforting his wife.

How could you do this? were the first words that sprang to his mind. Yet he couldn't say them. He knew the answer all too well, and if there were ever words he had no right to speak, those were the ones.

His legs went weak, and he grabbed the door frame to steady himself. *This is a nightmare. A monstrous nightmare. Any minute now it will end.*

But it didn't. The nightmare only grew, as a tall blond woman in a long black coat strode through a door at the other side of the room and crossed it to stand between him and Gina.

The woman laughed. "Oh, this is perfect!" she said, whipping off her leopard-print scarf. The coat fell open, revealing a gold necklace with the letter *A* at her chest.

"Even better than I'd hoped for," she said. "Mom's got a boyfriend, Daddy's got a mistress—"

She broke off at Gina's aghast expression. "You didn't know, Gina? Golly Molly, Paul, she didn't know! We must have been very good at hiding—well, never mind."

"Lacey," Paul said, his mouth so dry he could barely get the words out. "What the hell? What are you doing?"

"Lacey?" Rachel said, appearing at Paul's side. She looked with bewilderment at the other woman. "Who's Lacey?"

Paul couldn't answer. His mind had gone numb.

"Dad, don't you even recognize her?" Rachel asked. "It's Angela! I found her for you."

Lacey grinned. "She's right, Paul. Surprise! You too, Mommy. It's me—your long-lost little girl. Aren't you thrilled?"

21

This must be hell, then, Paul thought. There were times when he'd wondered if people created their own hell right here on earth, and now he was sure of it.

Lacey was here, in this room. She was here with Gina and Rachel.

And Rachel was calling her "Angela."

Had the whole world gone crazy?

Or was it Rachel who'd gone crazy? Rachel had brought Lacey here. Rachel, who had always been the "quiet" one. He recalled Vicky saying, "There are certain kinds of mental illnesses that only show themselves when a child is older."

But that didn't explain about Lacey. Why would she go along with such a thing? Had she sensed he was going to break it off with her? Had she been angrier than he'd ever imagined she would be—and was this her payback?

That was it. Rachel and Lacey had met somehow. Rachel had found out about his affair with Lacey, and she had been angry, too. Together, they had cooked up this meeting to teach him a lesson.

But why have her pretend to be Angela?

It took only seconds for so much confusion to whirl

through his brain, but the seconds seemed like hours. Then, through the muddle of his thoughts he heard a broken voice. "B-baby? Angela? Is—is it really you?"

He remembered Gina, who was still several yards away with a man he didn't recognize at first but who seemed familiar now, and who also seemed to have intimate knowledge of his wife. The man had stepped back, as if becoming an uneasy observer of this family play.

"Of course it's Angela!" Rachel said. There was a tone in her voice that Paul couldn't even begin to understand. Excitement? Fear? "I found her for you, Mom. You, too, Dad. I know how you always miss her at Christmas."

Gina's eyes widened, and her hand went to her mouth, which was trembling. "Found? You found Angela?"

Rachel nodded. "When I was in Spokane. She wanted to see you guys for the first time alone, where you wouldn't be bothered by work or anything, so I arranged for you all to come here."

Gina made a small, strangled noise in her throat. She stumbled forward, her hand outstretched. "Baby," she said softly. Her eyes scanned the other woman's face, wonderingly. "I can't believe it's you." She began to cry. "You've changed so much! I would never have recognized you. But it is you, isn't it?"

She turned to Rachel. "It is Angela, isn't it?"

"Yes, Mom. It's Angela."

It was only then that understanding dawned for Paul. Yet even with the evidence laid before him, he couldn't see it. Lacey's eyes were a deep green, not hazel, and her hair was blond, not brown. Those things were easily changeable, of course—contact lenses, hair color. Vicky had told him that Angela might have changed her appearance.

But beyond that—the nose, the chin—nothing about Lacey resembled the little girl Angela had been the last time he had seen her.

Of course, Angela had been only six years old that day. This person was a full-grown woman. *He of all people knew that.*

A deep flush rose to Paul's face. His stomach heaved, and black spots appeared before his eyes. For him, everyone else in the room disappeared. If he saw anything at all, it was only the gold *A* on the necklace he had given Lacey for Christmas.

A for Allison, her last name. That was what she had told him she wanted. Not *L* for Lacey, but *A* for Allison.

He knew, now, as that gold *A* flashed against her chest in the light from an overhead chandelier, what it really stood for.

"How could you have done this?" he cried. "I was your *father,* for God's sake! Do you know how sick—" Scenes flashed back to him—being in bed with Lacey, playing with her in a teasing way. Completely absorbed by her and, yes, even wondering if he should leave Gina for her.

"My God, Lacey—Angela—whoever the hell you are! Do you know how *dirty* that makes me feel?"

Her laughter mocked him. "In the first place, Paul, you were never my father. You were some guy who adopted me and then threw me away four years later. In the second place, I *want* you to feel dirty. Don't you get it? That's been the whole point!"

She laughed again, and the sound of it made him ill. "It's why I came to Seattle, why I set up our meeting in the bar that night, and why I became your vapid little mistress—always there ready to do your bidding, always waiting patiently till you had time for me. I did it all for this moment—this moment when I would see that look on your face, knowing you had been making love to your sweet little Angela."

She shoved her fists deep into the pockets of the black coat and paced frantically about the room, as if physically propelled by her rage. "Didn't you ever wonder why I didn't feel bad about you spending time with your family? Most mistresses would, you know."

"I thought...I just thought you didn't mind," Paul said, his voice as strangled as his thoughts. "You said you understood."

"God, you are stupid!" Angela cried, coming so close her eyes were only inches from his. Paul had a memory that tore through his gut, of Angela that Christmas Eve night, spitting into his face. The look in her eyes then was the same as this one tonight: pure evil.

"Sometimes you're so stupid I want to shake you," Angela said. "Do you have any idea how *I* felt when your dear Dr. Chase did things to me and made me do things to him? That's why he told you and Mom not to come back, you know. It's why he said I would never be normal, never go home. He wanted me for himself. By the time I was six, I was his little prostitute. 'Come here, Angela. Kneel down. Do this, do that. Ahh, yes, that's right. Not so hard, though. Do it softly.'"

She had squeezed her eyes shut and turned away, but now she whipped back, the long hair flying, and fixed a full charge of hatred on him. "He trained me, Paul. How the hell do you think I knew what to do with you? I'm twenty-one years old, *Daddy*. I'm barely legal, and I made you happier than your wife ever did! How do you think I learned all that?"

Gina cried out, and Paul came back to the rest of the room. His wife was on her knees on the floor, tears pouring down her cheeks. He had all but forgotten she was there. Rachel knelt next to her, an arm around her shoulders.

"I'm so sorry, Mom," she was saying. "I didn't know. I never would have…"

Paul wanted to go to them both, but he couldn't move. He barely heard the words Lacey continued to hurl at him, but he knew what they meant. He had committed the worst possible sin, and he would never be cleansed of it, no matter how many penances he made or how many prayers he offered to a God who could not possibly forgive what he'd done.

It wasn't just the sex, the betrayal of his marriage. That was terrible beyond imagining. But it wasn't the worst. The worst happened sixteen years ago when he left his little girl there in that monster's hands. When he didn't see what was happening to her.

How could he not have seen?

There was no answer to that, but Lacey—Angela— was right. He had thrown her away. What she had done to Rachel that Christmas Eve had been so terrible, so recent, he couldn't see beyond it. Much as he had loved Angela, he had become afraid of her. She was something he didn't want in his house, or even near him. The old Biblical word came to mind: *anathema.* Something to be abhorred. Cast off. Excommunicated.

We left her with no hope, he thought miserably. Helpless, with no one to protect her. He could only imagine how afraid she must have felt every time he and Gina had left. The image of her being taken back into Saint Sympatica's by Dr. Chase that last time, the way she had pulled away from his hand and run through the door alone, slamming it, came back in a rush of pity. Tears flooded his eyes as remorse filled his heart. When he looked at Lacey now he was startled to see that she was crying, too. Her entire body shook with silent sobs, and tears poured down her cheeks.

"My poor little girl," he whispered brokenly. "I am so sorry. Angela, I'm so sorry."

"Why did you leave me there?" she whimpered.

"We thought we had no choice. After what you did to Rachel—"

Quick as a flash her anger returned. "Don't you even get it now?" she cried. "It was *Rachel* who tried to kill *me!* All I did was defend myself. Why did I have to be the one to go away?"

With those words, the stunned tableau came back to life. Gina still knelt on the floor, but now covered her face with her hands, as if she could no longer bear to see what was going on. The man Paul now recognized as a former client bent over her and said in a low voice, "You know where to reach me if you need me." She nodded, and he hugged her and left the room. A few moments later Paul heard the sound of a car leaving the driveway.

Paul's gaze swung to Rachel. "Angela's right!" she said. Huge tears ran down her cheeks. "I'm the one who tried to kill her."

"Stop that!" Gina whispered harshly. "Don't listen to her!"

"Mom," Rachel said softly, "remember that summer you sent me away to the camp in Wisconsin?"

"We never sent you away," Gina cried. "Don't say that."

"Yes, you did. You sent me to music camp."

Gina raised her head. There was unabridged pain in

her eyes. "Rachel, we did that *for* you, not *to* you. It was what you wanted."

"Not at first," Rachel said. "I only decided to go to camp after I saw you were trying to get rid of me. Then I figured if I went to Wisconsin, I'd be that much closer to Minnesota and finding Angela. And that's what I did. I found Angela."

Gina stroked Rachel's hair. "Oh, honey, you were so difficult that summer. You kept asking questions we couldn't answer, and then you would take it out on us...."

She wiped her eyes with the back of her hand. "Honey, we thought we were supporting you."

She remembered though, that when Rachel came home from camp depressed, she had said to Roberta, "We never seem to be able to do enough for Rachel. No matter what we do, she always acts like we've got some secret agenda for doing it."

A bottomless well. She had always been a bottomless well.

"Why didn't you tell us," Gina said now, "that you'd seen Angela that summer?"

Rachel's eyes filled with tears. "I couldn't. You would have sent me away for good."

"What do you mean? Honey, we never would have—"

"You did Angela."

"But that was different! Angela was dangerous. Not only to you, but to everyone."

"No, Mom. That's what I've been trying to tell you.

It wasn't Angela—it was *me*. I remember it now. And I didn't just try to kill her. I'm pretty sure I killed that doctor, too.''

Angela planted her hands on her hips and laughed. ''I told you that you were stupid, Paul. You, too, Gina. See what you've been living with? And all this time you could have had me!''

Paul ignored her. ''Rachel, what in the name of God are you talking about? You didn't kill Dr. Chase. You couldn't have! This is some monstrous story Angela's made up.''

''I thought that, too, Daddy. But I'm starting to remember. I remember that night, and how I saw him doing things to Angela, and I couldn't stand it. I remember running over and beating on his back, but he turned around and grabbed my wrist. He had the most awful look on his face, and when he jumped up and put his hand on my throat I really thought he was going to kill me. Then I remembered a steak knife I'd taken from dinner the night before, in case anything bad happened on the road. It was in an open side pocket of my backpack, and I yanked it out and screamed at him to let go or I'd kill him...''

''Go on,'' Paul prompted softly. ''What do you remember next, Rachel?''

''I...'' She shook her head. ''Nothing. I can't remember anything after that.''

''Because you didn't kill him!'' Paul said. ''That's just one more lie of Angela's—''

''Lie?'' Angela interrupted, still pacing. ''You want

lies, Paul? How about all the ones you and Gina told, the ones where you said I'd be able to come home again? How about the times you said you'd come to see me and you didn't?''

She flung her hair back and laughed coldly. ''You know what I did on those visiting Sundays when you didn't show? I play-acted, Paul. That's what *he* called it. I play-acted with one of the other kids—Billy Rix. Poor Billy. He hated the good doctor as much as I did. And why wouldn't he? From the time I was eight and Billy was ten, Chase forced Billy and me to perform sexual acts with each other while he watched. Sometimes he'd just watch us take a bath together and touch each other, but there were other times…''

She broke off. ''You know what that is, Paul? When a psychiatrist likes to watch? Even if he never had touched me, they still call it incest. That's because a psychiatrist becomes like a father to his child patients. And fathers are people we're supposed to be able to trust.''

She stopped pacing just short of Paul and he was sure she was going to spit into his face, just as she had on that terrible Christmas Eve. Instead, she said in a soft, deadly tone, ''God, I hate men!''

All the moments he had spent with her as Lacey rushed back into Paul's mind. A woman so different, so good, so beautiful…and all of it lies. A performance. A staged play to bring them to this very moment, a moment when she could bring down the curtain and destroy him with the truth.

Paul made an angry motion toward her, but Angela backed up and was suddenly between him and the hallway. She drew her right hand from a pocket. In it she held a gun, which she grasped with both hands and pointed directly at him.

"Don't you dare come near me," she said.

"Why not? What will you do?" Paul said bitterly. "Kill me? Kill us all? Do you have any idea how many years I've thought about you and wondered if we'd done the right thing, sending you away? Well, now I know, thank God. I'll never have a sleepless night over you again."

"You told me you wouldn't hurt them!" Rachel cried.

"And you believed me," Angela said scornfully. "That's the difference between us. I don't believe anybody."

The cold smile Angela sent to Rachel twisted her beautiful face. "I even eliminated your little policeman friend. Too bad. He had potential, but I knew once I got rid of all three of you, he'd figure things out. Trouble with good old Al, he had too much time on his hands."

"What did you do?" Rachel cried. "Oh, my God! That's why he didn't answer his phone! What did you do to Al?" She swung back to her father. "Daddy, she's killed him!"

Paul stared. "Rachel, what are you talking about?"

"I...I set it up. This. Tonight. Daddy, I wasn't visiting a friend. Angela kidnapped me. She made me promise to get you and Mom together where you wouldn't be interrupted. She said she only wanted to talk to you, and she promised she wouldn't tell you it was me who tried to kill her, if I got you here. But then I got scared and I tried to call Al, but he didn't answer.''

"You were going to turn me in?" Angela said. "You little bitch!"

Rachel's eyes narrowed. "I can't believe I killed that doctor just to save you. You know what? You weren't worth it. I wish you were dead!"

She flew forward, her hands poised as if to grab Angela by the throat. Her movement was so unexpected it took Angela, who had turned the gun in Rachel's direction, by surprise. Rachel knocked her arm aside and barreled into her, shoving her to the floor.

Gina and Paul both rushed to help Rachel in a twisted déjà vu from years before. As they reached her, a siren echoed from the street. It grew louder and closer, whining more slowly as it reached the driveway. Red and blue lights flashed through the windows, reflecting against the walls. Almost immediately, someone knocked on the front door, followed by a pounding.

"Island County Sheriff! Open up!"

Paul held Angela's gun arm flat to the floor, while Gina fought off her other arm and tried to pull Rachel away from her throat. The pounding stopped, and two uniformed sheriff's deputies rushed from the entryway into the living room. One of them pulled Rachel away from Angela, while the other sat on Angela, shoving Paul aside and forcing the gun from her hand. Pulling her to her feet, the cop cuffed her wrists behind her.

The other deputy was still hanging on to Rachel, who was sobbing uncontrollably. Paul and Gina tried to put their arms around her, but she pushed them off. "D-don't touch me. I—I'm no better than she is. I almost got you killed."

Paul looked at the deputy, who answered his unspoken question. "We got a call from a Detective Al Duarte in Seattle. He asked us to get out here fast and see if you folks needed help. Are you Paul Bradley?"

Paul nodded.

"Well," the deputy continued, "Detective Duarte said your daughter Rachel left him a message. He wasn't sure what was going on, but he said if we ran into somebody with long blond hair—this one here with the gun, it looks like—we should grab her and bring her in."

"Al's alive?" Rachel cried. "Oh, thank God!" She let Paul take her into his arms then, while Gina put an arm around her and stroked her hair.

"Is he all right?" Paul asked.

"A bullet grazed the side of his head and knocked him out. They're keeping him overnight at Harborview, but he'll be okay." He looked at Angela. "You are Lacey Allison, right?"

She didn't answer, and the deputy looked at Paul.

"This is Lacey Allison," Paul said heavily. "Otherwise known as Angela Bradley. She was once my daughter.''

"Yeah? Well, the way I hear it, she's the one who took a nick out of the side of Al Duarte's head.''

He turned to her. "Al says to tell you that Lazybones is still sleeping off whatever drug you gave her, but when she wakes up she'll love that red-feather toy.''

He squinted as if trying to remember the rest of the message. "He said something about a pet-shop bag in your apartment, and you not having a pet. Then he remembered that Mr. Bradley, here, was supposed to get Lazybones something red and flashy. He figured you must have done the shopping for him. But when he saw the toy in his closet, he realized it was you who shot him and left that feather as a calling card.''

The deputy shook his head. "Funny thing, though. You couldn't have left a more obvious clue. Unless, of course, you didn't expect anyone to be left alive after tonight to point a finger at you. Is that it? You were going to make sure Duarte, and everyone here tonight, was dead?''

"Aren't you the smart little boy,'' Angela said scornfully. "Or, maybe I wanted to be caught. Isn't that what some idiot shrink might say?''

"I don't know about shrinks,'' the deputy said. "But if getting caught is what you wanted, we're more than happy to oblige.''

While one of the deputies kept an eye on Angela, the other talked to Paul, Gina and Rachel. Paul filled him in on what had happened earlier, and why they were there in the Albrights' house.

When Paul was finished the deputy said, "We'll need all of you to come into the office and make a statement about what happened here tonight. We're right down the road, so if you could stop by on your way home to Seattle, that would help."

Paul realized they were being unusually accommodating, probably at Al's request.

"Of course," he said. "I know where it is. Could you give us a little while?"

"No problem," the deputy said, standing.

He and the other deputy began to lead Angela out of the room, pushing her slightly ahead of them when she shook their hands off her arms. "Don't touch me!" she said angrily. "Get your filthy hands off me." There was an edge to her voice that sounded like tears.

"Wait," Paul said. "Wait, just a minute. Please."

They paused, and Paul said to Angela, "I still don't understand why you did it. Why did you have to set me up that way? Why—" He broke off, his voice so heavy with confusion and grief, he couldn't get the words out: *Why an affair?* "These past few months," he said. "Couldn't you have gotten your revenge some other way?"

"Sure," Angela said. "I could have done just about anything. But this way, Paul…this way was especially sweet. You want to know why?"

Paul didn't answer.

"Well, I'll tell you anyway," she said with a smile as brittle as ice. "This way, Paul? I got to have you in a way Rachel never could."

Paul, Gina and Rachel were alone in the room for the first time.

"I don't think I can get in the car and just drive home right now," Paul said. He was shaking all over, and he could barely look at Gina. "You think the Albrights would mind if I made some coffee?"

She shook her head and said in a monotone, "No. They won't mind."

Paul's heart ached in a way he had never thought possible. From this night on, it was over. Nothing would ever be the same between him and Gina again.

"Why don't we all go to the kitchen?" he suggested tiredly. "We can talk, try to get our energy back before we leave."

"I'll make the coffee," Gina said, her voice cold and distant. "I definitely do not want to talk."

Paul looked at Rachel, who was sitting on one of the two sofas and hadn't moved since the moment Angela was taken out. She sat with her head and shoulders bowed.

"They should have arrested me," she said softly. "It's just like before. I was the one."

Paul sat beside her and took her hands. "You didn't do anything, sweetheart. You just tried to stop her from using the gun."

"I mean...for killing Dr. Chase," she said, crying. "They took her away, and it should have been me."

Gina came to sit at her other side, putting an arm around her shoulders. "Don't say that, honey. That's just something Angela said to hurt you. It can't be true."

Rachel turned agonized eyes on Gina, who felt a shaft through her heart. "How do you know that? I don't even know it! All I remember is pulling out that steak knife and screaming at him. But Mom, I wouldn't have blocked out whatever happened next if I hadn't done it! I mean, why would I?"

"I can't answer that," a male voice said from the doorway. "But you didn't kill him, Rachel."

Paul whirled around. *"Daniel?"*

His manager from Soleil stepped into the room, his expression that of one who carried far too heavy a load for someone so young.

"I'm so sorry, Paul. I knew Angela was coming here tonight, and I should have warned you. I tried...but then I wasn't sure it was the right thing to do."

The young man turned to Rachel. "You told Angela you remembered a boy from that night in Dr. Chase's room. That was me, Rachel. I'm the one who killed him."

22

Rain pounded on the roof and slapped against the windows. Gina turned the heat on, and Paul made coffee, scrounging in the Albrights' cupboards for sugar and cups. Neither he nor Gina touched in the kitchen, or spoke to each other. It was as if Angela was still here in their midst, mocking them both and laughing that terrible spiteful laugh.

When the coffee was ready, they carried it into the dining room, where Rachel and Daniel were sitting at the table. Daniel was pale and shivering. He had witnessed the whole scene with Angela, he told them, and he'd waited on the terrace for the deputies to leave.

"Angela called me earlier today, and told me she was finally going to meet her parents," he said. "I didn't know what was going on, Paul. I hoped she was just coming here to see you for the first time after all these years. That's what she said. But the past few days, especially with Rachel disappearing…" He shook his head. "She swore she didn't have anything to do with that, but I was worried about the way she was acting. Not really crazy, but like she was right on the edge. I thought I should come up here and make sure you were okay."

He lifted the hot mug of coffee to his lips with shaking hands, then put it down without drinking it. "I got here just before Angela arrived. When I heard her say all those things to you, I was shocked. I had no idea you knew her..." He looked briefly at Gina, and flushed. "That you knew her now, I mean. At first it seemed like a family thing that I shouldn't interrupt. Then she pulled that gun, and you all went after her, and suddenly the sheriffs were here..."

Paul set his own coffee down with a thud and said shortly, "Back up. You said you were the boy Rachel remembered at Saint Sympatica's. And you say you killed Dr. Chase? What are you doing with Angela now? And why did you come to work for me? Daniel—who the hell *are* you?"

Daniel flinched, but then squared his shoulders and answered Paul's questions. "In the orphanage," he said, "I was Billy Rix, but I changed my name to Daniel Britt when I left Saint Sympatica's five years ago. The police had cleared all of us of Dr. Chase's murder, so it wasn't that I was trying to hide—except from myself, I guess. I was truly horrified by what I'd done. At the same time, I couldn't help telling myself I'd done the other kids at Saint Sympatica's a favor by getting rid of that..." He looked at Paul as if asking for understanding. "He really was a monster, you know. This isn't a justification. I'm just trying to tell you the way it was. When I left there a few months later, I wanted to forget everything that happened there, so I started by giving myself a new name."

Paul stared at the young man he had thought was oddly secretive about his past. Now he knew why. So many lies these past few months. Daniel, Gina, Angela...me. Even Rachel. Who of us, he wondered, is blameless?

"How did you come to kill Dr. Chase?" Paul asked.

"I'd been more worried than usual about Angela," Daniel said. "She turned sixteen that night, and Chase had promised her a 'special celebration.' That was the way he put it—the nights she spent with him. As if it was something *special* that she'd look forward to—"

He broke off, his voice failing, then began again. "I knew Angela had reached a point where she couldn't take it much longer. To be honest, I couldn't either."

He sighed and rubbed his hands over his face in a way that reminded Paul of himself. "I was sitting outside on the steps when Rachel came walking up the drive that night. I was older than most of the other kids, and sitting out there at night, looking at the stars, was the only kind of peace I ever got from the little kids playing and all the noise. I asked Rachel—who I didn't know then, of course—what she was doing there. She said she was looking for her sister, Angela. There was only one Angela at Saint Sympatica's, and I knew Chase had her in his room. I'd actually been sitting on those steps praying for some kind of sign, some way to help her, when Rachel appeared."

He turned to Rachel. "It seemed as if my prayers

had been answered. I thought that if you saw what was going on, you might blow the whistle on Chase.''

''Why didn't *you* do that?'' Rachel asked, an edge of hostility in her voice.

''I tried, believe me. Many times. The Ewings were no help at all. They were afraid that the board might get wind of any complaints by the kids, and they'd be fired for not taking care of them properly. Mrs. Ewing even accused me of being 'jealous' of the time Dr. Chase spent with Angela.'' His voice took on a bitter edge. ''She called me a pathological liar, and I found out later that she even put that in my records there. That's why no one wanted to adopt me.''

Rachel stared at him. ''That must have been awful for you,'' she said softly. ''People not believing you.''

''It was,'' he said, ''but only because it kept me from helping Angela. I knew I was getting out of there soon, and I hated the thought of leaving her there alone with Chase.''

Looking at Paul, he said, ''I took Rachel to Chase's room, and waited outside in the hall. I guess Chase had forgotten to lock his door, because Rachel didn't even knock, she just opened the door and walked right in. A minute or so later I heard her cry out, not too loud, but a soft, anguished kind of cry, and I ran in there. I saw Angela naked on the bed and Chase with his hand on Rachel's throat. Rachel had a knife, and Chase's other hand grabbed her wrist and made her drop it. I grabbed it off the floor and went after him, and…'' He shook his head. ''I don't really think I knew what I was doing until it was over.''

Paul looked at Daniel as if seeing him for the first time. ''He was *cut*, Mrs. Ewing said. Mutilated! You did that?''

''No! No, I would never—''

''Then who?''

Daniel's look was one of misery.

''Angela,'' Paul said.

He nodded. ''She told me to get Rachel out of there, and I left her alone with him while I sneaked Rachel through the grounds and outside the gate.''

He turned to Rachel. ''I heard you say a little while ago that you didn't remember actually killing him. Like I said, you couldn't have. It was me.''

Gina spoke up for the first time. ''You might have saved her a lot of heartache if you'd told her that sooner!''

''I'm sorry. I really am,'' Daniel said. ''I only knew Rachel from what Angela told me about her, and I didn't know that she didn't remember. I always wondered why she didn't tell someone about that night, though, and why the police didn't come after me.''

''About that,'' Gina said, her eyes narrowing. ''Why on earth would you come to work for Paul, if you knew he was Rachel's father and that you might run into her here? What were you going to do if she recognized you when she came home for Christmas?''

''I don't think I knew for sure. But Soleil is a big

place. I guess I hoped that she wouldn't see me there, at least not at first.''

Rachel shook her head. "It wouldn't have mattered. I just remember a boy. I don't even recognize you now, Daniel.''

"You were in a state of shock that night,'' he said. "Maybe it's best you don't remember.''

He stopped and reached for his coffee, but again he didn't touch it. Instead, he folded his arms against his chest as if to protect himself. "There are things I wish I didn't remember,'' he said softly. "When I got back to Chase's room, Angela was…she was there, and she was…''

He looked imploringly at Paul and Gina. "Please don't judge her too harshly. He'd been at her so long.''

"She told us he'd been at you, too,'' Paul said quietly.

Daniel's face turned beet-red.

"It's nothing to be ashamed of,'' Paul said. "You were a victim as much as Angela.''

"Speaking of Angela,'' Gina said, her tone not quite so kindly, "I notice you haven't answered the first part of my question. Why did you come to work for Paul in the first place?''

"I went to work for Paul,'' Daniel said, "because Angela asked me to. Given what's happened, of course, I realize now how wrong that was. I wish I'd told you sooner about her, but I swear I didn't know what she was planning, or anything she was doing.''

Paul's tone was disbelieving. "So you were innocent in all this," he said.

"I don't blame you for not believing me," Daniel said. "There's no reason in the world that you should. But I swear to you, this is the absolute truth. Angela contacted me one day last summer. We'd kept in touch over the years, but only on the phone, and only once a year or so. I hadn't actually seen her since we left Saint Sympatica's five years ago. Then, when she called last summer, she asked me if I'd do her a favor. She said she wanted to get in touch with the family who'd adopted her when she was a baby, but she didn't know what they were like now. She thought they might still hate her."

Gina gasped. "Hate her?"

Daniel nodded. "That's the way she put it. She always said she'd been taken back to Saint Sympatica's because the people who adopted her hated her."

"And you believed that?" Paul said.

"The thing is, I didn't know you then, so I didn't have any reason not to believe her," Daniel said. "Especially when she swore that you and your wife knew what Dr. Chase was doing to her, and didn't care. It sounds hard to believe, of course, but Angela had a way of making you trust her."

Gina flicked a look at Paul, but he couldn't meet her eyes. She turned away.

"Last summer," Daniel continued, "I was between jobs, and Angela called and asked me to offer to work for you as an intern. She said most people won't turn down an intern who shows a real interest in a business, because they don't have to pay them.''

"And you just willingly agreed to this?"

"Not right away. But even though I'd always done my best to take care of Angela at the orphanage, I felt guilty that I hadn't been able to keep Chase from her entirely. I mean, I'd sidetrack him somehow a lot of times, but it wasn't always possible—''

He broke off, swallowed and began again, looking at Gina as he spoke. "I know Saint Sympatica's had a reputation for being good with children. But that was before they lost funding from private donors and had to set up a board whose job it was to bring in government funding. Every *t* had to be crossed and every *i* dotted. They couldn't afford a scandal. Outsiders might not have seen the change in the Ewings, but I was one of the few kids old enough to know what was going on. They were nervous wrecks."

Paul agreed. "I saw some of that when I was there last week. But, to get back to you, what were you supposed to do when you came to work for me?"

"Well, in the first place, I thought I'd only be doing that for a couple of weeks, just until I could figure out what kind of people you and your wife were, and if you'd welcome Angela back. But it didn't take even a week to know that what Angela had said about you couldn't be true. I liked and respected you, Paul, and I love the business. I really wanted to keep working for you. So when you offered me a salary and a permanent position, I just couldn't turn it down."

"What did Angela think of that?" Paul asked.

"She thought it was great. In fact, she encouraged me to stay on."

"And why wouldn't she?" Paul said angrily. "It put you in a perfect position to—" He broke off. "My God! *You* let her in that night. She *is* the one who destroyed the Crystal Cave, and you're the one who let her in!"

Daniel flushed. "Paul, I swear to you, I didn't think she would do anything like that. I thought she just wanted to look at things, maybe even touch them, just to feel closer to you." Tears formed in his eyes. "I never dreamed she was capable of anything like that. I thought she really loved you and Gina. That's why I let her in, and when she asked me to leave her alone there, I thought it would be all right. It wasn't until the next morning—" He wiped beneath his eyes with a thumb. "I'm sorry, Paul. I've been such a fool! I swear, if you let me I'll spend the rest of my life making it up to you."

Paul's heart softened. "Well, don't feel too bad," he said. "You weren't the only one she fooled."

It was then he wondered if Daniel knew, and had known all along, about his affair with Lacey.

Daniel answered the question before he voiced it. "She never told me she had made contact with you, Paul. In fact, I thought it was odd that she'd go to the trouble of having me work for you, and then not even get in touch with you after I told her that you and your wife were good people. But then there was that business with...with the travel desk."

"Oh?"

"She asked me to bring it to you and tell you someone had left it on the counter in the lobby. It seemed a harmless enough white lie at the time. I thought she must have put a note in it for you, as a way of getting in touch with you. A surprise."

Paul sighed. "A surprise."

How could the woman he had known as Lacey possibly be Angela, a child he had raised from the ages of one through five and then mourned the loss of all these years? How could she have been so deceitful? And how could he not have known?

"The thing is," Daniel said, "once I saw what she did to the Crystal Cave, I knew how much she hated you, and I worried that she might do something worse. She even told me that the other day. 'His stupid Crystal Cave is just the beginning,' she said. I didn't know what she meant, but, Paul, I never dreamed she'd actually..." Again he looked quickly at Gina, then away. "I mean, you know..."

A silence fell over the table. Rachel laid her head on her arms and closed her eyes. Gina cried quietly into her cupped hands. Daniel studied his coffee cup, his expression one of misery, and Paul sat hunched over, holding back the angry cry of grief that had been threatening to explode for the past hour. The rain drummed on, banging against the windows like an angry spirit trying to get inside.

23

They came together the next day in Al Duarte's room at Harborview Medical Center: Paul, Gina and Victoria Lessing.

"Don't be too long," the nurse said. "He still needs plenty of rest."

"What I need is to get out of this place and back to work," Al grumped. His head was bandaged on one side where Angela's bullet had grazed it. "I've had worse injuries than this just raiding a cathouse."

He looked closely at Gina, then Paul. "You two look like you've been through hell and back."

"I'm not sure of the *back* part yet," Paul said. "We do agree with you, though, that it's a good idea to get together here and go over what's happened. That is, if you're sure you're up to it?"

"Up to it? For Pete's sake, man, I've been going nuts here alone, just wondering what's been going on."

"The sheriff's deputy said he'd call you last night," Paul said. "Didn't he tell you what happened?"

"All he said was that they had Lacey—Angela, that is—in custody and that the rest of you were all right. That's not the same thing as hearing it from you."

"Al," Gina said, sitting beside him in a chair and touching his arm gently, "it was awful, but it's over now. I can't believe you managed to call the sheriff's station even though you were wounded."

"Yeah, well, I almost went to the morgue instead. If Angela had been a better shot, I wouldn't even be here now." He smiled. "It was good thinking on Rachel's part to leave me a message. I picked it up when I came to and I called the precinct and the paramedics. Hal at the precinct called the Camano sheriff's office for me."

He looked around the room. "Which reminds me. There's somebody missing here. Where is Rachel? Is she all right?"

"She was great last night," Gina said, "but she fell apart on the way home. We put her straight to bed and called Vicky."

"I talked with her quite a while," Victoria said. "Then I went up to Coupeville on Whidbey and talked with Angela."

"Coupeville is the main precinct for Island County," Al told them. "She'll be charged with assault, at least, for tonight, and she'll have to stand trial in Island County. Seattle will probably want her after that, for abducting Rachel."

He sipped water from a glass, then pulled the straw out impatiently and tossed it aside. "How was she when you saw her?" he asked Vicky.

"I can't go into specifics, of course. I can tell you she was relatively docile. Almost too docile, in fact.

With a good lawyer, she may be able to convince a judge she's mentally incompetent to stand trial.''

"You mean she might get *off*?'' Gina exclaimed.

"Well, not completely, of course. She would certainly have to spend some time under psychiatric care.''

"Oh, God,'' Gina said. She was finding it hard, now, to remember that she had once loved Angela, the child. It was as if that little girl had never existed, as if she'd been a figment of her imagination.

Paul filled Duarte in on the events of the night before.

"Poor Rachel,'' Duarte said. "I should've been there for her.''

"Actually,'' Paul said with a smile, "she did pretty good on her own. I can't believe she came up there all by herself, just to protect us in case something went wrong.''

"That's what she said?'' Duarte asked.

"Yes. Apparently, Angela called the house after Gina had left that day. She told Rachel that she knew Gina and I would be at the Camano house that night, and she was going up there to see them and confess she was the one who kidnapped Rachel. She wanted to make it up to them somehow, she said, and hoped they could be a family again.''

Duarte raised a brow. "And Rachel?''

"She wasn't sure whether to believe her, so she went up there to protect us, just in case.''

There was a brief silence. "I guess that makes

sense," Duarte said finally, "since she called me for the same reason."

"Are you questioning Rachel's story?" Paul asked.

"Oh, I don't know. They've got me so full of drugs here, my mind isn't working right at all." But he frowned. "Vicky? What did Angela have to say?"

"She said it was all Rachel's idea for everyone to go up there last night."

"Hmm. What do you think?" Duarte said.

"Well, from what I know, now, of Angela, I think we can assume she's lying. I'm more concerned about Rachel, to be honest. It sounds like this has all taken quite a toll on her."

"She barely talked to us on the way home," Gina said.

"I've suggested she spend a few days at Falling Leaf," Vicky told Al, referring to the private psychiatric hospital she was affiliated with. "Rachel is tired, and terribly stressed. At Falling Leaf I can see her every day, and she'll get some respite from whatever memories might come up at home."

"How did she take that?" Al asked.

"She agreed, and I'm taking her out there later today. I'm also recommending she transfer out of Berkeley and up here to U-Dub. I feel very strongly that she should continue in therapy, either with me or someone else she trusts."

"But she'll be all right?" Duarte asked.

"I think she'll be fine." But Vicky's brow wrinkled. "The thing about RAD—if Rachel is suffering from some form of that, as I now suspect—is that it's difficult even for a psychiatrist to tell if someone is all right, or just pretending to be. Frankly, I'm feeling rather inept at the moment. I wish I had recognized how troubled Rachel really was, years ago. I wouldn't mind calling in a consultant, in fact.''

"If you feel that's the right thing, we can do that,'' Gina said. "You know we'll do anything for Rachel."

"Anything," Paul agreed. "Vicky, what about that Web site, and the note in Rachel's pocket? And was Angela the one who pushed us off the road that night?''

"She's admitted all of that to the police," Victoria said. "And she's given me permission to tell you about it. In fact, she seems almost proud of the things she's done. The way I see it, Paul, everything Angela has done is part of her illness. She got some kind of warped thrill out of setting up the Web site up in her name and then putting Rachel's bio on it, or rather, what she thought of as 'Rachel's perfect life.' In her mind, she would show the Web site to you and see how you reacted. She would sit there as Lacey, and you would share your doubts and fears with her. You would see her as a sort of heroine for 'helping' you, and you would end up loving her more than Rachel.''

Paul remembered Lacey's final words the night before: "*I had you in a way Rachel never could.*" Vicky was putting a kinder light on what Angela had told her, he thought—perhaps purposely, to help him save face in front of Gina. But he knew firsthand the games

Angela had played, and the fact that he was blind enough to fall for them shook him to the core.

"Paul," Vicky said, as if intuiting the way he felt, "you can't expect to make sense of many of the things Angela has done. I think I told you that these things often have no logical reason. It's part of an illness that we still haven't a clear picture of."

"All that aside," Paul said, "what I'm having a hard time with is that Daniel killed Dr. Chase."

"Well, I, for one, am glad he did it!" Gina said. "Daniel was right—Chase was a monster. He deserved whatever he got."

"For once, you've said something I agree with!" Roberta Evans remarked as she sashayed into the room. A green silky cape billowed around a tight purple cat suit. Her lipstick was pink this time, but her boots were chartreuse.

Peering at Duarte, she added, "You look like hell."

"Gee, thanks," he said. "I guess this is your idea of a mercy call?"

"As if I'd waste my mercy on the likes of you," Roberta said. She placed her palm over Al's forehead. "You don't have a temperature. How do you rate all this company?"

"Careful," he said, frowning. "We were just getting to the good part—where I tell them all about you."

Roberta withdrew her hand. "I have no idea what you're talking about."

"Or," Al said, "you could tell them yourself. You may make a better job of it."

"I don't know what you think you know—" she began.

"The support group?" Al said. "I have my sources."

Roberta fanned herself with an imaginary fan. "Oh, all right." She looked at Vicky. "I've just been doing what she told me to do."

"Meaning what?" Gina said.

"Meaning that Vicky told me, over and over the past few years, that I needed to wean myself away from my family—from you, Gina, and Paul and Rachel. She felt I'd become too involved in your problems, and I needed to have a life of my own."

"Mom, I didn't realize you felt that way," Gina said.

"Well, I didn't either. But I found myself slipping into a deep depression after we lost Angela, and then you and Paul started falling apart. Sorry," she said when Gina frowned, "but it's the truth.

"Anyway, I tried to focus all my love on Rachel, but you know how independent she was as a child. It wasn't until she was older that she even let me get to know her. I worried that she might have a mild form of RAD—nothing as severe as Angela's, of course, but something like it—so for the past year I've been going to a support group and conferences for families of children with RAD. That's why I've been gone so much. I've been visiting abused children in hospitals and women's shelters, too, sort of as a grandma, I guess. Anyway, that's what they call me.''

"But that's great, Mom! Why didn't you tell us?" Gina said.

"Because," Roberta said, her jaw firming, "I needed something that was my own and only my own. I didn't want it to become part of our everyday chats, with you asking me how it was going all the time, and wanting to know what it was like. If I was going to wean myself away, I figured the only way was to go all the way."

"But did that mean you couldn't even spend Christmas with us?"

"No, but to be frank, I was getting tired of spending Christmas with you," Roberta said.

Gina gasped. "Well, Mother, why don't you just tell us how you really feel?"

"I doubt that I have to," Roberta replied. "You must have grown tired of Paul's moodiness every Christmas season. The thing that really irritated me, however, is why you didn't try to do something about it."

"I can't control the way Paul acts, Mother!"

"No, of course you can't. But you don't even try. You just put up with it, year after year, and the longer it goes on, the more distant the two of you become."

"So you just left town? How nice and easy for you!"

"You're damned right," Roberta Evans said. "For once, someone in this family has done something nice and easy."

Epilogue

Six months later

Paul and Gina had lived apart since the incident on Camano Island, and Paul was nervous about seeing his wife now. He had no idea why she wanted to meet with him, or why the door to the Crystal Cave had been locked this morning when he came in.

Daniel had warned him not to try to open it. "Trust me," he had said.

That was precisely what Paul had decided to do. The murder of Dr. Chase had occurred several years ago and, the way Paul saw it, that moment in time was gone forever, as well as the motivation for it. Further, Daniel had redeemed himself since then in many ways. As far as Paul was concerned, Daniel was welcome to work at Soleil as long as he liked; in fact, Paul could imagine him taking over the business one day.

He wondered if the young man—who still went by the name of Daniel, although his past was now known—had prepared something in the Crystal Cave as a thank-you for being allowed to stay on. Daniel's relief was so great when he found that no charges would be brought against him for Chase's murder, he had thrown himself into his work with renewed fervor.

There was one person in particular responsible for Daniel's freedom, and that was Al Duarte. When Paul had talked to him about Daniel's past, and the things he'd been through, mentioning that he would like to keep him on at Soleil—give him a break, if possible— Al had said simply, "Let me think about it."

Since then, it seemed that Al somehow couldn't remember to do anything about it. In fact, when Paul had mentioned it again just before taking Daniel back on, Al had slapped the side of his head.

"It must be that bullet to the noggin I got that night," he'd said. "I just keep forgetting to mention anything about him to the lieutenant. In fact, I don't think I'll ever remember what you told me about Daniel and all that business with…who was it? A Doctor Something or other?"

As for Paul, Gina and Rachel, they had made a pact to tell no one. There had been enough suffering all the way around, and they would do nothing to prolong it.

There was still Angela, of course. And Vicky. But as far as Paul could tell, Angela had told no one, and Vicky had said that it was not her business to be a cop.

At Vicky's recommendation, he and Gina hadn't seen Angela since that night. They knew, however, that she had charmed a well-known Seattle criminal attorney into defending her pro bono—without charge. As expected, he'd advised her to plead mentally incompetent to stand trial. She had been sent to Trowbridge, a psychiatric facility in eastern Washington, for an unspecified period of time. When the doctors there felt she was well enough, she would stand trial. Meanwhile, Vicky would monitor her care and recovery, but had warned Paul and Gina that for Angela there would be no easy fixes; in fact, she might never be well enough to leave Trowbridge.

Paul's feelings were mixed about that. There were times when he remembered her as Lacey, and his heart hurt. Other times he remembered only her betrayal and his own. Thinking too much about that was like a steep descent into hell.

Otherwise, it seemed that the Bradleys' lives were settling down. Rachel had been under care at Falling Leaf for a month, and she seemed much better now. She was taking summer classes at the University of Washington and living at home. Vicky had assured Paul and Gina the other day that her weekly sessions with Rachel were going well; they could finally relax and stop waiting for the other shoe to drop.

Paul and Rachel often had lunch together at one of Rachel's preferred little out-of-the-way places, and as Vicky had suggested, they seldom talked about that night on Camano Island, but rather about the future. He and Rachel had never seemed closer.

As for Paul's suspense over the Crystal Cave's locked door, it ended when Gina breezed into Soleil at noon, carrying with her the scent of fresh air and summer flowers. They'd barely seen each other in the past six months, though they had talked on the phone several times about Rachel. Gina had seemed different to him, the few times he had seen her since that night. One time she was the woman he had met in college;

another time she was the loving mother who had held the twins in her arms the day they adopted them at Saint Sympatica's. And yet another time, she was the woman he'd held in his arms so many nights throughout their marriage.

Until Lacey.

At first, the memories of Angela as Lacey would overtake him, but little by little they had subsided, until the only memory left, now, was of the old days—Gina in his arms, Gina pressing close to him, Gina becoming one with him.

She stood next to him now at the door to the Crystal Cave, handing him the key. "Go ahead, open it," she said, a small uncertain smile in her eyes. "I, uh... sneaked something in last night."

Paul turned the key and braced himself, not knowing what to expect. He even half closed his eyes. But then he was inside the room and Gina was standing beside him, their arms touching, and he could barely catch his breath.

"What do you think?" she asked, as if not really sure she had done the right thing.

Paul could only stare in wonder. Over the past few months he had put the broken pieces of glass in boxes, then in the basement, as he hadn't the heart to just throw them away. He'd replaced them with a few new vases, plates and glasses on the shelves along the walls. He hadn't the usual passion for it, though, and hardly visited the Crystal Cave anymore.

Now, in the center of the room, stood a huge and breathtakingly beautiful sculpture of colored glass. It didn't take more than a second or two to realize that it had been put together from many of the pieces of art that had been broken by Angela.

"Daniel brought that box to me from the basement, and I had a local glass artist design this," Gina said. "I told her to be sure to incorporate the Gallès and Chihulys, because they were your favorites."

Remnants of the Chihuly sea forms were backlit from inside the sculpture, and looked extraordinarily beautiful that way. Fragments of Gallè cameo vases blended with them, in an astounding complementary honor to the originals.

"I can't believe you did this for me," Paul said, nearly overcome with emotion.

"Well, I know how much they meant to you," Gina said. "This seemed a fitting way to bring them all back. You like it, then?"

"I love it," Paul said in a hushed voice. He wanted to add, "I love you." It was too soon, however. The word "love" had taken on new meanings for him in the past year, some of which were just as soon forgotten. He would have to find a new meaning, a new way of expressing what he felt for his wife.

"This is incredibly beautiful in its own way," he said, walking around it and studying it from all sides. "Not the same, of course—but truly magnificent."

"I thought that, too," Gina said, following him. "It seems almost a metaphor for life. Dreams, relationships…they're all so fragile, and so easily broken. But in the hands of someone skilled—"

"Or someone who cares—" Paul added.

Gina met his eyes. "The damage may not be irredeemable?"

He touched her fingers, and she didn't draw away. Emboldened, he took her hand.

"Would you like to have lunch with me?" he asked, holding his breath for her answer.

After a moment she said, "Sure. I think that would be all right."

He almost suggested the Four Seasons, but caught himself. That would be the old them, the them that had never really worked.

"I know a great hole-in-the-wall for hot dogs," he said. "How does that sound?"

"Hot dogs sound wonderful," she said, looping her arm through his. "Lead the way."

It's going to be all right, Paul thought. Thank God! It's going to be all right.

Two weeks later

Rachel stood in the side yard of Trowbridge Psychiatric Hospital in eastern Washington. The night was pitch-black and bitter cold. Taking aim, she threw another stone at the window she believed was Angela's. She had pretended to be a volunteer and had slipped into the hospital this afternoon to see how the room numbers went on the second floor. From the outside, now, she counted left from room 201 to Angela's room, 207.

But what if she had gotten it wrong? What if she should have counted to the right and this wasn't Angela's room at all, but some really weird sicko's? What if some serial rapist looked out and saw her down here?

Oh, for heaven's sake, relax, Rachel, she admonished herself. They wouldn't be able to get out to catch me. No one but Angela would be smart enough to do that.

She threw another stone. There were bars on the windows, and they kept getting in the way. With the fourth try, however, Rachel was rewarded by a light coming on and Angela's face behind the glass.

The double-hung window slid open. Rachel stepped back a few paces so that Angela could see her better, and waved.

"What the hell are you doing here?" Angela called down in a low voice.

"I wanted to see you."

"Why aren't you locked up? I thought they put you somewhere."

"Only for a while," Rachel said. "I'm going to school now...or anyway, they think I am. Can you come down?"

Angela laughed the way Rachel remembered her laughing that night on the island: cold enough for icicles to form on her lips. Silently she laughed, too. *Icicles on her lips...like fangs. What a picture.*

"You mean, 'Slide down my rain barrel'?" Angela mocked. "You want me to come out and play, little sis?"

"Don't make fun of me," Rachel said in a hard voice. "Just tell me, dammit! Can you come out?"

"*Can* I?" Angela said. "Well, now, there's a challenge. You think there's anyone alive who can stop me from doing anything I damn well want?"

She shook back her long blond hair, dark now at

the roots, and closed the window. Four minutes later she was beside Rachel, under a tree and several yards away from the building.

"That was fast," Rachel said. "Didn't anybody see you?"

"Only one of the guards," Angela said nonchalantly.

"One of the guards? Really? He didn't stop you?"

"The guards here are a piece of cake after the good Dr. Chase," Angela said bitterly. "So what do you want? Haven't you done enough to mess up my life? *'Angela kidnapped me, Mom,'*" she mimicked. "*'She wanted to kill you, Dad.'*"

"I'm sorry I did all that," Rachel said. "I've missed you. I didn't realize how much I missed you till after we saw each other again."

She took one of Angela's hands and held it between her own. "You feel so cold," she said softly. "Look." There wasn't enough light to see well, so she held Angela's hand against hers, matching the length of the fingers. "We have the same hands," she said. "I didn't even know that till I saw you in that cabin."

Tears filled her eyes. "We're part of each other, Angela. Even if we're not identical, there are parts of me that are just like parts of you. Isn't that incredible?"

Angela yanked her hand away. "You're nothing like me! Why would I even want parts of a wimp like you inside me?"

"Don't say that! I'm not a wimp."

Angela's eyes narrowed, and Rachel thought they

looked like a wolf's. "What are you even doing here?" she asked.

"I just came to see you," Rachel said. "I thought we could be friends."

"Are you kidding?" Angela said scornfully. "How the hell are we supposed to be friends when I'm locked up in here?"

"But not forever," Rachel said. "Vicky told Mom and Dad that you're doing pretty good. Maybe you'll be able to get out someday soon."

"Yeah, and then I'll go to jail," Angela said. "You want to be my cell mate? I could tell the cops how you tried to kill me when we were kids. After all, what's the difference between me trying to kill you and Mom and Dad, and you trying to kill me?"

The tears spilled onto Rachel's cheeks. "I swear I never remembered till that night in the cabin when you told me. And I've been feeling so guilty ever since. All those years that you spent at Saint Sympatica's instead of me…"

"Don't remind me. I hate you enough as it is."

"Do you really, Angela? Do you hate me?"

"Oh, for God's sake, Rachel. You are such a leech. You suck people dry, you know that? Mom and Dad said so, last time they came to visit me."

"Mom and Dad? They came here? You're lying!"

"No, I'm not. They come to see me, and every time we talk about you. They know what you're really like now, Rachel. And by the time I get out of here, I'll be living with them and you'll be out the door."

"I will not! You're lying. You said it yourself, you'll be in jail."

"Not if Mom and Dad testify for me about what you did, and how my whole life was ruined because of it. My lawyer says he can get me off."

"That doesn't mean you can live with us at home."

"Sure it does. Mom and Dad already said so."

"Stop calling them Mom and Dad!" Rachel cried. "You never did that before."

"Things are changing, little sis." Angela shrugged. "I'm in. You're out."

"I don't believe you!"

But the truth was, she did. She had always known Angela was her parents' favorite, even after they had sent her back to Saint Sympatica's. Why had she thought anything would change that?

The truth was that coming out here, she hadn't really wished that she and Angela could be sisters again. There was only half of her that wished that. The other half, the half that went dark more often now, wanted Angela out of the way, once and for all.

"What if the doctors here, and Vicky, figure out you're still crazy?" Rachel asked. "They'll never let you out of here, no matter what Mom and Dad say."

Angela laughed. "Listen, dummy, by the time I meet with that panel of doctors six months from now, I'll have them all on my side—count on it! Vicky, too. They'll let me out of here, all right."

"You really think so?"

"I *know* so," Angela said.

"You can get a whole panel of doctors to believe you're well enough to leave?"

Angela sounded like she was smiling, Rachel thought, though she couldn't tell in the half-dark.

"You little fool," Angela said in a low voice. "I don't need them to *believe* anything! I've already got three of them wrapped around my little finger, and when the time comes...well, let's just say they'll back up whatever I say. And believe me, once I get out of here, Mom and Dad won't see you for dust."

Rachel was silent.

"What now?" Angela said irritably. She stomped her boots on the ground, as if to ward off the cold.

"I guess I hoped I was wrong about that."

"Well, you're not. Wake up, Rachel. Look at me! I'm back!"

Rachel searched her face in the dim light that spilled suddenly from a first-floor window. "You don't really love them, do you? You've just convinced them that you do, so you can wreck their lives even more. It wasn't enough that you and Daddy—"

Angela's voice grew hard. "He's forgiven me for that. Besides, it's none of your business what we did."

"It's my life, too, Angela. What they do is my life, too. Did you know they're getting back together?" she lied, just to get a reaction.

Angela seemed to stop breathing. "That's not true."

"It is. There will never be room for you." *And me,* Rachel thought. *When Angela comes home, there won't be room for me.*

But she had known that coming here.

Angela waved a hand in front of her face. "Earth to Rachel! Where'd you go?"

Rachel came back slowly. Her voice was distant. "Into the future," she said. "It's all in my hands now."

"Oh, for God's sake!" Angela pulled an apple from her jacket pocket and bit into it. "You know, Rachel, sometimes I think you're crazier than me. You're definitely dumber. Look, I've got to get back inside. They'll see I'm gone when they make rounds."

Rachel nodded. "Okay."

Angela patted her cheek. "I'll be seeing you soon. At home."

Rachel watched her turn and begin to walk away. *Maybe you're right,* she said to herself. *Maybe I am as crazy as you. But the one thing I'm not is a dummy.*

She reached into her pocket and pulled out the .22 caliber gun she had bought from a teenager that morning on a street in Seattle. Pointing it steadily at her sister's back, she said, "Angela?"

When Angela turned, Rachel pulled the trigger. The small gun made a loud popping noise, but no one seemed to hear it. There were no lights coming on, no excited voices calling out.

Rachel walked the few feet over to Angela and knelt beside her, checking for a pulse. Finding none, she wiped her fingerprints off the gun with the hem of her shirt and put the weapon in Angela's hand. Pressing it against Angela's chest where the bullet hole was already blooming red, she pulled the trigger again. Forensics and powder burns weren't something she knew much about, but she hoped this would at least confuse things.

Standing, she said, "You really should have listened to me when I said we think alike, Angela. I sort of figured you had a plan like that. And you know what you said about me being crazy? Well, I am crazy—

enough, anyway, to make sure you never mess with my life again.''

Her voice became a soft whisper. ''You should have died that Christmas Eve night. Why didn't you, *little sis?*''

Rachel smiled as she walked back to her car, which was parked just off the road at the end of the driveway. Her smile was cold, almost as cold as Angela's had been. Still, it wasn't as cold as Angela's would be, from now on and forever more.

On a warm September night, in a San Francisco law office,
a client and his attorney are gunned down.
It is just the start of what will be
the biggest squeeze play the city has ever seen....

Squeeze Play

Nick Sasso: A disgraced ex-cop whose brother has
been "borrowing" money from the family restaurant.

Billie Fox: A tough-talking defense attorney
whose ex-husband is murdered.

Dickson Hong: A homicide detective looking
for the case to finally make—or break—his career.

Henry Chin: A district attorney with his eye on the mayor's
office—unless the corruption scam he's at the center of is exposed.

Igor Sakharov: A retired hit man with a heart of
gold who's been offered one last job that he can't refuse.

Jolie Hays: A novice hooker who lands the wrong john and
comes away with a piece of information that will make her a target and
provide her with the opportunity to change her life...if she survives.

A novel filled with suspense, adventure, craziness—
and a cast of characters you'll never forget. Sit back,
take a deep breath and experience the unpredictable
trip that is SQUEEZE PLAY.

R.J. KAISER

MIRA®

*Available the first week of September 2002
wherever hardcovers are sold!*

MRJK936

Los Angeles Times **Bestselling Author**

SHIRLEY PALMER

DANGER ZONE

Maggie Cady is living the perfect life.

Her husband, Sam, is her soul mate: a kind and loving husband, a suppo
partner. Her four-year-old son, Jimmy, fulfills in her a lifelong desire to
mother. The life they have built together means everything to her. And Ma
has never been happier.

It's also the perfect lie.

But when Jimmy is kidnapped in a violent attack on their home, Maggie rea
the past she has kept a secret—from her husband, from everyone—has ca
up with her. As the pampered daughter of a Mafia kingpin, Maggie witne
the destruction of her family—of everyone she had once loved—becau
the lies and treachery her world was built on. Finally she escaped, lettin
everyone believe she was dead. Now someone has found her and they are
her son to draw her back into the danger zone. The only question now…is

Available the first week of October 2002 wherever hardcovers are s

Visit us at www.mirabooks.com

M

MEG O'BRIEN

66807	GATHERING LIES	___ $6.50 U.S.	___ $7.99 CAN.
66586	SACRED TRUST	___ $5.99 U.S.	___ $6.99 CAN.
66516	CRASHING DOWN	___ $5.99 U.S.	___ $6.99 CAN.

(limited quantities available)

TOTAL AMOUNT	$_____
POSTAGE & HANDLING	$_____
($1.00 for one book; 50¢ for each additional)	
APPLICABLE TAXES*	$_____
TOTAL PAYABLE	$_____

(check or money order—please do not send cash)

To order, complete this form and send it, along with a check or money order for the total above, payable to MIRA Books®, to: **In the U.S.:** 3010 Walden Avenue, P.O. Box 9077, Buffalo, NY 14269-9077; **In Canada:** P.O. Box 636, Fort Erie, Ontario, L2A 5X3.

Name:_____

Address:_____ City:_____

State/Prov.:_____ Zip/Postal Code:_____

Account Number (if applicable):_____

075 CSAS

*New York residents remit applicable sales taxes.
  Canadian residents remit applicable GST and provincial taxes.

MIRA®

MMO0902BL